# Pretty Lady

Morgan glanced down at the sunbonnet and plucked at the hard, fast knot. Even if anyone could untie it, the ribbon would never be the same.

"I ruined it. I'll pay for it." Charity pulled the rest of the pins from her hair, letting it fall down to the middle of her back. Turning, she scanned the men's hats on a nearby wall. "Let's see. I need something with a wide brim."

Morgan turned also, looking up at the display. "I can't rightly see you in a cowboy style."

She chuckled. "Me neither. But I can see me in that one up there." She pointed to a beige felt with a wide, droopy brim. Turning, she smiled impishly up at him. "Think that would do, Deputy Kaine?"

He returned her smile. "Yep." Stepping up to the wall, he stretched up on tiptoe and removed the hat from a long peg. Returning, he settled it on her head, then shook his own. She looked adorable. Horribly unfashionable, but adorable. Saucy. Kissable. "Let's face it, woman. There's no way I can make you look plain."

She slanted a glance from beneath the brim of the floppy work hat and made his pulse quicken. "Now, tell me the truth, Morgan Kaine, do you really want to?"

He looked at the twinkle in her eyes and the tiny smile on her lips and felt a grin spread across his face. "No, ma'am. I don't reckon I do."

Praise for *Country Kiss* by Sharon Harlow:

"Full of old-fashioned, homespun goodness that is sure to please."
—*Rendezvous*

*Diamond Books by Sharon Harlow*

COUNTRY KISS
YOURS TRULY

# YOURS TRULY

## SHARON HARLOW

DIAMOND BOOKS, NEW YORK

This book is a Diamond original edition,
and has never been previously published.

YOURS TRULY

A Diamond Book / published by arrangement with
the author

PRINTING HISTORY
Diamond edition /April 1994

ISBN: 0-7865-0001-8

Diamond Books are published by The Berkley Publishing Group,
200 Madison Avenue, New York, NY 10016.
DIAMOND and the "D" design
are trademarks belonging to Charter Communications, Inc.

PRINTED IN THE UNITED STATES OF AMERICA

10 9 8 7 6 5 4 3 2 1

To the people of Colorado City and Mitchell County, Texas—those of the past who left us a rich heritage and those of the present who keep that heritage alive. My thanks to all of you—family, friends, folks I've never met—for giving me a place to call home.

And in loving memory of Charles C. Thompson,
a kind and noble man,
lifelong friend and counselor.
We miss you, Mr. Charlie.

# Acknowledgments

My thanks for your assistance to everyone at the beautiful Heart of West Texas Museum in Colorado City, Texas, especially for letting me dig through things while you were still moving in.

And a very special thank-you to Jim Baum, friend and history buff extraordinaire, for answering my endless questions with patience and unflagging enthusiasm, and for all those entertaining and informative Chief Lone Wolf articles in the Colorado City *Record*.

I use dozens of research books in writing my novels, but this time there are three that deserve special mention: *Renderbrook* by Steve Kelton, *From Cattle Range to Cotton Patch* by Don H. Biggers, and *Lore and Legend, A Compilation of Documents Depicting the History of Colorado City and Mitchell County* compiled by J. Lee Jones, Jr., and his wife, Nona C. Jones.

# Prologue

Charity Brown took a deep, unsteady breath and opened the old trunk. A year of waiting had barely lessened the pain, but she couldn't put off going through the last of her mother's things any longer. It was time    time to remember, to cherish, to grieve still more.

A lump rose in her throat at the sight of the odds and ends Marion had held so dear. Blinking back tears, she carefully removed a bundle of letters from her Uncle Will, letters posted from all over the world. She didn't open them. She had read them all several times before.

A muslin pattern was next. It had been the first gown her mother had designed and sold. Beside it was the cloth doll Marion had made for Charity's fourth birthday. She had dragged it around with her for the next two years. She was slightly embarrassed to think how long she had slept with it. Her mother had also tucked away Charity's early attempts at art. Most of her other pictures decorated the walls of the apartment.

One corner of the trunk held a stack of *Century* magazines, containing articles Charity had written and illustrated. A tear trickled down her cheek. Her mother had been so proud of her success and had done so much to make it possible.

Charity was a strong person, but her mother's unexpected death had been devastating. Marion had been her dearest

1

friend, and Charity had admired and respected her more than anyone else she knew. She worked her way through the trunk, setting things out on the floor beside her, wiping her eyes often, sometimes barely restraining sobs of loneliness and loss.

For all practical purposes, she was alone. She had no brothers or sisters, and her father had died before she was born. Uncle Will was her only living relative, but it was not his nature to stay in one place for long. She had a number of friends, but that was not the same as having a family.

She removed her mother's satin-and-lace wedding gown from the bottom of the trunk and frowned. Beneath it was a small wooden chest, perhaps a foot long and six inches high.

"I don't remember this," she said out loud. Taking out the chest, Charity leaned back against the side of the bed and ran her fingers over the delicately carved leaves adorning the top of the walnut box. The wood glowed softly with a satin luster, telling of years of gentle care.

She lifted the lid and found a folded sheet of paper, yellowed with age, and a photograph of a handsome young man with fair hair and pale eyes. She opened up the sheet, reading the message inside with a twinge of guilt. Even though her mother was dead, she couldn't help feeling as if she were trespassing. According to the note, the little chest had been a gift from someone with the initials J. H., who had taken Marion to a play and was picking her up that night for a dance.

"Why, Mama, you never told me you had another beau besides Father," Charity said with a smile. She picked up the picture, holding it closer to the lamplight. Her smile faded, becoming a frown. "How odd." The man looked familiar, though she was certain she had never met him or seen the photograph before.

Laying the picture on the floor beside her, she looked back into the little chest. Uneasiness shivered down her back. *Why isn't this letter from Uncle Will with the rest of them?* She checked the postmark, and her frown deepened. "I don't remember getting a letter from Texas. I didn't even know he went to Texas."

With trembling fingers, she removed the pages from the envelope. Dated six months before Marion's death, the missive was shorter than most he had sent. Charity skimmed the brief description of West Texas and the small town he was visiting, but the last paragraph made her gasp. Her heart pounding, she read it again.

"I came here to see our old friend J.," he wrote. "He is doing well, happy and in good health. Don't worry, Mary, I didn't break my promise, although I was tempted to when he asked about you. I hope you will change your mind and write to him. If you send the letter here, he will get it."

An ink blot marred the page, as if he had absently let the pen linger there while he pondered what to say. "You are wrong to keep the truth from him and from Charity. They both have a right to know he is her father."

Even as she shook her head in denial, Charity's gaze drifted to the photograph—to those clear pale eyes, eyes that she was certain matched the clear pale green of her own.

# Chapter One

Amid the bustle and noises of Grand Central Station, Charity hugged her friend Helena Gilder. As they drew apart, Helena shook her head, her expression filled with worry. "Can't we change your mind?"

"No." Charity softened her refusal with a smile.

Helena's husband Richard put his arm around Charity's shoulders. "You know I'd hire the best detective in New York to look for your father. You don't have to go to Texas."

"But I want to." She smiled up at her mentor and friend. Through his guidance as editor of the *Century,* the most successful and influential magazine in the country, she had become a noted writer and illustrator. "And I know you want those articles on West Texas—almost as much as I want to write them."

"Well, I do admit I want the articles, but I could give the assignment to someone else."

"Don't you dare. It's my idea, and I'm going to do them. If you won't let me, I'll send them to *Harper's.*"

Richard smiled, giving her shoulders a squeeze, and stepped back. "And miss half your readers?"

"Might pick up some new ones. Not everyone reads the *Century.* Some folks like a little more adventure than they find in our staid, highbrow publication."

"Mark Twain a little too somber for your tastes?" he asked with a grin.

4

"Not mine. But I expect he makes some of our more genteel readers cringe."

Richard nodded in understanding, and his smile faded. "Promise me you'll be careful. Helena's not the only one who's worried about you going so far alone."

"You know I'm an experienced traveler."

"Yes, but your mother accompanied you most of the time."

"And she taught me well. I know who and what to watch out for, and how to take care of myself if anything should happen." She glanced at Helena, seeing her exasperation. "It will not ruin my reputation, not at the ripe old age of twenty-seven. Everyone we know considers me a spinster anyway, so it doesn't matter."

"And what about after you get to Texas?" Helena frowned, her eyes filled with concern and tenderness. "What if you find your father, and he doesn't want anything to do with you?"

"Then I'll come home a bit more bruised, but at least I'll know I've tried. Even if he won't publicly acknowledge me as his child, perhaps he will tell me about him and Mother. I need to know why she lied to me all these years."

"That's obvious," murmured Helena. "She didn't want to admit you were born on the wrong side of the blanket. She did it to protect you, Charity."

"I know. But why didn't she tell him eventually? Or me?" Charity paused. They had hashed through this several times. Obviously her dear friend still needed convincing. "With Uncle Will touring Africa, it could be months before my letter catches up with him and ages before I would get his reply. I can't wait that long. I have to get this settled, one way or the other, and get on with my life." She squeezed Helena's arm gently. "If I don't look for my father, I will always wonder what he is like and if there is a place for me in his heart and his life. When I was little, I sometimes cried myself to sleep because I wanted a daddy like my friends. I still do. He may not want me, but I'll never have peace until I know."

Helena sighed. "Promise me you'll send a telegram every week. And write often. I'll be sick with worry the whole time you're gone."

"And dying of curiosity."

"That, too." Helena finally smiled. "I want a detailed description of everything, not just the things you put in your articles for Richard. Send me dozens of tidbits about those wild cowboys. Than I'll at least have something entertaining to talk about."

"I will."

"All aboard!" The conductor's cry rang across the waiting area.

A shiver of nervous excitement raced down Charity's back. "Don't forget to send me the newspapers," she said. "I don't want to miss anything, either. I'll expect letters, too, nice, long gossipy ones."

Helena nodded and swiped a tear from her cheek.

"The sheriff promised to watch over you and provide any assistance. You let him do his job," Richard said gruffly.

"I will—as long as it doesn't interfere with mine." Charity smiled, blinking back a sudden tear, and hoped Helena wouldn't cry anymore. She really would hate to start off with her eyes and nose all red. "And, yes, I remember that he's supposed to meet the train. I'll wait for him to escort me to the hotel."

After one more round of hugs and listening to a few more admonitions regarding her welfare, Charity crossed the white marble floor toward the train. Glancing up at the sunlight pouring through the star-shaped windowpanes in the ceiling, she felt a sudden stab of loneliness. The last time she had boarded a train here, she had been with her mother.

Looking back at the Gilders, she flashed them a forced smile. It would not do to let them know she was having second thoughts about going. The conductor took her hand, guiding her up the steps to a first-class parlor car. Richard had insisted on paying for both the upper and lower berths in the sleeping compartment, insuring her a bit more privacy and comfort.

She sat down on the plush red-velvet seat. As Richard and Helena waved and smiled their encouragement, a long whistle pierced the air. Seconds later the car lurched, couplings groaned, and the train slowly began to move. Steam billowed; the engine chugged and gradually picked up speed. The engineer pulled the whistle with a heavy hand, and Charity plastered a smile on her face and waved happily at her friends until they disappeared from view.

She took a deep breath and tried to relax. In less than a week she would arrive in Texas. Would she regret this journey? Perhaps. She knew for a fact that she would be troubled all her days if she did not seek the truth.

Charity began the last leg of her journey in Dallas. There were no private compartments of first-class parlor cars on this particular train. She didn't mind since they would reach her destination before nightfall, and she enjoyed talking to the other passengers. The thick trees and hills of East Texas gradually gave way to the undulating grassland of West Texas. The winter grass rippled in the breeze, a knee-high sea of honey gold. In comparison to the vast rolling prairie, everything else seemed sparse and inconsequential. She spotted an occasional ranch house, scattered leafless trees— mesquites she was told—and a sprinkling of Longhorn cattle. They traveled through a few large towns, but many consisted of a handful of streets, the train station, a few stores, saloons, and a church. Others were only whistle stops, claiming a street or two.

At one point the train stopped miles from the nearest town. Like the rest of the passengers, Charity peered out the window, but she could see no water tower or other obvious reason for the delay. A brakeman climbed down and jogged across the prairie to a small ranch house about half a mile from the tracks. He returned shortly, again at a quick jog, and the train resumed its journey.

When Charity questioned the conductor about the stop, he explained that they had been delivering a message to the rancher's wife. While they had been in the last town, the telegraph operator received word from Fort Worth that the woman's mother was gravely ill. The quickest way to notify her was to stop the train and deliver the telegram. She would be ready and waiting at the tracks when the next eastbound train came through.

Two hours later, the conductor walked down the aisle, swaying gently with the train's motion. "Next stop, Colorado City."

Charity smoothed her fingers over her dark hair, making sure no strands of any significance had escaped from the coiled braid at the back of her head. She glanced down at her medium-brown cashmere traveling suit, thankful she had been able to arrange an overnight stay in Dallas. She'd had a hot bath and a good night's sleep, and for a small fee, the wrinkles had been pressed from a clean suit. Thus she had embarked on the last leg of her journey feeling refreshed and at ease. She looked crisp and polished, not at all like a young woman who had journeyed halfway across the country.

The train gradually slowed east of town, traveling past more than a dozen wooden corrals located next to the tracks. Although the corrals were currently empty, the trampled earth, piles of dry cow chips, and tiny tufts of animal hair caught in the cracks and slivers of the fence boards gave evidence of the vast number of cattle channeled through those pens and chutes for shipment to the beef-hungry East.

"It's a sight to see durin' spring and fall shippin' seasons," said the elderly man sitting across from her. She had learned earlier that he had once been a cowboy but now worked at one of the wagon yards in town. "I've known the railway agent to have as many as five hundred cars on order. They shipped over eighty thousand head of cattle out of here last year alone."

The train slowed, going past a second set of pens. Bits of white wool fluttered from the fence rails. The old-timer nodded. "Got sheep in these parts, too. Not nearly as many as cattle. Haven't had too much trouble so far. The herders purty much keep to their own range. Why, the wool in that fancy coat of yours might've come from here."

When the train started down a long, slight grade, the town unfolded before them, scattered across the valley. The courthouse, with its four-sided clock tower, was the first building Charity could identify, followed by a couple of churches. Several large, two-storied homes graced the gentle rise of land to the north and east of downtown. A few were decorated with gingerbread trim, but most, like the smaller homes around them, were built in simple, clean lines, with wide, inviting porches. She was surprised to see several brick homes mixed among the frame ones, and even an occasional tent.

As they got closer to the Texas and Pacific depot, a river could be seen running parallel to the tracks. She knew from her research that it was the Colorado River, not the one that had created the Grand Canyon, but one whose headwaters were some seventy miles northwest of the town. The small stream of reddish water flowed sedately along the riverbed, but it had taken high, swift currents to carve the wide chasm between the steep banks.

A cloud of smoke blew past the window, momentarily blocking her view. A loud, high-pitched whistle split the air. Charity's heart skipped a beat, then thudded against the wall of her chest. *Will I find happiness here? Or disappointment?* Fear raised its ugly head. For a split second, she shrank from her goal, then determination came to her rescue. No one knew the real reason she was there, and no one would find out unless she revealed it. The people here expected a writer, and that's what they were going to get.

The iron couplings between the cars clanged, the floor of the car rattled, and the couplings banged together again. Charity took a deep breath, willing her heartbeat to slow. Anticipation kept her from achieving the calm she desired.

The train rolled past the large Cameron and Company Lumber Yard and a block-long, two-story building made of dark red brick. The wheels locked in place, and another gust of smoke and steam drifted past the window, cloaking a second block of red brick buildings in a fleeting, ghostly fog. Wheels screeching, the train eased into the station.

The passengers gathered their belongings and clamored to their feet, anxious to depart—all except Charity. The floor beneath her feet rattled and hummed from the vibration of the train, but she did not move. Her gaze skimmed past the depot to the false-fronted buildings and boardwalks. The scene resembled the pictures she had seen of the wild West, except here more buildings were made of brick than of wood. Most of them had a flat top and false front, which gave the impression of another story. Often the fake storefront wasn't high enough to convince anyone the building had a second or third floor, but it did succeed in making it appear larger than it actually was. The town was much larger than her uncle had described. Evidently the past nineteen months had been prosperous ones.

"You comin', ma'am?" asked the old cowboy.

"In a few minutes."

"A mite different than what you're used to, I reckon."

"Yes, but interesting." After bidding him good-bye, she looked back at the passenger depot. It, too, was bigger than she had expected. It was made of bricks, although these were larger and a lighter shade of red than the buildings across the street. People filled the long wooden platform.

The fashionable style of the ladies' gowns came as a surprise. It was commonly believed back East that the West was a good ten years behind in fashion. Not these women. She spied one gown copied from a fashion plate that had appeared in *Harper's Bazaar* just two months before. Half the men were dressed in dark suits, typical of most business districts. Some were dressed like cowboys. Several combined the business suit with a Stetson and cowboy boots.

Practically none of the men, other than those departing the train, wore guns. That also came as a surprise. Charity thought every man in Texas packed a pistol.

Then she saw him.

He was too young to be her father and did not resemble him, but he captured her attention. He leaned against the side of the building, resting his shoulders and the sole of one boot against the bricks, elbows bent, his thumbs hooked over the top of a gun belt. The casual observer would have paid him little mind, thinking him indifferent to what was going on around him. Charity's trained eye detected the slow side-to-side movement of his head as he looked over the crowd.

From his cream-colored felt Stetson to his boots, he looked like any of the other cowboys—except for the bullet-filled gun belt and pair of Colt Peacemakers riding low on his hips. A railway worker lit a lamp near him, and the light reflected off the silver star on his chest.

*Is this the county sheriff I'm supposed to meet?* She waited, watching the lawman closely, hoping for a glimpse of his face. A glimpse was all she got. Suddenly he stopped his perusal of the crowd, his attention focused on someone departing the train.

"This might be interesting," she murmured, spotting two young men who looked like classic dime-novel ruffians. She kept her seat, waiting to see what the lawman was going to do.

Deputy Sheriff Morgan Kaine watched as the two men stepped down onto the platform. He didn't recognize their faces, but he had seen their type, which usually meant trouble. He pushed away from the wall and stepped into their path.

"Evenin'. You boys planning on staying long?"

"No, sir." One of the young men warily eyed the badge on Morgan's vest as the other one answered. "Just a few days. We come out to see my sister and her new baby boy." He named a local ranch foreman as his brother-in-law, and Morgan relaxed. The man would keep a tight rein on these two, both out at the ranch and in town.

"You know how to get there?"

"Yes, sir. We're going to get cleaned up, spend the night here in town, and then ride on out first thing in the morning." The young man grinned sheepishly. "Sis would throw me in the creek if she saw me lookin' like this. We were finishin' up some work on a ranch north of Fort Worth when I got her letter, so we just come on out here at a double trot. They been waitin' on that son a mighty long time. Already got three girls.''

"There's an ordinance against carrying weapons in the city limits, so stop at the marshal's and leave your guns. You can pick them up when you leave town. Have a good visit, and congratulate them on that boy for me." Morgan watched as they nervously walked away. There was no telling what they had been up to, but he hadn't seen any wanted posters bearing their likeness. Still, he would mention their presence to Sheriff Ware and the town marshal as a precaution.

He turned his attention back to the rest of the rumpled and tired passengers. A large crowd had gathered, although most weren't there to greet relatives or friends. Some folks had nothing better to do than meet the trains and see who was visiting, and everyone in town knew that a celebrated author was coming in on this one.

The word had spread like wildfire when the message came in over the telegraph a week before. The usual telegraph operator was pretty good at keeping things quiet, but there had been a substitute that day who couldn't resist the glory of telling the news.

Morgan enjoyed being a county deputy. He liked staying in one place. For the first time in years, he had a little house of his own and a good bed to sleep on instead of a cot or the ground. When he missed sleeping under the stars, he rode out to his uncle's ranch and spread his bedroll, picking any spot that suited his fancy. The job wasn't as dangerous as his previous one, but it came with enough excitement to make it interesting.

Like the sheriff, Dick Ware, he had been in Company B, Frontier Battalion of the Texas Rangers. He had spent nine years with the company, fighting Indians and chasing outlaws, before they had been assigned to keep the peace in the area when the county was first organized. After Dick was elected sheriff, Morgan stayed with the company for a few more years, then returned to Mitchell County to work for his old friend.

The Rangers weren't needed as much as they once had

been. The Indians were on the reservations, and there hadn't been a good bank or train robbery to occupy them in a couple of years. Morgan's last assignment with the state agency had been to infiltrate a group of fence cutters down in Central Texas. He'd hated it—he never could tolerate a liar, and that job had made him one. Sure enough, he slipped up. They found out who he was and promptly shot him in the back. When he lived through that one—and nobody thought he would, not even him—he decided to quit.

He hadn't liked cozying up to those fence cutters, and he wasn't a whole lot happier about this particular task. His job was to corral rambunctious cowboys and catch crooks—not play nursemaid to some old maid from the big city. She'd probably find fault with everyone and everything, and he'd spend the next few weeks listening to her bellyache. Just thinking about it made his head hurt.

And there would be the man problem to contend with. Women were so scarce, it wouldn't matter if she were as ugly as a buck-toothed buzzard. The vast majority of the unattached male population viewed a single female as an interesting female, regardless of size, shape, or disposition.

Morgan spotted two middle-aged women standing alone, one on each end of a passenger car, anxiously scanning the crowd. *Which one is Miss Pain-in-the-Neck?* The one on his left looked as if she could eat a side of beef for breakfast and still be hungry. Her large bosom heaved in consternation.

Preparing for a tongue lashing, he took a step forward but stopped when the woman's face broke into a smile. For a moment, he thought she was looking at him, but to his relief, he realized she was looking past him. He glanced over his shoulder to see a younger version of the woman rushing forward. Sidestepping quickly to avoid being crushed, he was momentarily deafened in one ear by squeals of delight and a cry of "Ma!"

He looked over at the other end of the train car, studying the tall, thin woman with a waspish expression on her face. Sighing softly, Morgan walked across the platform and stopped in front of her. Touching the brim of his hat with forefinger and thumb, he greeted her politely. "Miss Brown?"

"No, you impertinent young man, I am not Miss Brown. Now, step away from me, or I'll start screaming for the law."

"I am the law, ma'am. Deputy Sheriff Kaine." He pointed to the star on his chest. "Can I be of assistance?"

"No, thank you, Officer. My husband has stepped inside the depot for only a minute. We are visiting at the Matador Ranch, and our transportation has been arranged." A look of what might have been called amusement—if Morgan stretched his imagination—passed over her face. "I believe the woman you are looking for is right over there. She was the only Miss Brown on the train."

Morgan turned and barely stifled a curse as his gaze followed her pointed finger.

"Not what you expected, I gather." The woman chuckled. "You'd better hurry up, young man, or someone else will steal her away from you."

He barely heard the admonition. *Now I know why Dick kept grinnin' at me today. I'm going to skin him alive.* As a part of his mind registered the large, mostly male crowd around her and the difficult task that lay before him, another part took in her profile. Even in the fading afternoon light, it was easy to see she was no homely old maid.

Her dark brown hair was arranged in a thick, neatly braided coil at the back of her head and topped by a jauntily tipped camel-colored felt hat. It was small and round and not as fussy as most women's hats, with only a sprig of bright green silk leaves and a band of dark fur around the base for ornament. The shape of it reminded him of an upside-down stoneware bowl, with a thick lip around the top, like the one his aunt filled with mashed potatoes at family dinners.

The woman's figure was nicely curved, her slim waist accented by the stylish and obviously expensive brown traveling suit. He noted with grudging approval that her bustle was not as large as was the fashion, and that the dress wasn't decorated with a lot of folderols. The collar, cut similar to a man's suit coat, was accented with a small cream-colored cravat. Unlike her fellow passengers, she looked neat as a pin, as if she had just stepped out of her parlor for a Sunday afternoon stroll.

In their eagerness to escort the lovely celebrity to the hotel, several men—not all of them young and not all of them single—began shoving one another aside.

Morgan felt a bony finger nudge his back. "Go on, Deputy, before you have a riot on your hands."

# Chapter
# Two

"Gentlemen, please!"

Morgan was as startled by the firmness and volume of Miss Brown's voice, as were the men around her. The men instantly settled down and were rewarded by a pleasant smile. "You are very kind to be so helpful," she said quietly, draping a precisely folded camel coat over one arm. "I understand the sheriff is going to meet me. I think it would be best if I wait for him."

Her response surprised him. He had expected her to coyly choose an escort and encourage the others to try another time.

"Looks like he sent a deputy instead," someone called.

A path opened up as Morgan stepped into the crowd, walking slowly toward her. When she turned her head, meeting his gaze with a relieved expression, he quickened his pace. *Lord have mercy, no wonder the men were ready to fight.* Set against the background of dark hair, her pale green eyes were as clear as glass, her skin a creamy ivory and as smooth as porcelain. He knew he had seen more beautiful women, but at the moment he couldn't remember when.

"Welcome to Colorado City, Miss Brown. I'm Deputy Sheriff Morgan Kaine. Sheriff Ware sends his apologies and asked me to see you to the hotel. He was called to an unscheduled meeting of county commissioners." Annoyed by his own reaction to her beauty, he sounded gruff.

A soft blush filled her cheeks. Although he sounded mildly irritated, Charity took an instant liking to his deep voice and Texas drawl. She had spent the first seventeen years of her life in New Orleans and had never forgotten the charming, slower speech of the South. Texans had a bit more of a twang, but she liked it. "Thank you, Deputy Kaine. I apologize for the disturbance. I hadn't planned on making such an entrance."

When he stopped in front of her, Charity looked up at him—and up and up. *My goodness, they grow them tall in Texas*, she thought. Even without his hat, she guessed he would be almost a foot taller than her five feet, four inches. Her heart jumped a little when she looked him squarely in the face. Golden brown eyes studied her with a cool reserve that was mildly unnerving. They were nice eyes, she thought, but would be so much nicer if warmed by a smile. She couldn't see much of his hair beneath his hat, but it appeared to be a medium brown.

"You might want to put on your coat, ma'am." He didn't like the idea of parading her in front of the numerous saloons between the depot and the hotel, especially in a suit that emphasized her curves. "The wind is brisk once you get past the depot."

Charity nodded, lifting the coat from her arm. When he silently reached to help her, she handed it to him. He held it up, and she turned, slipping her arms in the sleeves. His hands brushed her shoulders as he settled the garment around her, sending a warm awareness curling through her. It had been a long time since she had responded to such a simple touch.

"Thank you," she murmured, glancing up at him over her shoulder.

His gaze held hers, a flicker of warmth shattering the coolness for a heartbeat. He nodded abruptly. "Shall I get your bags?"

"I just have this small satchel with me. I already asked the porter to take my trunk down to the hotel. I understand the weather this time of year is unpredictable, so I brought more clothes than I normally would."

"That was wise." He glanced at a leather case hanging

over her shoulder by a long strap. She also carried an alligator handbag.

She touched the leather case. "My drawing equipment. I'm so used to carrying it, I don't even think about it."

Her smile sent an unwelcome warmth rippling through him. He picked up her small case and turned toward the crowd. "Folks, why don't you go on home so Miss Brown can get settled in at the hotel? She'll be here long enough to make your acquaintance." Most of the crowd disbursed with smiles and well wishes, but a few of the men wandered away grumbling about interfering lawmen and missed opportunities.

Against his better judgment, Morgan offered her his arm. When she tucked her hand around it, he couldn't help but notice how small and delicate she seemed beside him. The top of her hat barely reached his shoulder. A couple of cowboys rode by the other side of the depot, whooping and hollering on their way to their favorite saloon. When they fired their guns into the air to add to the celebration, Charity jumped, her fingers tightening on Morgan's arm.

"It's all right, miss." Feeling a sudden protectiveness that had nothing to do with being a lawman, Morgan pressed her hand gently against his side. "The boys get a little rowdy now and then, but it's pretty safe up this way. Someone will be relieving them of their firearms directly. It's against the law to carry a pistol in town, and most of them know it."

"I'm fine, just tired from the trip." She thought about the derringer in her handbag but decided not to mention it. Surely a woman alone was allowed some protection.

He wondered how she could look so crisp and clean after traveling for so long, but he didn't ask. The less he knew about her personally, the better. A pretty woman only caused a man heartbreak—and sometimes worse.

They walked across the wooden platform and through a wide covered walkway at one end of the depot. A brisk, cold breeze hit them in the face as they paused, letting a buggy pass. Across the street stood the Grand Central Hotel and Saloon.

Morgan saw Charity's interest in the building. "This was

the first hotel in town. It's still popular with some of the cattlemen and cowboys."

"How many hotels are there?"

"Five. Besides the Grand Central, there's the Renderbrook, Planters, Pacific, and St. James. The Renderbrook is a two-story over on Walnut. It started out with twelve rooms, but by the time they had those built, they needed more, so the owner added twenty-four. A number of cattlemen keep rooms there all the time, so their families have a place to stay when they come to town. The Planters is smaller, a two-story house that was brought from Fort Griffin back in '81. The St. James is our newest and biggest. It has sixty rooms and caters to the more affluent cattlemen and important visitors."

"Like me." She smiled up at him. "I probably wouldn't be staying there if the *Century* weren't paying my expenses."

"Be glad they are. It's the only place in town—house or hotel—with indoor plumbing."

She laughed. "Thank heaven for unexpected blessings. Where do the other cowboys stay when they're in town?"

"Sometimes they go to one of the hotels, but more often they'll bed down in the wagon yards. It's a lot cheaper to throw out a bedroll on the ground or in a pile of hay. They don't usually come to town for a good night's sleep anyway."

As they stepped down the two stairs from the boardwalk to the dirt street, Charity gathered up her skirt in one hand, carefully keeping her ankles covered. Shopkeepers lit the coal oil lamps beside their doorways as darkness claimed the last rays of sunshine. She looked around in fascination at the people bustling to and fro, going in and out of dry goods stores, general merchandise stores, and a couple of furniture stores. Looking down the street, she realized that almost every other storefront housed a saloon, places with such names as the Senate, Page and Charlie's, Trivoli Hall, Ace and Henry's, the Favorite, and even one called the Little Church.

"Are there enough saloons?"

A tiny smile tugged at the corner of his lips. "Should be.

Twenty-eight at last count. All do a brisk business, too. I should warn you, ma'am. Even though we've got a law against carrying weapons, most men still carry a derringer or knife hidden away somewhere."

She shifted her handbag farther around to her side.

"If you see an argument going on, hightail it out of there."

"Hightail it?" She glanced up.

"It means to get away quick." He frowned at her still-questioning gaze. "When a cow gets spooked, she flicks her tail up in the air and runs, so cowboys call running away hightailing it."

"I see." She really didn't, since she hadn't been around cows much, but she tucked the phrase away for future reference.

After crossing the street, Morgan hustled her along the boardwalk past the Lone Wolf Saloon. The cattlemen and businessmen having their before-supper drinks quickly gathered around the windows. Many of those men were married, but he could speculate on the comments being made about the lady from New York City. Some would be complimentary, others crude. It would be the same at all the other saloons they passed.

He decided it was good he was out of hearing distance, even though he would have to make it clear that he would tolerate no disrespect for Miss Charity Brown. It was all part of the job—or so he told himself—and it might not be easy to do. A young woman traveling alone was a target for fast-talkers, rough customers, and just plain gossip. He supposed she was used to it. He hadn't read any of her articles, but Sheriff Ware had, and from what he said, she often went places a lady shouldn't.

As they moved along the boardwalk, Morgan was conscious of a hundred pair of eyes watching their progress. *Dang it, Boss. You might as well have handed me a sack full of rattlesnakes.*

"Are you in a hurry to get rid of me, Mr. Kaine?" She smiled at him. "If you keep up this pace, you'll soon be carrying me as well as my bag."

"Excuse me, ma'am." He immediately slowed down and shortened his stride, realizing guiltily that he had been walking fast because he wanted to deposit her at the hotel as quickly as he could. Yet the idea of carrying her cradled against his chest, her arms wrapped around his neck, was appealing. Too appealing. He frowned.

Charity chuckled. "Believe me, I'd lengthen my legs if I could, but I'm afraid I've been this height since I was twelve years old."

Other than a muffled grunt, he said nothing. He had been assigned to protect her because the sheriff trusted him to keep his hands off her. And that's exactly what he intended to do.

Charity was so busy looking at everything that she didn't pay much attention to Deputy Kaine's reticence. She noticed some tall poles evenly spaced along the streets and alleys, with wires stretched in between. Other lines connected them to several buildings. "You have a telephone system?" she asked in amazement.

"Yes, ma'am. It's only local, but we've got nearly seventy subscribers. Not many towns our size can boast of that."

"I should think not. I'm also surprised to see so many brick buildings," she said, noting a number of them mixed in with a few wooden ones along Oak Street.

"It's expensive to ship lumber out from East Texas, and, of course, there is more danger of fire with wood. Most of these bricks were made from clay taken from down by the Colorado River. The town's growing so fast, the kiln is going most of the time."

They slowed at the corner of Second and Oak to let a couple of riders go past before crossing the street. The Colorado National Bank was on the northwest corner, and the Snyder Building was on the northeast. It was a huge retail and wholesale mercantile that filled almost half a block. Several smaller shops were next to these businesses, including a few more saloons.

The south side of Second Street had several smaller shops on it, and one large two-story building. Across the intersection, on the southwest corner, was another two-story building, home of the local Masonic Temple. A sign on the same building indicated rooms for rent. Practically every building along this street was made of brick.

"I've learned what little I could about your area, from government records mostly, such as Colorado City being organized as the county seat in January 1881, and that the courthouse was completed in the spring of 1883."

"It was torn down last year."

"Why?" Charity looked away from her inspection of a window display of household goods, meeting his gaze. A tiny twinkle lurked there. She had been right. His eyes were even nicer when warmed by a smile. She wanted very much to keep it there.

"It was in the middle of Oak Street."

"A mistake in the survey?"

"Maybe. More than likely they didn't do a survey."

"Couldn't they run the street around it?"

"They did. But Senator Brown from Georgia was one of our prominent landholders. He donated the land for the courthouse, and when he came out to visit and saw it in the middle of the two lots, he became wildly indignant."

"Oh my, no one wants a wild senator on their hands." She smiled up at him and was rewarded with a smile in return. It warmed her all the way to her toes.

"No, ma'am. Indians and outlaws we can handle, but no one wants to take on a senator with a burr under his saddle."

She laughed. "So they tore it down to pacify him and built a new one."

"It's not quite done. Supposed to be finished early next month. It's bigger and nicer. Better be, since it cost almost three times as much as the first one."

"But I would assume there are more citizens to pay for it."

"That's a fact. Here we are. This is the St. James Hotel."

Charity turned her attention back to the street and smiled when she saw the three-story brick building. It covered half the block and had a balcony running across the front and around the corner. "Nice."

"It's the best hotel between Fort Worth and El Paso.

There's a courtyard out back. The veranda goes around back, too."

When they stepped through the hotel doorway, Morgan watched her face light up in delight and felt a swell of pride and pleasure at her reaction. He didn't know why it made him feel so good. He didn't own the hotel. He had never even stayed there. He didn't like admitting that he had a strong inclination to try to make her happy. Wanting to please a woman put a man in a dangerous position, and it was one he intended to avoid.

"Oh, this is lovely! I hadn't expected anything so grand." Charity noted the thick red carpet, highly polished mahogany staircase and woodwork, and ample, comfortable seating scattered around the spacious lobby.

The hotel manager hurried across the room to meet her. "Miss Brown, how wonderful to have you visiting us. Your trunk is upstairs in your room, and we have a table reserved for you in the dining room."

"Thank you. I'd like to freshen up a bit before dinner if you don't mind."

"Of course. If you would be so kind as to sign our guest register, I'll show you up to your room."

"Thank you. I'll be with you in just a moment." Charity turned to Morgan. "Thank you for meeting me at the train and for so nicely handling those enthusiastic gentlemen."

"You'll be seeing them again but probably not so many at one time. We're a mite short on women out here." A woman like her was liable to cause a stampede. And him a lot of trouble.

"I can probably handle a few at a time." She winced inwardly, thinking how vain that sounded. "But I was relieved when you took control of the situation. I seldom attract so much attention." At his raised eyebrow, Charity decided she was making matters worse. "Well, I'd better sign the register. Thank you, again."

"You're welcome, ma'am." Morgan politely touched the brim of his hat as she turned away and handed her valise to a young attendant hovering nearby. He figured she attracted attention wherever she went, and like most women he'd known, if her mere presence didn't cause a commotion, she would do something that did. *Yeah, I bet you can handle a few at a time,* he thought, watching her walk over to the front desk. *Just like my mother could.*

She signed her name with a little extra flourish as befitting her reception, and smiled at the desk clerk. "I'd like to send a telegram, please."

"Yes, ma'am." The gentleman handed her a piece of paper, on which she wrote a message to be sent to the Gilders: "Safe arrival. Hotel very nice. Deputy met train instead of sheriff." She paused, thinking about Morgan, and was glad he had been her escort. "Am in good hands," she concluded.

"I'd like this sent right away." Charity smiled at the clerk once again as she folded the paper and handed it to him.

"Yes, ma'am. Will there be anything else?"

"No, thank you." She turned around, waiting for the manager to show her to her room. A young man hurried past, her message clutched in his hand. Her gaze strayed to the deputy as he stopped to talk to a man coming in the front door.

She had admired his calm assurance in dealing with the young men at the depot, and the respect the townspeople gave him. His quickness when he avoided being crushed between the two heavy-set women had made her laugh and brought with it the unexpected wish to share her laughter with him.

Was he going to be the one to protect her? And was it wise to allow him to? She had caught the spark of interest in his eyes, the one he tried so quickly to hide. Charity was used to seeing interest, sometimes even lust, in men's eyes, but it had been a long time since she had felt an answer in her heart and body. She had been in love once long ago, and the experience had left her heartbroken and extremely cautious. *You came here to look for a man, but it wasn't Morgan Kaine,* she reminded herself sternly. She could not let anything distract her from what she has set out to do, not even a handsome guardian.

"I say, Miss Brown, this is a pleasure. I've been reading

your work this past year and never guessed those fine words flowed from the mind of such a lovely lady."

The strong English accent drew her out of her reverie. She knew there were a few British-owned ranches in the area, so even though the accent seemed strange, the sound did not surprise her. Turning, she came face-to-face with a very English gentleman. "You are very kind." She smiled politely, waiting for the man to supply his name, and title if he had one. The time spent at New York literary functions over the years had taught her that most noblemen were offended if addressed as a common man.

"Viscount Merryweather at your service, ma'am."

"And what brings you to Texas, my lord?"

"Cattle. Twenty thousand American dollars' worth of fine Texas stock. 'Tis only a meager portion of my fortune, you understand, but one must keep an eye on one's investments."

"Of course. Do you own a ranch here?"

The Englishman's chest swelled with pride. "One of the largest, my dear. I would be honored if you would ride out with me to see it. I have at my command the finest buggy the local wagon yard has to offer."

"Perhaps later. I shall be quite busy for the next several weeks, I'm afraid." Charity gave the viscount a cool smile. She had nothing against Englishmen, but the blatantly lecherous look in this one's eyes warned her to be careful.

"Not too long, I hope. I'm not a patient fellow."

His gaze dropped to her lips, then to the front of her dress, lingering there. Charity stiffened.

"Ma'am, we're mighty proud to have you come all the way out here to do a story," boomed another voice, one with a distinctive Texas flavor.

Charity pointedly turned her back on the viscount as several men approached her from the bar. They were dressed in fine suits and highly polished cowboy boots. "Thank you, sir. It's my pleasure to be here."

One of the men glanced at the nobleman, then met her gaze with understanding in his eyes. He introduced himself and the others with him. As she chatted with the cattlemen,

she learned that some had come into town from their
ranches for a few days, while others who lived in different
parts of the state or country made the St. James their
headquarters when they were in the area. These men treated
her with far more dignity and respect than the viscount had
shown.

Having sensed her perusal a few minutes before, Morgan
had turned his head in her direction, continuing his conversation with Sheriff Ware. He had watched her expression
soften as she looked at him. The hint of longing in her eyes
quickened his pulse and made him think of things he
shouldn't. Then, as the viscount approached her, the softness vanished from her face. Why should she be interested
in a lowly deputy when an aristocrat came calling?

She turned away, so he couldn't see her reaction to the
viscount's lewd gaze, but he did see the man's expression
clear enough, and it made his blood boil. It seemed to him
that she tolerated the Englishman longer than she should
have. Then she was surrounded by men, and from the looks
on their faces, she could have asked for the moon, and they
would have tried to pluck it from the sky.

"Looks like the little lady is going to be popular." Sheriff
Ware glanced at Morgan. "Nice to look at, isn't she?"

"Did you know she was young and pretty?"

"Well, as I recall, Gilder's message did mention something along those lines. That was one reason he was
concerned about her safety."

"But you didn't see fit to give me any warning."
Morgan's earlier irritation resurfaced, growing stronger as
Charity smiled and chatted, appearing completely at ease.
The poorest man in her captivated audience was worth at
least ten times more than Morgan was. Another one was a
millionaire. And he doubted if it made any difference that
half of them were married. A fancy woman like her would
probably just as soon be a man's mistress as his wife.

Morgan wasn't interested in a wife, or a mistress, either.
But a man would have to be blind not to be attracted to
her. Her soft laughter rang out, and he amended his assess-
ment. Even a blind man would not be immune to her charms.

"Are you listening to me?"

Morgan brought his attention back to the sheriff. "You were explaining why you didn't tell me what to expect."

The sheriff looked amused. "That wasn't exactly what I said, but I can see I made the right decision. If you'd known about her, you would have refused the assignment."

"Maybe I'll let someone else take over."

"I don't think so."

"Why not?"

"Well, in the first place, I don't have anybody free at the moment. Secondly, I think you'd wind up looking after her anyway, so why should I go to the trouble to put another man on the job?"

"You don't know me as well as you think you do."

"Maybe not. But I know you'll see the job through, regardless of your personal feelings. And I'm counting on that."

Morgan nodded. "I'll keep an eye on her, but I don't have to like it."

Dick chuckled softly. "Now I know you're lying." He glanced at his deputy, then looked across the room. "It's past time I met our guest. Want to join me?"

"Nope. I'm going over to Jake's and have a steak, then start my rounds. Unless you think Miss Brown needs me to ride herd on her this evening."

"No, I suspect she'll stay put tonight. Enjoy that steak."

Morgan hung around a few minutes, watching his friend introduce himself to the lady. Under the guise of glancing at a *Saturday Evening Post* on a nearby table, he moved closer so he could hear what was said.

"Mr. Gilder sends his best, Sheriff Ware. And we both appreciate your offer of assistance. He sent a letter for you, but I'll need to get it from my bag upstairs."

"You can send it over to the office anytime, ma'am. Just call the office when you're ready to start out in the morning, and Morgan will take you on a tour of the town."

"I would appreciate that. Once I know my way around, I can work on my own. Thank you."

Behind her, two men exchanged greetings as one was

leaving the dining room and the other was going in. "Why, J. H. Jones, you ol' coot! How are you?"

Charity swerved her head toward the men, but she was immediately disappointed. She had estimated that her father would be in his mid-fifties, but both of these gentlemen were at least seventy. Their hair was mostly silver now, but it was apparent both men had been dark-headed in their younger days. *You can't expect to find him so soon.*

In spite of her crisp appearance, Charity was tired and hungry. She knew she had been too obvious when she looked at the elderly men and was afraid the hope, followed by disappointment, had shown all too clearly on her face. She glanced at those around her. No one seemed to have noticed, yet she sensed someone watching her.

Looking past Sheriff Ware's shoulder, she met Morgan's penetrating gaze. He looked over at the two gray-haired gentlemen, who were laughing and talking in the dining room entrance, and studied them for a long moment. When his gaze came back to her, his brows were creased in a slight frown, his eyes thoughtful and questioning.

Charity turned away, sorely afraid she looked guilty as sin.

# Chapter
# Three

At eight o'clock the next morning, after a quick trip down the hall and a silent prayer of gratitude for the indoor plumbing, Charity went downstairs to the dining room for breakfast. When three of the cattlemen she had met the previous evening invited her to join them, she accepted their invitation, enjoying both the meal and their company. Afterward she left the men to their discussion of the cattle market and walked over to the front desk.

"Good morning, Miss Charity." The desk clerk beamed and straightened his waistcoat. "How may I help you?"

"Good morning. I'd like to use the telephone, please. I need to contact Sheriff Ware."

"This way, ma'am." The young man led her around a corner to the wall phone in a little alcove. "We even had long distance service for a while, but now it's just local. Tell Ester you want the sheriff's office. She'll put you right through." He pushed a wide, two-step stool over so she could reach the mouthpiece easier. "Anything else, ma'am?"

"No, nothing for now. Thank you." Charity stepped up to the phone and lifted the earpiece from the hook. A few quick turns of the hand crank brought the operator on the line. "Good morning. Could you put me through to Sheriff Ware's office?"

"His line's busy, ma'am. Is this an emergency?"

"No. I'll try again in a few minutes."

"Is this Miss Charity Brown from New York City?"

"Yes, it is, Ester."

"Thought so. You don't talk quite like you're from these

29

parts," she said with a chuckle. "Of course, we've got folks from all over, even a few Englishmen now and then. You met Viscount Merryweather yet?"

Charity smiled wryly. "Yes, I met him last night."

"I heard you were real pretty. I figured he'd be after you faster than a duck on a june bug."

Charity grinned. She had no idea what a june bug was, but it wasn't hard to imagine what Ester meant.

"If you'll excuse me for sayin' so, Miss Charity, you'll do well to stay away from that one."

"I fully intend to. Thanks for the advice."

"Sheriff's line is free now. I'll ring him for you. I hope you can stop by while you're in town. I run the switchboard from my house, so I'm always here. Don't get much of a chance to get out and visit with folks."

"I'll be sure to do that. Thanks, Ester."

Charity's conversation with the sheriff was equally brief. She hung up the telephone with a sense of anticipation mixed with wariness, a feeling which wasn't entirely due to her job or her search for her father. While she appreciated Deputy Kaine showing her around, she was well aware of his perceptiveness. She would have to be very careful, more so than she had been the night before, and not give him any reason to suspect she was there for a dual purpose.

When she was familiar enough with the town to go about on her own, she would feel more secure. Yet she looked forward to spending the morning with him and experienced a spark of pleasure when he walked through the hotel entrance.

There was something rakish about a man in Western clothes, but Morgan Kaine was in a class all by himself. He paused to speak to one of the ranchers, giving her a few moments to study him. Unlike the man he was talking to and the sheriff the previous evening, he did not wear a dark suit with a white shirt. Instead, his heavy dark-brown leather coat covered a Western-style flannel shirt of forest green. His faded blue denim Levi's were loose enough to be comfortable but tight enough to give a hint of muscular legs when he moved. The cream-colored Stetson had seen some use, but like his scuffed boots, it was worn with the comfort of an old friend. His clothes suited him, and his casual ruggedness appealed to her.

The leather gun belt riding low on his hips was another matter entirely. She had noticed the previous evening that it bore wrinkles and creases from years of wear. He shifted, and his coat swung open, revealing a Colt .45 revolver. The dark brown leather holster, worn shiny and smooth, lay against the side of his thigh like the gentle touch of a woman's caress. Charity blinked, surprised at such a thought. Hot color filled her cheeks, and she turned away quickly, pretending to check her drawing supplies.

Morgan ended the conversation with a handshake and looked across the lobby. He had spotted Charity the instant he walked through the doorway and had kept his glance from straying in her direction more than two or three times during the brief conversation. She had obviously dressed with care. On any other woman, the light green striped wool dress with its draped front and small bustle would have been considered modest. He suspected that with her eyes it would pack quite a wallop. Her matching green hat was simple enough, except for an ivory feather that curled provocatively over one ear.

As he walked up to her, he noted the soft blush in her cheeks. He hadn't spotted anything going on that would bring the color to a lady's face, but one minute she had been looking in his direction, and the next time he glanced her way, she had turned aside. He quickly scanned the lobby. It was empty except for the desk clerk, who would not have intentionally said or done anything to embarrass a lady.

"Mornin', Miss Charity. Everything all right?"

Morgan's quiet, deep voice wrapped around her like a shield against some unseen foe. She knew the note of concern she heard was a natural part of his job, but her heart did a little tap dance anyway. She met his gaze with a purposefully bright smile and closed the flap on her leather art bag. "Good morning. Yes, everything is fine. I'm anxious to get going."

Lethal. With her in that green dress, her eyes were more

deadly than a six-shooter in a gunslinger's hand. Morgan almost groaned out loud, but it had little to do with the fact that he knew of more than one fellow in town with a weak heart. Visions of kidnapping filled his mind, fracturing his well-disciplined, law-abiding thoughts. There was an abandoned line shack about thirty miles outside of town—no one would find them for days.

The intensity of his gaze held her motionless, evoking a longing unlike any she had ever known. He glanced at her mouth, sending goose bumps skimming over her, but when he met her gaze once again, anger glittered in his eyes.

Confused by his sudden change and mortified at her transparency, she looked away, dragging in a breath. The blood rushed to her cheeks for the second time that morning.

"Wear a coat. And button it up to your chin," he ordered curtly.

"Maybe I should throw a blanket over my head, too," she snapped. Usually Charity was slow to anger, but what had just transpired between them disturbed her in more ways than she could count. She grabbed her coat from a nearby chair and shoved one arm down a sleeve.

Suddenly he was helping her. He held the coat, taking care not to touch her, while she slipped the sleeve over her other arm. He surprised her again by straightening her collar, brushing the nape of her neck with his warm hand. Charity shivered but forced her fingers to jab a button through the buttonhole.

"Yeah, maybe you should." He dropped his hand to his side. "Although a gunnysack might be easier."

"You actually want me to wear a sack over my head?" Charity looked over her shoulder in disbelief and realized how close he was standing. He seemed to realize it, too, and stepped back.

"You might be safer. There are a lot of woman-hungry men in this country, ma'am, and someone like you comes along once in a blue moon. I reckon you want to look nice, but if you could keep from lookin' quite so pretty, it might help."

"I'll see what I can do, but I draw the line at wearing a

blanket or a sack." Smiling, she finished buttoning up her coat. His roundabout compliment pleased her much more than it should have.

"Fair enough. Where do you want to go first?"

"I want to see everything, so you choose."

"Let's start with the Opera House."

As they walked the block between the St. James and the Opera House, Charity noticed a track of narrow rails running down Second Street. "You have a streetcar?"

"Yep. Mule-drawn. Goes out to Phoenix Amusement Park east of town."

"Is it in the red light district?"

"No. The district is in the West End, mostly between Oak Street and the river. The amusement park has a beer garden, but it also has a dance pavilion, racetrack, baseball diamond, and zoo."

"A zoo?" She hadn't expected to find lions and elephants here on the fringes of civilization.

"Not the kind you're thinking of." A tiny sparkle lit his eyes. "Local animals—prairie dogs, coyotes, antelopes, and such. I've never figured out why it's so popular. If folks ran into those critters out on the prairie, they'd probably shoot 'em. But it gives people something to do. The family can go to a ball game or watch the horse races."

"I'll have to get out there before I leave."

Morgan unlocked the door to the Opera House and held it open for her to enter. Once inside, he lit a lamp and, carrying it, led her into the auditorium.

"My goodness, it's huge."

"Seats fifteen hundred. Dallas or Fort Worth don't even have one that big." Morgan was a little surprised at the pride he felt. Until he began showing her his adopted town the evening before, he had not realized how fond he had become of the place. "It opened last year with a week's performance by the St. Quinten Opera Company. They had eighty actors. Kept this town talkin' for months. Other theatrical groups come through now and then. And the third floor is one big ballroom."

Morgan almost mentioned the Stockman's Ball coming

up in a couple of weeks but decided against it. He hoped she would be gone before then. If the previous night was any indication, he wouldn't be getting enough sleep until she left town. No sense tempting her to stay for a fancy party. The last thing he needed was for the men around town to see her in a ball gown. His imagination was not kind—the image of shimmering green silk and creamy, smooth skin flashed across his mind. No, the last thing he needed was for him to see her in a ball gown.

"It's lovely. I'd like to come back sometime and sketch it. But since I'll need all the lamps lit, I'll arrange it with the manager."

"We can stop by his office this morning."

They left the Opera House, going across the street to Madame DeFontaine's shop, where the sign said dressmaking was done in the French style. The gown in the window was as fashionable as those Charity might buy in New York. A small sign on the door stated Madame had stepped out of the shop for half an hour. Peering through the window at the workmanship on the gown, Charity decided to come back another time.

By eleven, they had covered most of the downtown area, which encompassed some seventy-five merchants. Charity learned that the first businesses, started four years earlier, had been established on Oak Street between the train depot and the courthouse. Soon all the lots on Oak had been bought up, many by speculators—twenty-five-foot frontage lots sold for five or six thousand dollars each, and the asking price for corner lots had reached ten thousand dollars by 1884. Several important businessmen agreed among themselves to build on Second Street, where the lots were cheaper, so there would be more than one prominent street in town.

The stores provided all the necessities and quite a few luxuries. There were grocers, druggists, dry goods, and furniture stores. Some were more specialized, such as Mrs. Gilbert's. She owned a shop on the south side of the courthouse square and offered plain and simple dressmaking. Others were slightly more diversified. Nichols and Son, also on the public square, advertised as carpenters and undertakers who would make sheep-dipping vats and boilers on short notice.

There were several large general merchandise stores, such as Burns, Walker & Co. and the one owned by W. H. Snyder, carrying groceries, clothing, boots, shoes, and other staples. They furnished goods to the townspeople and served as wholesalers to the ranches scattered across West Texas, as far away as one hundred and fifty miles to the north and west and a hundred miles to the south.

Those same ranchers brought their cattle to Colorado City to be shipped out by rail. The days of cattle drives to other states had almost ended, stopped by progress and the westward-moving population.

Morgan gave her a bit of background on most of the businesses, which she jotted down in her notebook. She was ready to do some interviews and sketches. She had several interesting people in mind, such as J. Wright Mooar, a former buffalo hunter who owned a fine livery stable with his brother. Mr. Mooar had attained a certain fame by being one of the few men to shoot a white buffalo.

During the course of their walk, she had learned of three men with the initials J. H.—Mr. Colvin, who also owned a livery stable, Mr. Greene, who had a furniture store; and Mr. Mayfield, a blacksmith. She was anxious to meet them, but tried not to appear so.

"Well, that's most of the downtown area. Do you think you can find your way around?" asked Morgan as they strolled down Oak Street from the courthouse. They had spent a few minutes inside the new building, watching the workmen add the finishing touches. It appeared it would be ready near the deadline.

"Yes. You've been very helpful. Thank you." She enjoyed being with him, and even though she knew she shouldn't, she hoped they could spend more time together.

"I'll leave you at the hotel so you can change. You won't be needing that heavy coat this afternoon. But you might want a lighter one. The breeze isn't liable to die down."

She had several practical wool skirts and dresses in the hotel room, as well as two unfashionably loose light wool jackets. Her mother had designed the hip-length coats for her a few years before, nipping the waist in slightly instead of tightly. The sleeves were also wider than fashion dictated, but the extra room allowed more movement when she sketched.

While working, she often dressed as inconspicuously as possible. She had chosen the green dress that morning because she wanted to make a good impression on the townspeople—and on a certain deputy sheriff. She didn't like admitting it, even to herself, but she had wanted him to think she was pretty. *I guess I succeeded,* she thought ruefully.

"I'll see if I can find something appropriately drab to wear," she said with a smile.

"Good."

She glanced up at him, pleased to see a half smile. "I suppose I need a more practical hat, too. Something to keep the sun off my face."

He grinned. "I know just the thing. We'll stop off at Cupp's Mercantile."

Charity frowned but kept walking. Like the larger wholesalers, William Cupp & Company carried general merchandise, including clothing, but mostly men's work clothes. The few women's clothes she had seen there had been very utilitarian. She glanced at him again. The spark of mischief in his eyes mildly worried her.

When they reached the store, he led her to a small display of what appeared to be overgrown baby bonnets. She'd never seen anything quite like them. He took one off the shelf and ordered her to remove her hat.

"Why?" Her skeptical glance slid from the item in his hand to his face.

"So you can try on this sunbonnet," he said with exaggerated patience.

"You expect me to wear that?"

He frowned. "They're very popular around here. Keeps

the sun and wind off your face and neck. Women make fancy ones to wear to church."

She removed the long hat pin that held her hat in place. "I'll try it, but I don't think I'm going to like it." She eased her green hat from her head and handed it and the hat pin to him, exchanging them for the navy gingham sunbonnet.

Charity examined the design closely. Horizontal lines were stitched in the rigid, extremely wide brim, making casings which held inserts of either thin wood or perhaps cardboard. The brim was curved to fit around the sides of the face and over the top of the head. The back was gathered into a puff that stood above the brim, and attached to the bottom of both was a strip of material resembling a short cape.

She slipped the bonnet on and tied the ribbon beneath her chin. The brim stuck out a good four inches past her face, even on the sides. "I can't see anything except what's right in front of me."

He leaned down in front of her face, smiling smugly. "And nobody can see you," he said softly.

"Morgan, I can't wear this thing." She had the oddest feeling of being closed in. "It's like wearing blinders." When she started to untie the ribbon, he grabbed her hand, stopping her.

"Leave it on. It will keep you from getting sunburned."

"I don't like it." She jerked her hand from his, pulled the ribbon, and accidentally tied it into a knot. *Trapped.*

"Looks like you're stuck with it." He was standing in front of her but to one side, so she could hardly see him. Like his hand a moment before, his voice and the accompanying chuckle seemed to come out of nowhere.

She turned to face him squarely, fighting down a wave of unreasonable panic. It was only a hat, for pity's sake. She could hear other customers moving around nearby, but she couldn't see them unless she turned her head. Since the bonnet covered her ears, the sounds were slightly muffled.

A memory crashed into her thoughts—foul breath, an unwashed body, rough hands reaching for her, touching her. *Someone could sneak up on me.*

Panic swept over her again. She grabbed the ribbon, raking the taut strand up over her chin and the tip of her nose, and yanked the sunbonnet off her head. Hairpins flew with it as her dark hair tumbled around her shoulders.

Embarrassed, she met his bemused stare. "I have to see what is going on around me." She looked down at the crumpled sunbonnet in her hands, adding in a whisper, "To be safe."

Her vulnerability was unexpected. So was his reaction. Rage swept through him, directed toward the unknown man who had harmed her. His first impulse was to draw her into his arms, to tell her that she was safe, that he would protect her. But if he did, the tongues would be wagging before they left the store. Nor could he promise her complete protection; he couldn't be with her every minute.

Shifting, he blocked her from the view of anyone who might be looking. He brushed a long strand of hair back from her eyes, letting his fingertips trail along her temple as he tucked the silky lock behind her ear. "Who was he?"

She looked up in surprise, meeting his gaze. "Some hooligan."

"How bad did he hurt you?" He knew he had no right to ask, but he had to know.

She shook her head. "He didn't. He barely touched me. I got away, but I wouldn't have if I hadn't caught a glimpse of him as he stepped out of the alley."

"This happen in New York City?"

"Yes. I was doing an article on working women and had just interviewed some cigar-makers. I was on my way out of the tenements when he grabbed— uh, tried to grab me."

"Sounds like he did more than barely touch you."

He took a step closer. His size and strength alone were enough to put her on guard, never mind the anger she sensed churning beneath the surface. She should have been intimidated by him, but she wasn't. Tenderness, rough and little used, dwelled beneath his anger.

Charity had plenty of inner strength. It was part of her nature, but even if it hadn't been, she could never have been a weakling. Her mother would not have allowed it. Marion had taught her to be independent and self-sufficient, to take sole responsibility for herself. She had never leaned on anyone, yet she longed to do so now. More than anything, she wanted to rest her cheek against Morgan's broad, solid chest and tell him what had happened, tell him the story no one else knew.

Morgan covered her hand with his, squeezing gently. "How bad did he hurt you?" he repeated quietly.

"Bruised my arm and shoulder. Tore my gown. I stopped at a secondhand clothing store several blocks away and bought a shawl so I could go home without everybody seeing . . . without everybody knowing what had happened. The worst part was the nightmares. Sometimes I would dream about him grabbing me. Other times, I'd dream he was waiting outside my apartment building. I'd wake up and go look out the window to make sure he wasn't there. Silly, isn't it?"

"No, I expect that's a normal reaction." He glanced down at their joined hands and lightly caressed the back of hers. It was smooth, soft, and ice cold. "You never told anyone, did you? Not even that boss of yours."

"No. I was ashamed. I felt that I was somehow to blame."

"Had you seen the man earlier? Looked at him or talked to him?"

"No. I hadn't noticed him, but he evidently saw me. Still I must have done something to cause him to attack me, but I don't know what. I had worn a plain, inexpensive gown, but in the tenements, even that wasn't shabby enough. I looked out of place."

"The only thing you did wrong was to be alone. Being in a bad neighborhood didn't help, but it could have happened anywhere. He probably intended to rob you as well as molest you. It wasn't your fault."

She straightened her shoulders and took a deep breath, comforted by sharing the incident with him and cleansed by his assurance that she was not to blame. She thought she had gotten over it and had not realized that her terror and shame had simply been bottled up somewhere deep inside.

"I also didn't tell Richard, because he wouldn't have let me do my job if he'd known." She hoped he wouldn't make her regret sharing her secret by telling her she should work at something more suited to a woman.

He released her hand and pulled the sunbonnet from her fingers. "This job's real important to you."

"It's everything I've worked for since I was seventeen. And since my mother died over a year ago, it's all I've got."

Morgan handed the hat and hat pin back to her. He wanted to tell her that if she had a normal woman's job or a home and family, she wouldn't be taking so many risks. That would just make her mad at him, which in the long run might be a good thing. He kept his mouth shut, however. He would be better off without this attraction between them and without the tenderness he felt for her, but they were such unique feelings, he wasn't quite ready to give them up.

"I know how that is. There was a time when my job was all that kept me going." He glanced down at the sunbonnet and plucked at the hard, fast knot. Even if anyone could untie it, the ribbon would never be the same. "Looks like we bought a sunbonnet anyway."

"I ruined it. I'll pay for it." She pulled the rest of the pins from her hair, letting it fall down to the middle of her back. Turning, she scanned the men's hats on a nearby wall. "Let's see. I need something with a wide brim."

Morgan turned also, looking up at the display. "I can't rightly see you in a cowboy style."

She chuckled. "Me neither. But I can see me in that one up there." She pointed to a beige felt with a wide, droopy brim. Turning, she smiled impishly up at him. "Think that would do, Deputy Kaine?"

He returned her smile. "Yep." Stepping up to the wall, he stretched up on tiptoe and removed the hat from a long peg. Returning, he settled it on her head, then shook his own. She looked adorable. Horribly unfashionable, but adorable. Saucy. Kissable. "Let's face it, woman. There's no way I can make you look plain."

She slanted him a glance from beneath the brim of the

floppy work hat and made his pulse quicken. "Now, tell me the truth, Morgan Kaine, do you really want to?"

He looked at the twinkle in her eyes and the tiny smile on her lips and felt a grin spread across his face. "No, ma'am. I don't reckon I do."

# Chapter
# Four

Drawing whoever caught her fancy, Charity sketched some of the more interesting people in town, as well as some typical ones. A variety of characters graced the pages of her notebook—cattlemen and cowboys, businessmen and clerks, women doing their shopping. She was careful to explain to her subjects that she would not be able to use every picture or interview, but needed plenty to choose from. All accepted the fact with good grace.

Her visit with Mr. Colvin—one of the gentlemen on her possible father list—garnered some nice material for her assignment but no relative. Mr. Greene was out of town for approximately three weeks.

Later in the afternoon she stopped by the hotel for a brief rest in the lobby. As she studied one of her drawings, a young boy stepped up beside her chair.

"Hello." She smiled at the lad, touched by the awe and eagerness in his face. Glancing at the papers clutched close to his side, she knew immediately why he was there.

"Afternoon, ma'am. Are you Miss Charity Brown, the famous illustrator?"

"Well, I don't know how famous I am, but I'm Charity Brown. What's your name?"

"Sam Mayfield." He glanced around, a guilty look flickering across his face. "I'm supposed to be in school, but I couldn't stand waitin'. I sneaked off at recess. I just had to come find you."

Tenderness welled up in her heart. He looked to be about ten or eleven. Her talent had begun to show at that age. She hoped, for his sake, that his did, also. "Sit down for a bit, Sam. Do you like to draw?"

"Yes, ma'am." His face turned red as he sat down. "Well, I try. I ain't had no lessons or anything—except what Miss Jenkins, my teacher, has showed me. But she says I've got talent. Would . . . would you look at my pictures, Miss Charity, and tell me what you think?"

"Of course." He handed her the drawings, his young face intent and serious. *Please, dear Lord, let him be good,* she prayed silently. She looked down at the first page and smiled. He was more than good. His talent was exceptional. "This landscape is very nice. Is it near here?"

"Yes, ma'am. It's just west of town a little ways."

"About all we saw from the train was prairie. Are there many places like this in the area?"

"Not too many buttes or mesas, at least not big ones. There's some places south of here that have deep ravines. Some of them might even be canyons. Farther south, it gets hilly. We call 'em mountains, but Miss Jenkins said folks who have seen real mountains would call 'em hills."

"I like the way you shaded it. I'd guess it was late in the afternoon. Right?"

He grinned. "Right. Pa was out lookin' at a wagon that needed fixin', and me and Ma and my little sister went along for the ride."

She slid the sheet to the bottom of the stack, gasping softly when his drawing of a hawk in mid-flight came into view. "Oh, Sam, this is wonderful."

"I drew it from a picture I found in a book. Is that a bad thing to do?"

"Goodness, no. That's the way you learn. Was the picture the same size?"

"Naw, it was little. Maybe three inches across."

Charity smiled and shook her head, a little bit in awe herself. "You made it almost three times larger and kept it in perfect proportion. Excellent."

Next was a pair of cowboy boots, with a fancy feather design on the upper portion and across the toe. She had never carefully inspected a pair of boots, but it looked as if he had drawn them accurately. "Are these yours?"

He shook his head. "I was down at Mr. Myers's watchin' him work. He's one of the bootmakers here in town. They were on a shelf waiting to be picked up. A lot of the cowboys go to him. Come from all across Texas. They say he's the best in the business." Sam chuckled. "When he takes an order, he always tells the customer they'll be ready next Tuesday. The fellow that ordered those boots went off to Wyoming to work before they were done. When he came back a year or two later, he dropped in to pick them up. Mr. Myers told him they'd be ready on Tuesday."

Charity laughed with her new friend. "I'll have to make a point to stop by his shop. Is this design stitched in the leather?"

Sam nodded as she turned the page. "That's my cat, Whiskers. I didn't do too good on that one. He woke up before I was done and wanted to play. He wouldn't lay still after that."

"It's not bad. I think his ears are a bit small. A little thing like that can throw the whole picture off."

Next was a caricature of a cowboy, decked out in every kind of Western gear possible. The man was reaching up to adjust a precariously tipped, oversized hat. His chaps were wide and floppy above a pair of shiny boots and glistening, sharp-pointed spurs. He wore a bright red handkerchief tied around his neck and a long linen duster that dragged the ground. He looked dubiously at an old, swaybacked horse. The horse was staring in horror at the man's spurs.

"Friend of yours?" Charity grinned.

"Nope. He was some Philadelphia greenhorn. He didn't last long. First time he touched those Mexican spurs to that old mare's flanks, she pitched him right off. Next time I saw him, he was driving a buggy but still wearin' his cowboy rig."

Charity laughed and skimmed through the rest of the pictures. They were all good, but none were as delightful as the Philadelphia greenhorn.

"So what do you think, Miss Charity? Can I be an artist some day?"

"You already are an artist, Sam." She met his gaze, her expression growing serious. "I'll be honest with you. You could use a little training—we all do better with it—but I have never seen anyone with as much natural talent. I've taught several students and seen plenty of others' work. Not a one of them was as good as you are when they started out. And several of them weren't any better after two or three years' worth of lessons."

"What if I'm like them and can't get any better?"

"I don't think that will be a problem. I'd be glad to work with you. Maybe we could spend an hour together each day after school. You mustn't skip school anymore. I don't know how long I'll be here, so I would want to meet as often as possible."

He dropped his chin, staring at the floor. "My pa won't pay for lessons."

"I don't expect any payment. I'll do it for free."

Hope gleamed in his eyes when he looked up, but his brow furrowed in a worried frown. "I don't think Pa will let me. He says drawin' ain't manly. He wants me to be a blacksmith, like him."

A little twinge of apprehension skittered through her. Charity hadn't paid much attention to Sam's last name when he introduced himself, but there was a blacksmith on the list of men who might be her father. "What did you say your last name was?"

"Mayfield. You met my Pa?"

"No. Not yet." But she intended to. It was possible for her and Sam to have the same father, but not likely. With his brown hair and dark brown eyes, the boy certainly did not look like the man in the photograph. "Do you want to take me down to meet him?"

"I don't think that's a good idea. He's gonna be mad as all get out when he finds out I played hooky. I bet my teacher's already been there. I ain't gonna be able to sit down for a week." For a moment his expression was glum, but he quickly brightened. "But it was worth it to meet you, Miss Charity."

"I'll go speak to your father. You'd better go on home. By the way, you probably should learn another trade. Artists don't always make enough money to support themselves. Would you mind being a blacksmith?"

"Not as long as I could draw, too. Pa's real good. He's already been teaching me stuff. And I 'spect I could always find a job."

"You're a wise young man, Sam Mayfield. Let's hope you become a famous artist, but in the meantime, you'll be glad not to starve."

Sam laughed. "It would be a little hard to draw if I'm dead."

Charity laughed, too, and sent the boy on his way. She went the other direction.

Jack Hubert Mayfield did not look any more like her father than Mr. Colvin had. Everyone else she had chatted with during the afternoon had been pleased to talk with her or, as one of the ranchers put it, as happy as a pup with two tails. Mr. Mayfield's hospitality barely bordered on civility. She suspected Sam's teacher had already been by the blacksmith shop.

She decided to wait a bit before broaching the subject and took a seat on the top of a barrel, opening up her drawing pad, watching and sketching as he hammered a long, narrow length of iron over the anvil, forging it into a gentle curve at one end. Steam hissed into the air as he held the metal strip by long tongs and dipped it into a vat of water. He put the piece back into the fire until it was red hot, then transferred it to the anvil once again, hammering the other end into a deeper curve.

"What are you making?"

"A set of hames for a horse collar. I do the metalwork for the local collar maker. He does the rest," he said without a glance in her direction.

Charity continued to sketch as he worked, the drawing accurately depicting the power in his bare arms and shoulders, and the grace with which he swung the hammer. In his mid-thirties, he was an attractive man despite his thinning light brown hair. She included the area immediately around him, aware that there would not be room for more in the illustration.

"Do you do work for the ranches?"

"Some of the smaller ones."

"What about the large ones?"

"They each got a blacksmith shop and smithie. Keep a man busy full time."

She wondered if he was always this close-mouthed, or if he was angry with her because of Sam. "So most of your work is for the townspeople?"

"Yep."

"Shoeing horses?"

"Some. I can do most any metalwork they need."

"Mr. Mayfield, have I offended you in some way?"

He shoved the second piece of metal into the water and held it there. When it was properly cooled, he laid it on the workbench and walked toward her. He stopped in front of her, his sturdy legs spread wide in a defensive posture, and crossed his muscular arms in front of the leather apron covering his chest. Small scars speckled his hands and arms where bits of hot metal had burned them. "My son's teacher was here a few minutes ago. She said Sam ran off at recess to see you. Today was the first day of the new term."

"Oh, dear. I'm sorry he didn't wait until after school, but I am glad I met him. He's a very nice young man and a very talented one."

"You want to turn my son into a dude."

"Are you talking about Sam being an artist, Mr. Mayfield?"

He nodded. "I don't want my boy acting like some dandy."

"There's no reason he should. I know several artists who are big, burly men like yourself. Some of them have lived with the Indians or mountain men. One lived in a mining town. Another crossed the country with a survey crew ahead of the railroad. There is nothing foppish about them, yet they produce some of the most beautiful drawings and paintings I've ever seen."

She swung her legs around to the side and hopped down from the barrel to stand. Crossing over to his workbench, she picked up a three-foot-long piece of wrought iron with leaves curling between the framework. The pattern was intricate, the workmanship precise. "Did you make this?"

"Yeah." He shifted his weight and frowned, obviously uncomfortable.

"It's very beautiful." She returned the ironwork to the bench and walked back to his side. "And made by a true artist."

His eyes widened in surprise.

"Are you a dude, Mr. Mayfield?"

"Heck, no."

"Then why do you think Sam will be if he becomes an artist?"

"It don't seem manly."

"Because it doesn't take strength? Because it's something a woman can do, too?"

He shifted again, nodding curtly.

"I've met a woman blacksmith." She smiled at his expression of disbelief. "True, only one, a lady in upstate New York. Her husband had been the village smithie, and she assisted him. When he died, she kept the business going. She had help when it came to shoeing horses, but she did almost everything else herself.

"It is true that I draw well and can record what I see. But there are places I can't go, places that are too dangerous for a woman, or places that require more strength and stamina than I have. We need artists, Mr. Mayfield, both male and female, because we see the world in different ways.

"Your son has a very special gift. Please don't deny him the opportunity to develop it." She gave him her prettiest, most persuasive smile. "I'd be happy to help Sam as much as I can while I'm here. For free, of course, because I may never have another opportunity to work with someone so talented and because I'd like him to be my friend. I'm going to wire a friend to send some drawing instruction books for him. And you should know that I advised Sam to learn another trade, such as being a blacksmith, so he wouldn't starve."

Jack Mayfield's face broke into a smile for the first time since her arrival in the shop. He rubbed the back of one ear. "I guess that settles that."

Charity laughed. "Good. I promised him I would see him tomorrow after school. Will that be all right with you?"

"I don't know. He's got to be punished for leavin' school early. I could give him a lickin', but I don't like to. I'm afraid I might hit him too hard and hurt him. I think he'll have to wait a couple of days to see you again, ma'am. I expect that will get the message across more than a whippin' would."

"I understand. I'll look forward to seeing him when you think it's appropriate. Thank you for your time." She showed him the picture she had drawn of him at work.

His back straightened minutely as he looked at it. "You flatter a man, Miss Charity."

"I only draw what I see," she said softly.

He chuckled and handed the sketch pad back to her. "Then I'll have to tell my Nellie to drop by the shop a little more often while I'm working—just to impress her. Make sure she stays interested."

"You do that, Mr. Mayfield. I'm sure it will do the trick." Charity grinned at him and tucked the pad and pencil away in her leather bag. When she turned to go, Morgan was standing in the wide shop doorway, watching the exchange with a frown. It was the third time she had seen him since noon.

He fell into step beside her as she left the blacksmith shop. "Do you always do that?"

"What?"

"Charm a man into doing what you want."

"Not always. Sometimes it doesn't work with Richard." She glanced up at him. He was still frowning.

Jealousy pricked him. Again. Jack Mayfield was a God-fearing, happily married man who'd probably never thought once about cheating on his wife—until five, maybe ten minutes ago. He wondered if he could throw the enticing Miss Brown in jail as a threat to society before she disturbed the peace of half the marriages in town.

A little voice in the back of his mind told him he was being unreasonable. Jack wouldn't have mentioned his wife if he'd been thinking lecherous thoughts about another woman. And there had been nothing seductive about Charity's manner. He'd never been jealous in his life. Now he was ready to take on half the men in town for even looking at her. *Get this bronc under control, son, or you're gonna land facedown in the dirt.*

"You talkin' about your editor?" He tried to sound casual but didn't quite make it.

She looked at him, surprised at the trace of irritability in his tone. "Yes."

"The one you always persuade to your way of thinkin'. Why did he let you come out here?"

A heavily loaded wagon drawn by six teams of oxen drove up the street, distracting her. She halted abruptly and quickly pulled the sketch pad and a pencil from her bag of supplies. She flipped the pages to a clean sheet and began drawing the scene.

Morgan had glanced up at the supply wagon, too, and took three steps before he realized she had stopped. Muttering under his breath, he turned around and looked at her. She was absorbed in her task. He doubted if she even noticed where he was. Walking quietly, he moved behind her, watching over her shoulder as she worked. *She's good,* he admitted to himself. No, better than good. Although the tip of the pencil flew over the page, she didn't miss any of the tiny details that brought the picture to life.

As the wagon moved abreast of them, she took a step backward and bumped right into him. "Oh, excuse me."

"Sure."

She looked as if she expected him to step aside and give her more room. He didn't budge. A tiny frown wrinkled her brow, but she immediately turned back toward the street, standing at a slight angle, intent on finishing the picture before the wagon moved too far away.

He decided that since meeting the train last night he had gone loco. There was no sane reason for him to be standing there on the boardwalk enjoying himself so much. He was thankful they were on a side street, and hoped the few men who walked by would think he was merely watching her work. He wasn't.

Her shoulder brushed against his chest every now and then, and the side of her hip rested against his thigh, but she didn't seem to notice. He did.

The scent of lily of the valley drifted to his nostrils. He had never cared much for perfume. Most of the women he knew wore something that could be smelled ten feet away. But this fragrance was different, subtle and sweet. Pleasing. He breathed deeper.

Her hair was pinned up beneath that ugly hat, exposing the graceful line of her neck. Wispy little curls at her nape sidetracked him from his deliberation about perfume. When he exhaled, they fluttered gently. Just about the time he wondered if they tickled, she reached up and absently rubbed the spot, tipping her head a tiny bit to one side.

He grinned and peeked around at her face. When this woman set her mind to something, there was no stopping her. He eased back and blew softly.

She halted the movement of her hand and looked up from the drawing pad. Understanding dawned, and she turned her head slowly toward him, glancing down to where their bodies touched. Her gaze shot to his.

"Don't mind me," he said with a teasing smile and lazy, exaggerated drawl. "I'm just watchin'."

She raised an eyebrow and stepped away as three cowboys came around the corner, laughing and slapping one another on the back about a prank they had pulled on a shopkeeper. To avoid a collision, Morgan slid his arm around her, hauling her against him. One hand and the drawing pad were wedged between them. Her other hand, holding the pencil, rested against his chest. He stared down at her, vaguely aware of a "Pardon me, ma'am" coming from one of the cowboys as they passed by.

Irritation darted across her face, followed by a growing

awareness and a hint of yearning. When she made no attempt to pull away, he waited for a coy smile and murmured innuendo or perhaps an outright invitation to go someplace private. Instead she searched his eyes, uncertainty gradually filling her own. Her wariness confused him. Could it be she wasn't as wise in the ways of the world as he expected? She looked down, somewhere in the vicinity of his collar, as a deep blush spread from her throat up to her cheeks.

"Is the way clear now?" Her soft voice quivered slightly.

His gaze dropped to the rapid pulse visible in her throat. Did he frighten her? It might be safer for them both if he did, but he didn't want to. He glanced up at the boardwalk and nodded, reluctantly releasing her. "It's clear."

She stepped away, staying close to the building in case someone else came around the corner, and put an acceptable distance between them. "I should get back to the hotel."

"Before you go, will you show me what you drew today?"

"Of course." Charity handed him the sketch pad.

He leafed through it slowly, pausing longer when he came to a drawing of two cowboys standing in front of Page and Charley's Saloon on Oak Street. Their likenesses were perfect, from the Stetson hats, chaps, and spurs, down to the glint in the eye of the man doing the talking and the grin on the other one's face. "Looks like Lump Mooney was bendin' Blond Tom's ear as usual. Lump is full of homey wisdom. His sayings are quoted all over West Texas." The next page showed J. Wright Mooar and his white buffalo hide spread out on the wall. Once again, the portrait of the man was without flaw.

When he came to the picture of Jack Mayfield, he got jealous all over again. He expected more than one female heart would palpitate at the raw, masculine power radiating from the man. No wonder Jack's chest had swelled with pride. He shoved the sketch pad back into her hands. "You're real good, Miss Charity. I'll grant you that."

"Thank you." She glanced up at him before slipping the pad into the bag. He appeared mad again but not suspicious.

Exasperated, she wondered what she had done to irritate him this time. She decided she would let him mull over his problems—whatever they were—by himself. Turning, she started for the hotel.

"Is Richard more than your editor?"

She jumped when he suddenly appeared at her side. Frowning, she picked up the pace, but he easily matched it with his long stride. "He's a very close friend."

"How close?"

"He and his wife, Helena, are like family. Why?" She stopped abruptly, and so did he.

He glanced up the street, down at his boots—anywhere but at her face. "I just wondered."

What was he wondering? If Richard were her sweetheart or perhaps her lover? Just as importantly, why did he want to know? She thought she might be better off never asking those questions. When she started walking again, he fell in step beside her.

"You draw a lot of pictures of half-naked men?"

"No. Are you talking about Mr. Mayfield?"

He nodded curtly.

"Well, he really wasn't half-naked. His apron covered most of his chest." She wasn't sure what possessed her— later she would blame it on some unknown imp—but she couldn't resist teasing him. "Which is too bad, actually. Maybe I should ask him to pose for me without the apron."

Morgan glared at her. She smiled and poked his biceps with her finger. Nice. Curving her hand around his upper arm, she pressed the muscle a couple of times between her fingers and thumb. "Hmm. Not bad. Maybe I could get you to pose instead."

"Don't bank on it."

She gave him a look of pure innocence. "Why, you'd look every bit as good as the models in some of my art classes." She ignored his scowl. "Probably better," she murmured, momentarily lost in thought, the kind a lady wasn't sup-posed to have.

"How many of these models were there?"

"Huh? Oh, I think five or six. I don't remember. It was

years ago. We drew Greek and Roman statues first." Oh, how she had blushed at the beginning. "The kind that left little or nothing to the imagination, so we weren't embarrassed when the instructor brought in the live models." *Supposedly.*

The first man had looked like Adonis. Three of the other girls in the small class swooned at the sight. Charity didn't faint, but she didn't complete the picture, either. She was eighteen at the time, but because she and her mother had always lived alone, she had never seen a flesh-and-blood bare chest before, much less bare stomach, back, and legs. It was difficult to look at him without turning fifteen shades of red, especially when he was staring right at her. The next one wasn't as bad, and by the time the instructor had paraded three or four more in front of them, she could paint the pictures with a minimum of discomfort.

"What did they wear?"

"A large towel." She giggled at his shocked expression. "Carefully draped, I might add." *Shame on me.* She didn't want him to think she was too bad. "I haven't done anything like it since." At his skeptical snort, she added, "The blacksmith doesn't count. He was working. And had a lot more covered."

He made an exasperated noise low in his throat. It sounded suspiciously like a growl. "I ain't some fancy dude model."

"No, but I still would like to draw your picture." She smiled up at him, all traces of teasing gone. "I'll need it for the segment I'm planning on law enforcement."

"Maybe later. But I'm not takin' off my shirt—or anything else."

"Fair enough." *I wouldn't want the world to see you like that anyway. I'd keep you all to myself.*

# Chapter
# Five

Charity had quickly discovered that the St. James was often the site of business transactions, even for those ranchers who had homes in town. And financial transactions did not always have to do with business. The gossip racing around town the next morning was about a poker game in the hotel bar the night before where some four thousand dollars had changed hands on one play of the cards. Even though she knew times were good for the cattle industry, she was shocked that someone could wager so much and, as the story went, lose without batting an eye.

The other talk at breakfast was about the upcoming Stockman's Ball. She was relieved to hear that Viscount Merryweather had left town for his ranch the day before; otherwise he might have asked to take her to the party. The men at her table were married, but all offered to escort her along with their wives, unless some single fellow showed some intelligence and asked her.

The first thing after breakfast, Charity went to the Western Union office and wired Helena to send some drawing books. Like Charity, Helena was a graduate of the Cooper Union Art School, so she would know which ones to send.

Next she headed straight to Madame DeFontaine's shop. The cattlemen's cheerful complaining about what their wives were spending on ball gowns, coupled with the eye-opening information about the size of their card games, told Charity she needed something much fancier for the party than what she had brought with her. Although the seamstress was buried in work, she jumped at the chance to make Charity's gown, especially after being assured mention of her talents in the magazine article. Charity also paid her extra for creating something on such short notice.

She spent most of the morning going through the shipping records at the train station and the public records at the temporary courthouse, gathering general statistical information for her articles and searching for men who might be her father. She checked land deeds, title transfers, plat maps, and tax records as well as the death records. An Arthur James Hendrix was listed in the death records. He had died six months earlier, at age fifty. She prayed he wasn't the one. She found four names with the correct initials in the tax and deed records.

J. H. Jones, the elderly man she had seen her first night in town, was a small rancher. A man named Jonathan Harris owned a saloon called the Waterin' Hole. From the taxes paid, she could tell it wasn't as large as some of the others, but it appeared he made a tidy profit nonetheless. A check of the land deed and plat map told her his establishment was situated well into the red light district, not a place where she could casually walk by and peek in the window.

Two other men, Jacob and Joshua Hunter, owned a ranch south of town called the Double J. They owned a hundred sections, sixty-four thousand acres, and leased forty more sections, but Charity suspected, from the amount of taxes they paid and the number of cattle shipped the previous fall, that they also grazed their herds on some of the open range like most of the ranchers in West Texas. She studied the figures she had written down in her notebook and absently drew a little cowboy hat in the margin. Her breakfasts with the cattlemen provided lessons about the cattle industry right along with the food. Many of them owned little of their land, but others saw the need to buy or lease, especially with so many newcomers crowding the range.

She had been told that there were more millionaires in Colorado City than in all the rest of Texas, but it was difficult to tell for certain. Some of the county's citizens came close enough to make the story likely. Several of the men who were currently staying at the St. James had vast holdings in other counties but did their banking and business in Colorado City, so they were potential members of that elite group.

According to what she found, one of the gentlemen she had met upon her arrival was a millionaire. He hadn't seemed like one. Quite a few of the men she had eaten with or talked with in the hotel lobby were worth a hundred thousand dollars or more, and many of the others were not far behind. For reference, she made a list of the ranchers who owned land or paid taxes in the county, beginning with those whose holdings were small, working her way up through the median range, and topping it off with the wealthier ones.

The Hunters appeared to be worth well over one hundred thousand dollars, probably closer to two hundred. That bit of news stopped her cold. She had no idea if they were brothers or father and son. Nor did she know how old they were. But if one of them was her father, he would probably think she was only after money.

The shipping records at the depot yielded another name. Jefferson Davis Haley had sent out a load of sheep the year before. The railroad agent told her Mr. Haley had a sheep ranch some fifty miles north of town.

She skimmed over the County Commissioners' Court records but found them rather boring. The commissioners' main functions were to set tax rates and provide money where needed, such as caring for paupers and building bridges and the courthouse. These were important things, but she did not think her readers would find them particularly interesting.

The city council meeting minutes were more enlightening. Having always lived in cities, first New Orleans and then New York, Charity had never given much thought to what it took to establish a town. The first city ordinance dealt with regulating outhouses. They had to be over a vault four feet deep and cleaned once a month. This was later amended to being cleaned sufficiently often and kept in such a manner so that no stench or bad smell should arise.

Anyone caught throwing garbage or rubbish of any kind in the streets or alleys of the new town would be fined up to twenty-five dollars according to the second ordinance, and citizens could not let garbage remain on their property without a daily fine.

There were the usual ordinances against carrying weapons, assault and battery, disturbing the peace, drunkenness, and selling liquor to anyone under twenty-one, as well as a law prohibiting horse racing along public streets or alleys. There were regulations concerning stoves, outdoor burning, and fireworks—very important in a town where the only water available was pumped from Lone Wolf Creek, hauled in barrels from a group of springs called Seven Wells six miles south of town, or caught as rainwater in cisterns. Since there was no community water tower, the city was poorly equipped to fight fires. Water stored at businesses and homes might be adequate to extinguish a small blaze, but a large one could easily destroy most of the town. The council was currently preparing to sell bonds to build a waterworks.

During the town's earliest days, there appeared to have been a problem with hogs and pigs running loose. The town marshal picked them up and sold them after five days if the owner did not claim them and pay the fine. If the owner showed up within one week after the sale, the marshal would deduct the fine and all expenses and give the owner what was left. Otherwise the money went into the town treasury.

The city council wasn't as lenient on dogs. Dogs had to be licensed at the cost of one dollar each. If the marshal came across one without a tag, he was ordered to slay the lawbreaking varmint on the spot.

In addition to helping keep the peace, it was the marshal's job to collect fines and taxes. Ten men had served as town marshal in the two years since incorporation. One lasted only nine days. Another held out for eleven. "Maybe they didn't like chasing pigs and killing dogs," Charity said to herself.

The city council levied taxes and charged license fees for

doing business. A lawyer, doctor, or dentist paid two dollars and fifty cents a year, but a theater or dramatic representation was charged two-fifty for each day a show was performed unless the performance was for instruction or charitable purposes. Life, fire, and marine insurance companies paid five dollars per year to do business. Charity laughed when she read that one. Who would need boat insurance in the middle of the dry West Texas prairie?

Anyone keeping a hobby horse or flying jenny to be used for profit was charged ten dollars a year, and all billiard tables, pigeonholes, devil among the tailors, or Jenny Lind tables were worth ten dollars each to the city. Traveling patent medicine salesmen were hit for eighty-seven dollars and fifty cents, where clairvoyants only paid twenty-five dollars. The highest fee was five hundred dollars—charged to the owner of a nine- or ten-pin alley or a fortune teller. Either they were not welcome, or the councilmen thought they made a great deal of money.

Charity returned the ledgers to the county clerk and went outside. Sitting on a bench near the street, she drew a picture of the impressive courthouse. When she finished it, she walked over to the sheriff's office.

Sheriff Ware was at his desk. Morgan sat nearby, his long legs stretched out in front of him, a tin cup of coffee in his hand. She had never seen him without a hat. His hair was long and straight on top, combed back in a simple style, and shorter on the sides and in back. The sunlight coming through the window captured glistening copper strands sprinkled in among the brown. Both men stood when she entered the room.

"Good morning, Miss Charity. How are you today?" Sheriff Ware came around the desk and offered her a chair.

"Fine, thank you." She sat down, resting her handbag and leather art case on her lap, smiling first at the sheriff and then at Morgan as he resumed his seat. He leaned the chair back on two legs, and when he returned her smile, there was so much warmth in his eyes that she almost forgot why she stopped by.

"What can we do for you?"

Charity turned to the sheriff, catching a fleeting expression of amusement as he noted the exchange. He rested his hip against the edge of his desk and looked away briefly, scooting over a stack of papers.

"I want to go down to the West End this evening," she said matter-of-factly.

Morgan's chair crashed to the floor. He bit off a curse as the hot coffee sloshed over the rim of the cup and onto his hand. "You what?"

He shook his fingers and swiped them on the side of his pant leg, distracting her. "I need to get some information on the district for my story."

"Maybe we could tell you what you want to know," said the sheriff.

She shook her head. "I need to see it for myself. I couldn't possibly do any drawings from a description."

"You aren't going there." Morgan's tone declared the discussion finished.

She met his angry glare with a determined lift of her chin. "Yes, I am. I want to cover every aspect of this area for the magazine, and that includes something about the saloons, dance halls, and theaters."

"What about the parlor houses? Don't you want a firsthand look at them?"

"No, that would be a little too much for our readers, I'm afraid." She squirmed at his cynically raised eyebrow. "And for me. Although I've often wondered what makes women turn to that sort of life," she added thoughtfully. "I couldn't use it now, but perhaps later."

"Don't even think about it." Morgan stood, walked over to a little table beside the stove, and tossed his cup on it. "You set foot in a whorehouse, and not one decent woman in this town will give you the time of day. They won't let their husbands talk to you, either." He turned to face her. "Just going down to the district will be enough to ruin your reputation."

"Not if you take me."

"I don't know, ma'am. I'm afraid Morgan's right. Ladies don't go into saloons and such. There will be talk."

Feeling at a disadvantage with the two men towering over her, Charity rose gracefully, placing her bags on the chair. "Everyone knows I'm writing about settling the area and the growth of the town. Surely they would understand that I need to write about the whole town. On the one hand, you have the rowdy cowboys and a wide-open red light district. There can't be that many towns this size anywhere in the country with twenty-eight saloons. On the other hand, you have a thriving business district, two wonderful schools, four churches, an opera house, and solid, upright citizens. It's a clash of cultures, which my readers will find extremely interesting."

"It's more like uneasy tolerance of a mutually beneficial situation," said Sheriff Ware. "There are some who want to shut down the district, but most folks put up with it as long as the participants keep the mischief in that part of town." He looked at Morgan. "What do you think?"

"I think she's askin' for trouble, and it won't be just talk. I'm not takin' you." He crossed his arms and glared at her.

"Then I'll go on my own." She crossed her arms, too, and glared back. She had no intention of doing any such thing, of course, but if she ran a good bluff, he couldn't be certain.

*Independent little fool. Stubborn as a government mule. You'll get hurt, hurt bad.* Morgan had a reputation for being cool under fire—cold and hard as steel, most folks said. A single look usually stopped a man bent on mayhem. Occasionally it took a quiet, firm command. But with Charity he didn't feel cool or quiet. He was in unfamiliar territory, on uneven ground. So he yelled. "You will not!"

"I don't think you can stop me, unless you throw me in jail. And I don't believe I would be breaking any laws."

"You're not going down there." *Don't roar.* One long stride brought him within touching distance. Hands on her hips, she looked up, her gaze still locked with his. He bent down until they were practically nose to nose. With great effort, he kept his voice down. "You won't get twenty feet into the district before somebody propositions you. The first one might take no for an answer. A few others might, too, but you'll meet up with one who won't. He'll figure you're a prostitute just because of where you are. And nothing you say or do would stop him."

"But you could," she said softly. "No one would try anything if you were with me." Without thinking, she raised her hand to his chest in supplication. Beneath her palm, his heartbeat quickened. Hers sped up, too. "Please, Morgan. I need to go there, and I know I'd be safe with you."

Her soft answer turned away his wrath. He tried to renew his anger, but he couldn't—not with her looking up at him with such trust and tenderness in those beautiful green eyes. He ought to wring her neck, but he longed to caress it instead. He wanted—needed—to kiss her. He curved one hand around her waist and lowered his head—but a discrete cough brought him up short.

He jumped back, as if he'd touched a hot branding iron, and glanced at the sheriff. Dick hid a smile. Morgan turned away, trying to collect his jumbled thoughts. What in tarnation had come over him? Now Dick was liable to pull him off the assignment. *Good.* He surreptitiously glanced in her direction. *No, bad. I want to protect her. I want to be with her. And that's not good. Definitely not good.*

Out of the blue came something his Aunt Addie had once told him. "Not all pretty women are like your mother. Someday you'll find a woman you can admire and respect." She'd patted his cheek and smiled. "And when she makes you forget about everything else goin' on around you, you'll know she's the one."

He didn't want a woman who made him oblivious to what went on around him. He wouldn't be like his father. His aunt had uttered those words when he was seventeen, after he found his mother with one of her lovers. It hadn't been the first time. Nor was it the last. Morgan hadn't believed his aunt then. He refused to believe her now, even if a part of him wanted to.

"I think you'd better escort the lady down to Archie's after supper. He'll help you keep the boys in line."

Morgan's gaze shot to the sheriff. Dick's eyes were filled with understanding. Morgan had never told him about his mother, but they had talked enough over the years that Dick knew he didn't trust women and had never had much to do with them.

Charity turned back to the chair and picked up her things, trying to hide her blush. How could she have forgotten the sheriff was in the room? Easy, when Morgan looked at her with such need, such loneliness.

"Miss Charity, I don't want you going to the West End by yourself." Sheriff Warc's voice was stern.

She turned, meeting his gaze with more aplomb than she felt. "Yes, sir. I won't. I'm sure I'll get everything I need this evening."

"Good." The sheriff pulled his watch out of a vest pocket and checked the time. "If you'll excuse me, I have to be going. I'm due at the mayor's for supper in ten minutes. It was nice seeing you again, ma'am." He walked over to the wooden rack on the wall and removed his hat from a peg. "Have you had any problems? Anyone giving you any trouble?"

"No. Everyone has been wonderful. I spent most of the day with my nose buried in the city and county records, gathering statistics and general information."

Dick stopped by the door and settled his hat on his head. "You let me know if you need anything."

"Thank you. I will."

He left, shutting the door behind him. Silence reigned.

Morgan kept his back to her, his hands jammed in his pants pockets. She felt badly about embarrassing him in front of the sheriff. Reminding herself that he was as much to blame as she was didn't help much. "Morgan, could I buy your supper?"

He turned his head toward her, his expression aloof, and said nothing. No warmth burned in those lovely golden brown eyes.

"Everyone raves so about Jake's, I thought I'd try it. But I don't want to go alone."

"I don't let women buy me things."

Charity frowned, detecting a note of pain beneath his words. "It's only a meal. And I'm on an expense account, so if you want you could say Richard was buying it." She crossed the room to his side and smiled. "I'd like your company."

"Why?"

"Because beneath that huff-and-puff exterior, you're a nice man. With you I don't have to be Charity Brown, famous author. I can be me. And right now, Charity Brown, regular person, is feeling a long way from home and a little bit lonely. I need a friend."

He looked down at her smiling face and gentle eyes. As they so often did, her eyes reflected her feelings. His resolve melted. "You think I qualify?"

"I hope so." She grinned mischievously. "I wouldn't go places I shouldn't with just anyone."

"Don't remind me." He glanced down at her periwinkle-blue skirt and matching jacket. They were fashionable but not fancy. The fitted jacket hugged her curves, leaving no doubts about her full bosom and small waist. "You're not wearing that to the district." He frowned. "Don't you own anything baggy?"

She chuckled. "As a matter of fact, I do. I took a break from government records at noon and dropped in to see Mrs. Gilbert. She had a wool Mother Hubbard in her window display that you'll like. She shortened the hem and the sleeves and made a few minor alterations to the lining so it fits."

He plucked his hat from the wall peg and set it carefully on his head. He took a long tan duster from another peg and slipped it on.

Charity eyed the coat with interest and dropped her bags on the table beside his coffee cup. "Where can I buy one of those?"

"This is a man's coat."

"So?" She pulled the lapels together and studied the fit. He stood perfectly still and studied her.

"You've already got me wearing a man's hat half the time. I think one of these would come in handy. It looks warm, and since it fits loosely, it would be perfect for working outside. Or for wearing when I don't want to look my best."

She was standing close, still holding onto the coat. A slow smile eased across his face. "Like when you drop in at your local saloon?"

"Exactly."

"Most any of the dry goods stores have them."

"I'll pick one up after supper." She toyed with the lapel, absently rubbing the lightweight canvas between her finger and thumb. She knew she should move away from him, but she couldn't seem to get her legs to cooperate. Her gaze dropped to her fingers. She held them still and simply let her hand rest against his chest. "Morgan?"

"Hmm?"

"Since we're friends, would you drop the 'miss' and just call me Charity?" She avoided looking at him, suddenly feeling a little shy.

He nudged her chin upward with his knuckle, lightly caressing her jaw with the pad of his thumb. A soft light shone in his eyes; his expression was mellow. When he spoke, his voice was deep and low, his Texas drawl exaggerated. "Sure, Charity, darlin'. If it makes you happy."

She blinked in surprise, and he chuckled. During her brief time in West Texas, she had learned that cowboys—from cattle barons to lowly ranch hands—affectionately and respectfully liked to call the ladies "darlin'." She'd heard it so many times in the past two days that it had grown meaningless. Or so she had thought.

No one murmured the endearment quite the way Morgan did.

# Chapter
# Six

Jake Maurer's Restaurant was on Oak, not far from the train station. It was packed with cattlemen, cowboys, and freighters. Three women were also in the crowd, evidently escorted by their husbands. Morgan was such a regular customer, however, that a small table near the front window awaited him. The owner kept it available at all times, since the deputy never knew when he would be free to eat. After Morgan had politely helped Charity with her chair, Jake came over to personally take their orders.

"Evenin', ma'am." Jake smiled at Charity and grinned at Morgan. "How did you ever persuade a pretty lady like this to have supper with a scoundrel like you?"

Morgan smiled lazily. "I didn't have to. The lady invited me." He figured Jake already knew who she was, but he made the introductions anyway.

Charity liked Jake immediately. In his early thirties, immaculately dressed in black trousers with a freshly starched white shirt and black bow tie, he was a congenial host, not only to her but to everyone who came through the door. He recommended that Charity try the steak, then winked at Morgan, telling him they would be having some special entertainment.

When Jake left to greet another customer, Charity scanned the room. Between the diners and the men drinking at the bar, a singer might have been able to squeeze in next to the piano. There wasn't room for anything else. "What did he mean by entertainment?"

Morgan's eyes twinkled. "You'll see directly."

She was beginning to learn Texan, at least she thought she was. "Directly—as in soon, or am I going to be involved?"

He laughed. "As in soon. Course, you could get involved if you want to. Might be interesting."

"No, thanks. I'll remain a bystander—or bysitter, as the case may be." She glanced across the room, focusing her attention on Jake and a ragged-looking man she had seen eating a few minutes before. Instead of the man paying the proprietor for the meal, Jake fished in his pocket and handed him some money.

"He never turns anyone away," Morgan said quietly. "Not only does he give a man a free meal, or credit if he needs it, like as not he'll either loan him money to bed down someplace or give it to him outright. There are some good folks in this town. Jake is one of the best."

She whipped out her drawing pad and pencil, and quickly began sketching the scene. Jake's likeness was easily recognizable, but she purposely made the other man's face nondescript, only a symbol of a man down on his luck. When finished, she looked up to find Morgan watching her. He nodded in approval.

"How many of these drawings will you use?"

"I don't know yet. After I write the article, I go through my collection of pictures and send in the ones that are the most appropriate. Richard usually puts one per page. I don't have a set number of articles to do in the series, but I'll try for four to six."

"One a month?"

"Yes. I'll write them while I'm here, in case I need to check on something, and send them in to him as I'm done."

He played with the handle of a steak knife, nudging it back and forth with his finger. Watching the movement of the knife, he asked casually, "How long do you plan to stay?"

*Until I find my father.* "Until I run out of things to write about. It could take a month or two. Maybe longer. And sometimes I go back and touch up the drawings, or even do them over, if they don't seem right." She relaxed against the back of her chair and gazed out the window. The daylight was fading quickly. Like the other merchants, Jack walked outside and lit the coal oil lanterns beside his doorway. "I may stay in Texas awhile after my work is done."

He looked up at her. "I thought you were homesick."

"Not homesick. Just a little out of place. I miss my friends, but the change of scenery—and of people—is nice. Life can get so hectic in New York. I could go somewhere every night if I wanted, to the theater or to some literary or artistic function or to dinner. My friends rallied around me after my mother died, but most of them think the way to handle grief is to be so busy you don't have time to think about it." She took a deep breath and swallowed the sudden pain. "It didn't work very well for me."

"How long has she been gone?"

"A little over a year."

"You were close?"

"She was my best friend."

"What about your father?"

Her heart jumped, but she quelled the spurt of fear. "Henry died before I was born. He was a shopkeeper and was shot during a robbery. Mother and I lived in New Orleans until I was sixteen. Yes, that explains my odd accent. It's a mixture of Southern and New York. Mama was a dress designer for the society ladies in New Orleans, but when my teacher told her I should go to New York to study art and writing, she packed up and moved. She had such good references that it was easy for her to reestablish her business in New York City.

"She was a wise woman." *In some ways.* "She looked for clients among the literary and artistic elite and took every opportunity to brag on me, especially after I was accepted at the Cooper Union Art School. Richard's wife, Helena, was one of my mother's clients. She had attended the same school and took an interest in me. They included us in their literary meetings and took me to all the art shows. After I graduated, I gave private art lessons to youngsters and had some articles published in several small newspapers and magazines. When Richard became the editor at the *Century,* he suggested I submit something to him. I never dreamed he would actually publish it."

"And you've been writing for him ever since?"

"Yes. Although he doesn't always go along with my ideas."

"How did you convince him to let you come on this trip?"

She laughed. "I threatened to send the articles to *Harper's Monthly* instead."

He nudged the knife around a few more times. "Why did you want to come to Texas?"

Charity was certain he could hear her heart pounding above the noise in the room. She took too long to answer. His gaze narrowed as he looked at her. "I guess I could blame Mr. Twain."

He frowned. "Mark Twain?"

"Yes. He told me that I should get out to see the West before everything was civilized. Mother grew up near Brownsville, and she and Henry had lived in Galveston for a while. Texas seemed a logical place to follow Mr. Twain's advice, especially West Texas, since it is just now being settled."

Morgan stared at her. "You're friends with Mark Twain?"

"Not friends, merely acquaintances. When he is in New York, the Gilders have him as a guest. They often invite me to dinner or some function at their home while he is there—me and anywhere from twenty to fifty others. I've talked with him, and he even remembers me when he sees me, but that's about it."

She actually thought the man could forget her? "What's he like?"

"Humorous, friendly, opinionated. A little rough around the edges, but I like him. Some of his colleagues don't know what to think of him. But they're the old stuffed shirts who believe realism is vulgar. They think we should only write about or draw things that are beautiful or ideal."

"And you don't?"

"I have nothing against beautiful things or lofty ideals, but that shouldn't be the only thing people see or hear about. If we hide the problems, they will never be resolved. If we don't show people the commonplace in a way they can appreciate, they'll always be dissatisfied with what they have."

"Makes sense." He straightened and put the knife in its proper place. "Well, I don't think you could call Jake's grub beautiful, but I'll guarantee you it's not commonplace."

A waiter set the plates of piping hot food in front of them, adding a basket of fragrant yeast rolls and little bowls of canned peaches.

Charity looked at her plate, her delicate brows wrinkling in a frown. There was twice as much as she could possibly eat—twice as much of what, she didn't know. She recognized the mashed potatoes and spoonful of peas, but the meat—if it *was* meat—was covered with some kind of white gravy or sauce. She picked up her fork and pushed aside some of the gravy. Whatever it was had been coated in batter, which had been fried to a flaky crust.

She leaned toward Morgan and asked softly, "Didn't I order a steak?"

Amusement lit his eyes, and even though he was already chewing his first bite, she suspected he had watched her every move. He made her wait until he could swallow. "Yep. And that's what you've got. Chicken-fried."

"You mean the cook is a chicken?"

Morgan grinned. "Nope. But in Texas steak is cooked the same way you fry chicken. Most of the time, anyways. Your mother grew up in Texas. Didn't she ever cook it this way?"

"Mother seldom cooked. We either had someone do it for us or we ate out." She cut a small bite. "It seems tender enough. Well, here goes."

"Make sure you get some cream gravy. It tastes much better that way." Morgan watched as she dipped the meat in the gravy and raised the bite to her mouth. From the look on her face, it seemed she didn't expect to like it. The bite disappeared between those pretty pink lips. Her jaw moved slowly as her teeth carefully came together. Instantly her frown evaporated, her eyes widened, and she chewed in earnest, swallowing the bite quickly.

"This is wonderful."

He chuckled at the way she hastily cut another, bigger bite. She closed her eyes and made a little humming sound of pleasure when she tasted the food. Would she close her eyes and purr with delight when he kissed her? He knew it was inevitable. Maybe not tonight or even tomorrow, but before long, he would taste her lips and hold her close. He would probably regret it, but it was a temptation he couldn't resist. He'd give in. Once.

A movement outside the window caught his attention. "You'd better open your eyes, darlin', or you'll miss the show."

"What show?" She looked around and noted a man sitting at the piano. Seconds later he began pounding out a rousing tune. The crowd in the restaurant began to clap in time with the music, and a well-dressed middle-aged cattleman let out a Rebel yell that almost sent Charity flying into Morgan's lap. From outside came a woman's cheerful shout, followed by another. Charity spun toward the window.

"Oh, my stars!" Six young women, obviously dance hall girls from their mode of dress, trotted down the boardwalk from two directions, meeting in front of Jake's, swinging their calf-length satin skirts and ruffled petticoats with their hands, keeping time to the music. They hopped off the boardwalk and formed a line in the street. Swishing their skirts and petticoats back and forth in an arch at chest height, showing off their shapely legs, black mesh stockings, and lace-trimmed red drawers, they kicked right in to their own version of the cancan.

Charity laughed and joined in the clapping, though she refrained from stomping one foot, as many of the men were doing. Through the window, she could see cowboys pouring out of the numerous saloons up and down Oak Street. Someone fired in the air, and she jumped again, but that only made her laugh harder. The girls were rowdy and the crowd boisterous. When they finished the dance with the typical bottoms-up finale, they scampered back to their places of business amid whistles, catcalls, vigorous applause, and a few more Rebel yells.

"Oh my. Is it always this lively?" She beamed him a smile.

He almost dropped his coffee cup.

"No, but every so often, Mrs. Jake decides things are dull, and she rounds up some of the girls to wake everybody up." Morgan supposed he should be disappointed that she wasn't appalled by such behavior, as one of the other "proper" ladies in the eating establishment had been, but he had enjoyed watching her laugh too much to seriously think such a thing. It struck him that she needed to laugh, really laugh, more often. There had been such a sadness in her eyes when she talked about her mother, a hint of the depth of her loneliness.

"Is Jake's wife here?"

He nodded. "That's her."

Charity followed his gaze to a pretty young woman coming through the doorway.

"Georgienna Jalvery, or at least that was her maiden name."

"French?" Charity took a sip of coffee.

"French-Canadian from Quebec. She came into town last year with a wagonload of dance hall gals."

Charity choked.

Morgan grinned as she wiped her eyes and tried not to appear shocked. "Jake noticed her right away, but it took him about a year to marry her. Probably wanted to get the restaurant going good first. Everybody calls her Mrs. Jake . . . or Rowdy Kate."

Charity smiled wryly. "I can't imagine why."

They finished their supper in companionable silence. Charity thought he seemed uncomfortable when she paid for the meal, but he didn't say anything. On the way back to the hotel, they stopped in at the Riordan Dry Goods store on Oak and bought her a duster.

Arriving back at her room, Charity quickly changed her clothes. Although wrapper or Mother Hubbard—style dresses had been popular for years, she had never owned one. She had always worn her mother's designs, a walking advertisement of her expertise, and Marion's tastes had been more elaborate.

Although the dress itself was loose, the bodice contained a fitted lining, which according to Mrs. Gilbert made a corset unnecessary, even impractical. "That's one reason women out here like this style so much," the seamstress said. "It gets mighty hot in the summer, and women with their stays cinched up tend to faint. Most women around here are too busy to be swooning every time they turn around. They still lace up on Sundays or special days, and, of course, a few ladies wear them all the time—but not too tight. In this country, a woman's got to do her share, and that means being able to breathe and move."

Charity did not wear her corset extremely tight, but she had not gone out in public without one since she was eleven. She buttoned up the lining and wiggled around. Everything seemed to stay where it was supposed to, even if it wasn't quite as firmly held in place as she was accustomed to. When she buttoned the dress and added the belt, tying it loosely, she moved around again in front of the floor-length cheval mirror the hotel had provided especially for her.

"Well, I don't look indecent, even if I feel decadently free." She took a deep breath, releasing it with a smile. "I could get used to dressing like this." She smoothed the skirt over her very full stomach and shook her head. "I'll have to if I eat at Jake's many more times." She was embarrassed about how much she had eaten, but it had been so good that she made a glutton of herself.

Since a lady did not wander about town without a hat of some kind, she pinned a beret on top of her head. Besides, she thought, a hat pin might come in handy. It seemed unwise to carry money, so she put her alligator pocketbook inside the trunk and locked it, tucking the key safely away in her skirt pocket. Removing her derringer from the matching alligator handbag, she slid it into her leather shoulder bag with her drawing equipment. Carrying her duster because she liked it when Morgan helped her put on a coat, she hurried downstairs to the lobby, hoping he had not changed his mind and left her high and dry.

He was still there. She slowed her pace coming down the stairs so she could observe him before he noticed her. He was talking to another man—quite possibly the most handsome man she had ever seen, a fact she barely noted. He should have captured her attention immediately, but it was Morgan who held her interest—his broad shoulders and long legs, the way he threw his head back when he laughed, the warmth in his eyes when he looked up and saw her.

Both men stood as she approached. The stranger removed his hat—something these Texans seldom did unless being introduced to a lady—and gave her a smile that would have left Mrs. Astor blubbering. "Good evenin', Miss Charity. I'm Case McBride, Morgan's oldest and dearest amigo. I have to say, the rumors I've been hearin' are true. You're the prettiest little lady ever to set foot in the state of Texas."

Charity laughed at his outrageous flattery. "And you, sir, are one of those silver-tongued cowboys I've heard about."

"Just speakin' the gospel truth, ma'am. What do you think of our little town? Or shouldn't I ask?"

"I like it. The people are friendly, and the weather has been pleasant. The hotel is very comfortable, and I'll probably gain twenty pounds before I go home, the food is so good. It's very different from New York, but I find it fascinating."

"Good. Well, I've got to get going, but if this ol' boy gets too ornery, you let me know." He grinned and leaned a little closer, as if he were telling her a secret, one he made certain Morgan heard. "He can be replaced."

Charity grinned back, sensing that his banter was as much to tease Morgan as it was to flirt with her. "I'll keep that in mind, Mr. McBride."

"You do that, ma'am." He left with a wink and another make-'em-swoon smile.

"He seems like a nice man." Charity turned to Morgan, only to be met with a dark scowl.

"Yeah, he's a real sweetheart."

"Have you been friends a long time?"

"Too long."

Why, he sounded jealous. It shouldn't have pleased her, but it did. It showed he cared for her in some way, which she shouldn't have wanted. But she did.

"What do you think of my dress?"

"It's the wrong color."

"But I look good in pink."

"Exactly. And the belt's too tight."

She grimaced and untied the belt, muttering, "If I loosen it any more, people will think I'm expecting." Realizing what she had said, her gaze shot to his. "No, absolutely not. I will not tie a pillow around my waist."

His scowl faded, and she caught a tiny twitch at the corner of his lips. "You ready to go?"

He didn't sound as if he had almost smiled. It must have been irritation or maybe indigestion. He probably shouldn't have eaten the rest of her steak. She thrust her duster toward him. "Yes."

With a sigh Morgan took the duster and held it up for her. After she put it on, he rested his big hands on her shoulders, holding her firmly in place. "You stay with me every minute."

Tension radiated from him, flowing through his hands to her. For the first time, she had serious reservations about going to the West End. She glanced up at him over her shoulder, noting the worry in his eyes. "I'll stick to you like ivy on a courthouse wall."

"If I tell you to do something, you do it. No questions. No arguing. No hesitation. Just obey me. Understand?"

"Yes." He released her and stepped back. She picked up her bag and prayed that her stubbornness didn't get them into trouble.

# Chapter
# Seven

They didn't have to go far, hardly more than two blocks. Rounding a corner, they stepped into another world. Lamplight streamed from the windows up and down the streets, amid the tinkling sound of piano music, loud laughter, and an occasional burst of profanity. Cowboys, some already staggering, roamed the boardwalks.

Charity instinctively moved closer to Morgan. He put his arm across her back, resting his hand at her waist. "Sure you want to go on?"

"Yes. But I'm ready to run if you give the word."

"Good. Be ready to duck, too. We should be all right. It seems fairly calm tonight."

A door crashed open directly in front of them, and a cowboy came flying out backward, landing on his backside in the dusty street. A second wrangler barreled out of the saloon, fists clenched, fury on his face.

Morgan stepped in front of Charity and snagged the man by the back of the collar as he ran by. He came around swinging, but pulled the punch when he saw the deputy. He dropped his fists, and Morgan released him. "Havin' a problem, Smokey?"

"That son—"

"Hold it! There's a lady present, so watch your language." Morgan moved over so the young cowboy could see Charity.

"Oh, excuse me, ma'am." Smokey jerked his hat from his head and held it respectfully in front of him. He stared at Charity, reluctantly looking back at the deputy when Morgan repeated his question. "Huh? Joe called Miss Lucy a . . . a lady of the evenin'."

"She is, Smokey. You know that."

"Well, he don't have to go sayin' it so disrespectful and all. She's a fine woman. Just had a hard life."

"You sweet on her, son?"

"Yes, sir. I'm plannin' to ask that little filly to marry me."

The other cowboy struggled to his feet and knocked the dust off his pants with his hat. He stepped up on the boardwalk. "You didn't say nothin' about wantin' to marry her. I didn't mean no disrespect." He held out his hand to Smokey. "She's a mighty fine woman."

Morgan stepped back beside Charity as the two shook hands. He slid his arm around her again in a manner guaranteed to show possession as well as protection to Smokey and Joe and the other cowboys who had come out to watch the fight.

Joe tipped his hat to Charity. "Evenin', ma'am." He never took his eyes off her but mumbled a question to Smokey. "Who's the lady?"

"Don't know. Who's the lady, Deputy Kaine?"

"Miss Charity Brown from New York City. She's writing a magazine article about the town. You boys keep out of trouble." Without another word, Morgan pressed his hand against Charity's side in a signal to start moving.

As they stepped away, Joe turned to Smokey. "Can you beat that? I never thought I'd see a real lady down here."

"Miss Lucy's a real lady."

"Right. Besides her, I mean."

Morgan glanced over his shoulder, relieved to see Joe rest his arm across his friend's shoulders as they went back into the saloon.

"Who is Miss Lucy?"

"She works for Archie. I don't think she's been in the business long. Can't be more than eighteen."

They walked on in silence for a few minutes. Charity liked having his arm around her, but she could feel his tension growing the farther they got into the district. "These women actually find husbands out here?"

"Some do."

"And it doesn't matter to the men that they've been, uh, ladies of the evening?"

"Better to know she's a whore before they get married than to find out afterward," he said, his sharp words chiseled with bitterness.

Charity looked at him, struck by the underlying pain in his voice. "Are you married, Morgan?"

"No."

"Were you?"

"No. And I never will be."

"Why?" She stopped in the fringes of light from a window. He halted, too, only because he had to or knock her down.

"That's none of your business."

Charity hesitated. She wanted to know who had hurt him, but if she pushed him now, she would regret it. "You're right. I apologize. Are we close to Archie's?" She started walking again.

"Almost there."

During her strolls around the business district, Charity had peeked into several saloons. They were usually small and fairly simple, with a bar, a display case of cigars and tobacco, and tables throughout the room for gambling. None of them compared with Archie Johnson's place.

A horseshoe-shaped mahogany bar filled one wall, backed by bar-to-ceiling mirrors. A highly polished brass boot rail ran around the bottom of the bar. The room was large, fitted with gaming tables spaced comfortably apart. A stage curved out from the other side of the room, complete with velvet curtains across the back. A piano sat nearby.

The room was crowded with drinkers and gamblers. About ten or twelve women, dressed in extremely low-cut, calf-length satin gowns, mingled with the cowboys. The women leaned against them, hung onto their arms, sat on their laps, and gave them a kiss now and then. Charity tried not to let her discomfort show.

They stopped inside the doorway. "Archie is the overlord

of the district. Has his fingers in almost all of the action down here. He helps keep things orderly."

"Is that him at the bar?" Charity watched a burly man pour a drink.

"No, he's over there."

Charity looked across the room. "He runs the district?" she whispered, trying not to stare at the small man coming toward them. He looked meek and unassuming. Not at all as she had imagined.

"Yep. Some say he's an ex-Confederate soldier who never signed the oath of allegiance to the Union after the war. Drifted to the mining camps of the Northwest, back to Abilene and Dodge City, and finally to Fort Worth, where he heard about the boom here. He came out and set up business."

"Good evening, Deputy Kaine. Ma'am. Do I have the honor of meeting Miss Charity Brown?" asked Archie in a high falsetto voice.

Charity almost laughed. The man was definitely not a typical dime-novel saloon keeper. She nodded. "I'm pleased to meet you, Mr. Johnson."

"Call me Uncle Archie. Everyone does. What can I do for you?"

Charity noticed that the room had gradually gone silent. Everyone watched and listened. She glanced at Morgan. His eyes were hard and cold. His gaze scanned the room, sending a warning to one and all. His left hand rested against the small of her back, the other hung at his side—near his gun. "I'd like to sit someplace out of the way and draw some sketches of your establishment. It's beautiful, by the way. I want to get a sense of what goes on here so I can adequately convey it to my readers."

"Come sit by me, honey. I'll show you what goes on here," called a drunken cowboy from the other end of the room. Several men guffawed, but hushed the instant Morgan's icy gaze fell on them.

"I don't want to cause problems." Charity looked from Morgan to Archie. "If you think I should leave, I'll go."

"There won't be any problems, Miss Charity. I guarantee

it. You can sit right over here for as long as you want."
Archie took her arm and started to escort her across the
room.

"We'll take a table by the door." Morgan's tone was
implacable.

"Of course, Deputy." Archie winked at Charity as they
turned around. "With your back to the wall, I assume."

Morgan nodded curtly and turned, pinning four hapless
card players with a stare. A mad scramble ensued as they
gathered their cards, money, and drinks for the move to a
different table.

Archie seated Charity and smiled benignly. "Can I get
you anything to drink, ma'am? Deputy? No? Very well.
Stay as long as you like. Let us know if there is anything
you need." He nodded at a man in a striped shirt and bowler
hat, who immediately moved to the piano. "You're just in
time to see the girls do their show."

Morgan pulled his chair alongside Charity's, its back to
the wall. He sat down, facing the silent room. She set her
leather bag on her lap and opened it to take out her drawing
supplies. When she reached for the flap of the bag to close
it, his hand clamped down on her wrist.

"What are you doing with a derringer?" he asked, his lips
close to her ear.

Charity shivered, but she didn't know if it was from the
fear of having been caught with the gun or the pleasant
sensation of his warm breath on her skin. Sweet, lyrical
piano notes filled the room, and the customers turned their
attention to the stage as a buxom brunette stepped out.
Charity looked at Morgan with more bravado than she felt.
"I'm a woman alone. It's for protection."

"Then put it in your coat pocket. You'd never get it out of
that bag in time to do you any good."

"I thought of that, but I was afraid you'd see it."

"Afraid I'd arrest you?"

"No, but I thought you might take it away from me." His
grip had eased. He lightly moved his thumb in a small circle
on the inside of her wrist, like a caress. Charity was right in

the middle of telling herself to quit imagining things when his expression softened and warmth lit his eyes. It *was* a caress, one intended to make her brain fuzzy and her heart pound. He succeeded and he knew it. She pulled her hand from his hold.

He smiled in a knowing way. "Keep it."

"Aren't you afraid I'll use it on you?" she asked sweetly, slipping the small handgun out of the bag and into her pocket.

"You know better than to try." He settled back in the chair, resuming his unrelenting expression. "Get your work done so we can get out of here."

She made several drawings of the dancers, the soloist, the gamblers, and the men at the bar. Archie and the bartender were portrayed, too. The dancers were a bit raunchy, and one of the songs made her blush, but all in all she thought she was handling the situation rather well—until she realized the women were escorting some of the men upstairs, one by one, and disappearing behind closed doors. She knew she had a tendency to lose herself in her work, but how had she missed what was going on?

Hot color flooded her face. She closed the drawing pad with a snap. "I've got everything I need."

"And maybe a little more than you bargained for?"

Without looking at him, she couldn't decide if he was being sympathetic or taunting. And she wasn't about to look at him. "I'm done. Can we leave now?" She threw her pencils into the bag and buckled the flap.

"Not just yet." Morgan sat up straight, poised for action. Across the room, an obnoxious drunken freighter was trying to drag a pretty young girl upstairs with him. She adamantly refused. Charity gasped when she saw the young cowboy, Smokey, head toward the couple. "Is that Miss Lucy?"

"Yes. Wrap your fingers around that derringer. I'll be back in a minute." Morgan strode across the room, arriving at the scene a second after Smokey.

"I want this woman," snarled the drunk. "My money's as

good as anybody's. And I'm better than most." He laughed. Only his friends laughed with him.

"You're not takin' my Lucy anywhere." Smokey grabbed the man's hand and tried to pry it away from the girl's arm.

"Why, you little—"

Morgan caught the man's arm before he could take a swing. "Let him go, Smokey." The cowboy complied. "Release the lady, Carlson. She doesn't want to go with you."

Carlson hesitated. "I'm gonna pay for her. That's what she's here for."

"Do you want to spend a few days in the calaboose?"

"Can't. Gotta leave in the mornin'."

"Then take your hand off the lady, or I'll throw you in jail for being drunk and disorderly. And I'll ask the judge to keep you there for a week." Morgan never raised his voice, but no one in the room doubted that he would do what he threatened.

The man released Lucy with a shrug. "Go on. You ain't worth jail time."

"Smokey, take Miss Lucy into Archie's office. She's through working for the night."

"She's through workin' in a saloon for good. Come on, honey. We got some talkin' to do." Smokey tenderly put his arm around Lucy's shoulders as they went toward Archie's office. The girl was pale and shaken, but she looked at Smokey with adoring eyes.

Morgan turned to the troublemaker's friends. "You boys take him back to the wagon yard and sleep it off. I don't want to see any of you down here for the rest of the night."

"Yes, sir, Deputy," muttered another burly man. "Come on, boys." He got on one side of Carlson, and another man took his other arm. They guided him out of the saloon, and their two companions followed meekly behind them.

Charity breathed a sigh of relief when Morgan joined her. She had been standing by her chair, her bag hanging from her shoulder, her fingers coiled around the gun inside her pocket. She relaxed and pulled her hand free as she fell in step with him and left the saloon.

Morgan turned toward downtown.

She stopped, pulling on his arm. "Wait. There's one other place I want to go."

"Haven't you had enough excitement?"

"Well, yes. But I'd like to go to the Waterin' Hole."

Morgan studied her in the dim light. *Jonathan Harris's place.* Why was she so interested in men with the initials J. H.? There had been that old man in the St. James the night of her arrival. Two of the men she had first interviewed bore those initials. What was she up to?

"Why that one?"

"From what I read in the tax records, it's smaller than Archie's and it's in the district, so it would make a good comparison to his."

"So would a dozen others."

She grinned and hoped she looked mischievous. "And it's a great name. It sounds so Western. It would be perfect in the article."

Morgan didn't believe either reason was the main one, but the only way he would find out what she was doing was to play along. "All right. But it's several blocks from here, and there are no boardwalks over that way. You'll have to walk in the street."

"I don't mind. I'm wearing sturdy shoes."

"I noticed."

They walked down the street, going farther away from downtown. "You don't miss much, do you?"

"Nope. Not even when someone wants me to."

Charity swallowed hard, thankful for the encroaching darkness. A change of topic was in order. "Will Smokey be able to support Lucy? From what I've heard, cowboys don't make much."

"They don't, but he works for Case, and he'll take care of them. He'll give them a little house on the ranch and increase Smokey's salary since he won't be eating in the mess hall. It won't be an easy life, but they'll get by. Smokey's a hard worker and a good cowboy, so he'll have a job as long as Case has cows to tend."

"Is that usually the way it's done when a cowboy gets married?"

"Depends on the rancher. Some won't hire married men at all because they don't want the added responsibility of a man's family. Others prefer family men because they're more settled and liable to stay around. A lot of cowboys can't stay put for long. Wanderin' is in their blood."

They walked past two of the four dance-hall theaters in the district, several more saloons, and a few bordellos, or parlor houses as they were politely called. At one, a woman sat in a second-story open window, dangling one leg outside the building. She wore a knee-length chemise, stockings, and a shawl to ward off the evening chill.

Charity was mortified. Aware of her embarrassment, Morgan suggested crossing to the other side of the street and walking in the shadows of an empty lot. The buildings were more widely spaced, with only three or four businesses to a block, thus they often had only light from the full moon to guide their way.

"I thought there was an ordinance against prostitution."

"There is. One against gambling in the saloons, too. About once a month the marshal hauls all the girls, the gamblers, and the saloon keepers into court. They're found guilty, pay their fine, and go back to work. It's more a source of revenue than anything else."

"I also noticed that the city has trouble keeping its marshals. Why?"

"Various reasons. The salary was cut a few times when the town didn't have the money to pay it. Some men found they didn't like the job. There were some that the townspeople didn't like and a few that didn't seem to be quite honest. Could have been they just didn't know how to keep records on the fines and taxes they collected, or could be they helped themselves to the money. Hard to know. The man we've got now is doing a good job. He's been marshal almost a year."

The Waterin' Hole was a quarter the size of Archie's place. The furnishings were simple but not shabby. To

Charity's relief, there were few patrons in the saloon. They were a rough-looking bunch, not quite desperadoes, but close enough.

Her nerves were tied in knots. As much as she wanted to find her father, she did not want him to own a saloon. She didn't care if that made her moral or merely pompous. Jonathan Harris was short and fat with a wide, gray handlebar mustache and closely cropped black hair generously sprinkled with gray. He had to be at least sixty-five.

Charity almost cried in relief.

She made two quick drawings of the owner and his place of business, interviewed him briefly, and left gladly.

"Seen enough?" asked Morgan as they walked along the rutted dirt street.

"More than enough." Oddly, she felt disappointed as well as relieved. *I'm still alone.* Under the pretense of being unsure of her footing, she slipped her arm through his. She needed to be comforted by his strength, to let some of his assurance seep into her soul. "You won't have to worry about me coming back here. I'm not as open-minded as I thought I was. Could we go back a different way? I'd like to avoid the parlor houses."

"It'll take longer."

"I don't mind, if you don't." She glanced up at him.

"I'm not in a hurry. Turn right at the next corner." He smiled down at her, thinking that he had smiled more in the last three days—and gotten mad more often—then he had in months. He liked being with her. He knew better, but he still liked it.

"Morgan, is Case married?"

*Fool.* "No, his wife died a few years back."

"They were talking about the Stockman's Ball at breakfast this morning. Do you think Case would be my escort if I asked him?"

He wanted to tell her to keep away from Case, but he didn't get the chance. Six cowboys came racing down the street in a dust-churning dash. Morgan jerked his arm from hers and, grabbing her around the waist, hauled her over to the side of the road out of harm's way. He plopped her down next to an empty building and shielded her body with his as one horse and rider came perilously close to running them down.

Charity's bag slipped off her shoulder and slid down her arm. She let it fall to the ground as she buried her face against his chest. His hands were flat against the wood, his arms protecting her head. He held her against the building with his body, easing the pressure when the danger passed, and dropped his hands to her shoulders. He didn't step away or let her go. She didn't want him to. She wanted him to ask her to the ball.

"Do you think Case would take me?"

He put a little more distance between them without moving his feet. "He's taking someone else." He didn't see the need to tell her it was Case's mother.

Now she knew how a man sounded when he growled. "Oh. Well, maybe I could ask Viscount Merryweather."

"Stay away from him." He moved closer again.

Charity hid a smile. "He seems nice." If you liked the kind that made your skin crawl.

"I said stay away from him, Charity. He has a wife in England. And he likes to hurt women."

"Oh dear. Well, can you suggest someone else? Since it's a Stockman's Ball, I assume he would have to be a cattleman." Or perhaps a lawman there for security. He waited so long to answer that she thought he was going to ignore her question. "Morgan?"

"I'll take you."

"No, you won't. You sound like you'd rather face Billy the Kid in a shootout. I'll find someone who wants to go with me."

He stared down at her. She stared back—defiant, irritated, beautiful. He slid one hand down the outside of her arm, then to her waist. "I'll take you."

"No—"

She hushed when he caressed her cheek, and caught her breath when he spread his hand across the back of her head, tangling his fingers in her hair. He had wanted this kiss from the first moment he saw her. And, from the look in her eyes before her long lashes drifted over them, she wanted it, too. He brushed her lips with his, touching her with a gentleness he had felt for no other woman.

"Will you go with me?" he whispered against her lips.

She slid her hands up his chest and around his neck. "Convince me a little more," she whispered back.

With a low groan, he drew her tightly against him and kissed her the way he had in his daydreams.

Charity had been kissed before, but nothing in her experience or imagination had prepared her for the maelstrom exploding within her. For the first time, she understood the passion of which poets wrote. When he finally lifted his head, she slowly opened her eyes, dazed and filled with wonder. "Oh my."

Morgan was shaken to his very soul. In the interest of self-preservation, he wanted to lash out at her, accuse her of being a loose woman for letting him kiss her, but the amazement on her face stopped him. She was no schoolgirl, completely untouched, but the glow in her eyes, visible even in the moonlight, told him she had never known passion until that moment. Tenderness rose up inside him, a strange, unexpected feeling.

"You've been kissed before," he murmured, brushing her cheek with his knuckles.

"Never like that," she whispered, as if afraid of breaking the spell.

"Who was he?" he asked just as softly, almost wishing she'd say a lover, praying she wouldn't.

"My fiancé."

Pain shot through his heart, and he called himself a fool a second time.

"Ex-fiancé," she corrected quickly. "Five years ago, I was engaged for a short time, until I found out he was more interested in my connection with the Gilders than he was in me."

"Did you love him?" He frowned slightly, wondering why it mattered.

"Yes, but I got over him soon enough. I can't understand what I ever saw in him." Her curiosity—sometimes a curse, sometimes a blessing—was often rather unruly. Now was such a time. She ducked her head, then shyly glanced up at him. "I don't have much experience with this kind of thing, so please forgive me if I'm being impertinent, but do women always react as I did to your kisses?"

He chuckled, amused at her frankness and pleased that she didn't carry a torch for another man. "You mean do they go up like a keg of gunpowder hit with a bullet?"

"Yes." She toyed with the collar of his shirt and avoided his gaze.

"Of course, they do," he teased. "Didn't your mama ever warn you about cowboys?"

"I don't know if Mama knew any cowboys." *But if she had known a man like you, I think she would have been attracted to him.* His answer disappointed her, but she thought perhaps it was a safe answer, both for him and for her. "I suppose we'd better go back."

"I suppose we had." He straightened her hat, helped her tuck her hair back into place, and picked up her bag, sliding the strap up her arm to her shoulder. He offered her his arm, and she slipped hers around it.

The wind blew harder, coming from the north, as they walked back to the hotel in silence. The lobby was deserted, and after she picked up her key, he escorted her to the room. She opened the door and turned to tell him good night.

"Thank you," she said quietly, mindful of the late hour.

He nodded. "Where are you going tomorrow?"

"Nowhere. I'm going to stay inside and write."

"Good. There's a norther blowing in. It will be cold enough to freeze ducks to a pond tomorrow."

Charity grinned. "You Texans do have a way with words."

Morgan smiled. He glanced up and down the deserted hallway, his expression growing serious, and stepped closer. "I lied earlier."

"When?"

He smoothed away her frown with his fingertips. "When

I told you all the women I kiss react the way you did. I haven't kissed very many, but it's never been like that with anyone else."

Joy flooded her heart, but it was quickly stifled by a small voice of warning. "I'm glad, but it sounds dangerous."

"It is." He stepped back. "You know how to reach me if you need me." He was gone without another word.

# Chapter
# Eight

As Morgan had predicted, the following day was cloudy and cold. Sleet fell for part of the day, making the streets and boardwalks slick. Charity was more than happy to stay in her room. She buried herself in her work, writing about the conflicting facets of the town, making sure more emphasis was given to the genteel side than to the rowdy side.

She wrote of the merchants and how they kept a far-reaching territory supplied with necessities and sometimes luxuries, how much of the time the goods were never taken to the stores but were loaded directly from the railcars onto the freight wagons for shipment to ranches over a hundred miles away.

The teachers and preachers were mentioned, including the story of the town's first church service, which had been preached by a Presbyterian minister in a saloon with a wagon sheet covering the bar. The Methodists and Baptists established churches shortly thereafter, followed by the Episcopalians. She described the Opera House, hotels, homes, and the trials and tribulations of building the courthouse to suit all concerned.

All the while, she tried to block out thoughts of Morgan and memories of the previous evening, something she was unable to do for very long at a time. Seated at the small desk the hotel had provided, she would catch herself staring out the window at the winter sky, remembering the fire in his kiss and the tenderness in his touch.

During the week, she spent time with various ladies,

drinking tea, sharing talk, and satisfying their curiosity about her trip to the district—something the whole town had known about by the next morning. She was thankful that no one was aware of all the details. The ladies were nice, friendly, and accepted her trip to the bawdy side of town as part of her job. A few even confidentially expressed envy over her courage and her freedom. She received invitations to dinner and supper every day and gathered plenty of interesting tidbits to send to Helena in her long, gossipy letters.

A. H. Tolar, publisher of the local paper, *The Colorado Clipper,* interviewed her. When his article came out, she was a bit dismayed to find some things exaggerated, but felt better after talking to Ester, the telephone operator. Charity had dropped by for a visit and was assured that the newspaperman was known for his exuberant descriptions.

"According to him, a sprinkle is a slow rain, a good shower is a downpour, and a sandstorm is a cooling breeze," said Ester with a laugh.

Sam dropped by every afternoon after school. He was so eager to learn all he could about drawing and so diligent in doing the work she assigned that she worried about his school work. He assured her that he was keeping up with everything, and when she ran into his teacher at the bookstore, she said the same thing.

Every day they curled up together on a sofa in an out-of-the-way corner of the hotel lobby. A pretty coal oil lamp on the table next to the sofa and a large window behind it provided adequate light for the lessons. The other patrons of the hotel quickly grew accustomed to seeing Charity with the youngster and generally left them alone.

They were in their usual spot the day before the ball. "We were talking about magazines and books today in school. My teacher said someday photographs will replace drawings like you do."

"They probably will, but no one has been able to transfer them to the printed page yet. I'm sure it's only a matter of time before someone perfects the process so the pictures come out right. In the meantime, all the magazines and books depend on people like me."

"But how do they put a drawing in the magazines? I mean, it's not like something that's typeset. I watched the newspaper being printed off, and the type isn't flat. The typesetter said if it was, it wouldn't make the letters because the part that doesn't touch the paper is what comes out white."

Charity ruffled his hair. "You're a smart one, Sam Mayfield. When I send in my pictures, they go to the art department, where they are copied line for line on a very smooth piece of boxwood, except the pictures are drawn on in reverse."

"Reverse? You mean backwards?"

"Yes."

"Holy Moses, that sounds hard."

"I think it would be, but they have several artists who do it very well. In fact, they often specialize. One person will do the backgrounds, another the middle-distance figures, and someone else will do the foregrounds." As she talked, she pointed to the different sections of a drawing he had completed to reinforce what he had learned about depth in the pictures.

"Wouldn't that get boring?"

"I think it would, but that way, they get very good in their special area and can do them quickly. You have to remember that most of the stories are illustrated with several drawings, so there is a lot of work to be done."

"What happens after they draw the pictures on the wood?"

"Then an engraver takes over. He very carefully cuts away the portions of the picture that are to be white or lightly shadowed."

Sam looked dumbfounded. "You meant he cuts out everything between the lines? Even like on a buckskin shirt so the fringe shows up?"

"Yes. He looks through a powerful magnifying lens so he can see what he is doing and uses a steel cutting tool called a burin. It's very painstaking work."

Sam absently tapped the blunt end of his pencil against the paper. "I'll say. I think I'll stick to drawing. It's a lot easier."

"I agree with you, but the engravers make more money."

"And get stiff necks and go cross-eyed."

"Probably." Charity laughed and gave him another lesson in perspective, so his pictures would look three-dimensional. A whole box of drawing books had arrived on the train that morning from Helena, who had purchased them and expressed them out to Charity the same day she sent the telegram. She enjoyed being with Sam not only because he was talented and interested in art. He had a sweet, happy disposition and a good sense of humor, and he made her laugh often. He seemed to know everyone for miles around because at one time or another they all came to his father's shop. He had also been blessed with a good dose of common sense, so Charity felt entirely at ease asking the boy for advice.

"Sam, I want to stay on a ranch for a while. I'd like one not too far from town so it won't be too difficult to send in my articles. When I was gathering statistics from the courthouse records, I made a list of ranches that seemed reasonably close. I want something fairly large in size because there would be more to write about. Could you tell me what you know about them?"

"Sure. How close do you want to stay? Half a day's ride too far?"

"That's pushing it, but I certainly wouldn't want to be any farther than that."

"Who's on the list?"

She pulled a halfsheet of paper from her skirt pocket. "First is the Double Eagle."

"It's pretty far. It would take most of a day to get to town in a buggy."

She scratched out the name. "How about the Smithson place?"

"Naw. They still live in a dugout. You don't want to stay there."

"Flying Z?"

"Nope. He's an old bachelor. How about the Hunter place, the Double J? It's a little closer."

Charity's heart did a flip-flop. She'd been working up to that one. "What's it like?"

"Big. Jacob and Joshua Hunter own it. They're brothers. Jacob's married, and they got a boy named Lacy. They're real nice people. They got their own blacksmith, but they still bring work in for Pa to do, too."

"Is Lacy near your age?"

"Naw, he's old, around twenty."

Charity smiled. "I'll have you know, young man, that twenty is not old."

"It is to me." He grinned.

"It won't be when you're that age." She glanced at the watch pinned to her bodice. "Well, you'd better be running along so you can get your chores done. Remember, we won't have a lesson tomorrow."

"I remember. You gotta get ready for the big shindig." A teasing glint sparkled in his eyes. "Gotta get all spiffed up so you'll look pretty for the deputy. Say, you might visit Mr. McBride's ranch. It's about half a day's ride."

*Morgan would love that.* "I thought he was a widower."

"He is, but his mother lives with him, so it wouldn't cause no gossip."

"I'll keep it in mind."

Charity patted his shoulder, since hugs tended to embarrass him, and he went on his way.

She had run into Morgan a couple of times as she worked around town, but he had been cool, almost more reserved than before. He had not stopped by to see her since the night they went to the red light district. She was afraid he regretted the kisses they had shared, and she wondered if he still intended to escort her to the ball.

From his seat behind a large potted palm nearby, Morgan watched Sam leave the lobby. He had waited twenty minutes to talk to Charity, and the time had been enlightening. The beautiful women he had known had not been good with children. Most simply were not interested in them, spending their energies on perfecting their charms to attract men. Some, like his mother, were impatient and intolerant of the smallest offense, whether real or imagined. He couldn't remember one time in his life he had pleased her, no matter how hard he tried.

The boy seemed to please Charity with everything he did or said. From the time Morgan spotted them together until Sam left, no frown had crossed her face. Sheltered as he was, he had shamelessly eavesdropped, envying their banter and the easy laughter they shared and how close to her Sam sat.

He wished he could be that relaxed with her, but, he thought ruefully, the boy didn't have to contend with certain manly feelings yet. Morgan had avoided her as much as possible since their foray into the district, but it hadn't done much good. She filled his thoughts, night and day, awake or asleep.

So much about her lured him. The smile that had cracked open the door to his dark and weary soul, making him hunger for more of its joyful light. The way her eyes danced when she teased or got away with something she knew she shouldn't. Her walk. Her wit and intelligence. Her soft sighs when he kissed her, and the way she molded her body to his when he held her. Now he added to the list patience, gentleness, and affection for a young boy.

He had learned early in life not to trust women, and the lesson had been reinforced time and time again. On the surface, her conversation with Sam about the ranches seemed innocent enough, even logical. Added to the other instances concerning men with the same initials as the Hunter brothers, however, it appeared to be a carefully plotted strategy to gain information about them. While Morgan diligently guarded those in his jurisdiction, he fiercely protected the Hunters. They were family, and the only kin he acknowledged.

They would meet her tomorrow night whether he introduced them or not, and knowing his aunt Addie, she wouldn't give Charity a chance to ask about a visit before she extended an invitation for a nice, long stay. Addie loved their ranch, but she missed having more females to talk to, and she would take an instant liking to Charity.

He slipped out of the chair and worked his way around to the dining room door. Crossing the lobby toward Charity, his expression grew stern. He would find out, here and now, what she was up to.

She came out of her reverie and glanced up. When she saw him, her face lit up like a roman candle on Independence Day. His heart did a somersault, and he forgot about hammering her with questions.

"I was beginning to think I wasn't going to see you again." She smiled and patted the settee cushion beside her. "Sit down and take the load off."

He sat down before he fell down. He'd never been immune to her smiles, but why had this one made him go weak in the knees? She turned to look at him, her face glowing, and he realized what was different. She was happy to see him. Not the socially pleasant kind of happy but the feel-good-all-over kind.

"Don't mind if I do." He removed his hat and set it on the table beside the settee, next to the cut-glass lamp. Smoothing his fingers through his hair, he turned back to her and smiled. He couldn't help it. The sparkle in her eyes got to him. "How have you been?"

"Fine. Busy. I have the first article finished and off to Richard. And I'm giving Sam art lessons." Charity soaked up the sight of him and wished they were alone, instead of in the hotel lobby. She also knew that being in a public place was much wiser.

"I saw you two hard at work. I'm thinkin' about takin' art lessons myself." He leaned back in the corner of the settee, casually resting his arm along the cushioned back. His fingers were inches away from her jaw, his gaze lazy and seductive. His voice dropped to little more than a rumbling whisper. "Would I get to sit all snuggled up to the teacher if I did?"

"You might, but I doubt if you'd learn much about drawing." She had not seen this side of Morgan Kaine. It was hard to resist. She shifted her position, moving a fraction closer to where his hand rested. He didn't disappoint her.

With a wisp of a touch, he skimmed his fingertip along her jaw and back again. "Probably not, but I bet neither one of us would care a whole lot."

Cheeks flushed and heart pounding, she pulled away from his hand. She couldn't stand being so close, unable to get closer. She had engaged in an occasional trivial flirtation, at parties or on picnics, but there was no comparison between those simple games and this one. She took a deep breath to try and calm her nerves. "I picked up my ball gown today. Madame DeFontaine did wonders in such a short time."

"What color is it?"

"Violet."

He looked surprised. "Not green?"

"She didn't have the right shade." More truthfully, she had the perfect shade. Charity had declined it because she didn't want to draw any unnecessary attention to her eyes. "It's very pretty. I hope you'll be pleased."

"Can't be any other way. A gentleman always admires a lady dressed for a party."

She smiled. "Now I won't know if you truly like it or not. What time shall I be ready?"

"I'll come by at seven-thirty."

"I won't keep you waiting. I assume you'll be working, which is fine, because I will be, too."

"You're going to bring along your drawing equipment?"

"Only a small pad of paper and a couple of pencils. I can slip them into my handbag. Morgan, my next article will include the ball. I'll need some pictures of what it's like."

He leaned closer. His jaw tightened for a second, and his voice held a trace of anger. "When I asked you to go with me, I thought I'd be dancing with you."

"Oh, you will. I don't plan to sit on the sidelines all night. I'll just do my work whenever you're busy."

"Busy doing what? Stopping thieves? Breaking up gunfights?" Well, maybe a few fistfights.

Faint woodsy cologne mingled with the subtle scent of

his leather coat, an intriguing, all-male combination. For a second she lost the thread of the conversation. "Well, yes. Doing whatever deputies do. I thought you would be on duty."

Morgan sighed and sat back. "Tomorrow night, I'm officially off duty. If anything happens, of course, I'll help handle it, but I'm going to the party as a guest—a stockman, as in owner of cattle."

"You own a ranch?" She couldn't hide her surprise, although she certainly thought he was capable. It simply hadn't occurred to her that he was anything more than a lawman. It seemed like a big enough job in itself.

"No, not in the way you're thinking. Out here you don't necessarily have to own land to run cattle. It's still free range, so just about anybody can have a herd if he can find some empty space to graze them."

"But how do you care for them? Do you have cowboys to do the work? And where do they live?"

"Case and his men look after my herd, and I pay them something for their trouble." It irked him that she had thought the only reason he was going to the ball was because he was a deputy. Hadn't she figured out that practically every man in West Texas owned a herd of some size?

"How many cows do you have?"

"Not nearly as much as Case. Besides, you don't ask a man that question."

"Why not?"

"It's like askin' how much money he has."

"I'm sorry. I didn't think about that." She had offended him, perhaps not as much by asking about the size of his herd, as by not considering that he might have one. She glanced around the lobby. Most of the guests were in the dining room, so it was fairly empty. They were sitting in the corner, out of the view of anyone simply passing by.

His hand rested on the back of the settee. She reached up and curled her fingers around it. "Morgan, I beg your pardon if I offended you. I didn't mean to. It's just that you're so busy working with Sheriff Ware, I never thought about you doing anything else. I promise I won't spend much time working. I'll dance with you as much as you want."

Right then, he could easily forgive such a minor transgression, as long as her fingers kept moving softly across the back of his hand. He didn't think she realized she was doing it, which made the caress that much sweeter. "I'd like to claim every dance, but the other men would never let me get away with it. People will talk if I occupy too much of your time. Course, there's going to be a lot of champagne and sipping whiskey to go around, so after the first hour or so, most folks won't pay us any mind." He smiled, warmed by her touch and the tenderness in her eyes. "I want the first and the last dance, and half a dozen in between. You decide which ones. Any more and I'll be tarred and feathered."

"Well, we certainly don't want that to happen." She released his hand with a little squeeze. "I need your advice. I need to stay at a ranch for a while."

Morgan tensed, remembering that he had meant to confront her. "Why?"

Her face registered surprise, and a spark of fear flickered through her eyes.

"So I can write about it. I asked Sam about some of the ranches I found in the county records. He told me most of them are either too far away, or a bachelor runs it, or the house is a dugout or something like that. I briefly considered the one with the dugout, but decided it was much too primitive for me. He suggested I stay at Case's place or at the Double J with the Hunters. Which do you recommend?"

Instinct told him to keep her away from the Hunters, but he wasn't about to give Case a wide open door. When it came to charm, Morgan couldn't hold a candle to his friend. Case wasn't the kind to seduce her, but after a week in his company Charity wouldn't remember that Morgan Kaine existed. *I'd be better off,* he thought. *And have misery up to my armpits.*

"Either place is as good as the other. Case's ma is cantankerous, but I expect you'd get along. The Hunters are fine folks. Jacob and his wife are kind and hospitable, and she'd probably welcome the company of another woman. Joshua gets a mite rowdy now and then, but he wouldn't give you any problems. His prefers the company of Archie's gals to real ladies." She winced but didn't interrupt. "Mrs. McBride and the Hunters will be at the festivities. I'll introduce you." *And watch you like a hawk.*

# *Chapter*
# *Nine*

Charity checked her image in the cheval mirror one more time, twitching the short violet silk train that fell from a large bustle. The ball gown was one of the prettiest she had ever owned. The sleeveless violet silk bodice was smoothly covered in transparent ivory lace. A drapery of silk began at the right shoulder, crossed the front, and ended beneath a cluster of variegated pink silk roses on the left side of her hip. The bustle was of violet silk, as was the overskirt draping above a deep flounce of the ivory lace. Another cluster of roses and green satin ribbon filled in the triangle where the overskirt and train met.

At the sound of a sharp knock, Charity took a deep breath and crossed the room. When she opened the door, a small sigh escaped her lips. In his rugged cowboy clothes, Morgan had been all too appealing. Wearing dress clothes, he was overwhelming. The black suit, gray vest, crisp ivory shirt, and black tie were similar to what she had seen at other parties, although there was a distinctive Western cut to the suit coat. Add the highly polished black cowboy boots and a cream-colored Stetson he held in front of him, and she could do little more than gape.

Morgan didn't notice. He was too busy staring, his gaze slowly traveling over her. Her dark hair was piled in curls on the top of her head, with a small cluster of pink ostrich tips feathered across them. More curls cascaded down the back of her head, and a wide sweep of wavy locks nestled against her neck and upper back. Gold filigree earrings looped around her earlobes.

His gaze moved to her throat, soft porcelain skin caressed by a pale pink cameo on a glistening gold filigree chain; to her shoulders, smooth and creamy in the light; and down to the pointed neckline where an almost transparent strip of lace veiled the soft upper curves of her bosom. He swallowed hard and swore he wouldn't let any other man within ten feet of her. A useless vow, he knew. It would take a Gatling gun to keep them away.

He skimmed over her small waist, giving the skirt of the dress a quick glance, before taking in the long ivory gloves that reached above her elbows, the satin skin of her upper arms and shoulders, and finally her face. Her smile was warm, welcoming, and satisfied.

"I don't have to wonder if you like the gown," she said softly.

"I hardly noticed it." He glanced at it again. "It's very pretty, but not as lovely as you." He didn't want to let her set foot outside her room. Nor did he want to remain in the hall. He forced himself to relax, smile, and stay put.

She dipped into a little curtsy, her eyes sparkling. "Thank you, kind sir. And, if I may be so bold, you look dashing enough to make the ladies swoon."

He grinned. "I doubt that." He paused, his gaze dipping to her neckline again, and his grin disappeared. "Every waltz is mine, and all the slow dances."

His dictatorial tone surprised her. In some primitive way, it pleased her, too. "Is that Kaine's law, Deputy?"

"Yes, ma'am." He was being silly and stubborn, but he'd be hanged before he'd let another man hold her close. "And if you break it, I'll throw you in the hoosegow."

She had read enough stories about the West to know he was threatening to put her in jail. She giggled, and he rewarded her with a tiny smile.

"I always obey the law, sir." She smiled, slanting him a glance beneath half-lowered lashes. "And I'll be most happy to obey this one."

Pleasure coursed through him, and he relaxed. Smiling, he drew his hand from where he had been hiding it behind his hat and handed her a small wrist corsage of cream and pink rosebuds. "This is for you."

"Roses! Oh, Morgan, they're beautiful. Wherever did you get them?"

"From a hothouse in Fort Worth. They came in on the train this morning."

"Thank you." Her voice was soft and thick with some emotion deeper than a bouquet should bring. She looked up at him, her eyes glowing with admiration, shimmering with moisture.

He stepped closer and cupped her chin in his hand. "What's this, darlin'? Tears over a puny bunch of flowers?"

She closed her eyes, and he felt the faint pressure of her jaw against his fingers, as she reached out to his touch. She swallowed, then opened her eyes, blinking them once. He caressed her face tenderly and lowered his hand.

"Silly, isn't it? I'm touched because you went to all the trouble to have them sent out on the train." She cleared her throat and smiled. "It's been a long time since a man I admired brought me flowers."

He thought he might bust the buttons on his vest. "Does that mean you've recently had flowers from a man you didn't admire?" he teased.

She rolled her eyes. "Baskets of them. Bartholomew Pitney, a self-proclaimed art and literary power, decided after my last article to honor me with his undying devotion. Thank goodness, after I returned his tokens of affection for a week, his devotion died."

Morgan chuckled, glad to see her smiling. "What's wrong with ol' Bartholomew?"

"He's sixty, weighs about three hundred pounds, and writes bad poetry and atrocious plays. What's worse, he insists on starring in them." She laughed. "And he's awful!"

"You mean you went to see one?"

"Not exactly. He decided to give an impromptu performance at a restaurant one night. It was supposed to be a tragedy, but everyone laughed. One man laughed so hard he fell out of his chair."

"And did you laugh, Charity?" he asked quietly, holding her gaze with his. Somehow, he didn't think so.

"No, I didn't. I almost cried because I felt so sorry for him. He must be very lonely to go to such lengths to try to make people like him. But I had to send the flowers back. I thought about trying to be his friend, but that wasn't what he had in mind. Could you help me with this?" She pointed to the roses.

He put on his hat and tied the delicate ribbons around her wrist while she held the corsage in place. "You were expecting a marriage proposal?"

"No, he clearly wanted me to be his mistress."

He angrily mumbled something slightly impolite, and she laughed. "My thoughts exactly. Let me get my wrap."

He watched the gentle sway of her skirt as she crossed the room to the bed. Retrieving a long ivory velvet cape, she swung it around her shoulders and fastened it at her throat. A small pink velvet reticule completed her ensemble.

"You have drawing stuff in that little bag?"

She nodded. "I'll redraw the pictures and make them larger. I can do that anytime."

They joined a throng of other couples going down the polished mahogany stairs. Ladies of every age and description glided like princesses down the wide staircase. Their rainbow-colored gowns of silk and satin swished softly with each step; diamond necklaces, bracelets, and earrings sparkled like prisms in the lamplight, sending flashes of light flickering over the walls. The gentlemen walking beside them were clad in fine suits, and many boots tinkled with the sound of gold and silver inlaid spurs bearing rowels made from twenty-dollar gold pieces.

Charity glanced down at Morgan's feet. "No gold spurs?"

"Didn't want to tear a lady's gown." He leaned down, his warm breath whispering against her ear. "And I'm too old for such fancy riggin'."

"Not too old, but you don't need it." She squeezed his arm and sighed, caught up in the excitement and festive air. "This is already better than any ball I've ever been to."

He chuckled. "Wait until you step outside."

She looked up at his twinkling eyes. "Why? Morgan, what is it?"

"Hold your horses, sugar. I don't want to spoil the surprise. Let's just say Texans know how to treat a lady special."

When they finally walked through the east door of the hotel lobby, Charity gasped, staring ahead of her in amazement. A red carpet ran from the doorway across Walnut Street, down the boardwalk, and across Second Street to the front door of the Opera House. "Morgan, that's Brussels carpet," she murmured.

"Only the best for our ladies. Wouldn't want those pretty gowns or those fancy dancing slippers to get dirty."

She shook her head and grinned up at him. "I've never seen anything like it."

He grinned back. "We do know how to throw a party."

They joined the stream of people flowing to the Opera House. All the ladies were lovely, for on such a magical night even the homeliest spinster glowed. All the men were handsome, if not in countenance, then in the proud way they carried themselves, mindful of their success, men among men, who took risks and worked hard to achieve their dreams.

Others came from their homes and from the other hotels, since the St. James only had sixty rooms. Many disembarked their surreys at the St. James, simply so they could one day tell their grandchildren about the night they walked on a red carpet from the grand hotel to the Stockman's Ball at the Opera House.

Charity and Morgan climbed the stairs to the third-floor ballroom. He took her cloak, momentarily leaving her to check it and his hat with an attendant. Another attendant handed her a dance card. When Morgan returned, she was drawing furiously on her little pad, sketching the ladies and gentlemen walking along the carpeted boardwalk.

"Working already?"

"I wanted to do this one before I got distracted and lost my impression of it." She smiled, hoping to dispel the trace of annoyance on his face. "And before the dancing starts.

Morgan, this is wonderful. Where in the world did they find a fifty-piece orchestra out here?"

"They didn't. The musicians are from St. Louis."

"I wonder why I'm not too surprised." Many of these ranchers were wealthy men, and they weren't afraid to enjoy their money and let others benefit from it at the same time. "Not all of these men are rich, are they? There's not that much land even in Texas."

"No, some are just cowboys, and some are small-timers like me with little more than a herd to their names. Others have small ranches, land that they own and love. They won't ever be rich, but I reckon they have what they want most, a piece of land of their own where they can put down roots."

She detected a hint of wistfulness in his voice. "What about you? Do you want a ranch? A piece of land of your own?"

She put her sketch pad and pencil away and drew the strings on her handbag tight. When he didn't answer, she glanced up. For an instant, sorrow and deep loss haunted his eyes; then his jaw tensed, and bitterness replaced the other emotions.

"I've got no use for a ranch. Cattle are a good investment now, and my setup with Case works fine. I'm a good lawman. That's what I mean to keep doing."

"Do you plan to run for sheriff?"

"Not against Dick. I'll probably move on to another town next year and get established there, then run for sheriff. Eventually I'd like to be a United States marshal." *Now, why did I go shootin' my mouth off? Nobody knows about that.*

"You'd make a good marshal. I hope you get the job." Only because he wanted it. She understood about dreams and goals, and what it took to achieve them. "But isn't being a lawman dangerous?"

"It can be on occasion, but things are settling down. I haven't been shot in a couple of years."

"Shot?" Her eyes widened, and pain ran through her heart.

He chuckled. "Three times, and stabbed twice. I finally figured out how to get out of the way." He bit back a comment about showing her his scars someday. It revealed too much of the way he thought about her. "Did you get a dance card?"

"Yep."

"Sounds like we're convertin' you already. May I sign your card?" He held out his hand.

"Nope." Her eyes twinkled merrily. "But you can see which dances I filled in for you." She lightly dropped the card into his hand.

Morgan read down the list. She'd placed his initials beside the first and last dance and every waltz in between, plus several others. Something precious unfurled in his heart, warming him with its sweetness. It was a strange, new feeling, one he had no intention of investigating too deeply at the present.

"Thank you," he said gruffly, his gaze burning into hers.

"This is a fairy-tale night, Morgan, a once-in-a-lifetime dream, and I know whose arms I want around me. To make it happen. I'll defy convention if I have to."

"Woman, you keep talking like that, and I'm liable to carry you off someplace where nobody will find us for a week." The old line shack popped into his mind again.

She chuckled. "I'm not up to defying convention that much."

He smiled ruefully. "Well, part of me is glad to hear it."

"I'm not familiar with the Put Your Little Foot, the Heel-and-Toe Polka, or Two-Step, so I put you down for those. I feel more secure having you teach them to me."

"I'll trample your toes as good as the next fellow. I haven't danced in years."

"Once you learn, you don't forget." She smiled as he looked concerned. "I'm not worried."

"Well, I am, although I should know what I'm doing. My mother hired the best instructor in Austin." *But she wasn't just interested in improving my dancing skills.* When Charity's eyebrows arched in surprise, he realized he had spoken carelessly. That part of his life had been buried long ago. "Hope it pays off," he mumbled.

Charity was dying to ask him about his family and his

early years. Not only did it take money to hire noted dance instructors, but it required social prestige, too. His closed expression, however, told her he would not take kindly to any probing questions. To ease the silent tension stretching out between them, she opened her handbag and tucked the dance card inside.

"Come on, we'd better mingle before the boys decide to give me a necktie party because I'm keeping you all to myself."

"Necktie party?"

"A lynching."

They circulated through the crowd, with Morgan introducing her to those she didn't know. When she met several gentlemen from the Seven River Cattle Company in New Mexico, Charity realized for the first time how far Colorado City's influence and prestige extended. They chatted with Sheriff Ware, and he introduced her to his brothers.

She met a few others before Case McBride stepped up, asking for a dance. He had no sooner signed his name to her card than a dozen single men crowded around her, anxious for the chance to spend a few minutes with her. Morgan stood by patiently in case they got unruly. There were a few moans and good-natured protests when they noticed his name on the card so many times. Charity told them sweetly that Morgan had been so kind in helping her that she felt obliged to dance with him more than anyone else. No one believed her, especially when she sent a teasing smile in his direction when she said it.

Viscount Merryweather arrived a few minutes later and sought out Charity immediately. "My dear Miss Brown, how enchanting you look tonight. Your dance card, please. I must insist on a dance with the most beautiful lady at the ball."

"You flatter me, my lord. Unfortunately my card is full. I understand you're married. Do you have children?"

"Two." The viscount obviously did not like the turn of the conversation.

"How nice. You must miss your family dreadfully. It's a shame your wife didn't accompany you to Texas."

"My lady prefers England," he said curtly.

"I can see how she would . . . with the dust and all." The first dance, a Grand March, was announced. "Please excuse me, Viscount Merryweather." Charity turned away, pointedly dismissing him, and gave Morgan a beautiful smile.

Morgan put his hand to her back, guiding her toward the long line of couples, and leaned down close to her ear. "Well done."

When he offered her his arm, she placed her hand upon his forearm in a formal manner. All the other couples did likewise. When the music began, they promenaded down the ballroom until the lead couple formed an arch with their arms and whisked it back over the heads of all the other couples, who danced under it. Each couple in turn made an arch and followed them. When they reached the end of the line, they turned and ducked under the row of arched hands. Then the leaders turned and, trailed by the other dancers, doubled back alongside the column behind them. At the end of the room, they again doubled back, promenading until the song ended.

Morgan slipped his arm around Charity, resting his hand at her side as they walked off the dance floor. "Do you want something to drink?"

"I wouldn't mind." Charity spotted her next partner, a young cowboy, coming toward her. "The next dance is a polka, and I'll be dying of thirst by the end of it."

"I'll get you something and meet you back here after the dance. Want champagne?" When he saw the eager expression on her next partner's face, jealousy nudged him. He forced a smile. "They only have eighteen hundred pints on ice."

"Then I'll take a glass. Thank you."

He reluctantly handed her over to the grinning young buck and worked his way to the refreshment table. A bar had been set up nearby and was already doing a brisk business. Things would probably get rowdy later on, what with the necessary drinks, friendly drinks, throat-clearing ones, those pledging undying friendship, and those needed to clear up various and sundry misunderstandings of brands, fence lines, and water rights.

Morgan fetched them each a glass of champagne and wandered back to where he said he'd meet her, stopping occasionally to greet people he knew. He didn't spend too much time with them because he was more interested in watching Charity. Scanning the crowded dance floor, he spotted her across the room, laughing as she tried to keep up with the cowboy's exuberant rendition of the polka. When the dance ended, the young man was slow bringing her back to Morgan's side.

So he went to meet them. "Here's your champagne, darlin'."

Since the cowboy was telling her about his favorite horse, he was taken by surprise. He stopped in midsentence, glanced at the irritated glint in Morgan's eye, stammered his thanks for the dance, and scampered off.

Charity gratefully took the offered glass, sipping quickly. "Thank you. My goodness, that was the liveliest polka I've ever done."

"Some of these boys get a mite enthusiastic. They don't have enough opportunities to be with the ladies."

"I'm glad the next dance is a waltz. I'm ready for something slower."

He had been watching some activity across the room, but when he turned to meet her gaze, a fire burned in his eyes. "So am I."

Charity downed the rest of the champagne in one gulp. She looked at the glass in dismay. "Oh dear, I shouldn't have done that."

"Why? Are you going to faint on me?"

"No, but I'll probably start giggling any minute, or trip halfway through the dance." Or snuggle up indecently close. Warmth spread through her veins, either from the champagne or from the thought of being close to him, or both. She felt relaxed, yet very aware of him. Lethargy made her arms feel heavy, her brain a little fuzzy. Thoughts of being in his arms—not dancing but kissing—strolled across her mind. She slowly raised her gaze to his, and he sucked in a sharp breath.

"I think I'm going to like this waltz," he murmured.

"Me, too."

As the first notes of the song drifted across the room, he plucked the glass from her hand and put it, along with his, on a waiter's tray as the man walked by. "Come here, Charity."

She took a step toward him but stopped when a man hastily tapped Morgan on the shoulder.

"Excuse me, Deputy Kaine, but we've got trouble."

With great effort, Morgan tore his gaze away from her warm, limpid eyes. "What kind?"

"We've got about three thousand people in here. One of the boys went downstairs and said the floor over on the far end isn't just creaking, it's moanin' and groanin'. We're afraid it might give way."

Morgan stifled a curse. "Do we need to evacuate the building?"

"I don't think so. I've got men bringing some lumber over, but we need more help setting the braces in place."

"I'll gather up some men and meet you downstairs."

The man pulled a handkerchief from his pocket and mopped his brow. "Thanks, Deputy." He hurried toward the exit.

Morgan curled his fingers around Charity's upper arm. "Come on. I want you with me." Not only did he want her where he could get her out of harm's way if necessary, but he also wasn't about to leave her alone until the effects of the champagne wore off.

"Is there really a danger?" She scurried along beside him.

"Not if we get the braces up." He stopped, explaining the situation to Case and a dozen others who were in the midst of a discussion about the benefits and problems with fencing. They all quickly disposed of their drinks and followed Morgan and Charity down a back stairway.

On the floor below, workmen were hauling in load after load of lumber, while others hammered the heavy pieces into frames to support the floor. Morgan positioned Charity right beside the stairway door. "If something happens, you get outside. Understand?"

She nodded. Excitement and fear had quickly dispelled the hazy feeling brought on by the champagne. She took out her little sketch pad, recording the activity and quieting her nerves at the same time.

In a short time, Morgan and the others had the end of the floor they were most concerned about well secured, but occasional squeaks still came from other parts of the room. They put up additional bracing until they felt confident the whole floor was safe.

Under the pretense of making sure the door was locked and the area clear, Morgan stayed in the room after the other men left. They took the lanterns with them, leaving Morgan and Charity in only the dim light coming down the stairs from the hallway above.

"Sorry we missed our waltz."

"It's for the best. I'm afraid I would have embarrassed us both."

"It might have been worth it." His voice was low and rough.

"Probably not." She sighed softly. When he held out his hand, she took it, stepping up next to him.

"Still feeling the champagne?"

"No, all this scared it out of me."

"Too bad." He slid his arms loosely around her and silently cursed corsets. He wanted to feel her softness beneath his hands, not some piece of steel. "Sounds like you missed a couple more dances."

"Only one. That was Case's, and he was down here anyway. I left the next few free so I could work or talk to people. Besides, I'm too old to dance every dance."

He was quiet for a long moment before he urged her closer. "You don't look too old to me. Can't be a day over twenty-four."

"Flatterer. I'm twenty-seven." *A lonely old maid.* She had never thought much about her age until she met him. Being in his arms gave her an inkling of how much she was missing as a result of her solitary life. She brought the palms of her hands up, resting them on his chest. "Morgan . . ." Her heart ached with longing. "Would you think me wanton if I asked you to kiss me?" she whispered.

With any other woman, the answer would have been yes, but he couldn't bring himself to think of her that way. He felt her tremble and fought against the urge to crush her to him. She touched him in ways no woman ever had, made him hunger for things he knew only fools craved. He wanted the kiss as much as she did, maybe more. And that's what kept him from answering or doing as she asked.

She pushed against his chest, trying to pull away. "I'm sorry, I was much too forward."

He heard the pain in her voice, the embarrassment. He held her fast. "Shh. It's all right, Charity. I don't think you're wanton." She stopped trying to move, but he could still feel her tension. "The thought of kissing you right now makes me about as scared as a rabbit in a coyote's hip pocket." He barely saw her tiny, uncertain smile in the faint light.

"I might manage a gentle kiss, but I wouldn't be able to stop there, and the rest might not be so gentle." He pulled her close, cradling her head tenderly against his chest, and lightly touched his lips to her forehead. "Everybody would take one look at you and know exactly what we'd been up to."

"Then I guess we'd better not." She sighed quietly. "This is almost as good."

*Not hardly.* Her response, more than anything, told him the level of her experience. "We'd better get upstairs before your next partner comes lookin' for us." He slid his hand up, caressing her neck as she pulled away.

"Hey, Morgan, you still down there?" Case called quietly from halfway down the stairs.

"Yeah, we're here." They walked out of the room, and Morgan pulled the door closed behind them. He noted his friend's quick appraising glance at Charity and relaxed when Case didn't appear to see anything wrong—other than her deep blush.

"Your aunt is looking for you."

"It's about time they got here. Come on, Charity, there's someone I want you to meet." He hurried her up the stairs, briefly stopping at the door to the ballroom as he scanned the room. Spotting Addie in the crowd, he gently urged Charity in her direction.

Charity knew immediately which lady was his aunt because when the woman spotted them, her rather plain face broke into a beautiful smile.

"There you are, you scamp." She gave him the once-over. "You look good enough to give a sermon." She enveloped him in a warm hug, and he returned it with equal affection.

"We were downstairs helping brace up the floor."

"Are we in danger of falling through?" Her brow knit in a worried frown.

"Not anymore. Charity went down to watch. I think she drew a picture of it for her article." He slipped his arm around Charity, drawing her forward. "Aunt Addie, I'd like you to meet Charity Brown, the famous writer from New York. Charity, this is my Aunt Addie, the best cook in the country and the best aunt a man ever had."

Charity and Addie exchanged greetings. Charity liked the older woman immediately. She was warm, friendly, and obviously doted on Morgan.

"When this ornery nephew told me he was ridin' herd on the prettiest little gal to set foot in this town, I didn't believe him." Addie winked at Charity and grinned at Morgan as a dull red spread across his cheeks. "But now that I see you for myself, I understand. Has he been taking good care of you? He hasn't had much practice doing the pretty for the ladies. Most of his customers are scruffy cowboys who are three sheets to the wind."

Charity laughed and smiled at Morgan, sympathizing with his discomfort but finding it amusing, too. "He's taking very good care of me. He's answered about a thousand and one questions, shown me all around the town—even places he swore I didn't have any business going—and put up with my stubborn nature. I've tried his patience on occasion, but he's done rather well. He hasn't lost his temper too many times, and he only yelled at me once."

Addie looked stunned. "He lost his temper and actually yelled at you?"

"I fear I provoked him terribly. I wanted to visit the West End, and he was adamantly against it."

"Well, I should think so."

Charity noticed Morgan tugging at his necktie as his aunt studied him with a narrowed gaze.

"But I really needed to go there to get information for my article. So I told him I'd go on my own if he wouldn't take me. I never really intended to, of course."

"What!" He glared at her.

"Morgan, dear, don't bellow." Addie shook her head and smiled at several people nearby who were looking curiously in their direction. "Quit scowling and for heaven's sake loosen your necktie. Your face is turning purple." She put her arm around Charity's shoulders and turned her away from Morgan with a chuckle. "My dear, you've done something no other woman has ever done."

"What?"

"Broken through that icy shell of his. Oh, he gets mad just like the rest of us, but he doesn't let off steam like a fellow should. He just gets quiet as a shadow, and his eyes turn cold enough to chill a man's soul. I've only known him to yell one other time." When her voice trailed off, Charity glanced at her. Pain filled her eyes for a second, then she briskly blinked it away. She squeezed Charity's shoulders. "Knowin' you is good for that boy, Miss Charity Brown from New York City. It's time he met a woman who gave him what for."

"Are you two through tellin' secrets?"

"Yes, dear." Addie dropped her arm from Charity's shoulders, turned around, and was instantly greeted by a friend from out of town.

Charity cautiously met Morgan's gaze. No one would have any problem seeing that he was still irritated. She put her hand on his arm, squeezing lightly. "I'm sorry. Please don't be angry."

"I hate deceit, Charity. More than just about anything."

His eyes grew cold. Addie's description had been accurate. Charity felt the chill all the way to her soul.

"I only meant it as a bluff. Surely you've had to do that occasionally."

Some of the hardness left his face. "Yeah, I've run a bluff now and then. But I don't particularly like being on the receiving end of one."

"I don't suppose anyone does, but you have to admit part of the evening was very nice."

The corner of his lip lifted in a boyish half smile, and warmth chased the chill from his eyes. He put his hand over hers. "Yeah, it was." He glanced at his aunt, who was listening in delight to her friend's description of a grandchild's antics. "There are some other folks I want you to meet. We'll catch Addie again later."

Morgan guided her through the crowd. Charity was relieved he had gotten over his irritation, yet she sensed he had given her a warning. No one liked deceit, but Morgan clearly abhorred it. Did he see her untruthfulness? And if he did, how much had he figured out?

They approached a group listening to Lump Mooney telling a tale. Morgan tapped the shoulder of a tall man and said something in his ear. As he drew Charity to one side, the man broke away from the group, following them. "Charity, I'd like you to meet Jacob Hunter."

She barely stifled a gasp. Graying blond hair. Smiling clear green eyes, the same pale shade as her own. Nearly thirty years older than the man in the picture, but so much the same.

Her blood turned to ice, and her heart lodged in her throat. She had thought about this moment so much, and now that it was here, she had no idea what to say. *Remember your plan. Get to know him first. Tell him later.* Morgan's arm tightened around her stiff back. *Get control of yourself.*

"Jacob is Addie's husband."

*Oh, merciful heavens!*

"H-how do you do?"

"Fine, thanks. It's a pleasure to meet you, Miss Charity. This boy was bending my ear about you last Sunday evening." His eyes twinkled merrily. "Sounds to me like you've been keepin' him on his toes."

"He's been very kind. I'm sure he'd rather be chasing outlaws or something."

Jacob glanced at Morgan and grinned. "If he would, he's not nearly as smart as I thought he was. How do you like our part of the country?"

Charity rattled off a reply, giving him the same general answer she had given the one hundred or so other people who had asked that question during the past week and a half. While she carried on the conversation with a measure of social grace, her mind soaked up details—his attentiveness and sincere interest in what she had to say, the little crinkles around his eyes caused by smiles and squinting in the bright sunlight, the laugh lines around his mouth, and the way his face lit up when he spotted Addie coming toward him.

She was struck by the unabashed love shining in his eyes as he put his arm around his wife. She wondered if he had ever looked at her mother that way. Had he loved her? *Will he love me? Or hate me?*

Jacob waved to a young cowboy, who immediately came over to them. He introduced him as their son Lacy.

Charity automatically exchanged greetings with the handsome young man, and the small talk began again. A brother. *I have a brother.* He was in his early twenties, with brown hair and blue eyes like Addie's. The other features of his face and his tall, lean stature resembled his father's.

Jacob grinned and slapped his hand down on another man's shoulder, drawing him into their circle. "And this is the last member of the family here at the party. Miss Charity, this is my little brother, Joshua."

Graying blond hair. Smiling clear green eyes, the same pale shade as her own. Nearly thirty years older than the man in the picture, but so much the same.

Charity sagged against Morgan's arm. For the first time in her life, she thought she might faint.

# Chapter Ten

"Charity?" Morgan's firm voice held a note of concern. He supported her weight with his strong arm. "Do you feel ill?"

She took a deep breath, desperately gathering her scattered wits. "I'm sorry, I suddenly felt a little lightheaded. I'm afraid that glass of champagne is still bothering me."

"Those bubbles will get to you if you aren't careful." Lacy smiled sympathetically.

Charity's laugh was shaky. "That must be it. I was so thirsty I drank too quickly."

"Well, it's plenty warm in here with all these people. Are you feeling all right now, dear? Do you need to sit down?" Addie's face was wrinkled in concern.

"I'm fine, thank you." She straightened, sent Morgan a smile of thanks, and hoped he didn't feel her knees knocking. Evidently he did, because he kept his arm firmly around her. She looked back at Jacob and Joshua. "You look so much alike. Are you twins?"

The brothers chuckled, and Joshua poked Jacob in the ribs with his elbow. "See, I told you, you don't look your age."

"No, you've got it all wrong, brother. I look my age, but you do, too. All that hard livin' of yours is startin' to show." Jacob looked back at Charity with a warm smile. "We're not twins, ma'am. I'm eighteen months older than my baby brother here."

"Folks often have trouble telling these two apart," said

118

Addie with a smile. "Some used to have a problem with all three of them."

"There's another one?" asked Charity. Her voice had suddenly grown weak again.

"Yes, ma'am. Our big brother, Augustus. He lives down in San Antonio. There are two years between me and him. But most folks recognize him right off," said Jacob.

"That's 'cause his hair's a mite thin on top." Joshua laughed. "He's been bald since he was thirty."

"Except for havin' their mother's eyes, they all look like their pa," said Addie with an indulgent smile.

*Why do I have green eyes, Mama? Why aren't they blue like yours or brown like Father's? You have your grandmother's eyes, honey. Which grandma? Your father's mother.*

Until she found Will's letter and the picture in the little walnut chest, Charity had believed her father was Marion's husband, Henry Brown. Her mother had not been able to tell her the truth in person, but she had made certain Charity would understand, because Henry's death certificate was in the chest, too. Unlike the family Bible, which recorded his death as being six months before Charity's birth, the death certificate stated he had died three years earlier. Both Henry and Marion had been in their teens when their parents died, and Marion had not had pictures of any of them.

"That must please her," said Charity, realizing she had taken somewhat too long to speak.

"Yes, it does. She lives in San Antonio with Gus."

*A grandmother.* Charity reminded herself that she could be mistaken. Possibly neither of these men was her father. She glanced at the brothers again, knowing that was not likely. They looked too much like the picture, but which one was it?

The orchestra leader announced a waltz, and Lacy excused himself to go find his partner.

Morgan smiled down at Charity. "I believe this one is mine." He didn't give her a chance to say anything, but smiled at Jacob. "I was playing carpenter during our first waltz, so I don't intend to miss this one. We'll see y'all in a while." He guided her onto the dance floor, leaning down to speak softly in her ear. "Are you up to this, Charity? You still look like you've seen a ghost."

She cringed inwardly, wishing the man weren't so observant. Judging from his comment, she doubted he had been fooled by her excuse of the champagne. She smiled and turned to face him, resting her left hand on his shoulder. "A little exercise will clear my head."

He clasped her hand in his and put his arm around her. "Watch your feet."

"Don't worry, we'll do fine."

And they did. After the first two measures, Morgan relaxed. The lessons and the society parties of his youth paid off. He had never enjoyed a dance so much, but he doubted if he could say the same for his partner. She was an excellent dancer, following his lead easily. She seemed content in his arms and did not protest when he drew her closer. If he had been the romantic sort, he might have said they moved as one, except her mind was elsewhere.

After she barely responded to his first two attempts at conversation, he quit trying and let his mind drift also. Her reaction to meeting the Hunters troubled him. He didn't buy her excuse of the champagne. Seeing Jacob had shocked her—why else would the color drain from her face? Meeting Joshua, who did look enough like his brother to be a twin, had almost sent her into a swoon. Why was she so interested in men with the initials J. H.? And why had meeting the Hunters affected her so dramatically, when meeting Jonathan Harris at the Waterin' Hole had not bothered her at all?

He looked at her, noting the little frown wrinkling her brow. Sensing his gaze, she glanced up at him and smiled. He smiled back, enjoying the simple pleasure of holding her close, losing himself in her beautiful pale green eyes.

Suddenly Addie's words flashed across his mind—*Except for havin' their mother's eyes . . .*

He stepped on her toe.

"Ouch!"

"Sorry. You all right?"

She nodded. "I will be as soon as my big toe quits throbbing."

He vaguely noticed the music stop and automatically halted.

"Well, that was good timing, at least," she murmured, wiggling her foot.

He released her, staring at her face, trying to see a further resemblance to the Hunters. He couldn't detect anything other than her eyes, but they were strikingly similar to Jacob and Joshua's. Because her hair was so dark, however, the likeness wasn't particularly noticeable unless a man was looking for it. "Do you need to sit down?"

"No, it's already stopped hurting." She glanced at him, her expression quizzical, but she didn't say anything.

*She's smart. She knows I think something is amiss, but she's not about to ask what. We'll talk about it all right, after I study on the problem awhile.*

"Here comes my next partner. Will you excuse me, Morgan?"

He nodded absently. She tossed him a worried frown, then smiled at the bowlegged cowboy who took her in his arms for a schottishe. Morgan watched them dance away without a twinge of jealousy. Her red-faced partner was about the homeliest hombre he had ever seen. He wouldn't have any competition from him. Morgan scowled. Why in tarnation was he concerned about rivals?

He pushed the thought aside. There were more important things to concentrate on. Joshua was a rogue, a love-'em-and-leave-'em kind of man, and had been all his life. Could Charity possibly be his daughter, one nobody knew about? It wouldn't surprise him if Joshua had a string of children from Texas to Montana. He had spent enough time in parlor houses along the way to accomplish it.

If she was looking for her father, she obviously had not known his name—only initials. He figured she also had an idea what the man looked like—maybe that his eyes were the same color as hers. His gaze narrowed as she and her partner whirled within view. He doubted she'd mind if her father was a wealthy rancher.

Or she could be trying to pull a hoax. He had seen enough frauds to know they could be amazingly clever and resourceful. She could have been looking for someone whose eyes were a close match to hers, someone with enough money to interest her. She would cultivate his friendship, maybe even the family's. Under the guise of writing, she could learn about his past, finding out how wild he had been in his younger days. With a man like Joshua, she'd have it made. She would subtly learn where he had been and some of the women he'd slept with once or twice, women he had never seen or heard of again, and she'd have her mother picked out.

She would produce some fake letters her mother had written telling him about their child. Portraying the lonely daughter who had been diligently searching for her father, she'd feed him a sob story about how hard her life had been. She'd take him for everything she could and then suddenly disappear. The idea was farfetched, but he'd heard of some crazier schemes that worked. She would leave those who had grown to love her, like Addie, with a broken heart. Addie had been wounded enough. He wasn't about to let her be hurt again.

He wandered over to one of the refreshment tables and poured himself a cup of punch, taking a ribbing from some of the men clustered around the bar because he didn't drink something more potent. Morgan shied away from anything stronger than an occasional glass of wine or beer. Drinking, like love, could destroy a man. He had no intention of taking a chance with either one.

Strolling around the room during two more dances, he noted which men, and a few women, were imbibing too much. He dropped a gentle hint in an ear or two that certain people ought to be taken home or back to the hotel. His suggestions were immediately obeyed. All in all, folks behaved well. Many weren't drinking at all, merely enjoying the music or the dancing or visiting with friends they might not have seen in years. People had come from all over Texas, New Mexico, and several other states. Just about any man who branded cattle his own or anyone else's—had been invited to attend. The cowboys outnumbered the womenfolk, but the ladies were generous with the dances and tried to give everyone a chance to stomp and romp a little.

He picked up another cup of punch, this one for Charity, and angled across the room so he would be close to where she and her latest partner ended their polka. When the music faded, the man gave her a cocky smile and brushed her cheek with his fingertip. Charity laughed and shook her head, but the handsome cowboy continued to flirt with her. As Morgan stepped up beside her, the man asked if he could get her something to drink, and if she would sit out the next dance with him, maybe even step outside for a breath of air.

"She already has something to drink." Morgan handed the cup of punch to her and pinned the cowboy with his cold stare. "You're intrudin' on my time."

The other man grinned. "Sorry, Deputy. Can't blame a man for tryin'. Thank you for the dance, ma'am." He sauntered off and within seconds was whispering something in another young woman's ear.

"Oh my, what a rascal." Charity laughed and shook her head, taking a long sip of the punch. "This tastes wonderful. Thank you." She could hardly catch her breath. "Would you mind if we sat out the next dance? I'm not up to all of this exertion."

"No, I don't mind. Let's get you another glass of punch and go down to the auditorium and sit a spell. It will be quieter down there."

They picked up the punch and walked downstairs, meeting another couple coming out of the auditorium as they went in. It was much cooler there than in the ballroom, and softly illuminated, with only some of the lamps burning. They had the whole room to themselves.

"Are you enjoying the party?" Morgan asked, sitting down beside her in attached wooden chairs.

"It's grand. Thank you so much for inviting me. I'm going to have to quit playing soon, though, and do a couple more drawings. Have you seen some of those gowns? I overheard some ladies talking who said they ordered their dresses from Paris. I don't think they were lying. One gown had to be a Worth original. I've never seen anything so beautiful."

"Not even your mother's designs?" He wondered if her mother really had designed gowns for society women. Had she been a seamstress at all?

"Mother's gowns were beautiful, but she also worked to keep the cost within reason. Her clients were the elite of the literary and art world, not high society." She glanced down at her own gown. "Madam DeFontaine does lovely work. I don't feel the least bit shoddy, not even next to those Paris originals."

"You don't look shoddy at all," he said without a smile.

"I wasn't fishing for a compliment." She laughed, then studied him in the soft yellow light. "I don't think you're having a very good time. Are you disappointed that we're missing another waltz?"

"Maybe a little. But it's nice to get away from all the noise. Some of those war stories are gettin' a little loud."

"War stories? Civil War?"

"Some of them. Indian wars, trail drives." He smiled in spite of wanting to steer the conversation toward serious matters. "One of the loudest and funniest was about a fellow whose wife got mad at him for trackin' in mud—and some other extraneous matter from the corrals—on her new tapestry rug. She yelled at him good and proper, and he figured he'd been let off easy, until she nailed the outhouse door shut that night—with him inside."

"Oh no!" Charity giggled and felt a rush of warmth when he caught her hand in his and rested it on his thigh.

"He couldn't get the door open because she had wedged a big board up against it and nailed one clear across it. It was wintertime and colder than molasses in January."

"What did he do?" She smiled and shifted closer to him so her shoulder leaned against his arm.

"He finally kicked out one side—and left his boots on the back porch from then on." He was quiet for a long moment, listening to her husky chuckle and the muted music from the orchestra, feeling the warmth and smoothness of her gloved hand in his. "Why did you almost faint when you met the Hunters?" he asked softly.

"It must have been a combination of the champagne, the crowd, and the heat. I just suddenly felt light-headed."

"What kind of fraud are you up to, Charity?"

"I don't know what you mean." She tried to pull her hand from his, but he held tight. Fear of discovery sent the blood rushing through her ears, almost blocking out the music.

"Do you go from one area to another looking for men whose eyes are similar to yours? It's such an unusual color, it must take a while to find someone who fills the bill."

"I don't have the foggiest idea what you're talking about."

"Don't you? I'll cut to the bare bones." The more he thought about it, the more the idea of her running a con was as plausible as that of her being Joshua's daughter. All right, he admitted to himself, there were holes in the theory, but it could cause a lot more harm. "You find some poor sap who looks like you and is old enough to be your father. You convince him you're his long-lost daughter and take him for all you can get, then you up and disappear, moving on to some other territory to trick some other fool."

"And how am I supposed to convince him I'm his daughter?" She glared at him and tugged her hand free from his. "Just tell me that."

"You write a story about him, learn what he was like in his younger days, where he traveled. Most men have sown some wild oats. He tells you a story or two about his escapades, laughing about the time in such-and-such a town that he was too drunk to remember who he was with. You supply the name of the lady and point to your eyes, sweetly telling him how your mama always said they reminded her of him.

"For good measure, you might even have some 'old' letters your mother wrote to him, telling him about you. Of course, they never reached him and were returned to her unopened. You might even come up with a fake birth certificate with his name on it, once you decide who your 'father' is going to be, of course."

"That is the craziest story I've ever heard. You should try your hand at writing, Morgan. You'd make a fortune in dime novels."

He wanted to believe her. He wanted it to be nothing more than his imagination running rampant, but he wouldn't let Addie be hurt. This time he would stop things before they led to heartache. This time he would prevent it, not cause it.

"I'm not trying to defraud anybody, Morgan."

He gripped her chin, firmly but not painfully, and forced her to look at him. "Make me believe you, Charity. Tell me the truth. Don't try to deceive me."

The pain in his eyes was almost her undoing. She couldn't tell him yet. What if she figured out who her father was and decided not to reveal the relationship? It would be better if no one else, not even Morgan, knew about it. She met his gaze directly, admiring him for his loyalty to his family, envying them the fierce love he held for them. She didn't want to hurt him or anyone. Heartache was no stranger. Instinct told her it had intruded in Morgan's life, too, perhaps in ways she could not comprehend.

"I'm not trying to cheat anyone, Morgan," she said softly. "Mother left me a substantial inheritance. I have enough money of my own. I don't want to hurt anyone. Please believe me. Please trust me."

"I want to, sugar. I want to." His touch lightened, and he leaned toward her. His kiss was hard and quick. When he drew back, the promise of vengeance burned in his eyes. "If you're lying to me, Charity, if you try to cheat them or hurt them, I swear I'll nail your pretty little hide to the wall."

He rose swiftly, took two steps, and turned back toward her. "I'll be upstairs. Come find me if you want to dance."

She considered leaving the party but decided that would only make him more suspicious. It would also lessen her chances of getting better acquainted with the Hunters. She gathered her dignity, took several deep breaths, and walked upstairs with her head held high.

Charity danced the dances she was obligated to, except for the ones promised to Morgan. Worried by his suspicions and irritated by his distrust, even though she knew it was reasonable, she avoided him. She did her drawings and chatted with Addie, who found it amusing when Charity explained that she and Morgan had had a disagreement. He must have gone off somewhere to sulk.

Case overheard the comment and took the opportunity to fill his friend's boots and teach her the Two-Step. Afterward he introduced her to his mother. Mrs. McBride was outspoken and gruff, but Charity liked her anyway.

Addie invited Charity out to the ranch for a nice, long visit. She accepted the invitation with a surge of jubilant excitement followed by unexpected disappointment because she could not share her joy with anyone, especially Morgan.

She missed him. As the evening wore on and she sat alone during the slow dances, her loneliness and sadness grew. Spying him across the ballroom, looking every bit as unhappy as she felt, Charity called herself a fool. Pride had kept her from being with him; pride and distrust had cost her some of the most precious moments of her life. The last two dances were his—if he wanted them.

His gaze never left her as she made her way toward him, the lilting, almost plaintive notes of the music weaving a golden thread between them, drawing them together. She went most of the distance, but he met her partway. Neither spoke out loud, but as they searched each other's eyes and found regret and longing, words were not needed.

He took her hand in his and slid his arm around her. She placed her hand on his shoulder for a heartbeat, but when he drew her closer, she slid it up around his neck, resting her forehead against his chin with a soft sigh. Like many of the couples on the floor—some nearly worn out, some falling in love, and some already there—they danced almost in one spot, merely shifting from side to side. It was called a double-shuffle two-step, but in their case, as in some of the others, it was merely an excuse for a barely concealed embrace.

The song ended, but Morgan didn't release her. He allowed her to step back, putting a little more distance between them, but kept his hand firmly in place at the small of her back. "Don't worry," he murmured. "It's the wee hours of the morning. Anyone we might scandalize is already home asleep."

Charity glanced around. The crowd had thinned considerably during the last few hours, and no one was paying them any mind. Many couples were standing just as near to each other as they were. Several of the lamps had burned out or possibly been blown out, casting a soft, romantic glow over the room.

"This is the last waltz, folks." The announcer made a broad sweep with his hand. "The last chance to dance at the grand Stockman's Ball of 1885. We thank y'all for comin' and for makin' this shindig something folks will talk about for years to come. Now grab your sweetheart, ladies, or at least the fellow that brung ya, and we'll do our last bit of huggin' to music for tonight."

As the song began, Morgan gently urged Charity toward him, his smile tender yet rakish. "You heard the man, sugar, huggin' is allowed, as long as we shuffle our feet a little."

"Such scandalous behavior." She smiled and stepped forward, sliding her hand up his chest and around his neck. He pulled her gently but firmly against him. When he brushed her forehead with a kiss, her legs turned to jelly. "Morgan, I don't think I can dance like this," she whispered. "My feet refuse to shuffle."

"We'll just sway from side to side."

"That won't fool anybody." Her mind sent up a warning flag, but her body and heart ignored it. Even as she feebly protested, she yielded, letting him shift her from side to side.

"Does it matter?" he asked.

She felt the muscles in his shoulder tense. "No. I just don't want people to think I'm completely shameless."

He relaxed. "They won't. It's a magical night, remember?"

She smiled up at him. "Yes." She rested her cheek on his shoulder, closed her eyes, and surrendered to the enchantment, relaxing completely against him. His arm tightened around her, and he murmured something she didn't quite hear, something tender and filled with longing.

Everyone clapped when the song ended, and a few of the ladies shed a tear. Tired and subdued, but happy, they gathered their belongings and went back to their respective lodgings.

Morgan walked Charity up to her room, putting his arm around her when they reached her wing and saw that no one was in sight. Judging from the snores emanating from the other rooms on the floor, they were the last of the party-goers to return. She handed him the key, and he unlocked the door, stepping aside so she could enter.

As her heart began to pound, Charity looked at him. "I'm not asking you to stay, but would you come in for a minute?" she whispered. His eyes grew dark, and his gaze dropped to her lips. He nodded.

She held the door partly open so the light from the hall would show him the way to her desk. He took a match from the match safe and struck it against the rough edge. The second it flared to life, Charity quietly closed the door. When she turned, he was setting the lamp chimney back into place. He kept the light turned low. She crossed the room behind him, going over to her dresser.

Morgan slowly straightened and smiled, his gaze quickly scanning the room. Her shoes were lined up precisely beside the wardrobe, and everything on the dresser was neat and tidy. Her desk, however, looked as if a wild boar had run through it. He suspected she could instantly put her hands on any sketch or note she needed, even if no one else could make sense of the arrangement. He found this unexpected facet of her personality interesting, but it had not brought the smile to his face.

The smile and the warm, dangerous glow in the area of his heart had been brought about by her doodles—a likeness of him with his hat tipped back and a tiny smile lighting his eyes, and his name written several times in a flowing hand down the margin of a note page. He removed his hat, setting it on the desk, and turned, waiting to see what she would do.

Her hands trembled as she slid the delicate strings of her handbag over her hand and dropped the bag on the dresser.

The corsage came next. She pulled one strand of each ribbon, carefully untying them, and lifted the flowers from her wrist to her nose, inhaling their delicate scent. Pausing to run her fingertip along one smooth, delicate petal, she gently placed the bouquet beside her handbag.

Seeing how she treasured his simple gift brought bittersweet pain. His father had given everything he had—heart, soul, dignity, money—trying to please the woman he loved. Morgan doubted that his mother had ever touched any gift, no matter how simple or how expensive, with such tender appreciation.

He stayed where he was, watching as she fumbled briefly with the fastening on her ivory velvet cloak, then slipped it from her shoulders and laid it on the bed. She pulled off her gloves, slowly tugging each finger loose before easing the material down the length of her arms.

He'd never seen anything more seductive. He took a deep breath and exhaled slowly. She stood still, her back to him, her hands resting on the top of the dresser, her breathing shallow and fast. She waited for him to go to her, trusting him not to demand more than she was willing to give. By showing her faith in him, she was asking him to do the same for her.

His fists clenched. He did not give his trust freely, and she had not earned it. He hadn't known her long enough, didn't know enough about her. Everything she had told him could be a lie. His heart—that most unreliable, illogical part of his being—ordered him to grant her silent plea, give her more time, allow her to share her secrets when she felt she could. But his mind—keeper of the law, protector of the innocent, guardian of his heart—warned against it.

Slowly walking to her, he forced his fingers to relax, though he still did not know what he would do. He stopped behind her, lightly skimming his hands up her arms. She sighed. He bent down, feathering kisses from her shoulder up the side of her neck. She shivered and tipped her head to one side, and he kissed her neck again. Lifting the long sweep of hair curling down her back, he brushed it over her shoulder. When he dropped a kiss at the nape of her neck, she shivered again and made a tiny sound in her throat.

He started to slide his arms around her waist so he could hold her, but the large bustle got in the way. "Now I know why women wear these things," he muttered and stepped back. "Turn around, Charity." She did as he asked. When he put his arms around her, she brought her hands up to his chest, her palms pressing against him, clearly sending a message to stop. He fought against a spark of anger and frustration.

"I'm going to the Double J tomorrow with Addie and Jacob," she said quietly, looking at his necktie.

"I figured she'd invite you. How long are you planning to stay?"

"I don't know."

She met his gaze, her eyes troubled. He felt her hands slide higher up his chest, bringing her more fully against him. He tightened his hold, but she didn't try to pull away.

"There is a lot to write about, and there are things . . . things I have to check out. Morgan, will you trust me? I swear to you I'm not trying to cheat them out of anything."

He looked down at her lovely, sorrowful face, and settled on a compromise. "I'll trust you . . . for now. I won't push you for answers or give them any hints that you're up to something besides writing your articles." He would also wire *Century* magazine and confirm who she was. "But you have to understand, if it looks like you're going to stir up trouble, I won't hesitate to interfere. My first loyalty is to Addie and her family."

A beautiful smile lit her face. "I wouldn't have it any other way. She means a great deal to you, doesn't she?"

He nodded. "She's always loved me, always been there for me." Would he ever be free of the guilt? Would the pain ever go away? Or would it always be as fresh as the day he sent his father out to die? "Her well of forgiveness runs mighty deep," he whispered.

His pain and the dark remorse burdening his soul touched her heart. She wished with all her being that she could set him free. She, who lived by her words, found no words to give him peace. Stretching up on tiptoe, Charity kissed one corner of his mouth, then the other.

He lowered his head to make her quest easier, anticipation heightening his senses, and waited for passion to explode at her touch. She cupped his face with both hands and drew back to look at him. The tenderness and admiration in her eyes took his breath away.

"You're a good man, Morgan Kaine," she said softly.

"No." If she knew what he had done, she wouldn't think so.

"We all make mistakes. Forgive yourself," she whispered against his lips.

He'd never known a kiss could be so sweet, so gentle. Like the brush of angel's wings, it made him ache for what he had lost, what he didn't have, what he couldn't believe in.

"Let it go," she whispered, kissing him again.

It, too, was a cherished gift. Somewhere deep in his heart, tangled in with the guilt and the bitterness, the failure and the pain, her words settled like seeds on rocky soil. Instinctively he knew that without her to nurture them, they would never take root and grow.

Fear shook him. He didn't need her, not for healing his battered soul, not for anything. He broke off the kiss and released her. "I've got to go. The desk clerk saw us come up." She nodded, but he caught the disappointment in her eyes. "Charity, if I stay any longer, you'll be a ruined woman."

"Thank you for guarding my reputation and for not taking advantage of the situation. I know you have to leave." Her smile was wistful. "But I don't have to like it."

He didn't need her—wouldn't let himself need her.

He slid his arm around her waist and crushed her against him. Tangling his fingers in the curls at the back of her head, he slanted a hard kiss across her lips, angry because he couldn't simply walk away. He felt her tense and instantly softened the kiss, ashamed because he had frightened her. He eased his hold and gentled the kiss even more until it became little nibbles along her lower lip.

Finally, with effort, he raised his head. "I guess I don't

like leavin' much, either. I'll see you next week at Addie's."
He smiled. "I'm due for a good home-cooked Sunday
dinner."

When he released her and stepped back, she chuckled.
"Don't expect me to cook it. I could make the tea, but that's
about the extent of my expertise in the kitchen."

He walked over to the desk and retrieved his hat. "Better
learn to make coffee, darlin'. Cowboys don't drink tea."

She smiled and met him by the door. "Not even out of
dainty china cups?"

He smiled and shook his head. "Especially not out of
dainty china cups. Coffee, thick and black, preferably out of
a tin cup or at least a heavy mug."

She shivered. "With cream and lots of sugar, please."

"You'll never make a cowboy." His gaze raked over her.
"But can't say as I'd want you to. You're mighty fine just
the way you are. Now, open the door and make sure no one
is in the hall."

She opened the door and peeked out. "It's clear," she
whispered. As he stepped through the doorway, she put her
hand on his arm. "Thank you for taking me tonight. I'll
remember it always."

He caressed her cheek with the back of his fingers,
sadness entwined with his happiness. "I will, too. Thanks
for going."

He went on his way, wondering why he suddenly had the
intelligence of a cantaloupe. When had he lost control of his
life? More importantly, how could he be falling in love
when he knew what it might cost?

# Chapter
# Eleven

Charity hadn't known what to expect Jacob and Addie's house to look like, but she was drawn to it immediately. It was built of red brick that had been hauled out from the kiln in town and trimmed with white windows and doors. The porch posts were white, as were the gutters and gingerbread trim along the top of the front and back porches. It had a formal parlor, family parlor, four bedrooms, and even a bathroom, which held only a tin bathtub. Hot water had to be heated on the kitchen stove and carried to the tub. Cold water was brought by bucket from the hand pump nearby on the porch.

The front door opened into a small reception hall. To the right were two bedrooms. To the left were doors leading to the parlors. Across the reception hall, opposite the front door, was another door leading to the breezeway, or dog trot as it was called. This covered porch ran the length of the north side of the house, separating the kitchen and dining room from the other rooms. Addie explained that this was done to keep the kitchen heat away from the other rooms in summer and as fire prevention. With the front doors open to let the air flow through, it also served as a cool, shady spot to sit during a hot summer day.

The back porch connected with the dog trot, running along the west side of the house and curving around to the south side where a cozy sitting area was sheltered from the sun by a white lattice. Beneath this section of the porch was a large cistern. A pipe came up through the porch and attached to a hand pump. Gutters around the house collected

rainwater which was piped down into this cistern and
another one on the north side of the house. There was also
a springhouse between the Hunters' home and the bunkhouse. They usually used this fresh water to drink and cook
with, carrying it to the house or bunkhouse in buckets.

The floors were pine, polished to a high sheen. A wide
strip of white wallboard circled each room, separating the
floor from the floral wallpaper. The high ceilings were made
of beautiful beaded wood. Each room had at least two high,
narrow windows, and a strip of white wainscoting ran
around the room at the top of the windows. This was used
to hold the curtains and pictures. The pictures hung at eye
level, but were held up by wires attached to the wainscoting
so the wallpaper would not be damaged.

The furniture was tasteful and expensive, but not osten-
tatious. The red velvet settee and chairs, mahogany étagère,
and marble-topped tables in the formal parlor gave the room
an air of elegance. In the family parlor, the chairs and sofa
were designed more for comfort than to impress. A piano
stood along one wall, and a large desk almost filled another.

Little touches in every room gave the house a homey
feeling: embroidered throw pillows in the parlors; crocheted
doilies on the piano, the tables, and the dressers; patchwork
quilts or crocheted bedspreads in the bedrooms. A child's
rocker and a large box of toys sat in one corner of the family
parlor. "Just waitin' for our first grandchild," Addie said.

Charity wondered if that child would be hers. Then she
wondered where that thought had come from. She had never
given much consideration to having a home and family and
was surprised at how easily she could picture a little boy
with brown hair and golden-brown eyes sitting in that
rocker.

Of all the pretty and sometimes whimsical items in the
house, Charity's instant favorites were the doorstops. Some
were made of cast iron painted in pastel colors—ships,
flowers, a horse, a spaniel, and Longhorn cows that had
been specially made. Other doors had a brick sitting beside
them, covered in floral needlepoint and ready to be used
when needed.

"Can't have the doors banging closed every time we want a little air," said Addie.

As Charity had expected, the privy at the ranch house was in the backyard. She was amused to discover that it was a two-holer and hoped she never had to share it with anyone.

Joshua had his own house about a hundred and fifty feet away. It was a smaller version of the main ranch house, with only two bedrooms and one parlor. He usually ate with Jacob and Addie and often spent his evenings with them if he was at the ranch.

The morning after her arrival, Charity walked down to the corrals with Joshua and Jacob. The cowboys were scattering hay for the horses around the three fenced enclosures. "Where do you get the hay?" she asked, stepping back from the fence when a friendly horse stuck his head over it. She'd never been around horses, and they made her nervous.

"It's prairie grass. We've got a mowing machine down in the shed. A couple of the men know how to run it, so they cut a good supply when the grass gets tall. Then a crew comes along and gathers it up and stacks it behind the barn. They don't particularly like the work, but it helps keep the horses healthy during the winter."

Charity glanced around. There weren't any cattle in sight. "I didn't see many cattle on the way out from town. I heard the men at the St. James talking about a big drift last winter, but I didn't get the chance to have them explain exactly what they meant. I had the impression that most of the cattle wandered off somewhere else."

"We had some rough weather in December and January, some real blizzards. Cattle try to move away from freezing weather. When a storm comes in, they start walking and will go as far as they can to get out of the cold. Of course, they're looking for grass at the same time, and most of it around here was already gone. We usually send some men along to bring them back when the storm's over, but this year, since grass was already so sparse, all the cattlemen decided to let most of the herds drift until they could find shelter and something to eat. We think most of ours went south, down to the Devil's River."

"Along with everybody else's from this part of the country," added Joshua. "The cattle from up on the Plains, actually most of what was north of the railroad, wandered west toward the Pecos River."

"We've spotted about five hundred head of ours still here on the home range. All the ranches will be sending out crews to round up the rest before too long."

"We hope there's enough to bring back." Joshua scratched the horse's nose. "There's not a whole lot of grass even there."

"Then why would you let them drift?"

"Because there aren't as many ranchers down that way yet. It's pretty rough country. Truth is, Charity, we've got too many cattle in West Texas already, and more ranchers come in every year. We're plain overgrazing the land." Jacob shook his head, his expression sad. "Even if we get enough rain this year, we'll be overgrazed again by fall. We're comin' to a time when we'll have to fence just to provide enough grass for our herds."

"And what happens when the blizzards come, and the cattle can't get away from the cold?" asked Joshua. "They'll just stand there and freeze, that's what. We won't be any better off than if we let 'em drift."

Jacob's sober expression was softened by a tiny smile. "As you can see, it's not an easy problem to solve. We can't tell others not to come here when it's open range. We establish a territory, buying some of the land and leasing some from the state, which gives us grazing rights and water rights. That still leaves open land. Most of us also use some of what's not owned or leased, more by gentlemen's agreements than anything else. Our cowboys keep the herd generally within our territory, but they can't patrol every mile of the boundary all the time. Hungry cattle go where there's grass and water. They don't know if they're trespassing on another man's land." He smiled again, his eyes twinkling. "And what's more, they don't care."

\*     \*     \*

Charity spent much of her time during the next few days talking to the cowboys and drawing pictures of the ranch headquarters. The cowhands had finished up most of the winter chores, such as restocking the woodpile and gathering dried cow chips to use for fuel. They had mended the corrals and the fences around the horse pastures and fixed anything else that needed it. They were bored and anxious to get back to the business of taking care of cattle and riding the range. Her arrival and interest in them and their work went a long way to relieving their boredom.

She made a surprise visit to the bunkhouse—with Lacy going in first to make sure the men were decent—so she could sketch it as it normally was. The men were a little put out about that, and in some ways, she thought, they probably had a right to be. The place wasn't exactly what a woman would call tidy. As one cowboy put it, "Some of us hang our clothes up on the floor so they won't fall down and get lost."

The afternoon was warm, and she was glad the men had opened up the windows and door. As it was, the bunkhouse had an aroma all its own—a mix of old work boots and the dry cow manure that inevitably stuck to them, smoky coal oil lamps, licorice and other flavors from plugs of chewing tobacco, and sweaty men, some of whom thought bathing more than once every two or three months was a pure waste of time.

Once she got used to the smell, however, Charity found the bunkhouse a delightful example of ranch culture. The walls were papered with pages from newspapers, magazines, and mail-order catalogues. The men explained that even though this particular bunkhouse was put together better than most, the paper still added a bit of extra insulation and helped keep out the drafts.

"And it gives us something to read when we get real bored. By winter's end, most of us know every story in here. We'll save up this year's papers and magazines and start plastering them up next winter so we have something fresh to read."

The men had added various pictures, calendars, and even a valentine to the decorations on the wall. Each man's bunk was his personal domain, and the area around and below it often stored most of his worldly possessions—clothes, hat, a couple of pairs of boots and spurs, rifles and six-guns, perhaps even a book or two. His saddle and other equipment were kept along with everyone else's in a special tack room.

Charity made several sketches of the long room and went outside to draw four men engaged in a poker game. They had carried a wooden table and chairs outdoors to enjoy the sunshine and fresh air. They didn't play for money, since Jacob wouldn't allow it, and used kernels of corn as chips.

The bunkhouse was connected by a dog trot to the kitchen and mess hall. The cook was a small, wiry man who had quite a flair for keeping the cowboys happily fed. That night the main course would be fried antelope steaks, courtesy of an early morning hunt, but he hadn't forgotten about dessert. Charity took one look at the flaky golden crust on the peach cobbler and almost asked if she could stay for supper.

On her fourth evening at the Double J, Charity sat on the back porch steps of the ranch house, absorbing the breathtaking beauty of the sunset. She had watched it from her window at the hotel almost every day, but the view there was not as panoramic as this one because the business portion of town was in the valley. Here, no buildings impeded the scene. There was nothing but the magnificent sweep of horizon and prairie and endless sky. The sun dropped behind the horizon, leaving a layer of deep orange-red along the clear, dark edge of the land. The deep hue gradually faded into lighter orange and yellow-gold high in the western sky.

Beneath the brilliant splash of color, the gently rolling land spread out before her, shadowed dips and golden swells covered with pale dry winter grass waving in the breeze. The house stood on a rise above a wide, shallow valley. Beyond the valley, the land rose upward again, giving way here and there to small hills. Low, scattered mesquite trees dotted the landscape, their rough-hewn trunks and thorny limbs still winter bare.

Her gaze swept from one side of the horizon to the other

as a quiet stillness drifted over the land. Peace filled her soul.

"Pretty, isn't it?" asked Lacy, sitting down beside her.

"It's one of the most beautiful places I've ever seen. So quiet and peaceful. I feel like I'm being reborn." She glanced at him and smiled self-consciously. "I suppose that sounds silly."

"No, I know what you mean. I think that's why a lot of us stay. I go into town and enjoy the people and have a good time, but I'm always anxious to get back out here where a man can do his thinking without being disturbed. If I want to, I can ride off by myself and be alone, just me and the Almighty. Not see anybody for days at a time. Or I can sit here on the porch with the lingering smells from supper and soak up the peace and quiet. I figure I'm one of the luckiest men alive."

"Have you lived here long?"

"Almost five years. We brought a herd up in 1880, before the railroad came through. The hunters had killed off most of the buffalo by then, so the Indians weren't much of a threat. We had a ranch down in South Texas, but Dad and Uncle Josh were gettin' itchy feet. Said it was too crowded. They talked about moving to Montana, but Mom refused to go." He grinned. "Said she wasn't about to put up with Montana winters. Texas summers, she could live with, but not Montana winters. I think Dad wanted to move out here all along. He just talked about Montana so she'd agree to come here."

Charity laughed but wondered if she had misjudged Jacob. She had only known him for a short time, but he impressed her as a kind, hardworking man who didn't have a deceitful bone in his body. "Is he always so clever?"

"Well, I guess you could say he knows how to make things work to his advantage, but I've never known him to lie outright."

"What about Joshua?"

"Uncle Josh isn't above stretching the truth now and then, but never about anything serious. I'd call him an honest man." Lacy smiled and shifted, leaning back against the porch post, resting one foot on the porch and the other on the second step. "Usually his tales are so farfetched everyone knows he spinnin' a yarn. If there's a job to do, he'll get it done, but if there's a chance to go have a good time, he'll take off as soon as the job's finished."

"Were there many ranchers here when you first came?"

"Nope. Only a couple. Nobody had even thought of building a town."

"How did you get supplies?"

"Brought most of them with us. There were a couple of stores in the county that had supplied the buffalo hunters, so we could pick up a few things if we ran out. Too bad those stores are gone. You might have found them interesting. One was in a dugout, and another was made of buffalo hides stretched over poles."

Charity shifted, too, leaning against the opposite post, curling her legs up beside her on the porch floor. She studied Lacy's profile. He was his father's son in many ways, more in manner than in looks, with his brown hair and blue eyes. "How old were you when you moved the herd here?"

"Seventeen." He grinned. "Tryin' to find out how old I am, ma'am?"

She laughed. "Partly. So now you're twenty-two. Five years younger than I am."

"Whoo ee. That makes you a little too old for me." His eyes danced with mischief as he winked. "But just right for Morgan."

"Oh. And how old is he?" She tried to act nonchalant, but Lacy's grin told her she wasn't successful.

"Thirty. Time he settled down and started raising a family. He loves kids, but he'd never own up to it." His expression sobered. "I watched him at the ball the other night. He couldn't keep his eyes off of you, even after you had your spat." He held up a hand when she started to protest. "Change that to disagreement. I don't know what it was about—don't want to know, 'cause it ain't none of my business—but it was plain to see you were both miserable because of it.

"The point is, I've known Morgan all my life. He's a

good friend, kind of a big brother, and I've never seen him look at a woman the way he looked at you. Course, I wasn't around him much when he was off workin' for the Rangers, but he wasn't in any shape to be interested in a lady then anyway.''

"Why not?"

Lacy moved away from the post, sliding his foot down beside the other one on the step, and leaned his forearms on his thighs. "He joined the Rangers right after his dad died, and he was hurtin' awful bad. Dick Ware once said that Morgan was lookin' for a bullet, that he tempted death more times than a man had a right to and keep on livin'.''

"He told me he had been shot three times and stabbed twice." A shiver raced down her spine. "He laughed about it.''

"Every one of them was close, too. An inch this way or half an inch that way and he'd have been a dead man. The last gunshot wound would have killed any other man, but he was too cantankerous to die and lucky enough to be near a good doctor.

"He never had a chance that last time, never even saw who did it because he was shot in the back. I reckon he decided the good Lord wasn't going to put him out of his misery, so maybe life was worth livin' after all. He quit the Rangers as soon as he healed up enough to tell them adios.''

Charity's heart ached for him. What could have hurt him so badly that he wanted to die? "Is Addie his mother's sister?''

"No. Uncle Dave, Morgan's father, was Mother's brother.''

"Is Morgan's mother still alive?''

He nodded. "She's out in California someplace. The last I heard, she'd married some rich government official. None of us have seen her in ten years.''

"Not even Morgan?''

"I don't think so. They weren't ever close. She left right after his dad died." He took a deep breath and slowly released it. "I'm talkin' about things I probably shouldn't be. But I'll tell you a little bit more because it will help you understand Morgan's ways. His mother came from a well-to-do Austin family. She's beautiful and elegant, went to the finest finishing school back East, toured the Continent and England the year she turned eighteen. Maybe that's where she got her warped ideas, I don't know.

"She married Uncle Dave when she was twenty and had Morgan when she was twenty-two. Sometime after that, she started seein' other men."

"You mean she had lovers?" She knew it was done, but she had never understood it. Why would a woman risk everything of value with an affair?

He nodded gravely. "She changed men more often than most people change socks."

"And Morgan's father stayed with her?"

"He loved her too much, I guess. He did everything he could to try and make her happy, but she never was. I reckon some women just need to know they can have any man they want."

"And Morgan was aware of all this?"

"I don't know about when he was younger, but by the time he was twelve, he knew what was going on. He went fishin' one day and came across his mother and one of the cowboys down by the creek."

"How awful."

"He changed after that. I was only four, so I didn't learn what had happened until I was a lot older. But after it happened, I noticed he was different. He didn't laugh much anymore. He was real quiet most of the time, even when he was mad. Over the years, he grew hard and cold." He stared at the fading light, glancing up as the first stars appeared. "If he got close enough for a man to see his face, his opponent would back down every time.

"I watched him walk right between two fellows who were about to shoot it out. You could tell one man didn't want to fight, but the other one was bent on shedding blood. He already had a couple of notches on his gun and was out to make a reputation as a gunfighter. Morgan walked right up to him, his hand at his side, and ordered him to leave town. The man hesitated a minute—he had friends lookin' on— and decided that was the smartest thing to do.

"I was standing near his friends. They couldn't believe he had backed down. When they asked him about it, he said for the first time in his life he had looked death in the face. His hands were shaking so bad he could hardly pick up the reins. He decided then and there to give up his dream of being a gunslinger."

"Was that when Morgan was a Texas Ranger?"

"No, it was about six months ago in town. We don't get too many of that type through, but they show up every once in a while."

"So his job is more dangerous than he admitted." Charity felt a heavy weight drop on her shoulders. He was in danger every day, as she had feared.

"Being a lawman is always hazardous. Always will be, I suppose. But then, anytime a man goes up against a criminal, there's danger, whether he's a Ranger, sheriff, or ordinary citizen."

Charity thought of Henry Brown. He'd been an ordinary citizen, trying to talk a robber out of taking his money. The man killed him in cold blood. "That's true, but men like Morgan and Sheriff Ware make it safer for the rest of us."

"That's a fact." They were quiet for a while, both looking up at the stars in the black sky.

"I've never seen so many stars before. I'm sure they're up there, even over New York City." Charity smiled at Lacy's chuckle. "There's just so many lights we can't see them." She pointed to a light, cloudy strip across the sky. It looked as if an artist had flattened his brush and swept it across a black canvas, leaving behind a faint white trail with hundreds of stars twinkling across it. "What's that called?"

"The Milky Way. It's all stars, but a bunch of them are too faint to make out separately. There's the Big Dipper over there."

"That I have seen, even in New York."

"Do you miss the city?"

"A little. I miss the restaurants and art galleries and my friends. Most of them are artists or writers, and we get together often for some lively discussions. I don't miss the crowded streets and the noise. I didn't pay too much attention to it when I was there, but now I think it might bother me. And I don't miss the smoke from the chimneys or soot from the elevated train."

"Elevated train? What's that?"

"It's a train that connects the outskirts of the city to the downtown area. It's built above the streets on an elevated railroad track to save space. I don't live near it, but even if you have to walk or ride near it, you wind up covered in soot." She paused. Suddenly the night had come alive with sounds. "What are all those noises? Wild animals?"

"Yep. That howl is a coyote. In a second another one will answer." Sure enough, the same mournful sound came from a different direction. "Sometimes, one coyote will make so much noise you swear it's a whole pack of them. They do it to protect themselves. That was an owl. He's probably sittin' up on the hill, in that mesquite tree. He'll sit there for a spell, then go look for supper."

"What's that?" Charity tensed as another sound came from the end of the porch.

"A cricket. He's harmless. He's serenading us and his lady love." He stood up and offered her his hand. "Better come on inside. It's gettin' chilly out here."

Charity took his hand, and he pulled her to her feet. She was relieved that he seemed interested in her only as a friend. She would have felt uncomfortable if he'd had romantic notions. "Excuse me, but I think I may be your sister" would have been a shock to say the least. As it was, they had lapsed into a quick and easy friendship.

She and Lacy joined the others in the parlor. Addie was working on a needlepoint chair cover of muted pink roses. Jacob had his nose buried in a ranching magazine, and Joshua slouched in a big, overstuffed chair, snoozing.

"There you are." Addie smiled and patted the cushion on the sofa. "Sit down here beside me so we can visit."

Charity sat down next to her. "You do lovely work. Which chair will that go on?"

"One of the straight ones in the company parlor. I have the stuff to cover the footstool that goes with it."

"I've never tried needlework. For me it's easier to draw

something. Quicker, too. I don't think I'd have the patience to work so long on something."

Addie laughed. "Child, if I could draw like you, I'd never pick up a needle and thread. Since I can't, this gives me a way of being creative, even if I don't come up with the designs myself."

Jacob put his magazine on the table next to his chair. "Are you getting the information you need, Charity?"

"Yes, thank you. I've gotten some wonderful drawings, and the men have told me enough tales to fill a book."

"Don't believe most of them." Jacob smiled. "They sit around all winter tellin' each other stories, and by spring those tales have gotten bigger than they were in the fall."

"They said ranches often lay off a large number of men during the winter, but you don't. Why?"

"We get rid of some, the ones who haven't worked out as well as we thought they might. Sometimes a fellow turns out lazy or is too ornery. Doesn't pay to keep someone around with a hot temper, even if he's a good worker. Ends up causing trouble sooner or later.

"Most of our men have been with us for a while. It's hard to find good cowboys, and as long as we can afford to feed 'em and pay them something during the winter, we'll keep them on. Trying to pick up odd jobs on other ranches or renting a room with some other fellows in town can be difficult. Of course, there are a few who save enough to live in town during the winter by choice. Things are a bit more lively there than they are here."

She had heard much the same thing from the men who worked for the Double J. They told her the Hunters were fair, honest, and compassionate. They demanded a day's work for a day's pay, but were also likely to give an unexpected bonus or time off when the men needed it. Like most ranchers, they expected loyalty from their men, but they gave it back in return.

"While I was in town I heard about a sheep rancher who put green goggles on his sheep so they would eat the winter grass. Everyone swore it was true, but I can't quite believe it."

"I can," said Joshua. He opened his eyes and smiled at Charity with a lazy grin. "Saw them myself. Six thousand sheep, all wearing fancy little green goggles and eating away just like it was spring. Fattest sheep I ever saw. Some of them even had rubber boots on to keep their feet dry, and a couple were wearing yellow slickers. I asked one of the ewes if she was wearing wool socks, and she looked at me as if I had insulted her."

Charity joined in the laughter. "But was it true? Did someone actually try it?"

"I do believe a fellow south of here tried it on a small portion of his flock, but it didn't do any good. It might change the color of the grass, but it wouldn't change the taste any."

They chatted for a while longer. Every so often, Charity caught Jacob or Joshua gazing thoughtfully at her. She wondered if either man recognized some of her mother's features in her face, or if the color of her eyes stirred up questions.

When it was time for bed, Charity made a trip to the outhouse. The cold night air sent her scurrying back down the dog trot toward her bedroom. Joshua lounged against the porch railing in front of the door, obviously waiting for her. "Chilly night, isn't it?" she commented.

"Yep." He straightened and took a step toward her. "Charity, what's your mama's name?"

Her heart lurched and began to pound. She curled her trembling fingers into fists, digging her nails into her palms. "Her name was Marion."

"Was?"

"She died a little over a year ago."

"I'm sorry." He frowned. "Where were you born?"

"New Orleans."

"Did she always live there?"

"No, she lived in Galveston before that. She moved to New Orleans when she was carrying me." Charity took a deep breath. Surely it couldn't be this simple? "My mother was Will Davenport's sister."

Joshua whistled softly. "I didn't even know Will had a

sister. We met him that first night in Galveston. He and Jacob became fast friends, which suited me fine—left me free to seek my amusement where I liked. My big brother has never been fond of the same places as me. Jacob and I didn't get together again until the day we left for home, and I didn't see Will again until years later."

He studied her face in the light from the window, talking to himself, his frown deepening. "I knew a Marion down in Galveston. Or was it MaryAnne? A real pretty gal. Seems like she had blue eyes and red hair, or it might have been brown with a lot of red in it. Had a nice singing voice, that I remember for sure. I guess she could have been Will's sister, but it doesn't seem likely. I don't know any way to ask this except straight out, honey. Was your mama a saloon gal?"

"No." She swallowed her disappointment. "Why do you ask?"

Joshua looked chagrined. "Your eyes. I've never seen anyone with that same color eyes except in this family. I beg your pardon for askin' about your mama like that." He stepped back and leaned against the porch railing again, only this time his tall frame drooped. He looked tired, not work weary but life weary.

"Joshua, are you all right?" Charity put her hand on his arm.

He stared down at the wooden planks of the porch for a long minute. When he looked up at her, his expression was bemused. "Danged if I know. I reckon I'm disappointed. I kept watchin' you this evening, and somehow I got the crazy notion that you might be my daughter." He shrugged. "When a man lives like I have, he wonders sometimes if he's got some offspring somewhere that he doesn't know about. The thought of being tied down to a family and bein' responsible for them has always scared me. But sittin' there tonight, and thinkin' that you might be my daughter . . . well, the idea kinda grew on me." He shook his head. "Just listen to me, talkin' like a foolish old man."

"You're not old."

"Well, I'm not young, either. And I'm beginnin' to think

I've missed out on something important." He patted her hand. "You'd better get on inside, gal, before you freeze to death."

"I'm sorry, Joshua."

"Think nothin' of it. I've just got a good imagination."

She turned to go inside, but as her fingers wrapped around the glass-and-porcelain doorknob, he softly called her name, stopping her. She glanced back at him over her shoulder.

"Is your father still alive?"

"I think so."

"He didn't live with you and your mother?"

"No."

"Do you know who he is?"

She hesitated and decided to tell the truth. "No."

"Are you looking for him?"

She hedged. "I'd like to find him."

He glanced toward Jacob and Addie's bedroom, his expression troubled. "I hope you do." He grinned and gently squeezed her shoulder. "But if you don't, maybe I could adopt you."

"I think I'd like that." She returned his smile and opened the door to her bedroom. As she stepped inside and closed the door, a tremor shook her. She sat down on the bed before her legs collapsed, and ran the conversation through her mind.

It would be so easy. Joshua wanted her for his daughter. If he were her father, Addie wouldn't be hurt, and therefore Morgan wouldn't be angry or hurt. Joshua was a good man. Such a simple solution. Too bad it seemed to be the wrong one.

His description of the woman he knew, Marion or MaryAnne, came to mind, sending goosebumps down her arms. Ironically, he could have been describing her mother— pretty, with blue eyes, reddish-brown hair, and a nice singing voice. The description also probably fit many women. She couldn't imagine her mother ever setting foot in a saloon.

From the most remote recesses of her mind came a memory, a comment Marion had once made. *When you're hungry enough, you'll do just about anything to stay alive.*

She knew times had been hard after Henry died. He was deeply in debt, and his creditors demanded payment shortly after his death, not giving her a chance to pay them off over a long period of time. Charity was certain Marion had been pregnant with her when she moved to New Orleans. It had been confirmed through the years during various conversations with those who had known her mother since her arrival in the city.

But Charity knew little about her mother's life from the time she paid off Henry's debts until she moved to New Orleans. Was it possible she had not gone to work right away as a seamstress as she said she had? Could she have been so desperate that she went to work in a saloon? She had lied about other things. Surely she would not have told the truth about that.

Charity groaned and plopped back on the bed. She didn't know what to believe anymore.

# Chapter
## Twelve

After breakfast the next morning, Jacob swallowed the last of his coffee, set the cup on the table, and scooted back his chair. "Good breakfast, sweetheart, like always." He grabbed Addie's hand as she walked by, and pulled her down on his lap to give her a kiss.

"Jacob Allan Hunter, whatever will Charity think with you kissing me here in the dining room? Stop that!" Addie playfully swatted at his hand as he pretended to pull out one of her hairpins.

"I reckon she'll think I'm in love with my wife. Right, Charity?"

"Right." Charity smiled at them in spite of a twinge of sadness. If Jacob was her father, she didn't see how he could have cared for her mother the way he did Addie. Was it possible to love two women with so grand a passion?

"I thought I'd take Charity for a tour of the ranch this mornin'. Is that all right with you?" asked Jacob.

"Of course, it is. I don't have anything special planned."

"Charity, would you like the grand tour of the Double J?"

"I'd love it. Unless I need to stay here and help you with something, Addie?"

"Land's sake, child, I don't expect you to help with anything unless you particularly want to. You're company. Workin' company, at that. You've got your own job to do. You just go on with Jacob and see the sights." She gave her husband a peck on the lips. "Don't get to jawin' about this and that and be late for dinner. I want you comin' in that door no later than noon."

151

"Yes, ma'am." He grinned at Charity. "Bossy, ain't she?"

Charity laughed. "No comment. I know better than to take sides."

They laughed, and Jacob boosted Addie off his lap and stood up. "You know how to ride, Charity?"

"I'm afraid not. There never was a need for me to learn. And to be honest, horses scare me."

"That's because you've probably never been around them. Maybe after you get used to them, we can give you some riding lessons." He smiled kindly when her little frown revealed her worry. "It's all right if you never try to ride. We'll take the buggy this morning. We can go most places in it. You'll need a hat and maybe a light jacket. It's going to warm up later, but it'll be a little breezy for a while. Half an hour give you enough time?"

"Plenty. I'll be ready." Charity rose from the table and stacked up the plates. When Addie protested, she didn't back down. "The least I can do is help you with the dishes. I'm not much of a cook, but I know how to wash dishes."

She carried the plates and silverware into the kitchen and set them in the dry sink. Taking an apron from a peg on the wall, she tied it around her waist, then poured some hot water from a teakettle on the stove into a graniteware dishpan. Adding a dipperful of cold water from a bucket on the cabinet nearby, she brought the dish water to a temperature she could stand. She filled a second dishpan with water to use for rinsing. After adding soap, she plunged the plates into the water and quickly did the task, letting the dishes dry on a wooden drainer at the back of the sink.

Addie set the crocks of butter and jam and a stoneware pitcher of milk on a small table by the back door so they could be carried to the springhouse. After the dishes were done, she and Charity walked down the well-traveled dirt path. The small stone building was built over the spring to keep the cattle away from it. Some of the cold water was channeled through wide stone troughs. By setting the covered stoneware crocks in the cold running water, the milk, butter, cheese, jam, and anything else that might easily spoil were kept cold. The food couldn't be left there indefinitely, but it was usually eaten up before it could spoil.

"I bet I know where you go on a hot summer day." Charity trailed her hands in the icy water.

"I confess I do find more excuses to come down here in July and August than I do the rest of the year. Of course, it's often above one hundred degrees during those months, so any relief is welcome. One nice thing, though, we don't get high humidity out here like we did down in South Texas. I can take the heat as long as it's not humid along with it. That hair of yours would curl up tighter than sheep's wool if you were to go down to the coast."

"Oh dear. I was thinking about going to Galveston before I went back to New York. My mother lived there when she was young, and I thought it would be fun to visit. Have you ever been there?"

"No, never have. You might ask Jacob or Joshua about it. They spent some time there years ago." Addie closed the door on the springhouse and turned a small piece of wood nailed to the door frame so it went across both the frame and the door, holding the door in place. "Twenty-eight years ago, to be exact. Guess things have changed a right smart since then."

Charity's pulse rate jumped, and she looked away, afraid Addie might notice the excitement in her eyes. "How do you remember exactly how long it's been? Were you a young bride or something?" She prayed that wasn't the case.

"No, but I met Jacob at a dance in Austin right before he left. I had just turned eighteen, and he was the handsomest young man I'd ever laid eyes on." Addie gazed out across the prairie, her eyes glowing at the memory. "I fell in love with him the moment I saw him walkin' across that dance floor toward me, but it didn't hit him so quick. I never was the type to turn a man's head. He and Josh went off to Galveston. They weren't in any big hurry goin' and comin', so the whole trip took about a month."

"Did he come courting when he got home?"

"That rascal waited a whole month before he came callin'. I turned away another suitor in the meantime and just about gave up on him." Addie laughed softly. "Two whole months without seeing him almost drove me crazy. I was afraid he'd found a sweetheart in Galveston."

Maybe he had, thought Charity. Had he missed Marion? Or had he felt guilty about his little fling with her? Charity couldn't believe her mother had been with Joshua. She couldn't have worked as a prostitute. It went against everything Marion had believed in, everything she had taught Charity. Her father had to be Jacob. *Then, why,* she wondered for the thousandth time, *didn't she tell him about me?*

"When he did come courtin', he said work had kept him away, but I don't think that was all of it. He was only twenty-two. Any man thinks twice about gettin' married, but one that young has to be sure he's ready to settle down. Jacob's not the kind to cheat on his wife. Once he made up his mind, though, he didn't waste any time. Of course, I was more than ready to claim him for my own, so we were married two months later."

Charity did some quick mental arithmetic. Just about the time Jacob and Addie got married, Marion probably realized she was carrying a child. As far as she knew, her mother had never been pregnant while she was married to Henry, so she would have assumed that she couldn't have children. She had told Charity she was an unexpected blessing, one she had never regretted and had always cherished. Charity believed her. She never questioned her mother's love, not even now.

Marion had been ten years older than Jacob, twelve years older than Joshua. Charity had suspected her mother was older than her father because the picture was of a younger man, but she didn't know for certain when the picture had been taken. She had not quite anticipated so much difference in their ages. That could be one reason Marion never told Charity's father about the baby. It was common for an older man to marry a younger woman, but seldom did it go the other way and then not without ridicule.

"Whirlwind courtship, huh?"

"That it was," said Addie with a happy smile. "And it

hasn't changed much since. I thank the good Lord every day for that man. He's never been unfaithful, not once. Even when he goes off on business, I don't worry. Josh might find some woman to keep him occupied, but not my Jacob. When it comes to loyalty and livin' the upright life, you won't find anyone better at it than my husband."

When they reached the house, Charity went to her bedroom and slipped on her jacket and floppy work hat. Taking her bag of supplies, she walked out back to wait for Jacob, wondering if there would be an opportunity to mention her mother during their drive. She wasn't sure she wanted to.

"That's some hat," said Addie with a smile. "Latest New York City fashion?"

"Nope. Latest Colorado City fashion, courtesy of Deputy Morgan Kaine."

"Morgan picked out that thing?" Addie stared at Charity, resting her hands on her hips. "He knows women around here wear sunbonnets."

"Actually, I picked out the hat. He tried to get me to wear a sunbonnet, but I didn't like it. It limited my vision too much. I was afraid I might miss something interesting. This one is comfortable and keeps the sun off my face."

"Well, it's practical, I'll grant you, although you probably could have found one at the milliner's shop that was a little more ladylike. Something with just as wide a brim."

"I'm sure I would have, but Morgan was trying to make me look plain."

Addie cackled with laughter. "Now I know that boy's taken a shine to you. Not much of a chance that he could keep the other men from admirin' you, but it tickles me that he tried. He must have been fit to be tied the night of the ball. You were the prettiest gal there."

"I don't know about that, but thanks for the compliment. Here comes Jacob. I'll see you at noon." Charity hurried to the buggy and climbed in so Jacob wouldn't think he had to help her in and out. She didn't want to be a bother.

"I see you're ready to go," he said with a smile. "Afraid Addie will put you to work?"

Charity smiled back. "I doubt if I would be much help. I'm not very domestic, especially in the kitchen."

Jacob waved to his wife, then he tapped the horse's back with the reins. "Didn't your mama teach you how to cook?"

"No. She didn't do too much of it herself. We always lived in the city, so there were plenty of places to eat nearby. Sometimes we had a lady who kept the house part-time and did some of the cooking for us. When I was little, my mother had a dressmaking shop, so she worked very hard. By the time I was twelve, she had gained quite a reputation for design and had a good business. She had several seamstresses working for her, so she didn't have to put in so many long hours."

"This was in New York City?" Jacob guided the horse and buggy across the prairie without need of a road.

"We lived in New Orleans then. We moved to New York later so I could go to art school." Charity noticed that the land gradually sloped downward as they drove into a long, wide valley.

"What about your father? What did he do?"

Charity hesitated. Here was the opportunity. What would happen if she came right out and told him who she was? Her courage failed her. She decided it was good sense not to hit him with too much at a time. "I never knew my father. Mother was widowed before I was born."

"That's a shame. She never remarried?"

"No. I don't know why. She was intelligent, friendly, and pretty, with reddish-brown hair and lovely sky-blue eyes. I think she liked running her own life. She had an independent streak a mile wide." She smiled sadly and wondered if she would ever quit missing her. "She said she was content with just the two of us. She was thirty-two when I was born. I think she had given up on having children. I was something of a surprise." To put it mildly.

"Is your mama dead, too, Charity?" he asked gently.

She nodded, sudden tears burning her eyes. "She died a little over a year ago of a heart attack."

"I'm sorry, honey. You sound like you were real close."

"We were. She was the best friend I ever had."

He gently pulled on the reins, slowing the horse. "You have any other family?"

"An uncle, my mother's brother, but he travels a lot, so I don't see him very often."

"Sounds like it's time to find a husband and have a family of your own."

Charity laughed softly. "Maybe, but I'm not so sure I'd be a very good wife. I'm afraid I inherited Mama's independent streak. I love my job and want to travel. There's so much to see in the world."

"Being married doesn't always mean you can't travel." He smiled. "You have to find a husband who'll go along or else pay the bills if you want to go. As far as being independent, just make sure you pick a man who's as strong as you are. Don't pick a fellow who'll let you run roughshod over him. You'll both be miserable."

"Like you and Addie are miserable?" she teased, smiling at him.

He chuckled. "Oh, she doesn't run my life as much as I let on. I just let her think she's boss."

"Something tells me she's well aware of that."

"Yeah, I reckon so." He stopped the horse at the edge of a bluff and pointed to his left. "Look down there," he said quietly.

Charity followed his instructions and gasped softly. A large herd of animals—antelope, she thought—was spread out along a shallow running river. Some were drinking from the stream that trickled down the middle of the riverbed, and some were grazing the green grass that grew between the mesquites and weeping willows on both sides of the bank. "Antelope?" she whispered.

"Yep. Looks like about fifty of them. You got drawing stuff in that bag of yours?"

"Never go anywhere without it." She carefully opened the leather case and withdrew her sketch pad and pencil. Seconds later, she was recording what she saw. A few of the animals were close enough for her to see the details of their markings. They warily watched the humans for a few minutes, then went back to eating, except for one lone male, who kept a close eye on the intruders. Charity drew him and the others closest to them, then sketched the whole scene.

She had filled in about half the details when the horse shook her head, jangling the harness. The antelope took to their heels, dashing across the water and up the opposite riverbank, fleeing over the windswept grassland until they were mere specks in the distance.

"Will you be able to finish it?"

"Yes. Only the minor detail work is left, and I can fill that in. I got the main idea. Sometimes that's all I have time for."

Jacob studied the drawing. "I'll bet you'll sign that C. M. Brown."

"That's right. You're familiar with my work?"

"Now, darlin', we're more cultured out here than you might think. We've subscribed to the *Century* for the past three years. Addie ran across a copy somewhere and liked it. She said we needed a bit of refining, so she sent off for it. I've enjoyed it, too. And I've gotten a lot out of your articles. You're one of my favorite writers. Even Josh reads it, although I doubt he'd ever own up to it. He likes folks to think he raises Cain more than he does anything else, but he's mellowing out in his old age." He clucked to the horse and flicked the reins. "Let's go see if we can find you a cow or two to draw."

"What river is this?"

"Colorado. Same one that's in town. Winds around some before it gets here."

They forded the river and drove up a steep slope on the other side. Jacob took them across a wide, flat stretch that ran alongside the river, then up and down hills and ravines as if it were commonplace to ride over the rough terrain in a buggy. Hanging on, Charity laughed and squealed like a child as they bounced over rocks and ruts and tipped precariously as they went through the gullies. Jacob chuckled at her joyful whoops. "It's a sight easier to get there on horseback, but I'm going to show you a Texas Longhorn even if I have to dump you out on your head before we find one."

They finally came to a small box canyon where twenty

Longhorns had staked a claim on a patch of grass. "There's a little spring over there that keeps this spot nice and green. Unfortunately it's not big enough to support very many head. These ornery critters have camped out here all winter. Even when the others took off in the blizzard, they huddled up under that overhang of rocks and stayed warm. Probably the smartest ones in the bunch." He pulled up fairly close. "There you are, ma'am. My herd."

She caught an odd note in his voice and turned to face him. "You're really worried about how your herd survived the winter, aren't you?"

He nodded. "After we shipped last fall, we had close to fifteen thousand head left. I'm afraid of what the boys will find when they ride out to the Devil's River country in a few weeks."

"You won't go with them?"

"No, Lacy will run the outfit. He'll take most of the men with him. All the ranches join up in the spring for the roundup. We usually divide the counties up into districts, but because everybody let their herds drift so far this year, there will only be two divisions, one for the ranches north of the railroad and one for those south of it. Since we're south of the railroad, we'll join up with the outfits workin' the Devil's River. There's a good chance most of our stock went that way. Course they're all branded, so they'll get sorted out even if some went to the Pecos.

"The Devil's River is mighty rough country, a lot of draws and canyons for shelter. Trouble is, there's not any water between there and the Concho. They've got miles of desert to cross. It's the same, maybe even worse, coming back from the Pecos. If the animals are already weak, we'll lose some to thirst."

"So fencing probably would be the best solution?"

"In some ways. Many of us are thinkin' about bringing in Shorthorns for crossbreeding to improve the quality of the herd. Longhorn beef isn't as tender as some of the other breeds, but they're hardy, so they survive well here. Charles Goodnight has brought in Herefords on the JA Ranch, but he's up in the Palo Duro Canyon where there's shelter, and he can keep them confined. We can't do that unless we fence. Wouldn't have control over the situation. Up on the Plains part of the Panhandle, the cattle are liable to freeze to death if they can't get down off the Caprock."

"What's the Caprock?"

"Northwest of here, about sixty, seventy miles or so, the land elevation goes up several hundred feet. It's a high ridge line, called the Caprock, that runs pretty much north and south through six or seven counties. Once you get to the top, the land is as flat as a pancake for as far as you can see and then some. It's rich land, plenty of good grass, but when a blue norther blows in, there's nothin' to break the wind. No hills, canyons, or trees. Not even a stump.

"And boy howdy, can the wind blow. Just about knocks you off your feet. So when the temperature drops down to the teens or lower, and the wind's blowing the snow or sleet straight in their faces, those old cows put their tails to the wind and come down off the Caprock like a waterfall. Some of 'em find shelter in the breaks and canyons down below, and some of 'em just keep on movin' until they get warm or can't move anymore."

"So if the land is fenced, they'll probably freeze unless they have some kind of shelter," said Charity.

He nodded. "And how does a man build a shed big enough to hold thousands of head of cattle? Down here, we've got more places for them to hide out from the cold, so if we fenced, they might have enough shelter to survive. At least some places would. A lot of this county is flat, too, so we could lose some."

He sighed. "But who's to say we won't lose as many trying to bring them back across the desert country? If we get some good rains in the next month, we'll be all right. If we don't, I hate to think what'll happen. It's a hard thing to see animals die like that."

After Charity drew a couple of pictures of the cattle, Jacob drove up a steep plateau. At the top, the land in front of them was fairly level for some distance before it became the same type of undulating prairie she had seen most of the way from town and from the ranch house. He turned the buggy around so they could look at where they'd been.

"Oh, Jacob, it's beautiful." Charity felt a swell of awe and reverence. From their vantage point, the whole valley sprawled out a hundred feet below. In a wild mix of small isolated buttes, canyons, ravines, and boulders, the land dropped off sharply then became low-lying hills and more ravines—draws, Jacob called them—gradually sloping away toward the valley floor or the flats—again, his term.

She couldn't see the water in the river, only the mesquites and weeping willows that grew alongside it. The willows had already turned green, but the mesquites were still bare. Addie had told her earlier that they were the last things to put on leaves in the spring. The opposite riverbank was higher than where they had crossed. Studying it, Charity realized that for several miles the riverbank was actually another plateau. No sloping valley there, just an abrupt fifty-foot drop. Maybe more. "Anybody ever fall off on the other side of the river?"

"Not that I've heard of. That's one reason I have a rule against drinkin' here at the ranch. If the boys want to go to town and blow their money, that's their business, but they'd better be sober as a watched preacher when they head toward the ranch."

Charity laughed softly. "Sober as a watched preacher. I'll have to remember that one."

Jacob grinned and checked the angle of the sun. "We'd better head back home, or we'll be late for dinner. That old woman will have my hide if I bring you in after the biscuits get cold."

Jacob took a slightly different route back down the side of the plateau, one fraught with dips, bumps, wild tilts, hoots, and hollers. Charity laughed so hard that by the time they got to the bottom, she was gasping for breath. Jacob had done his fair share of laughing and yelling, too.

"Bet you can't do that in New York City," he said with a broad grin.

"Nope." Charity grinned back, her eyes shining with

affection for the man she so desperately wanted to be her father.

Jacob's grin faded, an odd look flickering over his face. He stared at her for several seconds before turning to concentrate on driving the buggy. They rode in silence for most of the way back to the ranch house. He pointed out clumps of prickly pear cactus and straight spiky bear grass along the way, and showed her a gray-and-white mockingbird and a red cardinal in a nearby mesquite tree. As they approached the house, Charity realized she hadn't mentioned that her mother had lived in Galveston. Now she couldn't think of a good way to say it.

"I'll drop you off here and take the buggy back down to the shed. Tell Addie I'll be up directly for dinner."

"I will. Thank you for a wonderful morning, Jacob. I enjoyed it very much." Charity climbed down from the buggy. As she started to walk away, he called her name softly.

"Yes?" She stopped and turned back toward him.

He studied her face for a long moment. "Your name— what does the M stand for?"

"Marie." She watched him closely. "Why?"

"No reason in particular. I just wondered." His smile held a tiny hint of sadness as he glanced away. "That's not quite true." He looked back at her, his expression tender and a little bemused. "It's funny, but sometimes you remind me of someone I knew a long time ago. She was a lovely lady." He took a deep breath. "A special lady," he murmured, as if he were thinking out loud and didn't realize it.

"Before you met Addie?" she asked softly.

He nodded.

"It didn't work out?"

He was quiet for a minute, his thoughts far away. "No, it didn't work out."

*Tell him now.*

"Jacob Hunter, are you goin' to keep that poor child standin' out there all day?" called Addie from the back porch. "Hurry up. The biscuits are almost done."

He smiled at his wife, his eyes full of love. "We'll be right there, sugar. Don't have a hissy fit." Still smiling, he glanced at Charity. "Looks like I made out all right anyway."

Somehow she smiled back. "Yes, I think you did."

She turned and walked toward the house, watching Addie laugh and shake her finger in mock chastisement at Jacob.

"Did you have a good time?" Addie waited for her on the porch, her smile warm and welcoming. "You must have, from the color in your cheeks and the way your hat's sittin' on the back of your head. Did that man bounce you over every rock and down every gully between here and there?"

"I think so. It was a wild ride but fun. I laughed so much my sides ache."

"Well, you passed muster, then. Come on in and get a cold glass of spring water."

Charity followed her inside the kitchen, thinking how well Addie and Jacob got along, how well she knew her husband. But Addie didn't know everything about him. He had kept a few things to himself. What would happen if those secrets came to light? Would she gain a father's love? Or would she destroy what he held most dear?

# Chapter Thirteen

Charity spent the afternoon watching and sketching as Addie baked bread.

"You know anything about makin' bread?"

Charity shook her head and smiled. "I only know how to eat it with great enthusiasm. We always bought ours from a bakery."

"Lots of city folk do. Lasky's Bakery in town does a good business. We don't always get into town every week, but I buy some there occasionally. I enjoy making my own. It's good hard work. Helps me keep my girlish figure." She gathered the dough into a smooth lump. Pushing against it with the heels of her hands, she flattened it out; then she folded the edges back toward the center and pounded on it again.

"How long do you knead it?" asked Charity, glancing up from her sketch pad.

"Twenty to thirty minutes."

"You can't be serious. You're working awfully hard to go that long."

"I get a little slower toward the end, but that's what it takes."

Charity flipped a page on her drawing pad and started a new picture. She sketched for a few minutes and paused. "You ever do that when you're mad?"

Addie laughed. "Sometimes. Works as good to get rid of my anger as beatin' my husband over the head with a broom. Doesn't leave his face all bruised up, either."

Charity laughed and continued to draw. When Addie

164

decided she had kneaded enough, she formed the dough into four loaves and put them in the pans.

"Do they go in the oven now?" Charity relaxed and tucked her pencil over one ear.

"Nope. Have to let 'em rise again. Doesn't take as long this time, though. Half an hour to forty-five minutes." She set the pans on a counter in the corner and covered them with a towel. "Whew! Time for a break." She poured herself a cup of coffee from the pot sitting on the back of the stove and dropped down in a chair across from Charity.

"Is four loaves all you make?"

Addie nodded. "That's all for today. I usually bake a couple of times a week. That's all I need just for the family if I make some biscuits, too. If we're goin' to have company, I make sure to get the sponge, that's the first part of the dough, started at night and usually mix up another batch in the morning."

"What's in that other bowl over there?" Charity pointed to another stoneware bowl on the counter. The towel over the top of it covered another mound.

"A sweet dough. We're makin' doughnuts."

"I have a feeling I'm going to gain even more weight while I'm here. I've already put on a few pounds eatin' at Jake's and at the St. James. Both have wonderful food."

"Don't think you need to worry." Addie gave her a once-over. "Looks like a few pounds won't hurt you any."

"Can I help this time?"

"Sure. Grab an apron. You can be the puncher and the cutter."

Charity put her drawing things away and took an apron from the wall peg. In addition to covering the front and sides of her skirt, it had a bib to protect the front of her torso. "Shall I get started?" she asked as she pumped a bit of water into the dishpan and washed her hands.

"Go right ahead."

Charity brought the bowl over to the table and lifted the towel. Inhaling deeply, she smiled. "It smells good even before it's cooked. My mouth is watering already." She rubbed flour on her hands as Addie had done and punched down the dough. "Does this have to be kneaded as long?"

"No. Just a little bit to make it smooth." Addie set a deep cast-iron pan on the stove. "I'll put the grease on to heat."

"What spices did you put in?"

"I grated some nutmeg and added some cinnamon. We'll roll some of the doughnuts in cinnamon and sugar after they're cooked." She smiled at Charity and gave her a smug nod. "You'll want to learn how to do those. Morgan likes any kind of doughnut, but that's his favorite."

Charity kneaded the dough for a few minutes, until Addie told her she'd done enough. "Now sprinkle some flour on your board, dump out the dough, and roll it out into a square with the rolling pin. You want it to be about a quarter-inch thick. Rub some flour over the rolling pin first."

Charity did as she was instructed, laughing at the lopsided edges to her square. "I hope this doesn't have to be perfectly straight."

"Nope. We can cut 'em any way we want to. They don't last long enough around here for anybody to pass judgment on the shape. The men in this house work hard and they eat plenty."

Charity cut the dough into small squares, and Addie showed her how to cook them in the hot fat. When the first batch was puffed and a nice golden brown, Addie told her how to take them out with a skimmer and put them to drain on an inverted sieve over a plate.

"While this batch is cooking, you can mix up some sugar and cinnamon in that small bowl. Pour some out on a plate and roll the doughnuts in it when they get cool. The cook gets to help herself to a sample whenever she wants."

Charity followed her instructions to the letter, especially the one about sampling the product. "Mmm, this is good. Nothing you buy at the bakery tastes this good unless you happen to walk in when they're taking the loaves out of the pan."

She doubted if she would ever become much of a cook, but she fully enjoyed spending the afternoon with Addie in the kitchen. Addie was warm and caring, a person who gave her affection easily and wholeheartedly. It was impossible not to return that fondness. She could see why Jacob adored her, as did everyone who knew her.

There was enough time before supper to write a letter to Helena and Richard, giving them the details about the ball and about moving out to the ranch. She related her belief that Jacob was her father, telling them about his comments that she reminded him of someone he had once cared about. She also confessed that there was a remote possibility that Joshua was her father. She couldn't bring herself to ask if they thought her mother might have worked in a saloon.

After supper the family played a couple of games of dominoes, with Lacy winning both times, although Charity came close in the last one. "Want to try again? Or do you want to get whupped three times in a row?" Lacy grinned at Charity and tweaked a bouncy curl at the back of her head.

"I've never been one to back away from a challenge." Charity laughed and ducked as he went after her curl again. She grabbed a double-blank domino and dropped it into her skirt pocket. "I'm bound to win this time, and I might not even have to cheat. But just in case, I'll keep this one handy."

"You stinker. Put that back in the boneyard."

"Nope. That's my security."

"Now, children, behave yourselves," Addie scolded affectionately.

"Yes, ma'am," they said in unison, and both burst into laughter.

Charity glanced at Jacob and wished she hadn't. Eyes narrowed, he intently studied Lacy's face, then hers. Her gaze skidded away from his and crashed right into Joshua's. He looked questioningly from her to Lacy to Jacob and finally back to her. She gave him a tiny shrug and held her breath, hoping he wouldn't say anything and that Addie wouldn't notice the sudden undercurrents flowing around the table.

"I think I'll ride into town," said Joshua abruptly. Every pair of eyes in the room turned to him. "I'll be back in a few days." He pushed away from the table, grabbed his hat from the rack near the kitchen door, and left without another word.

Charity glanced around the table. The others appeared disturbed but were trying not to show it. "Is something wrong?"

"I don't think so," said Addie as she glanced at her husband.

Charity prayed silently, asking God not to let Jacob start asking questions that might bring them all heartache. If she did decide to tell him about her mother, she wanted to do it in private.

"He hasn't left like that in a long time," said Jacob. "It used to mean he'd come back with a black eye and split lip and owing half the saloons in town money for broken tables and mirrors."

"Did we do something to make him angry?" asked Charity.

"Not that I know of," said Jacob thoughtfully. "He'll probably go have a rip-roarin' drunk and come home hung over but fine. Dad-blast his ornery hide. He's gettin' too old for that."

"Charity, I think I'll pass on that domino game. I'm out of the mood." Lacy began putting the dominoes back in their wooden box.

She handed him the one she had spirited away earlier. "Another time." She pushed away from the table. "Would you excuse me for a few minutes? I think I'll ask Joshua to send a letter for me and pick up my mail while he's in town."

"Tell him to remind Morgan to come out for dinner Sunday," said Addie with a sparkle in her eye. "Not that he'll need reminding, I expect."

Charity hurried to her bedroom for the letter. After a moment's hesitation, she took her father's picture from the chest and tucked it inside the pocket of her skirt. She threw a warm shawl around her shoulders, and then walked the short distance to Joshua's house. The moon shone brightly, lighting her way. He came to the door promptly at her knock.

"I hope I didn't disturb you. Would you mind mailing this letter for me?"

"No, I don't mind." Joshua stepped out onto the porch. "Do you want me to check for your mail at the hotel?"

"Yes, please. Oh, and Addie said to remind Morgan that he's supposed to come to dinner on Sunday."

Joshua chuckled. "As if he would forget."

Charity pulled the shawl tighter, holding her arms in front of her. The night wasn't particularly cold, but she felt chilled. "Last night I told you my mother had not worked in a saloon. I answered quickly because the idea was inconceivable to me. I've thought about it, and I realized I can't be sure. If she did, I never knew about it. I can't imagine her working as a . . . a lady of the evening, but I've learned in the last few months that she lied to me about other things."

"Tonight you and Lacy sounded just like Jacob and I used to when we were your age or younger. Jacob noticed it, too. I was watchin' him. He saw somethin' in your face, Charity, or maybe I should say someone, someone he remembers well. As much as I'd like for you to be my daughter, honey, I don't think you are. I'm not sayin' it's impossible, because it's not, but my gut feeling is that Jacob is your daddy. The more I try to remember that little gal in Galveston, the more uncertain I am as to what she looked like. It's been too long. All I know for sure is that she had blue eyes and was young—maybe eighteen or nineteen."

"Then she couldn't have been my mother. Mama was thirty-two when I was born." Relief mingled with disappointment. She knew Joshua would have been happy if she had been his daughter. She wouldn't have minded having him as a father, but it would have been hard for her to accept the fact that her mother had been a prostitute. She thought of her mother's walnut chest and the note from J. H. "Did Jacob ever talk about being with a special woman in Galveston?"

"No. He never mentioned a woman, but that doesn't surprise me. He never was one to talk about the ladies. As I recall, he was pretty closemouthed about the whole visit. Just said he and Will had a good time, played some cards, and did a lot of talkin'. I do remember that he seemed troubled on the way home and for a while after that—until about the time he started courtin' Addie. I may have asked him what was eatin' him, but I don't remember if he said anything. He probably shrugged it off. That's what he used to always do. Still keeps his own counsel on most things." He rested one hand on the porch post. His expression was tender.

"I'm pretty sure of one thing, honey. If Jacob is your daddy, then your mama wasn't any dance hall gal. He always had a high standard where women were concerned. Fine, genteel ladies were the ones that interested him— which adds to the puzzle in a way. How did you find out about your daddy?"

She told him about going through her mother's things and finding Will's letter and the picture. With trembling fingers, she withdrew the photograph from her pocket and handed it to Joshua.

He moved closer to the window and held the portrait up to the light. Drawing a deep breath, he met her gaze. "That's Jacob. But I can see how you'd have a hard time decidin' which one of us it was." He shook his head. "No wonder you almost fainted when you saw the two of us. Poor Charity." He put his arm around her shoulders and hugged her. "Why don't you go in there and talk to him? I'll go with you."

"Thank you, but no. I want to wait awhile, let him think about it." She suddenly realized the only acceptable way to resolve the problem was to let Jacob figure out who she was. "I don't want to confront him, put him on the defensive. I don't want to force him to accept or reject me. I want him to have the time to decide what to do. If I drop enough hints, maybe he will realize who I am and can make his choice without pressure from me. I want a father, a family, but I don't want to take a chance of destroying the family he already has."

He squeezed her shoulders again. "You're a good woman, Charity Brown. I wish to heaven you were my child. It'd make everything a lot simpler, and me a lot happier."

"What you need is a good woman to love you, Joshua Hunter. Someone to make a family man out of you."

He snorted. "I'm too old for that, gal. Besides, no decent woman will come within twenty feet of me." He grimaced. "I don't have the kind of reputation to inspire women to marriage."

"Marry someone from the saloon, then. Morgan says it's done."

"Some men get away with it, but that's not the kind of woman I'd want for a wife. I don't want a woman who's been with other men. Hypocritical of me, ain't it?" He shook his head. "No, honey, I set my feet to the wrong path a long time ago. There's not much chance of me gettin' on the right one now."

"Surely the distance between those paths isn't too wide to cross." She smiled and stepped away. "Some women love to reform a rake, don't you know?"

He chuckled. "No, I didn't know. I don't think I want a reformer for a wife anyway. Nag, nag, nag." He shook his head. "I'll just stay the same old reprobate. That's what folks expect, what they're comfortable with. What I'm comfortable with. I'm too old to change now."

"I don't believe it. I'd better get back to the house. Tell Morgan hello for me."

"I will. Want me to tell him you miss him?"

"Matchmaker. You're as bad as Addie."

"Well, it's the truth, isn't it?"

"Yes, I miss him. Just tell him I look forward to his visit on Sunday." She smiled impishly as she stepped off the porch. "And tell him to come prepared to teach me how to drive a buggy."

"Sounds like an excuse for you two to be alone."

"Why, Joshua, I never thought of that."

"Yeah, and Longhorns can fly."

# Chapter Fourteen

Joshua stared at the cards in his hand in disgust. By the time he'd reached town, he had convinced himself that all he needed was a little gambling, a little drinking, and a lot of loving. He'd tried monte, faro, and now poker, and lost every time. He'd had a glass of the Senate Saloon's best whiskey and hadn't enjoyed it. He threw down his cards and shoved back his chair, scraping the legs against the wooden floor. "I'm out. My luck's gone fishin'. See you boys another day."

He wandered down to the West End, stopping in at Archie's place. He ordered another drink and sat down at a table, watching the show. Every one of the dancers flirted with him from the stage. Afterward, each pretty woman stopped by to see him, draped an arm across his shoulders or sat down on his lap, and extended a warm, eager invitation. The women liked spending their time upstairs with Joshua, and it wasn't just because he tipped them well.

He turned down every offer with kindness. When he left the saloon half an hour after entering it, his drink sat untouched on the table. He didn't want to go back to the hotel, and he didn't feel like going home. Stopping by the sheriff's office, he learned that Morgan had gone off duty a short while before, so he decided to walk over to his house and shoot the breeze.

As he walked up Fourth, he heard a commotion up ahead. It was after eleven, and hearing a ruckus at that time of night wasn't so unusual, except that this was the more sedate part of town.

"Let me go!"

At the sound of a woman's cry, Joshua broke into a run. Turning the corner on Walnut, he came upon three young, drunk cowboys circling around the woman like wolves moving in for the kill. "What's going on here?"

The cowboys stopped and glared at him. "Don't try hornin' in. This one's ours. Go find your own woman." One of the men, who was a little steadier on his feet than the others, grabbed hold of her arm.

"Take your hands off me, you ugly galoot."

The other cowboys hooted with laughter. "She's got you pegged," said one between guffaws.

Joshua stopped in front of them, quickly making sure they weren't wearing gunbelts. Knowing they probably had weapons of some sort stashed away—as he did—he didn't relax. "Take your hands off the lady and step aside."

Two of the cowboys fell back, but the one holding onto the woman's arm wasn't ready to give up his prize. "Why don't you make me, old man?"

"Don't push it, boy, or you'll regret it." The menace in Joshua's voice made the younger man blink. "I came to town lookin' for a fight. You goin' to give me one?"

One of the other cowboys stepped closer, squinting in the moonlight. "That you, Mr. Hunter?"

"It is."

"Joshua or Jacob?"

"Joshua. Now, tell your friend to release the lady, and you boys get goin'. Head on down to the district if you want some female attention."

"But she came from that way." Her captor eased his grip on the woman's arm. She jerked it out of his grasp and moved next to Joshua.

"That doesn't make her a prostitute, son. Now, get out of here before I run out of patience."

The man who had recognized Joshua pulled on the other one's arm. "Come on, let's go. That there's Joshua Hunter, owner of the Double J. Cross him and you'll never get a job anywhere in this country." He tugged harder. "Besides that, he can whip his weight in wildcats." Grumbling, the man let his friends lead him away.

"Kin to Davy Crockett?"

The woman's soft, gentle voice made Joshua think of twilight settling over the prairie, and his tension evaporated. "No, ma'am. The boy was stretchin' it. You all right?"

"I think so." Her voice wobbled a bit. She tried to laugh but didn't quite pull it off. "I guess I'm one of those people who fall apart when everything's over. I'm shaking like a leaf."

He slid one arm around her and very slowly and carefully drew her against him. He put his other arm around her, holding her tenderly. Never had a woman felt so good, so right in his embrace. "Nobody's going to hurt you now. You're safe."

She rested her cheek against his chest, her fingers curled around the lapels of his jacket, and let him hold her close until her trembling stopped. Leaning back against his arms, she looked up at him in the moonlight. "Am I safe?"

She'd heard of him. Disappointment filled him, along with deep regret. There was no fear in her voice, no accusation, simply contemplation. He said nothing, for in spite of his self-recriminations, he wanted to kiss her more than he'd ever wanted to kiss any woman. She wasn't especially pretty, but she was beautiful. Her eyes glowed with an inner peace and beauty that soothed his soul, wrapping him in warmth and tenderness. He eased his hold, and she took one small step backward.

"I've heard about you, Joshua Hunter—that you're a gambler, a fighter, a hard drinker, and a womanizer." She brushed his cheek with her fingertips. "Are you all those things?"

"I was, but earlier tonight I found I didn't want any of it anymore. The whiskey hurt my stomach. I didn't win a cent. The women didn't interest me." He smiled. "And I actually talked my way out of a fight. That's got to be a first."

"And did you figure out what you wanted?" Her hands rested against his chest, and she looked directly into his eyes.

"You." The word was out of his mouth before he could stop it.

She smiled. "What else?"

How could she look so seductive and so angelic at the same time? Who was she? "I want to know your name."

"Serena Weaver."

"Are you married, Serena Weaver?" he asked softly. The nearest houses were at the other end of the block. The street was deserted. He felt as if the whole world had disappeared except for the two of them.

"Widowed."

"Children?"

"Not so blessed."

"How long were you married?"

"A year. My husband was killed in a buggy accident five years ago."

"What are you doing out here at this time of night?"

"I took some soup to May Campbell earlier and stayed with her awhile."

"May Campbell that works down in the district?"

"Same one. Only she doesn't work there anymore. She's going to have a baby and hasn't been doing well. She has to stay in bed most of the time. Poor child, she has no family. The girls keep an eye on her, but she doesn't really have anyone to care for her. She's barely eighteen."

"How did you meet her?" It occurred to him that he ought to quit holding her. He'd sooner have been dragged through a prickly pear cactus.

"Dr. Coleman told me about her."

"So you went to her, knowin' what she is?"

"We're all God's children, Joshua. How can she change unless someone treats her kindly and shows her the way?"

He pulled her a hairsbreadth closer. When she didn't resist, his heart soared. He felt like a young buck with his first love. He also knew the kind of man that would normally be attracted to someone like Serena. "What did your husband do for a livin'?"

"He was a minister."

Joshua sighed. Just what he'd suspected. There was no chance for him. How could he compete with a man of God?

"So was my father."

He groaned and dropped his arms. Instead of stepping away, she moved closer and slid her hands up to his shoulders. He put his arms back around her, holding tight.

"I've heard other things about you—that you're kind, generous, a hard worker, and as honest as the day is long."

"They must have been talking about my brother."

"No, you were the subject of discussion, and it didn't come from the girls in the district." She smiled. "Didn't know you were admired by churchgoing ladies, did you?"

"No, ma'am. That comes as a big surprise."

"What did you figure out you wanted, Joshua?" she asked softly.

"A home, not a house where I hang my hat and sometimes sleep, but a place filled with the laughter of children and the sweet, soft sighs of a satisfied woman. I want to wake up every morning with the same woman by my side—a woman who loves me, who will forgive me when I make mistakes, who will laugh with me and be there as I grow old." He frowned, staring down at her smooth, unwrinkled skin. "How old are you?"

"Thirty-two."

"I'm almost forty-eight, Serena."

"I don't have a problem with that."

He threw back his head and laughed. "Do you realize we're standing here holding each other in the middle of the street?"

She smiled. "Actually we're over to the side. And nobody ever comes through here this time of night anyway."

"Why haven't you remarried?"

"No one's asked me. There's something you should know. I broke my leg in the accident that killed my husband. It didn't heal right. I have a limp."

"I don't think that will bother me."

"I'll let you reserve judgment until you see me in daylight." She laughed. "I know what you look like, but I doubt if you've noticed me. I tend to fade into the

woodwork." When he started to protest, she put her finger to
his lips. "By choice."

"Then it's been my loss. I like what I see in the
moonlight." He shook his head, bemused by what was
happening between them. He felt as if he had been looking
for her forever, had known her for a lifetime. "Do you
believe in love at first sight?"

"Yes. And I believe in God's Providence. I also know you
may feel differently after you've slept on it. If you don't feel
this way tomorrow, I won't raise a stink."

"May I kiss you before I escort you home?"

"Why, sir, such forward behavior." She smiled. "I thought
you'd never ask."

He lowered his head slowly, touched her lips reverently.
At her soft sigh, his heart leapt, and he deepened the kiss.
Gentle and kind she might be, but passion lurked below the
surface. He kissed her with expertise learned from the best,
but no other woman had ever tasted the love in his heart.
And love her he did, crazy though it was. He knew with a
surety born in the depths of his soul that the light of day
would bring no changes in his feelings. He had found his
salvation.

He slowly raised his head and smiled as she struggled to
open her eyes. "Think I'll change my mind?"

"If you do, I may shoot you." She took a deep breath and
leaned her forehead against his chin. "I think I may be glad
you've been a womanizer."

He laughed and hugged her. "*Been* is right, sweetheart.
This cowboy's roamin' days are done."

The sun was barely up when Joshua knocked on Morgan's door. He answered it in his stocking feet. "What in
tarnation are you doin' up at this hour?" Morgan peered at
Joshua's grin and his eyes. "You look too good to have a
hangover, but you're grinnin' too much to be sober. What
did you do, drink real slow all night?"

"Nope. What's for breakfast?"

Morgan raised an eyebrow. "Bacon and eggs."

"No biscuits?" Joshua walked into the tiny front room as Morgan stepped aside.

Morgan shook his head. "I might let you have a slice of bakery bread if you don't complain too much."

"That'll do. Ain't in the mood to be complainin' about anything this morning." Joshua took off his hat and sent it sailing across the room, where it landed brim-down, crown-up on the settee. He turned back to Morgan with a silly grin.

"What have you been drinkin'? If it makes you that happy, I might even try it."

"Nothing. I'm drunk on love, boy. Drunk on love." He strolled into the kitchen.

Staring at him in disbelief, Morgan followed. "You been with that new gal at Archie's?"

"Nope. Have you?"

"Of course not," snapped Morgan. He walked over to the table, sliced six pieces from a slab of bacon, and put them in a black cast-iron skillet on the small wood-burning cookstove. "So who's the lady?"

"Serena Weaver. Know her?" Joshua picked up two eggs and, holding them in one hand, cracked them together expertly, dumping the yolks and whites into a mixing bowl and tossing the shells aside.

"Yeah, I know her." Morgan watched Joshua break four more eggs in the same one-handed way. He never had been able to learn that trick. "She moved here about six months ago from East Texas. She does some sewing for Mrs. Gilbert and works two days a week at the bookstore." He turned the bacon strips over in the pan. "Goes to the Baptist church. She does a lot of tending the sick and elderly, takin' them meals, sitting with them, and such, especially the ones that can't pay or don't have anyone to look after them. She goes about her business quietly. Most folks don't know what all she does, but the doctors and ministers know who to call on if they need help."

"You that well acquainted with everyone's business?" Joshua used a whisk to beat the eggs.

Morgan grinned. "Practically everyone in the county. In

my work it pays to know as much about folks as I can. Fewer surprises that way." He lifted the bacon from the frying pan with a spatula and set it on a plate. Having drained off the grease into an empty tin can, he set the pan back on the stove and took the bowl of eggs from Joshua. Pouring the eggs in the pan, he asked casually, "How did you meet her?"

"Meaning how did a scoundrel like me become acquainted with a saint like her? Well, I reckon you could say the good Lord put me in the right place at the right time. I was coming up here to see you last night, walkin' up from the district, and I came across her being accosted by three men."

Morgan's gaze shot to his. "Was she hurt?"

"No. Just scared. She had been down to the district to see May Campbell, and those young whippersnappers thought she was one of the girls. Luckily I came along before they got rough. They were three sheets and a pillowcase to the wind. Couldn't seem to get it through their heads that she wasn't interested in going with them." He cut four thick slices of bread, leaving them on the breadboard on the table.

Morgan carried the frying pan to the table and evenly divided the eggs between his plate and Joshua's. He set the pan in the dry sink, picked up the bacon, and returned to the table, sitting down. Joshua poured them each a cup of coffee and joined him.

"So you met her last night," said Morgan around his first bite. He frowned at his friend. "Rescued her from certain harm, then demanded a night of lovin' as payment? That's low, Josh. At least you had the decency to sneak out before the sun came up."

"You've got it wrong." Joshua's voice was quiet and calm. That in itself brought a befuddled expression to Morgan's face. "I didn't make love to her, though heaven knows I wanted to. I didn't even go inside her house. We sat on the front porch in the dark for a couple of hours and talked, then I went back to the St. James and went to bed. Can't say I slept a whole lot," he added with a grin. He shook his head and speared a chunk of scrambled egg with his fork.

"It's the strangest thing that's ever happened to me. She handled the situation with those boys well, but afterward she started shaking. I put my arms around her, just meanin' to comfort her, help her calm down. I swear Cupid must have been sitting in one of the elm trees, 'cause within five minutes I was in love." He looked up at Morgan. "Not in lust. In love. I wanted her in the worst possible way, but I never even suggested going to bed with her. And I won't either, until she's got my weddin' band on her finger. I won't insult her by asking."

Morgan stared at him, his fork halfway to his mouth. Finally he set the fork and the bite of egg back on his plate. "You're serious. Does she know how you feel?"

"Yep."

"And what about her?"

"She feels the same. She believes in love at first sight, and in Providence, too. I'm goin' to see her about mid-morning and I intend to have a wedding ring in my pocket."

"Just like that?"

"Just like that. If she's willin', I'll be taking my bride home in the next day or two."

Morgan shook his head, thoroughly confused. Of all the people he knew, Joshua was the last one he had expected to get married. It didn't surprise him too much that once Joshua had decided to do it, he would rush into it. Patience wasn't one of his virtues. More often than not, he went with his instincts. Oddly enough, they were usually right. "You been lookin' for a wife?"

"No, but I been doing some studying of my life lately. I didn't like what I saw, not now or what was ahead of me." Both men ate while they talked. In the company of another bachelor, politeness wasn't much of a requirement.

"How lately?"

"Mostly since Charity moved out to the ranch, although I've been thinkin' about things for a while."

Morgan scooped some butter from a crock with his knife

and smeared it on a slice of bread. Trying to sound casual, he asked, "What did Charity have to do with it?"

"Well, with those green eyes of hers, I got to thinkin' she might be my daughter."

Morgan set his knife down on the edge of the plate and looked at him. "Is she?"

"No. I wish she was, but that time I wasn't in the right place. But before we talked about it, I kept thinkin' she might be, and I got to liking the idea." He took a sip of coffee. "All my life I've worked hard and played hard. Why bother havin' a wife when I had a choice of women? If I didn't like one, I didn't have to go see her anymore. But the last year or so, the good times weren't as good. I had to work at having fun." He chuckled at Morgan's raised eyebrow.

"I realize nobody would have guessed the truth. I ain't sayin' I didn't enjoy the gals down in the district, but I got tired of being one of many. I want a woman that's mine alone, one I can curl up with every night and know there's not some cowboy waitin' downstairs to take my place."

Morgan snorted. "Even if you put a ring on a woman's finger, there's no guarantee she'll be faithful."

"No, there's not—unless you marry the right woman. They aren't all like your mama, Morgan. You know as well as I do that Addie has never looked at another man. Serena won't, either. She's pure goodness itself." He grinned. "Besides, I intend to keep her so happy and satisfied, she won't have time to think about goin' on the prowl.

"After I got the idea that Charity might be my offspring, I realized what had been missing. I never thought I'd want a family, but I do. I want to leave a part of me behind when I go."

"I've heard mighty good things about Serena and never anything bad. I'd say you're a lucky man."

"So you do believe in love?" Joshua chewed his last bite of bacon and picked up his coffee cup.

Morgan took his time answering. "I know it exists. It's obvious that Addie and Jacob love each other. My father loved my mother too much. What I have a hard time with is trusting a woman enough to love her."

"I don't think we choose to love someone. I think it just happens, and there's not much we can do about it. The trick is trusting a woman enough to believe in her."

Morgan nodded, thinking about Charity. He wanted to trust her, wanted to believe in her, wanted her to tell him the truth. "Some women don't make it easy. Some like to keep secrets."

"Sometimes they're afraid not to." Joshua drained his cup and set it on the table. He knew who Morgan was talking about. "Charity's mother was Will Davenport's sister, Marion."

Morgan exhaled slowly. He had met Will when he visited the Double J and knew Will and Jacob had been friends for almost thirty years. "Did you know her?"

"Nope, never met her. I didn't even know he had a sister."

"Do you think Charity is Jacob's daughter?"

"Yes, but I don't know it for a fact. Jacob never mentioned Marion or being with her, but it clarifies a few things. He was unhappy when we left Galveston, but as usual, he didn't talk about it. Lookin' back, I figure he was bothered by what happened. Charity found his picture in her mother's things. She showed it to me last night."

"Did she come right out and ask you about it?"

"No, I asked her. She doesn't want to say anything to Jacob. She wants him to figure it out on his own."

"Do you think he will?"

"He's wondering about it. I can see it in his face when he looks at her. If he is her father, he'll do what's right."

"What's right for Charity? Or what's right for Addie?" Morgan pushed back from the table and grabbed the plates and silverware. "How's she gonna feel if he up and tells her he's got a daughter he didn't know about?"

"Addie adores Charity. Course, she's thinkin' about finding a wife for you, not about havin' a stepdaughter. Jacob met Addie right before we went to Galveston, and as far as I know, he didn't make her any promises. Charity would have been conceived before he ever courted Addie."

"You think that'll make a difference? He gave another woman a child, a girl. You know how much she wanted another daughter after she lost little Carrie."

"Maybe now she'll have one." Joshua carried the rest of the dishes over to the dry sink and put his hand on Morgan's shoulder. "Let it be, son. It'll work out. Charity's not trying to harm anybody. That's why she wants Jacob to ask her about it, instead of her confronting him. She's a good woman, Morgan.

"Now, I'm goin' to skedaddle. Never did like doin' dishes." He grinned at Morgan's scowl. "Thanks for breakfast. I've got to go buy a ring." Joshua slapped Morgan on the back and went to get his hat. He stopped back by the kitchen door on his way out, his expression somber. "Take it from one who knows what growin' old alone is like. If you love her, don't let that little gal get away from you. Don't reach my age and find your life empty.

"Oh, I almost forgot to tell you. Addie said to remind you about comin' out to dinner Sunday. And Charity misses you. She said to tell you to be prepared to teach her how to drive the buggy. Judging from the sparkle in her eye, I'd say she's anxious to be alone with you." He grinned. "Take advantage of the opportunity, son, but don't get carried away. That's probably my niece you're spoonin'."

# Chapter
# Fifteen

"I sure appreciate you askin' me to come along, Mr. Kaine." Sam grinned at Morgan as they rode under the high arched gate of the Double J. "Ma wouldn't let me come out here on my own, and I've been lonesome to see Miss Charity."

"I expect she's missed you, too, son. It'll be fun to surprise her." Morgan had decided the day before to invite the boy to go out to the ranch with him on Sunday, mainly because Sam had stopped by the office every day that week asking if he had heard from Charity. "Have you been doing the art lessons in your book?"

"Yep. I got a whole stack of things to show her. I think I'm doin' it right, but I want her to check 'em for me."

Charity stood on the front porch as they neared the ranch house. Morgan couldn't take his eyes off her. The stiff breeze whipped the skirt of her soft, pink cotton wrapper against her legs, revealing enough womanly curves to quicken his heartbeat and make him draw a deep breath. The wind tugged little wisps of hair free from the chignon at the back of her neck, forming angel curls around her face. Her smile was like sunshine on a dark, cloudy day.

He couldn't believe how much he had missed her, or the joy that filled his heart at the sight of her. Years of controlling his emotions kept him from jumping off his horse and racing up the walkway to hug and kiss her—that and the fact that Sam beat him to it. The boy tossed the reins around the hitching post, barely making a complete loop, and ran up the walkway. He didn't kiss Charity, but he gave her a big hug before he remembered such displays of affection were embarrassing.

"Oh, Sam, it's so good to see you." Charity wanted to hug him again, but settled for resting her hand on his shoulder. "What a pleasant surprise." She glanced at Morgan as he swung down off his horse, her joy shining in her eyes.

"When I stopped by the sheriff's office yesterday, Mr. Kaine invited me to come, too. He said Mrs. Hunter wouldn't mind one more person."

"I'm sure she won't. She loves company. How have you been?"

"Good. School's goin' okay. Our teacher is reading *The Adventures of Robin Hood* to us. Wow, what a story! She's going to loan me the book when we're through so I can copy some of the pictures. I've done a bunch of stuff from the art book you gave me. I've been doin' the lessons in order like you told me to."

"Did you bring something for me to see?" She smiled, knowing he most certainly had.

"You bet. I got a whole stack of stuff in my saddlebag."

"Why don't you take it into the parlor, and we'll look at it after we eat. I think Addie has dinner almost ready."

"Okay." Sam grinned. "I'll take my horse down to the corral first, and you can go say hello to Mr. Kaine." He leaned closer. "I think he's kinda missed you."

"Thank you, Sam. You're being very considerate." They strolled down the walk together but parted at the gate. Sam unfastened the horse's reins from the hitching post and led it off toward the corrals. Charity walked around Morgan's horse, bravely rubbing the animal's nose when he nickered a greeting. Morgan stood beside the horse, unbuckling his saddlebag. She stepped up beside him, her eyes shining with happiness. "Good afternoon, Deputy Kaine."

He turned to her and smiled. "Afternoon, ma'am. Looks like the country agrees with you." He nudged her chin up with his knuckle. "What's this? A freckle or two? You've been going without your hat, pretty lady."

"Guilty as charged, but only a few times. And not for long at a time. Addie nags me when I forget," she said with a smile. "I confess I enjoy the warmth of the sun on my face. How have you been?"

*Lonely.* "Not bad. Things have been quiet in town. Reckon everybody wore themselves out at the ball." He leaned closer and almost gave in to the temptation to kiss her. "Can you keep a secret?"

"If you want me to. What is it?" Her gaze dropped to his lips, but she forced herself to focus on his eyes.

"I have a message from Joshua. He told me to tell you he took your advice. He found a good woman to love him. He got married yesterday."

She blinked. "He did?" she squeaked, then quickly lowered her voice. "Who? How? Where?"

Morgan chuckled and straightened before his resistance dissolved. "Her name is Serena Weaver. She's a good Christian woman, widow of a preacher. They met the other night when he came into town. He rescued her from some men who were hassling her."

"They just met? Oh, Morgan, how can he marry her so quickly?" Charity frowned, her eyes troubled. "What if she's only after his money?"

"Why would you think that?" *Is that what you're after?* He tried to ignore the pain that came with the thought and wished he didn't find it hard to trust her. He wondered if he'd never gone into law enforcement, if he would still be as suspicious of people.

"It's so quick. He doesn't really know her. Of course, knowing someone for a while doesn't always tell you much, either. I was certainly fooled by my fiancé. Maybe I'm worrying for nothing. He's so lonely, and I don't want to see him hurt. Does he love her?"

"Yes."

"Have you seen them together? Do you think she loves him?"

"I was at the wedding, and if she doesn't love him, she's the world's greatest actress."

Her smile touched her mouth first, then her eyes. "I'm very happy for him. Is she young enough to have children?"

"Probably. I think she's in her early thirties."

"Oh, I hope so. I think he truly wants a family."

Morgan relaxed. She was concerned because she had once been used by someone she loved. He believed she wasn't after money, and that felt good.

He flipped open the flap on his saddlebag to get her mail. As usual, he carried some carrots in the leather pouch, and his horse, Cactus, knew it. Cactus turned his head, looking for a carrot, and smacked Charity in the back, shoving her up against Morgan. He laughed and threw his arm around her. "Why, darlin', if I'd known you were this glad to see me, I'd have given you a hug sooner."

"Did you teach him to do that?" She tried to frown or at least sound prim, but being so close to him made either one impossible.

"Not me." He was the picture of innocence, although his arm tightened, holding her in place. "Of course, I bought him from Case, so there's no tellin' what he taught him." The mischief in his eyes slowly gave way to heat. His voice dropped as he moved his hand slowly up and down her back. "So soft. Ah, sweet woman, you make me think about things I shouldn't. Now, step away from me, sugar. I figure we're being watched, at least by one lovable, nosy aunt, and if you don't move soon, I'm going to embarrass you by kissing you."

"I can't go anywhere until you move your arm."

She sounded slightly breathless, and her voice skimmed over his nerve endings like a caress. He squeezed quickly before he released her, and she moved away from him. "Josh asked me to bring you the mail. He and Serena are planning to come out later this afternoon, but he wanted me to give it to you in case they decided to stay in town another night." He reached into the saddlebag and withdrew a large packet of newspapers, magazines, and several letters.

"Oh, my goodness! Now I can catch up on what's happening at home." She flipped through the letters. There were two from Helena, one from Richard, and three from some of her other friends. "Oh my!"

Her awed voice brought Morgan's gaze her way. "What is it?"

"I got a note from Samuel Clemens." She glanced up, reading the question in his eyes. "That's Mark Twain's real name." She tucked the other mail underneath her arm and tore open his letter. It was only one page long.

Morgan noted her sweet smile and was jealous of a man he greatly admired. "What does he have to say? Or is it too personal?"

"He was in New York a few weeks ago. He's sorry he missed me but is glad to hear I took his advice and went out to see the West. He said to do as many drawings as possible, since I do them so well." She blushed slightly.

"Sounds good. Any more words of wisdom?"

Her blush deepened. "And to beware of sweet-talkin' Texas cowboys who might hogtie me and carry me off to the middle of nowhere."

Morgan glanced at the wide open country and chuckled. "Now, why didn't I think of that?"

She gave him a saucy smile. "Because you know all you have to do is ask."

His breath came out in a rush. "Careful, woman, or I'll move those buggy-driving lessons up on the schedule, and you won't get any dinner."

"And miss Addie's cooking?" She patted his stomach well above his belt buckle. "I don't believe it." She turned away, glancing coquettishly at him over her shoulder.

He shook his head and laughed. "I'll take this critter down to the corrals. Tell Addie I'll be back directly."

Charity watched him lead the horse away, her face glowing softly from an inward smile. It was so good to see him again. She couldn't wait to be alone with him, yet she knew she had to be careful. Morgan Kaine had a way of making her forget everything but him and the way he made her feel.

She went back into the house and mashed the potatoes while Addie made cream gravy from the chicken drippings. Morgan and Sam came in a few minutes later, having stopped on the back porch to wash up in the basin that sat on a stand beside the hand pump.

Addie made fried chicken after church because all her

menfolk liked it, especially Morgan. Besides the huge bowl of mashed potatoes and gravy, there were green beans, carrots, and sweet cherries. Rolls, freshly baked the day before, completed the main portion of the meal.

"We don't have a lot of different courses even on Sunday," said Addie, after Jacob asked the blessing. She sat at one end of the table, her husband at the other. Under her direction, Charity and Sam sat on one side of the table, Morgan and Lacy on the other. "I suppose if we had fancy dinner parties and servants, I'd be inclined to have more things, but we've never seen the need."

"This is perfect," Charity said. "The only thing I see wrong with this meal is that I love everything you've prepared. I'll be stuffed."

"If these men leave you enough to eat," said Addie with a laugh. She nodded at Morgan and Lacy. "These two have a way of wiping the plates clean."

All through dinner, Charity wondered if Morgan intended to tell the others about Joshua. Finally, when they had finished dessert and were drinking one last cup of coffee, he glanced at her. She knew instantly he had decided to break the news.

"Addie, do you know Serena Weaver?" He stretched his legs out in front of him beneath the table and accidentally bumped Charity's foot with his boot. He met her gaze, apologizing with his eyes, then smiled when she rubbed the side of his boot with the toe of her shoe. She pulled her foot back quickly, tucking it beneath her chair.

"Yes, I've met her. Seems like a nice lady. I've heard very kind things about her from Doc Coleman and others. Why?"

"Well . . ." He paused, glancing around the table to make sure no one had a coffee cup in midair. "Joshua married her yesterday."

"What!" cried Jacob, Addie, and Lacy in unison.

"Josh married? You've got to be kidding," roared Jacob.

"To Serena Weaver? How on earth did he meet her?" Addie slumped against the back of her chair and fanned herself with her napkin. "Morgan, didn't anyone ever tell you to bring things up subtly?"

He shrugged and looked at Jacob. The older man turned three different shades of purple. "You all right, Uncle Jacob?"

"Heckfire, no, I'm not all right. Are you tellin' me my baby brother went and got married and didn't even tell us about it?"

"I think he's planning on telling you later today."

"But I didn't even know he was thinking about it. He's never mentioned the lady."

"That's because he didn't meet her until Wednesday."

Addie gasped. Lacy grinned. Jacob shook his head and closed his eyes, the bright color draining from his face. "Was this a shotgun wedding?"

Morgan tried not to grin. "No, sir. Her daddy wasn't even there. Josh was walking up to my place the other night when he came across her being accosted by three young rowdies. Serena had been down to the district to tend to a little gal who is sick, and was going home about eleven o'clock. The boys figured that since she came from that way, she was from one of the saloons. Course, she didn't want nothin' to do with them, and they weren't takin' no for an answer. That's when Josh stepped in."

Lacy grinned. "Did he whip all three of them?"

"Not if it was eleven o'clock," growled Jacob. "He would've been drunk himself by then."

"Funny thing was, he hadn't had much at all to drink. I'd seen him earlier at the Senate, and he didn't touch his glass the whole time I was there. And he was losing every hand."

"Uncle Josh?" Lacy stared at him incredulously. "He almost never loses at anything."

"Well, he did that night. And the way he was rubbin' his belly, I don't think the whiskey was sittin' too well either. The way he tells it, he took one look at Serena and ol' Cupid dumped a whole quiver of arrows on him. It was love at first sight for the both of them." Morgan chuckled. "He says he even talked those boys out of a fight and sent them on their way."

"I'll be danged." Jacob stared first at Morgan, then at Addie. "He's gone and got himself married." He was clearly befuddled. "How could he marry a woman he just met?"

"Sometimes a man and a woman know right off they're meant for each other," said Addie with a soft, reminiscent smile.

Jacob was too upset to notice. "Love at first sight, my foot. I've never heard of anything so stupid."

Hurt clouded Addie's happy expression. "Why, Jacob, what a thing to say."

"Well, it's a bunch of foolishness. It takes more than five minutes to decide if you want to spend the rest of your life with someone."

Addie shoved her chair back from the table and stood, stacking up the dirty plates with a vengeance. "I'll have you know, Jacob Hunter, I fell in love with you the first time I ever saw you. You hadn't even spoken to me, and I knew I wanted to spend my life with you."

Stunned silence filled the room. She turned and bustled off to the kitchen in a huff, dropping two spoons and a fork on her way. She left them on the rug, a sure sign of how upset she was.

Jacob frowned and pushed back from the table. "Aw, Addie." He hurried after her, pausing only long enough to pick up the silverware she had dropped.

"Sam, why don't we go look at your drawings?" said Charity quietly, scooting back her chair.

"Yes, ma'am." He carefully slid away from the table and headed for the door leading to the dog trot. Lacy got there before him, clearly uncomfortable and troubled by his parents' argument. As they left the room, Morgan stood, waiting at the end of the table to walk with Charity. When they stepped outside, Addie's angry words reached them through the open window.

"And what's more, I thought you had a good idea that night how you felt about me, but I guess I was wrong. You didn't exactly come runnin' to see me right away. I thought you were deciding whether to settle down or not, but maybe I was wrong about that, too. Maybe you were holdin' out for some other woman—one you already had your eye on or maybe someone you met in Galveston—and when she turned you down, you had to settle for me."

Charity gasped softly. Her stricken face told Morgan more than he wanted to know. This was as much her fault as anyone's. Addie wasn't blind. She could see the similarity between Charity's eyes and Jacob's as easily as the rest of them. Surely she had wondered at the coincidence of Charity turning up here at the ranch. Strictly speaking, Addie was not a pretty woman and never had been. Her beauty had more to do with her inner qualities than the attractiveness of her face. Morgan suspected it was natural for her to have doubts.

He felt like wringing Charity's neck, but she didn't give him the chance. She fled down the breezeway to her bedroom. He almost followed her, but at the last second changed his mind. Father or not, Jacob would have a fit if he found him there.


Jacob walked across the kitchen and stopped behind Addie, laying the silverware in the dry sink. She ignored him. He put his big hands on her shoulders and rested his chin against the top of her head.

He had never told her about Marion. It hadn't seemed necessary or even right. He hadn't waited to court Addie because he was holding out for Marion. She had already turned him down. He had only been trying to get over her, to accept the fact that she wouldn't have him because he was too young. Marion had been his first love, but she hadn't loved him. She was only a faded dream from long ago. He couldn't see any sense in telling Addie about her now.

"Honey, I wasn't waitin' to see if I could get someone else. I did have strong feelings about you right from the start." That wasn't a lie, but after only one dance, those feelings hadn't been strong enough to keep him from being enchanted by Marion. "I waited to come courtin' because I wanted to be sure it was the right thing to do. We were both young. I'm sorry if I didn't fall head over heels in love with you the first time I saw you." He slid his arms around her waist, pulling her back against him.

"You know how I am, sweetheart. I don't make snap

decisions about much of anything, especially if it's important. I like to take my time with things." He caressed her gently, roaming places only his hands had touched, and bent down to nibble on her earlobe. "Things like makin' love."

She sniffed and tipped her head away from him. He leaned his face against hers. "Addie, I love you more than I could love any woman." His voice was low and thick with emotion. "It may have taken me a little while to make up my mind, but once I did, I knew you were the only woman for me, the one I wanted to spend my life with. You've given me more joy than any man has a right to have." He turned her around to face him. "I love you with all my heart."

"I know you do." She blinked back the tears burning her eyes and gave him a small smile, feeling foolish. "And I love you, too."

Jacob lowered his head, kissing her gently at first but growing more passionate by the second. She moaned softly and broke off the kiss. "Darn you, Jacob Hunter, this isn't the time to start something."

"Isn't it?" His eyes twinkled as he boldly caressed her bottom. "I think we should go over to Josh's house and make sure it's clean. He wouldn't want to bring a new bride home to a pigsty."

She snuggled closer. "It was cleaned on Friday, just like always."

"Well, we'd better check to see if the job was done well. It needs airing out. It's been shut up almost a week."

"Tighter than a drum. I wouldn't want Serena to come home to a musty-smellin' house." She met his gaze, her good humor restored, her self-worth secure. "I've always wondered what a sheepskin rug would feel like beneath my back."

"It's time you found out. Wouldn't want to mess up their bed." He lowered his head again, kissing her deeply. "And if you like it, sugar, I'll carpet our whole bedroom with sheepskin."

"Not necessary, but we might pick up a couple of rugs." They tiptoed out the back door like a couple of young lovers, only to find Morgan leaning against the railing at the far end of the dog trot, a heavy scowl on his face. It lessened when he saw them arm in arm and disappeared altogether when they looked at each other and Addie burst into giggles, burying her face in her husband's shoulder.

"Looks like you two made up. Goin' someplace?"

"Uh, we thought we'd go over and straighten up Josh's house. Don't want him bringing his bride home to a mess."

"Nope, wouldn't want that," Morgan said softly, his eyes twinkling. "Now, git. I'll tell the others you've resolved your differences and gone for a walk."

Jacob winked at him over Addie's head. "Thanks. And if you take Charity for a drive before we get back, mind your manners. She's our guest."

"I'll keep that in mind." Morgan didn't smile. She was more than a guest, and he suspected Jacob knew it. Or at least he was thinking about it. "She's checking over Sam's art lessons right now. I'll see you later." He waited a few minutes before going into the parlor, to give Jacob and Addie time to get away from the house. When he stepped through the door, both Charity and Lacy looked up.

"Are they all right?"

"They're fine. Smiling and holdin' hands. They've gone for a walk."

Lacy blew out a deep breath. "Thank goodness. I haven't seen Ma that riled up in years."

Charity was noticeably silent. She had avoided Morgan earlier, going directly from her bedroom through the formal parlor to the family parlor. He glanced at her, and she looked away, clearly uncomfortable. They needed to talk, but not here with the others. It could wait until they were alone. "So how's the young artist doing?"

Relief filled her face, and she sent him a skittish glance. "Wonderful. I can't see a thing more I need to correct." She smiled at Sam, who sat next to her on the sofa. Her eyes glowed with affection. "I'm so proud of you, and so glad you came out today. I've missed you."

"I've missed you, too." He grinned at Morgan. "Just ask Deputy Kaine. I've been pesterin' him all week to see if he knew when you were comin' back to town."

"I'll be here a while longer. He brought me some newspapers from New York. Would you like to look at them?"

"They got art stuff in them?"

"They might have something about art shows. Let's look." She picked up the packet of papers, which Helena had wrapped in brown paper, and unwrapped it. "These are copies of the *New York Times*. This one is for Sunday, February fifteenth." She opened the paper to the section titled "Amusements" and scanned the page, "No, I don't see anything about any galleries. Bangs and Company Auctioneers sold the extensive library of Rezin A. Wight, Esquire."

"Who's he?"

"I don't know, but it sounds like he might have had some interesting books—numerous curious and rare books, including an extraordinary collection of books of and on proverbs, books of emblems, jest books, early printed books, and the classics."

"Sounds expensive," muttered Morgan, stretching his legs out comfortably in front of him and picking up Charity's drawing pad from a table by his chair. As he listened to the conversation, he thumbed through her drawings.

"Probably was. We could have gone to the theater. *Adonis* was still at the Bijou Opera House. It's an amusing play, with the same man portraying a statue, milkman, ballet dancer, barber, and the dry goods clerk. *The Private Secretary* was still at the Madison-Square Theater. That was another good one." A little frown creased her forehead. "Fiddle. There's one I missed, and now it's closed. It was supposed to be a good one, too."

"Are there lots of theaters in New York City?" asked Sam.

"Dozens. I've never stopped to count."

"Holy Moses, do they all have plays and stuff every weekend?"

"They have some kind of entertainment every day—matinees during the day and regular performances at night. There are a variety of things to choose from—dramas, comedies, operas, orchestras, and solo concerts. Some of them change fairly often, so new things are available. There is almost always something to go see."

Sam mouthed a silent "Wow!" and shook his head in amazement.

Charity continued to scan the paper. "*The Prophet* was staged at the Metropolitan Opera House to good reviews. That doesn't always happen when there isn't a star performer in the show."

"Do you like operas, Miss Charity?" asked Sam.

She wrinkled her nose. "Occasionally. I prefer to go to plays or orchestra concerts."

That surprised Morgan. He had assumed she would like the opera. His mother had insisted on going during their rare visits to the East. To her, it had been the epitome of culture and a good place for a woman to show off her beauty and to seek new conquests. Once again, he had unwittingly measured Charity against his mother. Charity had come out ahead.

"The Philharmonic Society gave a concert at the Academy of Music. They played a new song by Hugo Reinhold. The reviewer says it has a pretty and refreshing effect, but that the dainty motive and treatment of the minuet are the only really noticeable features of the number."

Lacy hooted. "Pretty and refreshing?"

Sam giggled. Morgan threw back his head and laughed. "Can't you just see the *Colorado Clipper* printing a review of Old Bill's fiddle playing for the next dance?" Lacy assumed a falsetto voice. "Mr. Bill's dainty motive and treatment of 'Old Dan Tucker' were the only noticeable features of the number."

Morgan grinned at Charity. Her most noticeable feature at the moment was a miffed expression. He was about to tease her, too, but Sam spoke first.

The boy was obviously trying to be nice, but his curiosity was more than he could contain. "Is that the way they really talk in New York City?"

"No, men don't go around talking in a high voice." She glared at Lacy, but her love of the ridiculous overcame her irritation. "At least most of them don't." A tiny smile tugged at her lip, but she kept it under control.

Sam giggled again. "I figured that. I meant, is that how they describe music and stuff? Or is that just the way they put it in the papers?"

She shifted, fidgeting under Morgan's amused glance. "Both. Some critics do get a bit fancy with their words. Art or music usually evokes some kind of emotion in people, and they often describe it by the way it makes them feel."

"Like what you see in the face of a mother and her child." Morgan's gaze locked with Charity's. "Come here, Sam, and I'll show you what she means." Morgan looked back down at the drawing in front of him. A young mother sat on a bench outside Waldo and Wells Hardware store, holding a sleeping toddler curled up on her lap. Weariness etched her face as she leaned her head against the brick building and gazed at nothing in particular. When Sam stood beside his chair studying the picture, Morgan asked him what he saw.

"She's tired. From the angle of the light, it's probably late afternoon."

Morgan smiled. He hadn't noticed that part. "What else?"

"They've been in town most of the day, and her husband's probably been in the hardware store for an hour, looking at tools and chewin' the fat with his cronies."

Morgan chuckled. "You're probably right."

"The little girl was fussy before she went to sleep, and that tired the woman out even more." Sam peered closer at the picture. "And she's going to have a baby," he whispered.

Morgan glanced at Charity. She was beaming like a proud aunt. "That's right. She doesn't look very happy there, does she?"

"No, sir. Got ruffled feathers, but she's too tired to squawk."

"You, sir, can read people like a book," Morgan said with a smile. His gaze drifted to Charity. "Like someone else I know. Now, look at this." He turned the page. It was the same woman, still sitting on the bench, but the little girl had awakened. She stood on the boardwalk, resting her hand on the woman's big round belly. The child looked up at her mother, her face alight with excitement. The woman gazed down at the little girl, and the joy and love in her face touched Morgan's soul. That was the way a mother was supposed to look. He glanced at Charity, and his heart did a somersault. She was watching Sam, and if her tender expression was any indication, that was the kind of mother she would be.

"Wow. She looks really different. She's happy now and not feeling so tired." Sam cocked his head. "She loves that little girl a bunch, doesn't she?"

"Yes, she does. What do you think has just happened?" His voice held a trace of huskiness that brought Charity's gaze to his. He pictured her pregnant, his large hand resting on her round belly to feel the kick of their child. Desperate, sweet longing filled him, an ache that caught him by surprise. The love she obviously had for this boy and the love he had for her made Morgan ache for things he had never thought he would want.

Foolish wishes. Her life was in New York, with the theaters and artists and people like Mark Twain as friends. She would never be happy stuck in a small town out in the middle of the prairie with only common, everyday folk. His mother certainly hadn't liked living on his father's ranch or in the small town nearby, even with Austin only a two-hour ride away. He wondered if boredom had triggered her infidelity, or if something else had driven her to seek the attention of strangers, friends, even family.

Sam glanced at Charity, uncertain if he should talk about pregnancy, which some people considered a taboo subject. When she nodded, he relaxed. "Looks to me like her baby just kicked. When Ma was carryin' my little sister she let me feel her stomach sometimes when the baby was movin' around. That kid could pack a wallop." Sam walked back over to the couch and plopped down next to Charity. "I can't do faces yet. Not real faces, anyway. I reckon I don't do too bad at cartooning, though."

"No, you don't. You're very good, in fact. Drawing real people will come in time and with training. Faces are often the hardest part to learn, but once you get them down, they will come easily."

Charity explained the basics of drawing people to Sam, and Morgan continued to look at her sketchbook. When he came to a perfect likeness of Jacob, he halted. Jacob's lips were curved in a tiny smile, one corner higher than the other. An impish glint danced in his eyes as he looked at someone other than the artist. Addie, probably.

Morgan had seen that expression on his uncle's face many times, but it was not unique to him. He had seen it on Charity's face more than once before she ever met Jacob Hunter. Staring at the drawing, a moment captured in time, he could easily see Charity's resemblance to Jacob. Besides her eyes, it was there in the shape of her face, the lift of her smile, the tilt of her head.

He turned the page. Addie gazed back at him, a sweet, tender smile lighting her eyes and her mouth. She was beautiful, with a glow that seemed to come from her soul. This was the Addie he loved, the woman who had never failed him, who had seen him through the blackest depths of despair and guilt with never a condemning word, who forgave his most grievous sin without a thought of her own suffering.

The drawings weren't simply the creations of a master artist, someone with the innate ability to capture the feelings and fleeting thoughts of her subjects and bring them to life. He had seen some of those earlier in the sketchbook. Those other drawings were outstanding works of art, but the ones of Jacob and Addie had a quality the others lacked—subtle, yet to his eyes very obvious. Love. Each pencil stroke was a testimony of what Charity felt for Jacob and Addie, especially Jacob.

He turned back several pages to some earlier sketches of the whole family. Even there, he could sense her affection for them all. "If that person is important to you personally, you'll probably see them differently than others would," he commented during a lull in the conversation. He returned to the latest pictures of Jacob and Addie, making sure Charity noticed what he was doing.

Charity looked from the drawings to the knowledge in Morgan's eyes. It was past time to tell him everything she knew. He had guessed the truth, or perhaps Joshua had talked to him. She should have told him everything the night of the ball, but would that have brought his trust, or would he have interfered? He closed the sketch pad with a slight frown, drilling her with his intense gaze. Would he interfere now?

# Chapter
# Sixteen

Morgan checked the harness one last time. He had taken Charity through the process of hitching the horse to the buggy, carefully showing her each step. "Think you can do it on your own?"

"Probably not. But I'll get someone to supervise until I can. I wouldn't want the thing to fall apart on me out on the range."

"You plannin' on going out by yourself?"

"Some. There are several scenes I saw when Jacob took me on a tour that I'd like to go back and sketch. Although I wouldn't dare go some of the places he did in a buggy. It was a little like being on a tiny boat in the middle of a storm." She grinned as he handed her up into the buggy. "But I had more fun than I've had in a long time. I laughed so hard, I almost cried."

Morgan climbed into the buggy. "Do you want to start off?"

"No, you drive now. I'd like to wait until I'm out of sight of the others before I make a fool of myself."

He made a clicking sound with his tongue and flicked the reins. The sweet-tempered horse, Biscuit, trotted away from the buggy shed, happy as you please. Morgan drove down the road and through the ranch gate. When the road curved around a small hill and the ranch headquarters disappeared from view, he gently drew the horse to a stop. "Your turn."

Charity took the reins when Morgan handed them to her. "Tell me what to do. I know you just flick the reins when you want to go, but what do you do after that?"

"If you want to stop, you pull back on them. You don't want to jerk them because that will hurt the horse's mouth. Just pull back firmly. Once you're stopped, you shouldn't have to keep pulling, just hold the lines taut. For normal straight driving, you keep even tension on both reins but try to relax, otherwise you'll make the horse tense and skittish. If you want to go to the left, you ease the tension in your right hand. If you want to go to the right, you ease the tension in the left hand. That's about all there is to it."

"It sounds too easy."

"It's not too hard, unless the horse gets spooked and runs away. Then it's hard to stop her. Now, relax, take a deep breath, and let it out slowly. Okay, shake the lines a little."

Charity did as instructed and clicked her tongue as Morgan had done earlier. Biscuit took off at a fast trot. A grin flashed across Charity's face as she concentrated on keeping the tension even. Her right hand was stronger than her left, and before she realized it, they were heading off across the prairie.

"Ease up with the right hand," yelled Morgan, grabbing his hat with one hand and the side of the buggy with the other as they dropped into an old buffalo wallow and his backside flew off the seat. "A little more." He grinned as they lurched up the other side of the dip, and the front end of the buggy tipped upward at a steep angle for a second. Once on level ground, he took a deep breath and blew it out in a whoosh. "That's it. Now, even them up when we get back on the road."

Frowning in concentration, Charity pressed her lips tightly together and successfully guided the horse and buggy back onto the road. When they had gone about a quarter mile with no further mishap, she relaxed slightly.

"You're doin' good. See that intersecting road up ahead?"

She glanced way down the road and nodded, bringing her gaze back to the straight stretch in front of them.

"Turn right on that road. It goes over to the Davis place, but it's miles away, so you won't see anybody. Now start easing back on the reins. That's it. Good. Relax the left one a little."

The horse shifted slightly to the right—but not enough. Off they went across the prairie again.

"Ease up more. No! Wait, watch out for that draw!" He grabbed the side of the buggy with one hand and slid his other arm protectively around her waist to keep her from being thrown out the other side.

Charity missed the deep gully but took them through a shallow wash, then up over a rocky hill With a great flapping of wings, a quail flew up in Biscuit's face, startling the horse. She didn't break into an all-out run, but she definitely picked up speed. Bouncing so hard her teeth rattled, Charity choked out, "Help!"

Morgan shifted closer, his arm still around her, and covered her hands with his, grasping the reins. His voice vibrated as they pounded over another stretch of rocks. "Bring her to a stop." Together, they pulled on the reins, which brought Charity back against his chest. Biscuit slowed and stopped at the bottom of the hill, next to a leafless mesquite tree. The horse's sides heaved with exertion and fright.

"Take her over by that wild plum thicket. There's a little creek there, and she can get a drink and calm down." He felt Charity tremble. "Looks like someone else needs to calm down, too," he murmured against her ear.

She shivered again and leaned against him. "It's more fun to bounce around when someone else is handling the horse. We didn't go that fast when Jacob was climbing hills and diving into gullies." She took a deep, steadying breath and gently flicked the lines. "Come on, Biscuit. That's a good girl. Let's go get you a drink." Morgan moved his hands, but stayed close and kept his arm around her. Charity guided the horse to the trickle of water without further mishap.

When they stopped, Morgan helped Charity down from the buggy and showed her how to keep the horse from running away. He took a heavy cast-iron weight from the back of the buggy and set it down in front of the horse. A rope was tied to a ring on top of the weight. He tied the other end of the rope to the reins. Once Biscuit was secured where she could get a drink or nibble on the sparse, tiny grass beside the creek, they climbed back into the buggy.

"Whooo-ee. That was some ride, lady." Morgan pushed his hat back off his forehead with his forefinger and grinned. "You didn't do half-bad for the first time."

Charity rolled her eyes and relaxed against the back cushion of the buggy, pulling off her floppy hat with trembling fingers and fanning her face with it. "I need a lot more practice."

Morgan slid his arm across her shoulders, patting her upper arm in reassurance. "We'll do some more in a little while. Biscuit needs a rest." He relaxed, his gaze resting on her lips. A sweet warmth sprang to life, curling through her body. "And I need a kiss," he murmured, peeling off his hat and setting it on the floorboard by his feet. "Come here, woman."

She dropped her hat, not caring where it landed, and went willingly. He wrapped his arms around her, crushing her to him, and slanted his mouth over hers in a searing kiss. When he deepened the kiss, she whimpered softly, pressing against him, clutching the back of his head with her hand.

Her desire fueled his own. Never had kisses been so sweet yet filled with so much passion. Never had he wanted a woman the way he wanted her, but never had there been a greater reason not to make love to her. He broke away, and she made a tiny sound of protest. "Shh, darlin'. We're not goin' to stop just yet," he murmured softly, trailing a finger slowly down her cheek. "But we'd better slow down or we'll wind up in trouble."

He smiled and lowered his head, touching her lips with his. He took his time, brushing tiny, nibbling kisses along her bottom lip before settling his mouth fully over hers. She spread her fingers through his hair, delighting in its softness, and gently ran her fingertips along his scalp.

He took his time, caressing her gently, boldly. Charity gasped with pleasure, but she felt no shame. How could she, when he touched her as if she were a precious treasure? When he finally lifted his head, she buried her face against his throat, clutching his shirt in her fist. He wrapped his arms around her and simply held her, resting his jaw against her hair.

He held her for a long time, saying nothing. Even after her heartbeat had returned to normal and the blood no longer raced through her veins, he held her. Finally she felt him tense slightly and knew the time had come to be done with secrets. "Will you tell me why you're here?" he asked.

She slowly straightened and looked into his eyes. "Yes." She reached under the seat for her art bag. Opening it, she carefully withdrew her mother's little wooden chest and set it in her lap. After sliding the bag out of the way, she turned slightly in his direction, but looked out over the grassland.

"All my life I believed Henry Brown, my mother's husband, was my father. Mother told me he died while she was carrying me. I had no reason not to believe her. The records in the family Bible indicated he was my father and supported her claim as to when he died. Funny how a child can grow up loving a father she's never known, but he was more than just a face in a picture. Mama talked about him often, and I felt like I knew him.

"My mother was the most honest person I've ever known. She firmly believed in doing the best work she could, and if someone overpaid her or if a store clerk gave her too much change, she would make a special trip if necessary to return the money. She obeyed every law, never gossiped or said a bad word against anyone. She went to church every Sunday, brought me up by a strict code of morality, and made certain I abided by it.

"Mother was very independent and raised me to be the same way. She often said she saw no reason why a woman with any intelligence should be subjugated to a man, when she was perfectly capable of handling her own business and life. She was also very loving and patient when I made mistakes. We laughed and played together. We were very close, perhaps because it always was just the two of us."

She glanced at him. He gave her his undivided attention, his expression controlled and giving no hint to what he was thinking. She was sure he not only listened, but also watched every tiny movement and expression to see if they belied what she was saying. His years of training and experience had taught him well.

"I loved my mother very much. She was my ideal and my best friend. When she died suddenly of a heart attack, I was devastated." Tears burned her eyes, but she held them back. "We were dining at the Gilders' one Saturday evening. We had finished the meal and were on our way to the drawing room when Mama collapsed. Richard sent for a doctor, but she was gone before he arrived." She swallowed hard and wiped her eyes with her fingertips. Clearing her throat, she continued. "She died in my arms."

She closed her eyes, dragging in a ragged breath. "I miss her."

Morgan covered her hand with his, feeling her pain. He knew all too well the agony of losing a beloved parent.

She regained her composure, and he moved his hand to rest on the back of the seat cushion. "As I was holding her, she whispered that she loved me and said she had meant to tell me something. She didn't say what it was she had intended to tell me. She asked me for forgiveness. I had no idea what she was talking about, but of course, I forgave her. Then she died."

She paused, drawing in another deep breath, trying to bury the painful memory. "I learned from the doctor that he had been concerned about her heart for several months, but she had asked him not to mention it to me. I thought that was what she had meant. It was months before I could even go into her room, much less go through her things. It was difficult, and I could only do a little at a time, often skipping weeks in between. I kept busy with my work, taking on more assignments than I probably should have so I would have something to think about.

"A few months ago, I finally had the courage to go through her trunk. I knew there was nothing in it that anyone else could use, only memories. When I got to the bottom of the trunk, I found this little box. As close as we were, I'd never seen it before." She opened the lid. "When I looked inside, I found this picture." She took it out and handed it to Morgan.

He stared at it for several minutes. Just by looking, he couldn't tell for certain if it was Jacob or Joshua, but it was definitely one of them. Since Joshua said he had never met Charity's mother, he knew it had to be Jacob. A dull ache spread through his chest.

"There was a note in the box from someone with the initials J. H. He thanked Mother for going to a play with him and told her he had bought this little chest because when he saw it, it made him think of her. He said he would pick her up that night at seven for a dance.

"There was also a death certificate for Henry Brown stating that he had died three years before I was born. And a letter from my Uncle Will. Mama always shared his letters with me, but I had never seen this one." She handed him the envelope, taking the picture in return. "I don't know if Joshua told you or not, but my mother was Will Davenport's sister."

Morgan noted the postmark on the envelope, both the city and date, before slipping the letter out of it. He read it quickly, doing as Charity had done, rereading the part about J. H. being her father. He felt sick. He stared at the letter, wishing he could make it say something different. He glanced at the note lying open in Charity's hand, recognizing the bold scrawl. Joshua was right. She was Jacob's daughter.

He thought of Addie's words at dinner. She had been in love with Jacob, and he had gone off to Galveston and had an affair. Anger boiled up inside of him, and he silently shouted at the man he loved almost as much as a father. Barely resisting the urge to crumple the letter and throw it to the wind, he handed it back to Charity. "Have you told him?"

"No." She took one look at his hard expression and the glittering anger in his eyes and knew the rest of the afternoon wasn't going to be nearly as nice as the first half had been. There might not be any more nice days with him at all.

"Why not?"

"I'm hoping he will realize it on his own."

"Why?" he asked harshly. "Why not just confront him? Get it out in the open?" *Break Addie's heart.*

"I want him to acknowledge me because he wants to. I can't force him to be my father. That wouldn't accomplish anything."

"Wouldn't it?" His voice was cold, contemptuous. He wasn't being fair or even logical, but he couldn't help it. He was angry at Jacob for betraying Addie. Even though he knew Jacob had not been in love with her then, he should have been. She loved him. Why couldn't Jacob have gone to a parlor house like Joshua? Addie wouldn't have liked it, but she would have understood. Why did he have to wind up in the bed of a lady—and give her a child? "What about a nice big inheritance?"

That stung. "I told you I'm not after money."

"And I'm supposed to believe you?" he snarled. Trouble was, he did, but he was still mad at her. Why did she have to come along and stir up trouble? Why did people have to be hurt just so she could have what she wanted?

She glared at him and didn't bother answering him out loud.

"Why is it so important for him to admit you're his child? Why can't you just be friends?" He knew. He'd seen the loneliness she hid from the world. Rarely could friends become substitutes for family.

She took so long answering that he finally glanced back at her and wished he hadn't. The naked pain in her eyes and the bleak sadness on her face twisted his heart.

"I've always longed to have a father. When I was a little girl, I sometimes pretended he was just away on a business trip, and that he would be coming home soon. He would lift me up to sit on his knee and tell me all about what he had done and where he had been. He would take me on walks and carriage rides and trips to the park. He would teach me to dance and indulge my whims and stand at the door looking stern-faced and foreboding when some young gentleman came to call. Those were the things my friends' fathers did."

Morgan sighed and looked away. Why did life have to be

complicated? Why did one person have to hurt another to gain happiness? "What if he doesn't want to acknowledge the kinship?"

"I won't say anything. Morgan, I don't want to cause strife between him and Addie. They have a very special, precious love. I don't want to jeopardize that. Yet I can't help wondering what happened between him and my mother." Pink tinged her cheeks. "I can't see either of them involved in that kind of relationship without caring for each other."

"Maybe she didn't want to live on a ranch."

"She loved the city, but I can't believe that was the only reason. She was ten years older than Jacob. That's not exactly ideal for marriage. I expect that had something to do with it."

"Do you honestly think you can stay here and not say something to him? Not let something slip to Addie?"

"I couldn't keep up the pretense forever, but I could for a while." She hesitated, then plunged ahead. She had to know if he was going to try to stop her. "Do you think I'm doing the wrong thing? Do you think I should go to Jacob and tell him who I am?"

He turned to her, his gaze slowly moving over her face, storing away its contours and colors and textures in his memory. His loyalty belonged to Addie. His debt to her could never be fulfilled, but he would spend his life trying. She came first, even above what he yearned for most. He forced his voice to remain steady. "Let him be, Charity. Don't turn their lives upside down. Take the next train back to New York City and stay there."

*And tear out my heart.*

# *Chapter Seventeen*

Stunned, Charity stared at him, then turned away before he could see the tears burning her eyes. She slowly put the chest and its contents back into her bag. She thought he cared for her. *Idiot!* He'd just been playing with her, passing the time with nothing better to do. He found her amusing, allowing him kisses and caresses like some wanton, a silly city woman who thought she could interest a rough, tough Texan like him. Well, she wasn't rough, but she could be tough in her own way. If he thought she would simply take the next train to New York and pretend she had not found her father, he was gravely mistaken.

"I can't do that," she said, her tone cold, her expression like stone.

She climbed down from the buggy and stepped on her hat. With the dignity of a royal monarch, she picked it up, brushed it off, and eased it onto her head. Removing the rope from Biscuit's reins, she lugged the heavy weight to the boot of the buggy.

Morgan sat silently with his arms crossed in front of his chest, watching every movement she made. He felt like a coyote with his foot caught in a trap—he had two options, and neither one was good.

When Charity was seated once again, she picked up the lines. It galled her to no end, but she had to ask. "How do we get back to the ranch?"

His instructions were terse. She followed them precisely, handling the horse with amazing accuracy—no way on earth would she ask for his help—and got them back to the ranch house in hardly more than half an hour. A cowboy met them as they drove up to the buggy shed. When he offered to take care of the horse and buggy, Charity managed a tight smile and thanked him.

Without a glance in Morgan's direction, she marched straight toward her bedroom. He was right behind her, his boots clomping on the wooden floor of the dog trot. She paused at the entryway.

"Thank you for teaching me to drive the buggy." Icicles would be warmer than her voice now. "As for the other . . . instruction, you can take your expertise elsewhere, down to the West End where it belongs. I have no interest in any further lessons." Chin held high, she went through the entryway to her bedroom. Before she could close the door, however, a scuffed brown boot blocked her way. She looked up, glaring at Morgan.

"Get down off your high horse," he ordered in a low voice.

"You put me there," she whispered, still furious. "And don't order me around." She threw her weight against the door, but he didn't budge.

"Joshua and his new bride are in the parlor with the rest of the family."

"Oh." All the fight went out of her. She quit trying to crush his foot and opened the door. "I'll put my things away. We wouldn't want to spoil their homecoming."

"No, we wouldn't." She had wilted right in front of him. He felt like a heel. "Take a few minutes to freshen up. I'll meet you inside."

Charity did as he suggested and begrudged him every splash of cold water, even if she did feel better for having washed her hands and face. She smoothed her hair and, calling on years of training in being sociable even if she didn't feel like it, plastered a smile on her face and stepped into the parlor.

"There she is." Joshua jumped to his feet with a grin. "Charity, I'd like you to meet my wife, Serena."

Charity stepped in front of the sofa and extended her hand

to Serena. "I'm very pleased to meet you." Her smile finally lit her eyes. "I can see you've made Joshua happy."

Serena took her hand in both of hers and returned her smile with a gentleness that went right to Charity's heart. "It's so nice to meet you, too, Charity. Joshua has told me so much about you." Her eyes spoke volumes, and Charity knew instantly that Serena was well aware of the situation. "Here, sit beside me."

Charity sat down on one side of her on the sofa. Joshua took the space on the other side of his wife, immediately clasping her hand and resting it on his thigh.

"Morgan bragged on you." Addie smiled at the two of them. Charity could almost hear her cluck like a mother hen. "He said you had a gentle touch and learned quickly."

Charity slanted him a glance. How could he look at his aunt so innocently? His gaze flickered to Charity. Amusement twinkled in his eyes. The cad. How dare he laugh at her! He hadn't been talking about driving the buggy, and they both knew it. She glanced at Jacob and almost died. From his frown, he knew it, too. "I'm afraid I missed a couple of turns and we went dashing across the prairie." She smiled at Jacob and prayed her cheeks weren't as pink as they felt. "It's a lot more fun to bounce around when you aren't driving. But I did better coming back. I actually kept us on the road all the way here."

"Yes, you did." Morgan's expression had sobered. "You might want to have Lacy take you out one more time before you go off on your own. You still need a little practice on the turns."

"I will." She turned to Serena. "Are you going to settle out here right away or are you going on a honeymoon?"

"Stay here for now. We might go somewhere later. We would have come out sooner, but there were a few people in town I had been tending to. We had to arrange for someone else to take care of them."

"It's not always easy to find volunteers to care for folks if they need a lot of help. Did you have any problems?" asked Addie.

"Some of the ladies from church are going to take turns

looking after Mrs. Jones. She's not sick, just elderly and can't quite manage on her own." She smiled at Joshua, her face glowing with love. "And Josh hired some ladies to nurse the sick ones. We moved May out of the district to Mrs. Harvey's boardinghouse. She was very kind to her, for which I'm grateful. She's so young and very frightened." She looked at Addie. "She's only eighteen and pregnant. Dr. Coleman has ordered her to stay in bed until the baby is born. She has five long months ahead of her. She likes to sew and is very good at it."

"Serena has been teaching her," said Joshua. "That's why she's so good at it."

She only smiled at him. "Mrs. Gilbert has hired her to do handiwork. It will help May pass the time, save up a little money, and point her toward a new profession." Her smile was tranquil. "And knowing Mrs. Harvey, by the time the girl is on her feet, she'll be going to church."

Joshua chuckled. "Speakin' of church —you should have seen the faces when I walked in there this morning." He laughed at his family's shocked expressions. "Addie's been after me for years to go to worship services," he explained to Charity. "I was too bullheaded. Hard to get up on Sunday morning and go to church when you've got a hangover." He brought Serena's hand to his lips, kissing her palm. "But since my drinkin' days are over, it seemed like a good thing to do when Serena asked me to go."

She laughed softly. "The preacher had a hand in convincing him. When we went to get married, he refused to do it unless Josh promised to go to church every Sunday—either there or the one out here—for the next six months."

"I don't believe it." Jacob shook his head. Could a woman change his wild brother this much overnight? Or was she in for a rude awakening the first time things didn't go right?

Joshua seemed to read his mind. "I would have promised for a year if I had to so we could get married. It will probably be like training an old bronc to pull a buggy. I may veer off the road every once in a while and bounce around a mite, but I'll do all right, as long as I've got Serena to steer me back onto the path."

"If he gets too ornery, Serena, just let me know. Lacy and I'll throw him in the river." Jacob winked at his son and grinned at his brother. "I'm not too old to handle you."

"Not if you have help," chortled Joshua. "Couldn't do it on your own, old man."

"That remains to be seen."

"How you two go on." Addie smiled and shook her head. "Don't pay them any mind, Serena. They kid each other like this all the time."

They continued to chat, and no one seemed to notice that Morgan and Charity had little to contribute to the conversation or that she wouldn't look at him. No one except Sam. He sat quietly for as long as a ten-year-old could. He sidled up to Charity. "Lacy taught me some rope tricks while you were gone. Want to see them?" he asked softly.

"Of course." She glanced at the others, except for Morgan. "Please excuse us. We're going outside for a while."

They walked out to the backyard, where Sam showed her how well he could rope a fence post and spin a wide loop around in a circle near the ground. "I read some more of your newspaper, too. They had two inches of snow on February thirteenth. And on the morning of the eleventh it was two degrees. I don't think I've ever been where it was that cold."

"I haven't many times. You sure wouldn't want to be outside, would you?"

"Nope. There was another article about a man who died. He had thirty children."

"Thirty? My goodness."

"His name was Martin Blanchard, and he lived in New Jersey. Got married when he was fourteen and had nineteen children with his first wife. She died—"

"I wonder why," murmured Charity.

Sam grinned. "And he remarried. They had eleven children. He said during the war he could muster a full company with just his own male children and grandchildren. He was a grandfather before he was thirty. They think he had between six hundred and seven hundred descendants."

"That's enough for a town."

"Yep. Do you play badminton? I read an article about it, but it didn't say how it was played. They just said it was a delightful game and could be played with little practice. They mentioned pretty prizes given at the Badminton Club for the winners." He grinned. "There they go, talking fancy again—delightful game, pretty prizes."

"Sounds a little silly out here, doesn't it? I've never played badminton. I've seen it done, though. It's similar to lawn tennis. You use a racket to hit a fancy little thing called a shuttlecock over a net to someone on the other side. They're supposed to hit it back. When someone misses or hits it into the net, the other side wins a point. The shuttlecock is kind of like a half ball with feathers attached, so it flies up in the air but doesn't go too far. It can be played by two people or by four. It looked like it would be fun."

"I think I'll stick to ropin'." His expression grew serious. "Miss Charity, did you and Mr. Kaine have a fight?"

Charity tried to hide her dismay. "Why do you ask?"

"Well, you ain't hardly looked at him since you got back, and you were lookin' at him a lot, all happy like, before you left. My ma does that when she's mad at Pa. She kinda ignores him."

"We had a disagreement."

"I think he wants to kiss and make up." When she looked at him in surprise, he shrugged. "That's what my ma and pa do. He's been watchin' you, almost the whole time since you got back, and sometimes he looked real sad. Downright dismal, as my granny would say."

Morgan stepped out onto the back porch. He certainly didn't look downright dismal now. His cold glance raked over her. She barely controlled a shiver. When that man wanted to be hard, he certainly didn't have to work at it.

"Get your stuff together, Sam. We'd better head back. I promised your mother we'd be home before dark."

"Yes, sir." Sam turned back to Charity with pleading eyes.

"Make up with him, Miss Charity," he begged softly. "It ain't good for you two to be mad at each other."

"We'll have to see what happens, Sam. Now, go get your things. Don't keep the deputy waiting."

Morgan spoke to Sam briefly, telling him he wanted to talk to Charity and asking him to meet him at the corral in about fifteen or twenty minutes. The boy nodded and went inside. Morgan came down the porch steps. "Walk with me a ways."

Charity looked up at him and raised one delicate brow.

"Please."

"Very well."

They walked slowly toward the corrals. Morgan debated what to do. She had shared her secrets with him. He certainly had some of his own. If she knew them, maybe she would understand why he tried to protect Addie. "My daddy was Addie's twin brother. They were as close as two peas in a pod. They had another brother, Silas, who was two years older. He and my dad never got along. They were always tryin' to best each other. Had since they were boys, as I understand. Over the years, they got to where they couldn't stand each other. They couldn't be in the same room without gettin' into an argument.

"My mother was a witch." He glanced at her shocked look. "Not nice talk from a son, I know, but she was. My father thought she was the most important thing in the world, and he did everything he could to make her happy. Even when she started seeing other men, he didn't interfere. He said she always came back to him, and that proved who she loved. By then he'd started drinking heavy. He bought her expensive gifts, anything that caught her fancy or he thought she might like, things we didn't have the money to buy.

"I discovered all this when I was twelve, and I think it had been going on several years before that. It continued for the next eight years. Dad even moved to Austin, leaving the foreman to run the ranch. He thought maybe she'd be happier there, but it didn't help. Over time my father got to where he was drunk all the time, and my mother was gone morc and more. At one time she had been reasonably discrete, but she got to where she paraded her lovers openly. She wasn't particular who she was with, Charity. It might be one of the ranch hands or a neighbor's gardener or a close family friend or our attorney. Looking back, I think she wanted Dad to stand up to her, wanted him to stop her. But he never did, and if she'd ever had any respect for him, she quickly lost it."

He paused, trying to block out the pain. He started to speak but had to stop and clear his throat. "When I was seventeen, I moved back to the ranch. I liked it there. Liked the work. Liked being able to visit my parents but not live with them. I loved my father and couldn't stand being away from him for too long at a time. It broke my heart to see what was happening to him. One afternoon when I was twenty I made the trip to Austin. Dad was drinkin' real bad. I decided to find my mother and drag her home, make them have it out once and for all and try to settle things between them.

"It took money, but I finally persuaded the coachman to tell me where Mother had gone. She was with Uncle Silas."

"Oh no!" Charity laid her hand on his arm, forgetting her anger, only mindful of the stark pain in his eyes.

"I stormed over there in righteous indignation, but they didn't care what I had to say. I meant nothing to either of them. They laughed at me, mocked me, humiliated me in front of the servants. She taunted me about my father and said she was going to stay with Uncle Silas. He was the only real man in the family. She said I was weak like my father." He shuddered. "She caressed him and kissed him in front of me. I went outside and got sick. She stood in the doorway and laughed."

"Oh, Morgan." She leaned her head against his shoulder and wrapped her arm around his waist. "What did you do?"

He dragged in a rough breath. "I went home and threw their affair in my father's face. I was furious because he'd put up with her all those years, never lifting a finger to stop her when she humiliated and embarrassed the whole family. I was ashamed to be their child."

"You were hurting."

"Yeah, I hurt. I had for years and had kept it all inside. I exploded. I don't even know what I said. I ranted and raved and vented my spleen. I demanded he put an end to it once and for all. Then I stormed out of the house. I tore him apart and walked away. I killed him."

"How? What happened?" She moved in front of him and slid both arms around him. He swallowed hard. His eyes were misty.

"Dad went to see Silas as I had demanded. They argued, and Dad pulled a gun on him. I doubt if he meant to use it, but it gave Silas the opportunity he wanted. He had slipped a gun in his coat pocket when he heard Dad arrive. He drew his gun and shot my father. According to Mother and the housekeeper, who both saw the whole thing, Dad pulled the trigger as he was going down. They both died. I didn't find out about it until the next morning when one of the servants rode out to the ranch to tell me."

She hugged him tight, resting her cheek against his chest, wishing she could take his pain.

"Because of me, both of Addie's brothers died. They were her only family, and being Addie, she adored them both. I broke her heart."

"And your own."

"Mine doesn't count." He put his arms around her, holding her close. Lord help him, she was his anchor. How could he stand it if she left? "I killed them both as surely as if I'd pulled the trigger." Guilt crashed over him, suffocating him, blinding him to everything but his obligation to the one person who had truly loved him all his life. "I have to protect her from more pain, Charity. I have to. I owe her."

She raised her head, gazing into his eyes with all the compassion and caring in her heart. "I don't think Addie would agree with you."

"Without her I would have gone insane. This time I can protect her."

She cradled his face with both her hands, willing him to listen to a different portion of his heart. "You're a noble, loyal man, Morgan. But you're only a man. You aren't God.

You can't control everything that happens even if you try. How do you know that by sending me away you aren't going to hurt her more? I love her dearly, Morgan, and she loves me. Don't you think she might want a daughter?" She dropped her hands to her sides.

"Not if getting one hurts her," he said stubbornly.

"Does she blame you for what happened to her brothers?"

He hesitated. "No, but she should."

"If she loves you in spite of what happened, don't you think she'll love and forgive Jacob for something that took place before he courted her?"

"She already loved him."

"But he didn't know it, and he didn't love her. I'm not saying she won't be hurt. She probably will be at first, but Addie's an intelligent, logical person. After all, he married her instead of my mother. She's the woman who won his heart." She could see he wasn't convinced, but that he was thinking about what she had said.

"Morgan, do you want me to leave?"

"It would be better all the way around." The desolation in his eyes belied his words.

"Better. Let's see. Addie wouldn't find out about Jacob's indiscretion, that's true. There wouldn't be any hurt feelings or angry words. Jacob would never learn he has a daughter, one who loves and respects him. Addie wouldn't have a chance to be a stepmother, and Lacy wouldn't have a sister. They would go on just as they have been—a happy family, none the wiser.

"I would be alone. No father. No stepmother. No brother. I'd be walking away from my own family. Sure I have Uncle Will, but he's off in Africa. Next year, he'll probably be in Tibet or someplace just as remote. I may not choose to live here, but at least I'd have a family to visit, someone to spend Thanksgiving and Christmas with. Maybe even the Fourth of July."

Her voice grew softer, and he had to listen carefully, turning his head away from the breeze to hear it.

"But I would be walking away from something else just as important." She dropped her gaze, resting it on the middle of his chest. "I'd be leaving the one man I think I could love." She saw his quick intake of breath and raised her gaze to his. "I don't know much about love, but I know what we have is uncommon. I know it goes beyond physical attraction, perhaps beyond friendship. I'd like to see what happens. Do you truly want me to go, Morgan?"

He should tell her yes. Instead, he lost himself in her beautiful clear green eyes, and what he saw there stopped him cold. She could fill the black, lonely hollows of his heart with joy—in truth, she had already touched those dark depths with light, with life. She could help him resolve his guilt, bring healing to his tattered soul. She could be there in the night to hold him when the nightmares still haunted him. She had already taught him how to laugh again, how to feel. She made him mad sometimes, but at least he was no longer a hard, empty shell of a man going through the motions of life.

They might not make it. They might decide marriage was wrong for them. She had her career. He had his, but he had some questions about a lawman having a family. If she left now, they'd never know if they would have found a love like Addie and Jacob's, like Joshua and Serena's. They would both go through life wondering what might have been.

He had wandered through life too long already. He couldn't make her go. A tiny smile touched his heart. He couldn't make her go even if he wanted to, not this independent, stubborn woman. He prayed it would all work out. "No, darlin', I want you to stay."

He lowered his head and brushed her lips with his. He put his arms around her and was drawing her close when a young voice rang out.

"See, I told you they'd probably kissed and made up by now."

They guiltily jumped apart and turned to find Sam and Lacy grinning at them.

"I think they got it backward, pardner. Looks like they made up first and were just gettin' to the kissin' part." Lacy smiled at Charity. "Sorry to interrupt."

"That's all right," said Morgan, chagrined. "This isn't the place to be kissin' a lady anyway."

"Well, I guess it doesn't rightly matter as long as the lady isn't offended." He winked at Morgan. "And I get the feeling she didn't mind at all. Come on, Sam, let's go saddle the horses. Quit spittin' on the handle, Morgan." They strolled out of sight around the corner of the barn.

Charity looked at Morgan. "Quit spittin' on the handle?"

He smiled and put his arms around her again. "He was tellin' me to get to work."

So he did.

# Chapter
# Eighteen

On Monday morning, Lacy took her out again in the buggy. He corrected a few minor problems and let her drive wherever she wanted. After an hour or so, he felt she was capable of driving it on her own. He showed her a few other places that were particularly pretty. He gave her instructions to avoid walking on rocky hills, because they sometimes sheltered rattlesnake dens, and he pointed one out to her, explaining how a rattler sounded and how to back away from it if she should stumble across one. Since the days were getting warmer, she needed to be careful even in the grass, in case she ran across a rattler roaming away from the den.

"Don't park the buggy in a ravine or even stop in one. A hard rain twenty miles away can send a gully washer ripping through here, and it could carry you and the buggy with it. When it's dry like this, the dirt gets hard, and water takes a long time to soak in. The rain runs off into the draws, and they fill up mighty quick."

Charity promised him she would be careful and said the same thing again to Addie and Jacob when she drove off by herself early in the afternoon. She told Jacob where she would be and promised Addie she would wear her hat. Charity wanted to go up on the high ridge where Jacob had taken her, but she didn't feel confident enough to try it alone. She settled for stopping various places along the river and drawing those scenes as well as one of the ridge from the valley. The mesquites had put out their pale green lacy leaves, dotting the still-dry prairie with little splotches of color.

Sometimes she sat in the buggy or on a large rock—after carefully checking around it for snakes—and simply listened. She had never known such quiet, yet after a few minutes, she realized that the silence wasn't complete at all. The breeze rustled the dry grass, birds flitted about, and a hawk gave a piercing cry high overhead, a bee or dragonfly buzzed by. It was a hushed but vibrant world, teeming with life. Charity loved it. She wanted to stay forever.

Once a jackrabbit hopped within ten feet of her. Afraid to frighten it by turning the page, she drew it on one corner of the picture she was already working on so she could recopy it later. Lacy had showed her a safe place to park the buggy in the riverbed. It was wide enough that even if the water began to rise from a distant rain, she would have time to get to safety.

Having tethered Biscuit so the horse could eat to her heart's content or get a drink if she wanted, Charity walked around the bend of the river. The high wall of the opposite bank towered above her, casting the river in shadows and making her feel small, insignificant, and very aware of being alone. No breeze stirred the grass or cooled her face, and in the stillness, she realized how much sound the wind made blowing across the grassland. The birds were just as busy, cavorting in the green mesquites and weeping willows that grew along the riverbed and up one bank, the side that sloped gently upward to the flats. A mockingbird sang from a tree nearby, going through all the melodies he had copied from other birds as well as a chicken's cluck, and something that sounded like a gate creaking.

She paused at a small, shallow pool and watched tadpoles swimming furiously away at her approach. A little farther down, where the river spread out to a wider, deeper pool, she spotted a bewhiskered catfish swimming lazily about in the clear water. She took a seat on a clump of dried grass and sketched the fish. While she was there, a coyote ventured down for a drink some thirty feet away, and he was captured on the page, too. A flock of brown-and-white killdeer raced along the water's edge in hurried but short starts and stops. Their loud calls pierced the silence, but they quickly moved on down the river, leaving only the chatter of the other birds and the mockingbird's song.

Charity leaned back on the grass, lazily gazing up at the cloudless deep-blue sky, lost in thought. Just as she was remembering Morgan's passionate kisses of the day before—and wondering if a man came by such a skill naturally or if he'd had lots of practice—she got a whiff of something pungent. Bolting upright, she scanned the area, and spotted the black kitty with twin white stripes from head to tail. He was still some distance away but moving in her general direction. Grabbing her hat and drawing supplies, she hightailed it back to the ranch house.

The next day, Jacob stopped her as she walked out the back door. "Don't go out today, honey. Looks like we're in for a sandstorm." He pointed to the thick dirty line along the northeast horizon. "You don't want to get caught out in that."

As the storm moved closer, she watched the line grow wider until it looked like a giant brown cloud rolling between earth and sky. Addie carried a heavy dutch oven outside and propped it up against the north side of the house so the inside of it would face the wind. Her eyes twinkled when Charity asked her what she was doing.

"I burned our dinner about a month ago. Got busy and forgot to check on it. I've scrubbed and scoured that pan until I was red in the face but haven't been able to get it clean. I tucked it away, waiting for the next sandstorm. That blowing sand does wonders, just blasts all the burned part off. It will be as shiny as new."

The horses were secured in the corrals, where they could find shelter in the three-sided sheds. Even before the sand hit, the volume of the wind grew. The cowboys hurried to finish their chores, the last one holding his hat on his head and chasing a cranky, clucking old hen into the chicken coop before he raced to the bunkhouse.

Jacob and Lacy stayed inside, going over the books and deciding on the provisions they would need to send with their crew on the roundup. Addie sewed on buttons and patched holes in work shirts, and Charity answered her mail and began her next article. The sand-filled air dimmed the sunlight, so they all worked by the golden glow of kerosene lamps. Joshua and Serena stayed at home, doing what newlyweds do when they aren't likely to be interrupted. They didn't need a lamp.

The wind blew all day, waning at times, only to come back with window-rattling gusts. Charity took a short break from her work at mid-afternoon, watching the scene from her bedroom window. Tumbleweeds raced along the ground, bouncing and leaping until brought to a stop by the side of a building or a fence.

She thought of Addie's pan and decided to see if it was coming clean. She went into the bedroom next to hers and peered out the window. Sure enough, all the burned-on particles had been chiseled away. She very briefly toyed with the idea of stepping out on the porch to see what it was like to be buffeted by driving sand but decided firsthand knowledge was not necessary to write about it. She could well imagine how it would feel to have thousands of grains of sand stinging her skin and eyes. Someone could always fill her in on the details if she needed any.

After sunset the wind died down, leaving behind deep drifts of sand along the buildings and fences. Tumbleweeds nestled among the drifts, perfectly content to rest a spell from their long journey.

A thin layer of sand covered every piece of furniture, every knickknack, even the clothes they were wearing. The house was well built, but the wind had driven the fine grains through the tiniest cracks around the windows and doors. They didn't try to clean much that night except for changing the bedding.

The next morning, a good breeze blew from the south as usual, so they knew there probably wouldn't be another sandstorm. After breakfast Jacob and Lacy hauled the quilts outside and gave them a good shaking before venturing off to see how the rest of the ranch had fared. Joshua stayed behind to help Serena.

Addie and Charity shook the small rugs and hung them over the porch railing. While Addie swept the bedrooms, kitchen, and dining rooms, Charity pushed the Bissell carpet sweeper over the larger carpets in both the parlors. They met several times on the back porch as they went outside to empty the sweeper and the dustpan.

Charity chuckled over Addie's dustpan. It was made of tin, with a long wooden handle so she wouldn't have to bend over, but the back and sides were higher than normal. "Texas size," said Addie with a grin. "Made for West Texas sandstorms and men who track half the cow lot through the back door."

For dinner Addie baked some white potatoes in the oven and fried up some ham slices. She opened a can of green beans and a can of pears and made a pan of biscuits. Jacob and Lacy ate more biscuits dripping with butter and oozing with jam for dessert.

In the afternoon Charity and Addie teamed up on the dusting, doing each room together so they could chat. Usually one of the cowboys' wives helped Addie with the cleaning once a week, but she and her husband had taken a brief trip to visit relatives before he left for the roundup.

Everything in the house had been shaken, swept, or dusted by evening. Lacy came in, glanced at the shiny clean house and the two exhausted women sprawled in the parlor, and volunteered to cook hotcakes for supper. Addie told him to be her guest. The men even did the dishes. Charity wondered how Addie had managed to train them so well.

Shortly before bedtime, she found Addie in the kitchen. "What are you doing?"

"Putting some red beans on to soak. If they don't soak overnight, we'll have to eat them for supper instead of dinner." She spread the dried beans out on the table, picking through them quickly to remove any tiny rocks that had been gathered along with them. Then she swished them around in a bowl of water to rinse them. A few rocks she had missed in her first sorting sank to the bottom of the bowl. Skimming up the beans with her hand, she poured them into a large pot of water.

"I'll put them on to cook early in the morning. It makes a nice no-fuss meal for wash day."

Charity groaned. "How can you wash tomorrow after all the work you did today?"

"Don't have much choice. Clothes have to get clean. Besides, Bessie Martin always comes over and helps. Her husband, Tom, and Randy Hill are the only married cowboys we've got. Randy's wife, Annie, helps with the cleaning, and Bessie helps with the washing. It makes things easier for me and gives them a bit more money, too."

"Who washes all the other cowboys' clothes?" Charity hadn't thought about that when she interviewed them.

"Some of the men do their own, especially in the winter when things are slow. There are some big washtubs out behind the bunkhouse, and they team up once every couple of weeks to get the wash done." She wrinkled her nose. "In case you didn't notice, several of those boys don't mind wearing their clothes for a while at a time. A long while. The others take their things to the Chinese laundry in town. Sam Sing does a real good job. I've sent a few things to him myself when I didn't feel up to doing 'em. Would you hold this light for me? I want to take these out to the washtub."

Charity carried the lantern as Addie lugged a big laundry basket of Jacob and Lacy's work clothes out to the backyard. A few years earlier, Jacob had run a water pipe from the cistern under the back porch out to the wash house. The hand pump was on the outside of the little house because Addie preferred doing the wash outdoors except on cold or stormy days. She dumped the clothes in a wooden washtub and pumped in enough water to cover them. She soaped the collars, cuffs, and extra soiled places before returning to the house.

"I use the cistern water because it's rainwater, which is very soft. Does a good job on the clothes. We'll be running out, though, if we don't get some rain soon. Jacob is going to try to lay a pipe from the springhouse, so I won't have to haul so much water if the cistern does go dry."

The next morning Charity helped Addie and Bessie carry out the big laundry baskets. Once outside, they built a fire around two big, black cast-iron wash pots and filled them with water, carrying it bucket by bucket from the nearby hand pump.

"Those ol' pots have seen a lot of use." Addie grinned and straightened after pouring in the last bucket of water. "I got them when we were first married. Over the years, we've used them for laundry, makin' soap and lard, melting wax for candles, and once or twice for bobbing for apples at a party. I don't bother with making soap or lard or candles now. No need when we can buy store-bought goods that work just as well."

She might shun one of the newfangled dough mixers and make bread by hand, but she took as much advantage of modern technology as she could when it came to the laundry. As Charity watched, Addie and Bessie carefully lifted the wood-and-tin box that covered her Union washing machine and combined wringer. It was several years old, but Addie liked it just fine, thank you. "It's a sight better than doing everything on the rub board. Some things still have to have a little extra elbow grease, but most things can go right in."

Within the washtub the washing machine had a perforated cylinder that held the clothes. The revolving cylinder was turned by a crank on the outside, and the movement agitated the clothes in the water. Next to the machine, on the wringer side, was a long workbench. It held two large wooden tubs with another wringer attached to each. These were the rinse tubs. At a right angle to the workbench and washer was another, shorter bench. It held another washtub and the infamous rub board, where an industrious person could rub away particularly dirty stains.

Addie shooed Charity away, telling her that she and Bessie had a system, and another person would just mess it up. So Charity brought a chair down from the sitting area on the back porch and did sketches of them as they worked.

"I don't boil my clothes. Used to, but I couldn't see that it did much good, especially since I got the washing machine," said Addie as she dipped a bucketful of hot water from the pot and poured it into the machine. "I just use the wash pots to heat the water now."

Since Charity had never been involved in more than washing out a few things in the kitchen sink, she was amazed and appalled at how much work was involved. Heat the water. Pour some cold water in the tubs first. Add hot water until they were full. Help brighten and whiten the clothes by adding a bit of Mrs. Stewart's Liquid Bluing in the last rinse water. Yes, the water was supposed to be bright blue.

Fill the machine with hot water. Shave or chip enough Ivory Soap from the big laundry bar into the machine to make good suds. Load the delicate white clothes. Turn the crank—over and over, again and again, swirling the clothes around in the sudsy water. Dip the clothes out of the hot water with a smooth stick and run them, one at a time, through the wringer—crank another handle that turns the close-fitting heavy rollers, which press the water from the clothes.

The water flows back into the machine. The flattened clothes ooze out the other side of the wringer. Splash. Into the first tub of rinse water they go. Swish each piece by hand, up and down, over and over, then up they go, into the next wringer, turn the crank, rollers press—watch the fingers!—water gushes, clothes slither away from torture . . . splash . . . into the second rinse tub. Quick, stir the water or the clothes will be bright and white with blue spots, rinse same as the first time, run through the wringer, clothes escape . . . plop . . . into the laundry basket.

Separate items to be starched from things ready to hang. Dip collars, cuffs, and shirt bosoms in the starch, as well as anything else that might need it. Carry heavy basket to line.

Wipe dirt, bugs, spiders, and cobwebs off clothesline with clean, damp rag. Shake out each item, hang it on the line with clothespins. Basket empty? Heavens, don't stop. Go back for the next load. Sheets and pillowcases. Tablecloths and napkins. Underwear and white socks. Fine colored clothes. Regular colored clothes. Towels. Grubby, smelly work clothes.

The work lasted all morning. Charity couldn't sit still and let the other women work so hard. She helped hang things on the line and spent time cranking the washing machine or running clothes through the wringer. Addie took advantage of her help to dash into the house and mix up a batch of corn bread to go with the beans.

After the noon meal, the whole process started again, and lasted until late afternoon. But they still weren't done. The clean, fresh-smelling laundry had to be brought inside, folded and put away. Everything that needed ironing, except the sheets, was sprinkled with water, rolled up tightly in separate rolls, placed in the ironing basket, and covered with a special blanket. The sheets were folded carefully and stacked together.

They ate an even simpler meal for supper—corn bread crumbled up in tall glasses of cold, sweet milk. That hadn't sounded very appetizing, but Charity discovered on the first bite that it was delicious. Physically exhausted for the second day in a row, she crawled into bed and lost herself to sleep and dreams of Morgan.

The next day was ironing day. While the sadirons heated on top of the stove, Addie showed her a room off the kitchen, which Charity had thought was only a storage room. Various household items were stored there, but the prize Addie wanted her to see was the mangle. It greatly resembled a wringer, except it was much larger, and the rollers were much heavier.

"I iron all the linens with this thing. Just slip a sheet between the rollers, turn the crank slowly, and it comes out as smooth as if I'd spent an hour on it with the sadiron. Cuts our work in half."

Charity insisted on ironing her own clothes and some of theirs while Addie ran the mangle on the sheets and tablecloths. Ironing and general cleaning were the only domestic tasks Charity could do with some confidence. She didn't particularly enjoy the ironing, but it gave her time to think about her article, and daydream a little about ironing Morgan's shirts instead of Lacy's.

Early in the afternoon, Charity took off in the buggy to

see more scenery. She traveled farther than she had on
Monday, going to Honeysuckle Springs. A man who lived in
Mississippi had leased the section but had never done
anything with it, so he had given Jacob permission to use the
spring for his cattle. The lease was due to expire in a few
weeks, and the Hunters had plans to buy the land. They
already owned the section next to it. The spring was half a
mile from the border of their property.

Charity drove the buggy up over a little rise and drew
Biscuit to a halt. In the long, narrow valley below, a group
of cowboys, all armed with rifles, formed a circle around a
small pond, keeping some forty or fifty head of cattle away
from it.

Puzzled, she checked the map Lacy had drawn and
studied the lay of the land. The pond sat in the middle of a
tiny oasis of gray-green grass in a sea of honey-gold. A
stand of chinaberry trees grew to the left of the water, and
three big mesquites were on the right. She was at her
destination.

She didn't recognize any of the cowboys. Farther down
the valley, on her side, was another group of men. She
shaded her eyes with one hand, squinting in the bright
sunlight. "My stars! They're putting up a fence!"

As she debated whether to go down and talk to them, the
matter was taken out of her hands. A lone cowboy mounted
up and rode toward her. Charity took off her floppy hat so
there would be no mistake that she was a woman and rested
one hand on her skirt, right over the pocket holding her
derringer.

"Afternoon, ma'am." The solemn cowboy touched the
brim of his hat in greeting and brought his horse to a halt
beside the buggy. "What brings you so far out this way?"

She gave him her prettiest smile. "I'm an artist. I
understood Honeysuckle Springs was a very pretty spot, and
I thought I might sketch it. I am in the right place, aren't I?"

"Yes, ma'am. But I can't let you go down there."

"Why not? Is something wrong with it?"

A tiny smile touched his face. "No, ma'am. You might
say there's too much right with it. It's the only reliable

source of water in this area. Mr. Davis wants to make sure he has water available when we bring the herd back from the roundup. He doesn't want anyone else using it."

She smiled again. "Would that be Zeke Davis over at the Flying Z?"

He nodded. "Are you acquainted with him?"

"I met him at the Stockman's Ball. Unfortunately we only talked briefly." The Hunters didn't think too highly of Zeke Davis. They said he'd had no business bringing his herd into the area in the first place. All he did was add to the over-stocking problem. Morgan had him pegged as someone who was going to cause a problem. Judging from what she'd just heard, Charity figured he was right.

The cowboy grinned. "He ain't exactly a ladies' man. You that writer and illustrator from New York City?"

"Yes. I'm sorry, I should have introduced myself. I'm Charity Brown."

"Tate Barkley. I heard you were stayin' at the Double J."

"For a while. Mr. Barkley, I thought the Hunters used this spring."

"They have been." He glanced at the men putting up fence. "But they won't be anymore. They don't own it."

"I understand the land was leased, and they had the man's permission to use it."

"I don't know anything about that, except that the lease runs out soon, and Mr. Davis is claiming this section. He means to fence the whole thing, with gates only on his side."

"You mean he's going to buy it?"

"I couldn't say." He sighed heavily. "I just know there's bound to be trouble. The Hunters aren't going to take this lightly."

"And you and the other cowboys will be caught in the middle."

"That's a fact, but when a man signs on to an outfit, he's pledging his loyalty to it and his employer. I don't have to like what's bein' done, I just have to do what's asked or lose my job." He met her gaze. "And jobs are hard to come by these days."

She looked down at the armed men. "Will there be violence?" Acid singed her stomach at the thought.

"We got orders to shoot any cow or horse that won't turn back. That's not much of a worry. They wouldn't go down there unless they were half-dead, not with us there. We haven't been told to fire at people yet, unless they shoot first, of course. Mr. Davis is a stubborn man. From what I hear, the Hunters don't back down easy, either. I'm prayin' there won't be gunplay."

Charity knew she had to get back to the ranch and tell Jacob, yet she didn't want to. The men would rush out here to right a wrong and might get themselves killed. Biscuit snorted and pawed the ground, staring at the water. "It's a long way back to the ranch house, Mr. Barkley. Would you let my horse get a drink? I brought a canteen for myself, but I had planned on using the spring for her."

He took off his hat and swiped his forehead on his sleeve. "Well, ma'am, I can't see how Mr. Davis would want me turning away a lady. I'll escort you down there, but as soon as your horse drinks her fill, you'll have to be on your way."

"Thank you." Charity followed him down to the water, uneasy under the other men's watchful eyes. She stopped Biscuit, and the horse drank nervously, keeping her ears on the twitch.

Charity glanced around, counting men and taking stock of the situation. Most of the men looked nervous, some scared. One man stood out because he didn't look either. Dressed all in black, he reminded her of every picture she had ever seen of a gunslinger. His gaze never left her. His eyes were hard and mean, his interest in her plain. He wasn't a man she would want to come across by herself.

"I'll ride back up the hill a ways with you, Miss Charity," said Barkley when Biscuit had slaked her thirst. He caught hold of the bridle and guided the horse and the buggy around in a tight circle. Releasing the bridle, he dropped back to ride beside Charity as they moved up the hill. At the top they halted.

"I know you have to tell Mr. Hunter what's goin' on. Make sure he knows we're armed and prepared for trouble.

We don't want a fight, but we'll give him one if he starts something."

Charity held the man's gaze. If they hurt Jacob before he found out he was her father, she might personally come gunning for them. When she spoke, her voice was firm, revealing none of her fear. "I'm afraid you're fooling yourself, Mr. Barkley. The fight has already begun, and the Hunters didn't start it."

# Chapter
# Nineteen

Charity stopped the buggy by the back fence, looped the reins over the hitching post, and raced inside. Addie was in the kitchen ironing, putting the finishing touches on an everyday dress. Serena was keeping her company and baking a cake.

"Charity, dear. What is it?" Addie set the sadiron on the stand and hurried to Charity's side.

"Zeke Davis's men have surrounded Honeysuckle Springs. I talked to a man named Barkley. He said Zeke wants the spring for his cattle and won't let anyone else use it. His men are armed with rifles, and more men are fencing the section with barbed wire."

"Barbed wire! He can't fence something he doesn't own. Did he buy the land?"

"Barkley didn't know. He just knows he intends to use it. He's stringing barbed wire down the valley a quarter of a mile this side of the spring, but he hasn't reached the spring yet."

"I don't know where he got the money to buy it if he did. Jacob is on the board of directors at the bank, and knows Zeke Davis is mortgaged to the hilt and being hounded by his creditors. How many men did you see?"

"Twelve at the spring and another six or seven working on the fence. Barkley let me give Biscuit a drink at the spring, so I got a better view. I think they were all out in the open. I didn't see anyone hiding behind the trees. Most of them were tense and edgy. Each man had a rifle, two pistols, and a full supply of bullets in his belt. I think one man might have been a gunfighter. There was a cook and a chuck wagon and a pile of bedrolls."

"Sounds like he plans to keep all his men there around the clock. I sure don't like hearin' about a gunfighter." Addie chewed on her thumbnail, her brow wrinkled in thought. "Our menfolk have gone over to see Case. Lacy went, too. I'll need to send someone after them. Oh, dang Zeke Davis! He's just a good-for-nothing who's too big for his britches."

"Shouldn't we send for Morgan or the sheriff? Isn't this something the law should take care of?" asked Charity.

"Yes, it is, but these cattlemen have a way of tryin' to settle things on their own. I can't send any of the cowboys for Morgan. Jacob will need everyone when he rides over to see Zeke."

"I'll go." Charity started for the door.

"Do you know the way?"

Charity mentally retraced the trip out from town. "Take a right at the next road and a left at the second one after that."

"Third one. There are two places between us and the main road."

"I'll be all right. Do you think Biscuit will?"

"No. Take Princess. Have one of the men get her for you. She's as good with the buggy as Biscuit. Sweet-tempered but fast." Addie crossed the room and hugged her. "Be careful, child. Don't say anything to the cowboys. I'll give you half an hour's head start before I send for the men. That way, maybe Morgan or the sheriff can get out here before too much happens."

Serena was clearly worried. "We'll try to get them to wait until the sheriff comes." Addie shook her head, and Serena nodded. "I know they won't wait, but I'm not anxious to be a widow for the second time. What if we didn't send for them, but Charity went for the sheriff? Then they could go see Zeke together."

"I promised Jacob a long time ago that I wouldn't interfere or question his judgment on ranch business. I'm pushing it by waiting to send for him and letting Charity go for the sheriff."

"The only way you could stop me is to tie me up. If he

questions you about it, tell him it was my decision, not yours." Charity opened the back door with a decisive yank.

"If Dr. Coleman is in, ask him to come, too," said Serena. "We'll be glad to pay him even if we don't need him. If he's not there, try Dr. Terrell or one of the others. I'd rather be prepared and not need help than need it desperately and not have it."

Charity felt a wave of fear. She loved these people so much. She couldn't bear losing any of them. "Don't let them get hurt." She looked first at Addie, then at Serena, her eyes filled with worry. "Please."

Addie's gaze narrowed for a second before she tried to smile. "We'll do our best, dear. Now, hurry."

Charity tried not to let the cowboy see her impatience as he brought Princess in from the corral and harnessed her to the buggy. He noticed, but he didn't question her. The instant the horse and buggy were ready, she jumped in and raced out of ranch headquarters. Princess liked to run, and Charity let her go as fast as she dared. Fear made her heart thud as they approached the first turn, but her worries were for naught. Princess slowed at her command and took the turn at a fast trot. More confident, Charity urged her back up to speed.

She slowed the horse as they neared town, but she was still breaking the law. No one was supposed to go faster than a normal gait in town and over the wooden bridges. She didn't care as long as she didn't run someone down or crash into another vehicle.

Morgan looked out the window of the sheriff's office and saw her racing down the street. A tiny smile touched his face as he shook his head. "She's goin' to be a menace to society." He stood and put on his hat, watching her bring the horse to a sharp halt in front of the office. Her worried face sent a jolt of fear shooting through him.

Bolting out the door, he startled Princess. He quickly brought the horse under control and was at Charity's side in seconds. "What's wrong?" When she reached out to him, he grabbed her hand and held it tight.

"Zeke Davis has posted armed guards at Honeysuckle

Springs, and he's building a fence to block it from Double J land." She related the situation as quickly as she could, ending with "Addie said she would give me a thirty-minute head start before she sent someone after Jacob." Tears filled her eyes. "Morgan, please don't let anything happen to them. Don't let any of them get hurt." The tears slid down her cheeks, and her voice broke. "Please don't let anything happen to my father."

He gathered her in his arms, holding her close, feeling her pain as if it were his own. "I'll do all I can, sweetheart."

She only let him hold her for a minute before she pushed him away. "Go."

"Are you all right?"

"No, but I'll manage." She wiped her cheeks with her fingers. "Hurry. Stop this madness. I promised Serena I'd ask a doctor to come out."

"Did you see any gunfighters?"

"One man might have been, but I've never actually seen a gunfighter."

"What did he look like?"

"Cold and confident. He strutted around when I drove the buggy down to the spring. Swaggered like he was someone important. He was dressed all in black while the other men wore regular cowboy working clothes. They didn't have anything to do with him." She shivered. "His eyes were hard. I don't think he would have any problem shooting a man. He never came close to me, but he tried to intimidate me anyway."

"What about the others?"

"Tense and nervous. Several of them looked frightened, as if they had gotten into something they hadn't expected. Barkley didn't like what was going on, but he said men owed their loyalty to the man who hired them. It's either obey or be fired, and jobs are scarce."

"Loyalty to the brand. It goes a long way out here."

"Even to fighting for something you think is wrong?"

"Sometimes. Depends on how hard up a man is. You go get the doctor. I'll ride out to the Double J. With the good Lord's help, things won't get out of hand."

"Shouldn't the sheriff or another deputy go with you?"

"No one's around who can go. I have to leave one man here, and Dick went to Abilene this morning. The others are scattered around the county today."

"I'll be there as quickly as I can."

"You stay at the ranch house." It was an order, one that demanded no refusal. She tried to protest anyway, but he silenced her with a look. "Charity, you could get hurt. I don't have time to worry about you."

He had hurt her feelings, not hard to do considering her overwrought emotions. He didn't have the time to be tender, but he took it anyway. "Sugar, I can't be distracted during a situation like this, and I would be if you were there. I'd be worrying too much about keeping you safe." He lightly ran a finger down her cheek. "That's got to count for something."

"It does. I'll stay at the ranch house."

"Thanks." Morgan went back into the office and loaded his Winchester rifle. When he came out, Charity was still sitting there.

"Go with God," she said softly. It was on the tip of her tongue to tell him she loved him, but she didn't. Now was not the time for such a revelation, especially when she couldn't be sure she meant it, or if she was merely being emotional. He nodded and headed off toward the livery stable. She watched him walk down the street and said a prayer for his safety as well as that of the others. It was one of many messages that had flown to heaven in the past hour.

Dr. Coleman was out at another ranch delivering a baby, but Dr. Terrell was in the office. After Charity explained the situation, he quickly excused himself from a patient with a case of sniffles and told Charity he would be on his way as soon as his buggy was ready. She stopped by the livery stable so Princess could get a drink at the water trough, then hurried back to the ranch.

When Morgan arrived at the springs, it appeared that shooting might erupt any minute. The men from the Flying Z were lined up in front of the water, rifles in hand, although they were not exactly pointing them at anyone. The Hunters and their men were still mounted and had spread out in a line opposite the other cowboys. The Hunters were in the middle, slightly in front of their men. Zeke stood directly across from them, in an even line with his men. The gunman stood beside him. Morgan noted that Joshua never took his eyes off the man in black.

Morgan rode in slowly. He sensed that Jacob was aware of his presence, but Zeke was too caught up in the confrontation to notice. Zeke was a man with big dreams. Unfortunately he didn't have the ability needed to make them succeed.

"I've got a right to this water," said Zeke. "I ain't lettin' you turn my cattle away."

"We've never stopped your cattle from drinking here. You know that." Jacob was calm, but it was clear he had no intention of backing down. "We could have. We have written permission from Smith to water our stock here. He didn't say anything about yours."

"That lease expires next week. And I ain't lettin' nobody else get this water." Desperation burned in Zeke's eyes. "I'll go belly-up without it."

Morgan moved into Zeke's line of vision but said nothing.

"You'll go under even if you have the water. You're not a cattleman, Zeke. It's time you accepted that fact."

"I'm not gonna stand here and listen to your insults." Zeke nudged the gunman in the arm. "Shoot him."

"Don't move." Morgan's order cut through the tense silence.

The gunman met his implacable gaze. The man's fingers twitched, and he went for his gun. Morgan had his Colt leveled at the gunfighter's heart before he could get his pistol halfway out of the holster.

"Drop it to the ground."

With hate and fear in his eyes, the man obeyed.

"Now the other one."

The second one hit the ground.

"Anyone else interested in tryin' their luck?"

Eighteen men shook their heads. Morgan kept his gun

drawn as a precaution. "Barkley, pick up those pistols for me. You can give them to him back at the bunkhouse. I don't want your friend gettin' any ideas."

"He ain't no friend of mine, Deputy." Barkley did as Morgan asked, handing the guns to another cowboy and quietly telling him to take them to the chuck wagon. The younger man did as instructed.

Morgan pinned the self proclaimed gunfighter with his gaze. "I want you out of the county—now. If I see you again, I'll throw you in jail."

"On what charge?"

"I don't expect it will be too hard to think of something. Josh, are you keeping an eye on this hombre?"

"Yep."

"Mr. Hunter is as fast as I am, so if you're thinking about going for that derringer you've got tucked away, I'd advise against it. Keep your hands out away from your body."

A trace of surprise flickered across the man's face, and he glanced uneasily at Joshua. Joshua grinned back.

"You waitin' for an engraved invitation?" Morgan asked softly.

Glaring at Morgan, the gunfighter turned and walked away, keeping his hands out where Josh could see them. When he got to his horse, he looked back to find Josh calmly holding his gun on him. With a string of curses, he began saddling his mount.

Morgan looked down the row of Flying Z cowboys, making brief eye contact with each man. Most of them were young, but there were a few old-timers who should have known better. "You boys load on up and head back to the ranch, except for the ones working on that fence. You're going to go undo your work. You're trespassing, and if I had room, I'd throw every one of you in jail. A man has to have some integrity and draw limits on ridin' for the brand. When your boss is askin' you to do something illegal or immoral, don't do it. A man who stands up for what's right won't have trouble finding another job."

The cowboys looked sheepish and started gathering up

their gear, ignoring Zeke's sputtered order to stay where they were.

"It's over, Zeke. You can't just decide you want something and try to take it with guns. Jacob's got first right to use this water because he had permission from Smith, and because he had established this part of the range and claimed the water rights before you came. If you want to use it, you buy or lease the section. Unless you own or lease it, you can't fence it, and you can't turn anyone or anything away. Whoever owns it can do what they want with it."

"I ain't just going to sit still and let him have all the water," shouted Zeke.

"Then you'd best buy it or settle it in court. But don't fence or set up guards around the spring until the court says you can. If I catch you over here again, I'll throw you in jail for trespassing. It's what I ought to do now, but I don't think Jacob would want a neighbor disgraced by being hauled into town hogtied like an outlaw." He actually thought Jacob might enjoy it. "I want that fence dug up. When I ride out here tomorrow afternoon, I don't want to see a post or a piece of wire. And fill in those post holes. Understood?"

Zeke nodded curtly. "You haven't heard the last of me, Hunter. I'm not going to let you run me out of business."

"I'm not trying to run you out of business, Davis. I never have."

"You've never wanted me here."

"That's true. I wasn't the only one who told you at the start that this part of the country was being overgrazed already. You can't blame your failure on me or anybody else. We tried to give you fair warning."

"You just want it all for yourself."

"We want what we've worked hard for, I'll not deny it. When we came here, you could still see moccasin prints in the mud down by that spring. We've earned the right to be here, Zeke."

Zeke had no comeback. He just stared at Jacob and Joshua with hate in his eyes until one of the cowboys brought him his saddled horse. He mounted, sending them all one last glare, and rode off beside the gunman. The rest of the cowboys left a few minutes later.

Joshua grinned at Morgan as they turned their horses toward home. "Not bad timing."

"Just lucky."

Jacob snorted. "Luck shaped like your aunt and a certain little gal from New York. Addie knows better than to interfere in ranch business."

"Seems to me she has a right to protect her husband if she can. Besides, I don't think she could have stopped Charity from comin' after me."

"You know darn well she didn't try."

Morgan smiled at him. "Probably not. Glad I came?"

Jacob frowned and grudgingly admitted he was. "I guess a man thinks twice about startin' a fight when he sees you draw a gun. None of those other boys were lookin' for trouble."

"I probably could have taken him," said Joshua. "But I'm glad I didn't have to try. I sure would hate takin' the chance of making Serena a widow again so soon. I got me a lot of livin' to do."

"I figured you'd start a knockdown brawl before I got here. I was surprised everybody wasn't covered with mud."

Joshua chuckled. "I've lost interest in fightin'. Hard to kiss a sweet woman with a busted lip."

Morgan glanced at Jacob. His uncle was still mad. He didn't see that very often. "Who's got you so lathered up? Zeke?"

"That cussed fool. Who does he think he is?"

"A man about to lose everything."

"Well, he ain't got enough sense to spit downwind. And I guess I'm irritated at Charity. Surprised, too. She had no business racin' off to town like that. It's a wonder she didn't wreck the buggy and break her neck."

"She's a good driver, Dad. I had her push Biscuit to a run a couple of times, and she handled her without any problems." Lacy grinned at Morgan. "I made sure she knew how to turn before we went fast."

Jacob grumbled something under his breath. "She's too

independent and headstrong. Sticking her nose where it don't belong. Who gave her the right to meddle in my business?"

Morgan almost told him. If he had still harbored any doubts about her feelings for Jacob, they had vanished when she risked her neck to get help and begged him not to let anything happen to her father. Pure love had motivated her actions.

"She's grown real attached to all of you. Almost like a second family."

Joshua glanced at Morgan, then Jacob. "You may not realize it, big brother, but you're real special to her. She looks up to you, kind of like a father."

Jacob looked surprised—and touched. "I don't reckon I'll say much, then," he said gruffly. "This time."

"Why are we goin' so slow when we got womenfolk home worryin'?" asked Joshua, kicking his horse to an easy gallop. The others matched his pace.

They met Dr. Terrell before they reached the house. When he learned that no one had been hurt, he turned his buggy around and headed back to town, promising to send Jacob his bill. They both knew he wouldn't.

All the women, including Bessie, were waiting on the back porch. They breathed a collective sigh of relief when they saw the men racing home, each one sitting tall and riding easy. The women rushed down to the corrals to meet them.

Joshua swept Serena up in a wild embrace and kiss. Jacob was more sedate, but love and relief were visible in his face as he hugged his wife, squeezing tightly. Charity watched them embrace, feeling relief and thankfulness all mixed up with regret that she couldn't let her love for Jacob show. She turned away, looking for Morgan, and found him watching her. Her gaze locked with his, she walked quickly to his side.

Once there, she looked him over. "You aren't hurt, are you?"

"Nope. No one was. They might have been if I hadn't

gotten there when I did. You were right to come for me, Charity. Davis had a hired gun."

Her eyes grew wide. "Did he try to shoot you?"

"He tried." He grinned lazily. "But he wasn't nearly as fast as he thought he was."

She sank against him, resting her cheek on his solid, warm chest, forgetting about her family and all the cowboys who might be watching. "Thank God you're safe. I was so worried about you."

He slid one arm around her, mindful of the smiles and speculation on the cowboys' faces, knowing how easy it would be to lose himself in her scent, her touch, and the way she felt pressed up against him. "I'm glad," he murmured. And he was. He couldn't remember any time in his life when a woman besides Addie had worried about him. It felt good to know someone cared enough to worry.

She looked up at him. "Thank you, Morgan. Thank you for risking your life to keep them safe."

"It's my job. Besides, they're the only family I've got. I'm not about to let some fool hothead harm them if I can help it."

"Is it over?"

"Maybe. Maybe not. Davis was still pretty riled up. He's about to lose his shirt. A man is liable to try just about anything when he's desperate."

"Hey, Morgan. You two coming to the house, or are you gonna stand there huggin' all afternoon?" Lacy grinned at them and pointed toward the house with his thumb. The rest of the family was already walking that way.

"We'll come along." They kept one arm around each other as they walked. Why not—everyone on the ranch had seen them embrace. "I'm going to stay out here for a while. I've got some time coming, and I'd like to be around to keep an eye on Zeke."

"And on me?" She looked up at him, concern wrinkling her brow.

"And on you." He squeezed her middle and smiled. "In case you haven't noticed, I like looking at you, lady."

She smiled back. "I kind of like lookin' at you, too."

"As for Jacob—you do what you have to do."

"Thank you." She broke away from his penetrating gaze, afraid the love she felt for him showed in her eyes. If the past few hours and moments had taught her anything, it was that her earlier feelings hadn't been due merely to emotional turmoil. She loved Morgan Kaine.

# Chapter Twenty

Morgan rode back into town and explained the situation to Sheriff Ware. He agreed that Morgan should stay at the Double J and keep an eye on things, but he gave it to him as an assignment instead of letting him take time off. "When they get things worked out, you can stay on awhile if you want and count that as time off. You haven't had any vacation since you came to work for me, so you're overdue. Enjoy your family—and Charity." Dick smiled at his old friend. "I couldn't help but notice that something is brewing between you two. Hope it works out the way you want it to."

"Me, too. Now all I have to do is figure out what I want." He considered telling Dick about Charity being Jacob's daughter, but decided against it. He'd find out soon enough if he was supposed to. "Seems like life can get mighty complicated."

"Sometimes it can. Other times we just make it that way. You have to decide what's most important and cut through all the clutter."

Morgan remembered those words several times during the following days. The next afternoon he rode back to Honeysuckle Springs with Lacy, while Jacob and Joshua went to town and started the process of buying that section of land. To Morgan's relief, Zeke had obeyed his orders and removed the fence. Not a post, piece of wire, or unfilled hole could be found.

That evening Jacob and Joshua decided to try to buy Zeke out. Unless he asked a ridiculously high price, they could

247

afford what he and the bank owned. It would be worth it not to have any more trouble and to secure all the land nearest the springs. When it came right down to it, they didn't like to see a man go bankrupt, even if they thought he had brought it on himself.

Morgan went with them to the Davis place the next morning. Zeke met them on the front porch of the small board-and-batten house with hatred in his eyes. Tate Barkley stood uneasily at his side. One other cowboy was down at the corrals feeding the horses. There wasn't a sign of anyone else.

Morgan nodded a greeting to the two men. "Did your hired gun leave like I told him to?"

"He left. I would have fired him anyway. Couldn't do the job."

"You'd better be thankful he couldn't."

Zeke paled slightly at the hard glint in Morgan's eyes. "You come out here to push your weight around some more?"

"I came to make sure you listened to what these gentlemen have to say."

"I ain't interested in anything they got to say."

"Not even an offer to buy you out?" asked Jacob. Dumbfounded, Zeke stared at him. "You know I'm on the board at the bank, Zeke, so I'm aware of just how deep in debt you are. We know you paid cash for the land, then mortgaged it to buy cattle and make improvements." He looked around, studying the house, corrals, and the few sheds that had been built since Zeke set up the ranch. "We'll give you six thousand dollars for the land and buildings and ten dollars a head on the cattle—head count, not book count. We only pay for cattle actually delivered or brought back during the roundup."

"Ten dollars a head! I paid twenty."

"You paid too much. They aren't worth anywhere near that now."

"Ten thousand for the place and fifteen dollars a head on the cattle."

Jacob shook his head. "Too high. Eight thousand and

twelve dollars a head. Take it now and you don't have to send any men on the roundup. That's my last offer." It was more than fair but worth it to get rid of Zeke. He wouldn't be the wealthy man he wanted to be, but they wouldn't leave him a pauper either.

Zeke studied Jacob and Joshua for a long moment. Gradually relief filled his eyes. "I'll take it on one condition."

"What?"

"That you give Tate and that other feller down at the corrals a job. They're the only two men I've got left, the best ones in the bunch. Paid off the rest yesterday."

Morgan was surprised by Zeke's concern for his men. He could see Joshua and Jacob were, too. Maybe Addie was right. She always said there was a speck of good in just about everybody.

"If they want to work for the Double J, they're welcome," said Joshua. Jacob usually handled the money negotiations, but Joshua did most of the hiring. He looked at Tate. The man's grin was a mile wide. Joshua smiled at him. "I reckon that means you're interested?"

"Yes, sir. And I'm sure Shorty will be, too. He's young but a good hand, Mr. Hunter. Works real hard."

"Come on over when things are finished up here." He glanced at Zeke. "I'd like them to go on the roundup."

"They'll be done in plenty of time. We don't have more'n a handful of cows left around here. The rest drifted south."

"How about if we meet at the bank in the morning at ten o'clock to tidy up all the legalities?"

"I'll be there." Zeke held out his hand to Jacob. "I appreciate what you're doin'." They shook hands, and Zeke turned to Joshua and shook his hand, too. "I reckon I went a little loco the other day. I feel bad about that."

"It's hard to lose a dream," said Joshua. "We've been close a few times ourselves, so we know what it's like. What will you do now?"

"I've been thinkin' about goin' up to Eastern Colorado. Got a brother up there, and he says they can always use good horses. I've got some good stock, and I know horses a whole lot better than I know cows."

"Good luck." Morgan smiled, and almost laughed out loud at Zeke's look of surprise. He'd been doing that a lot the last month or so. Most folks had thought he didn't know how to smile.

When Jacob and Joshua went to town, Morgan sent a message to Dick advising him that everything was settled, and that he was officially on vacation.

With the exception of his last undercover assignment with the Rangers, he hadn't spent any length of time on a ranch since his father died. There wasn't much work to be done other than preparing for the roundup. Some of the men worked with the horses that had been out to pasture all winter, reacquainting them with saddles and riders. Others mended harnesses and bridles or weaved new lariats.

Morgan did a bit of everything, including hauling hay to the corrals and spreading it out for the horses. He quickly realized he had gone a little soft working as a deputy. Strolling around town looking for trouble or riding out to settle an occasional range dispute didn't keep him as fit as he should have been.

At first working around the ranch brought painful memories of the life he had once loved, reminding him of both good times and bad. Gradually enjoyment of the work and the pleasure of being with his family and Charity dispelled his sadness.

He helped round up about a hundred Double J cattle still on the home range and spent a couple of days cutting cows and calves from the herd to give both the cowboys and horses practice. Morgan enjoyed that part of the work and was very good at it. Cactus had a natural talent for directing cows exactly where he wanted them to go, and like his master, did well even though he hadn't used the ability in a long time.

One afternoon Morgan did something that made him question his own intelligence. Wanting to see if he still had the touch—and in an impulsive, juvenile attempt to impress Charity—he decided to help break some new cow ponies.

Four seconds after he climbed onto the back of an angry and terrified sorrel, he realized two things: He wasn't as young as he used to be, and he wasn't going to stay in the saddle for five seconds. He landed facedown in the dirt. Only pride—and knowing Charity was watching—made him get up, spit out a mouthful of dirt, and climb back on the wild-eyed, snorting horse.

He lasted a little longer that time and hit a little harder. When he flew off the third time, landing on his back, he was sure he had jarred the ground hard enough to knock a few boards off the fence posts. He lay there awhile, trying to name the multicolored constellations drifting across his eyelids, and did a woozy bone count. About the time he came to the conclusion that all his appendages were still attached, Lacy bent over him.

"You still alive down there, pardner?"

"No." Morgan opened one eye and peered up at him.

Lacy grinned. "Charity said to tell you she isn't impressed. You'll never make it as a circus acrobat, and she's gone back to the house, so you can stop trying to kill yourself for her benefit."

"She said all that?" Morgan groaned as he pushed himself to a sitting position. It wouldn't have mattered if she were still watching. He wasn't dumb enough to get on that bronc for a fourth time.

"Yep." Lacy helped him to his feet. "She was also about to cry."

Morgan looked at him to see if he was serious. He was.

"It didn't bother her near as much when I got bucked off half a dozen times." Lacy grinned again. "Course, I'm a bit more nimble-footed than you are. I didn't lay there like a waterlogged stump."

"Wait and see how spry you are when you reach a hundred and ten." Morgan moaned again as he made a feeble attempt to brush the dust off his backside with his hat. "I'm leavin' you to it."

"Giving up so soon?" Lacy's eyes danced, and the other cowboys snickered.

"Yep. I'm goin' to find a bottle of liniment." Morgan

waited until the chuckles and good-natured jibes died down. "And a pair of smooth, soft hands to rub it on." He turned and walked away, grinning as the others groaned with envy.

From her seat on the back porch, Charity watched him slowly and painfully limp toward the house. She didn't know whether to chew him out or cry. As he got closer, and she saw the blood trickling down his cheek and a dark red splotch on the elbow of his torn shirtsleeve, she thought she might do both.

By the time he reached the steps, she had clean washcloths and a basin of warm water waiting on the porch table. He unbuttoned his shirt with one hand as he hauled himself up the steps with the other. One knee was already swelling and going stiff. He took one look at her and smiled. She was mad enough to kick a hog barefooted, but she didn't look like she was going to cry.

"Idiot." She glared at him.

"Yes, ma'am." He tossed his hat on the table in the shaded sitting alcove. "That's a fact."

When he tried to shrug out of his shirt, she sighed heavily and went to help him, tugging it from his pants and easing it over a scrape on one shoulder and a cut on his elbow. When she peeled the cotton material down the other arm, a chunk of skin from his elbow came with it. "Didn't you have anything better to do?" she muttered.

"Yeah, but now I'm too skinned up to do it."

His voice was close, low, and intimate. Only inches away from his bare chest, she was tempted to run her fingers through all that curly brown hair. His arms and chest were a little lighter than his hands, neck, and face, but not much. Then she looked closer. The man was covered with fine dust. He didn't need a washbasin, he needed a water trough. "I'll wash your cuts. You can take care of the rest."

"That's no fun."

"You don't deserve any fun for scaring me half to death."

"Sorry, sugar. I used to be pretty good at bustin' broncs, but I guess I'm out of practice."

She pointed to a chair, and he gladly sat down, leaning his head against the high back. Wetting a cloth in the water, she gingerly cleaned the blood away from a small cut on his cheekbone and wiped the dust from his face. "You don't need practice. You need to stay off unbroken horses."

"Bossy woman." He rested his hand at her waist. "I don't know, I may take some convincing." She met his gaze. "I seem to remember a method of persuasion that works well."

"Lean forward so I can clean your shoulder." Her order came out less commanding and sharp than she wanted it to, but at least she didn't completely melt at his reminder of their first kisses. When he obeyed, she realized she had made a mistake. He was much too close. As she bent over his shoulder to see what she was doing, he turned his face toward hers. His breath was warm on her neck.

"You haven't been sleeping well," he murmured.

"I've been sleeping fine," she lied. How could she with him in the next room? Only a thin wall separated them. And his bed squeaked. It would be worse now that she knew how he looked without a shirt.

"You've been tossing and turning a lot." She glanced at him, but her denial died on her lips when she saw the warm tenderness in his eyes. "Your bed squeaks," he whispered.

"So does yours." Her face turned bright red, and he grinned.

"Been listenin'?"

"It's hard not to."

"Yeah, I know." Out of the corner of his eye, he saw Addie come to the kitchen door and look their way. She quickly moved away from the door with a wide grin. "Want to go for a moonlight drive tonight?"

"You're going to be too sore to go anywhere." She stepped back. "Hold your elbow up here." When he did she made a face. "I think you'd better soak that one. It's full of dirt." He leaned up, dipping the cut in the water with a grimace. "Hurt?"

"Stings, but that's all right. Wash it out good. I don't want to die of lockjaw."

She shuddered. "Morgan, please don't ride those horses again."

He forgot about trying to wangle a kiss. Her soft, heartfelt entreaty was all the persuasion he needed. "I won't. I'll leave that to the youngsters."

"Thank you." She leaned down, touching her lips gently to his. When she raised her head, he stared up at her. For a heartbeat, she thought she saw love in his eyes.

His lips formed a silent whistle. "Remind me to let you do the kissin' more often."

She merely smiled. She had enjoyed it, too, although she thought an equal exchange was best. "Let me wash your elbow now. I'm sorry. It's going to hurt."

It did, but he was very brave and only "ouched" and complained five or six times. Then he held it up for her to kiss—on a clean, unwounded spot—and she complied. They went through the same routine with the other elbow, but when he suggested she fix his sore knee, she declined, telling him he would have to tend to it himself. Then she made him wash the dust off his chest and arms, threatening to throw the basin of water at him if he didn't. With the dirt gone, she could see a definite line along his neck and throat where his shirt collar went and his tan stopped. Another line ran around his wrists, separating his dark brown hands from the lighter skin of his arms.

He went to his bedroom and changed clothes, examining his knee carefully. It was bruised and swollen, but it didn't appear too damaged. It would be stiff and sore for a few days, but he'd had far worse. By the time they finished supper, however, he deeply regretted having stepped into that corral. He hurt in places he hadn't known could hurt, but he didn't complain much; otherwise Lacy would never let him live it down.

Joshua and Serena stopped by for a few minutes after dinner, but they were working on plans for enlarging their house, so they didn't stay long. Morgan sat in one of the big, overstuffed chairs, with his feet propped up on a footstool, watching Jacob, Addie, Lacy, and Charity play a game of dominoes. Seeing them all together, laughing, teasing, and competing in high-spirited fun, he didn't know how Jacob could miss Charity's kinship to the family.

The longer he observed them, the more he believed his

uncle suspected who she was. When the others were absorbed in the game, Jacob studied her face, his eyes searching, questioning. Once, when the other three were in the midst of a cheerful argument over a play, Charity gazed at Jacob with such undisguised love that Morgan silently begged his uncle to look at her. That was when he decided to help her, to think of some way to force Jacob's hand.

He closed his eyes and thought about the problem for a while. Near the time Addie was declared domino champion for the evening, he had come up with a plan, one guaranteed to make a woman's father object in righteous indignation.

He caught Charity's hand as she walked by and pulled her down to sit on the wide arm of the chair. "Sugar, I was thinkin' I might take you down to Tom Green County so you could see the start of the roundup. Would you like that?"

He expected her to consider it and decline since it would take her away from Jacob. She couldn't very well talk to her father about their relationship if she wasn't there. He glanced at Jacob. Sure enough, his face looked like a thundercloud.

"I'd love to go. It would make a wonderful article to add to the series. I've been listening to Lacy and the cowboys talk about it ever since I got here, and I'm sure my imagination doesn't do it justice. Would we go with Lacy and the others?"

He nodded.

"You can take the buggy," said Addie, beaming at them. "Even if Charity knew how to ride, it wouldn't be smart for her to go that far on horseback."

Lacy smiled in approval. "It would be fun for you to go along, and taking the buggy wouldn't cause any problems. We'll be moving slow so the horses won't tire out before the roundup starts. You'd better take lots of pencils and paper." He grinned and winked at Morgan. "I can just see her now when she catches sight of three or four hundred cowboys all in one place, gettin' ready to ride out on one of the biggest roundups in the history of Texas. There may not be anything like it ever again."

"It's no place for a lady." Jacob's stern voice silenced the others—for about half a second.

"Don't be silly. There are bound to be other lady visitors at the ranch, and I'm sure Charity can stay at the main house. It's not as if she would be camping out with the cowboys." Addie patted her husband's arm.

"She would be on the way down." Jacob clearly was not pleased.

"Morgan and Lacy will look after me, and your men would never do anything to offend me. They always treat me with the utmost respect." Charity smiled at Jacob, too excited about the trip to realize what Morgan was trying to do.

Jacob glared at Morgan. "And what about on the way back?"

"No cowboys. It would just be the two of us." He let the statement hang in the air, measuring his uncle's reaction. Jacob glanced at Charity and Morgan's clasped hands, and his own fingers curled into a fist. Morgan waited for him to say she couldn't go, intending to suggest that the rest of them leave the room and let Charity and Jacob hash it out. He never got the chance.

"Well, by that time Charity would know how to help him set up camp," Addie said, "and you know Morgan will take good care of her. If she can't be safe with a deputy sheriff, who would she be safe with? They'll do just fine—as long as you do the cookin', Morgan. This gal's biscuits are hard as rocks." Addie winked at Charity and smiled lovingly at the two of them, obviously determined to play the matchmaker, yet trusting Morgan completely to behave himself.

He was sorely afraid her faith was misplaced. He had a feeling his idea wasn't so good after all.

"But she's a fair hand at washin' the dishes. I think it's a fine idea. Otherwise, this roundup might never get recorded in history. Oh, Charity, just think of the pictures you'll be able to draw. We'll have to get up in the morning and decide what you should take. You'll need comfortable clothes and sturdy shoes."

Morgan watched Jacob. When he glanced at his wife,

pain filled his eyes. Looking at Charity, the pain deepened. He appeared confused and bewildered, but neither of the women noticed. They were too busy making plans.

"And don't forget your Cashmere Bouquet soap and some good cold cream. Traveling all day in the sun and air will dry out your skin somethin' awful."

Jacob turned to Morgan. Anger instantly overshadowed all other emotions. "I want to see you outside. Now." He spun on his heel and stormed out the back door.

As he struggled to stand, Morgan glanced at Charity and Addie. They hadn't noticed Jacob's anger or his departure. Lacy caught his eye, his expression concerned. Morgan shrugged and limped out the door, thinking he'd made a big mistake.

"You've got no business taking her down there."

"She'll be all right. You know the men will go out of their way to be polite."

"It's not the men I'm worried about, and you know it. You can't keep your hands off her. How many nights do you think you can spend alone with her without things gettin' out of control?"

Morgan had been wondering the same thing for the last few minutes. Getting bucked off that horse must have knocked what little sense he possessed right out his ears.

When he didn't answer right away, Jacob sighed heavily and leaned on the porch railing. "She's lonely, son. Loneliness eats at a woman just like it does a man. Maybe it's even worse for them. They're made to be held, to be loved and treated with tenderness. And when a woman needs a man, when she needs someone to show her a little caring, it's easy to take advantage of her. Even if you don't mean to."

"I think I can handle it."

"It's hard to turn away from temptation, especially when you have feelings for the woman."

Morgan knew his uncle was right. Being alone on the trail for several days and nights was an open invitation to trouble. He wished he could reassure Jacob, give him his word that he wouldn't make love to Charity, but it was a promise he couldn't make. He wanted to believe he would do what was right, but Charity wasn't a young girl. She was a desirable, passionate woman, and if she gave him much encouragement, he wasn't sure he had the willpower to resist.

Besides, if he promised not to take advantage of her, Jacob would have no reason to worry. It wouldn't push him into admitting that Charity was his daughter. He leaned against the railing beside his uncle and shrugged. "I don't intend to seduce her."

"What you intend and what you wind up doin' are often a whole lot different."

"She's a grown woman, Jacob. What if she decides to seduce me?"

"She'd better not."

*Spoken like a father.* Morgan bet Jacob had silently added something about tanning her backside if she did. "Like you said, she's alone. She has no family, no one to answer to . . . no one to care."

"Well, I care."

"Why?"

Jacob practically sputtered. "Because she's a good, decent woman," he said finally. "She's a good friend, and I don't want to see her hurt. I don't want to see you hurt, either." His voice dropped to a ragged whisper. "If you make love to a woman like Charity without benefit of marriage vows, you'll regret it. And if you go your separate ways, it will be painful for both of you."

"That sounds like experience talkin'," Morgan said quietly.

"It is. And it's not a lesson you ever forget."

Morgan waited, hoping Jacob would open up more, but he didn't. "I'll keep what you said in mind. I'll do my best not to disappoint you." He started to walk away, but stopped and looked back at his uncle. "Where does Addie keep the liniment?"

"Top left-hand side of that old pie safe by the bathtub."

Morgan found the bottle and thought about how Charity's soft hands would feel smoothing the liquid along his skin, how nice it would be to have her rub away the pain in his shoulders and back. Then he thought about thin walls and squeaky beds and the kind of dreams he'd have if she touched him like that. With a wistful sigh, he went looking for Addie.

# Chapter
# Twenty-one

Charity had been told what to expect at the VP Ranch in Tom Green County, but even her vivid imagination had not stretched far enough. The Double J outfit attending the roundup consisted of thirty men, a remuda of one hundred and fifty saddle horses, and a chuck wagon pulled by six mules and loaded with all the food and gear necessary to support these men and a few others for over a month. She had tried to envision this picture multiplied several times, but as they came up over a rise and saw the encampment, she realized her vision had been lacking.

She counted ten different outfits that had already set up camp, with the men lounging near the chuck wagons or wandering around visiting with friends from other ranches. Hundreds of horses grazed nearby, loosely segregated by ranch. They weren't in corrals, but each herd generally stayed together. As she watched, another outfit with a dozen cowboys rode across the valley from the opposite direction. Their remuda was smaller than the Double J's, but their chuck wagon appeared to be just as loaded.

From the left came a single rider driving a string of four saddle horses and a packhorse, and from the right a trio of men rode in with their packs and small herd of horses. Those cowboys, and others like them, represented the smaller cattlemen whose holdings weren't large enough to justify the great expense of a chuck wagon. Occasionally the lone rider would be the rancher himself.

It was an exciting, boisterous concoction of thundering

hooves, whinnying horses, creaking wagons, clanging pots, blustering cooks, laughter, shouts, and even singing.

Morgan drew Biscuit to a halt. Princess and Cactus were tied to the back of the buggy. He had alternated the buggy horses each day so neither one would get too tired. When Charity grew bored of simply sitting, he had ridden Cactus while she handled the buggy. He surveyed the scene in front of them, looked at Charity, and grinned. "Shut your mouth, darlin', or you're gonna catch flies."

She looked at him and smiled, then surprised him by leaning over and giving him a lingering kiss. For most of the trip he had kept ahead of Lacy and the others by about fifteen minutes to avoid eating dust, but he had quickly realized that this also afforded them the only privacy they were going to get until they started home. He had taken advantage of it on occasion, but this was the first time she had initiated the kiss.

"What was that for?" he asked with a pleased smile, slipping his arm around her.

"For bringing me here. I wouldn't have missed it for anything."

"Then you'd better pay up twice."

"You'd better set the brake." She laughed at his shocked expression. "Well, it's the last chance we'll have. I figured you'd want to make it a good one."

"Yes, ma'am." He set the brake and looped the reins over the iron arm of the seat. The top of the buggy was raised to protect Charity's skin from the afternoon sun, and it conveniently sheltered them on three sides. He gathered her in his arms and touched her lips in a soft kiss filled with promises of sweetness and delight. When he finally raised his head, he smiled tenderly. "Think that'll hold you for a while?"

She nodded and leaned her head against his shoulder. "I think I'm becoming addicted."

He chuckled softly. "Me, too." When he untied the reins and released the brake, she sat up straight, ready for a big adventure and a few nights' sleep in a real bed. She had gained a new sympathy for anyone who had to sleep on the ground.

"And yes, I remember the conditions. I'm not to go anywhere away from the ranch house unless you or Lacy goes with me. When I'm in the cowboy camp, I stay right by your side."

"And I promise that if you see something interesting, all you have to do is let me know, and if it's safe, we'll go look at it." He smiled, remembering that when he laid down the rules, she had added a few of her own. "I'll bring you down here bright and early in the morning and let you stay as long as you want to at night—unless I decide it's not proper or safe."

"Only not safe. I'll decide if it's proper or not. I'm a big girl, Morgan."

"Too big for your britches." He gave her the once-over. "Everything else looks just right to me. If I see something is going to get too raunchy, Miss Know-it-all, I'm gettin' you out of there."

"You say git, and I git, huh?"

"That's right."

"I'll think about it if and when the situation comes up." She smiled smugly, knowing she was getting his goat. He was such a stuffed shirt sometimes that she couldn't resist teasing him.

"Don't think on it too long, sweetheart, or you might find yourself thrown over my shoulder like a sack of flour and hauled out of there."

"You wouldn't dare."

"Try me."

They continued to bicker playfully as he drove up to the ranch house. Morgan had wired the VP Ranch before they left to make sure it would be acceptable to bring Charity. Ranch Manager Kenny Mayes, who was in charge of the roundup, had immediately sent a telegram inviting her to be their guest. They freshened up and visited at the ranch house for a while, chatting with a few folks from Paint Rock who had come out to see all the commotion.

Mr. Mayes understood why Charity was there and gave

her permission to go anywhere she wanted. "There might not be any man here who would cause you harm or be rude to you, Miss Charity, but since they come from so many different spreads, I can't personally vouch for them. Just to be safe, I have to ask you not to go anywhere near the men without Morgan or Lacy or one of the other Double J men accompanyin' you. Our door is always open, so feel free to come and go as you like. You're welcome to eat here at the house or down at the camp, whichever suits your fancy at the time. Just show up if you're hungry."

About four o'clock, Morgan drove her down to where Lacy and his men had set up camp. Being in charge of the Double J outfit was an important job for one as young as Lacy, but he had been trained well. His father and uncle had taught him ranching from the time he could walk. His men knew that for all his fun-loving ways, the ranch came first. He had learned from the best and usually made the right decisions. When he didn't, he took full responsibility. He had earned the men's respect, and they gave it, obeying his command just as they would Jacob or Joshua's.

For the next couple of days, while the men relaxed, Lacy would join the other bosses in conference with Mr. Mayes. Plans would be perfected, and he would learn what would be required of him and his men. During the evenings, however, he was free to enjoy himself like everybody else. He met Charity with a big grin.

"I think everyone in camp has heard you're here, and I swear they all want to meet you, or at least look at you. Shall we take a stroll? I know of fifteen or sixteen cooks who have invited you to sample their fare."

Charity laughed. "I heard that everybody walks around and samples the cooking."

"True. But you got special invitations. They've been coming in from every outfit in the camp ever since we got here." His expression grew serious. "Some of these men live miles away from the nearest town. If they see a female face at all, it's usually the owner or manager's wife. You're going to make the next few days real special for them." He surprised her by putting his arm around her shoulders and giving her a hug. "I'm glad you came, Charity."

"I'm glad I did, too." She smiled up at him. Robust singing began from the men nearby, and the bellowed "Tribute to the Trail" quickly spread throughout the camp. The volume would have made a sinner sit up and take notice, while the tune—or varying tunes—would have made a choir director cry.

"The frivolity has begun, ma'am." Lacy turned and grinned at Morgan and, with a gallant sweep of his arm, offered him the privilege of escorting Charity.

Morgan didn't need any prodding. He'd been jealous of Lacy when he hugged her, which should have made him feel silly since the man was her brother. Only Lacy didn't know that. As he stepped toward her, Lacy met him and leaned close to his ear.

"It was just a brotherly hug, Morgan."

Shocked, Morgan stared at him. How did he know?

Lacy shrugged. "Well, she seems like a sister to me, at least the way I think one would be. We're real good friends, nothin' more."

*That's what you think.* Morgan realized he would be very glad when Charity's secret was out in the open. Maybe she was right. Maybe the hurt it initially caused would be healed by the love she brought to the family. He sure hoped so.

They strolled from camp to camp, speaking to the men they knew, introducing themselves to the ones they didn't, sampling fried steak, biscuits, beans, or stew whenever the food was offered, which was at every chuck wagon. The chorus died down after a couple of songs, although here and there musicians, some with talent and some without, continued to serenade those around them. They came upon poker games and discussions on everything from baseball to politics to religion.

Everywhere they went, the reaction of the men was basically the same as soon as they caught sight of Charity—awed silence until someone, usually the cook, broke the ice. Hushed murmurs followed as they admired her beauty and expressed amazement that such a fine lady would pay them a visit. Sometimes a man who hadn't learned the Western code of respect for a lady, or perhaps didn't care, commented on his desire to get to know her better. One piercing look from Morgan quelled his interest immediately.

Once, when she heard such a comment but Morgan didn't, another man's words made her glow with pleasure. The cowboy looked at his friend as if he were the dumbest man alive. "You know who she's with? That's Morgan Kaine, deputy sheriff from up in Mitchell County and an ex-Ranger. See the way he looks at her? The way he stays real close and touches her like he's got the right and nobody else had better try? You're droolin' over his woman, boy, and he ain't gonna like it. You don't want to mess with him."

The other man gulped and murmured, "Beg your pardon, ma'am."

They laid the foundation that night so she could work fairly unhampered the next few days. She wanted to record life as it was in the camp and encouraged the men not to let her presence hamper their festivities. They obliged her, within reason. Rough language or stories, even those only slightly impolite, ended abruptly when she stepped within hearing range, and the practical jokers in the bunch felt it was their duty to restrict their pranks to milder forms of fun than in the past. In turn, Charity left the camp early the next two nights, so the men could completely relax.

With Morgan constantly at her side, she roamed about the camp at will, talking to the cowboys and bosses—men with names like Chunk, Boots, Tubb, and Burr—writing down much of what they had to say, and drawing innumerable pictures. She recorded horse races ridden between jammed rows of onlookers, both on foot and mounted, who closed in behind the racers as they passed, yelling and shooting their pistols.

Another favorite pastime was the convening of the kangaroo court. The will of the high-muck-a-muck of the kangaroo court ruled the camp, with jurisdiction over all minor offenses, such as fistfights and cheating at mumblety-peg, poker, fuzzy-wuzzy, chuck-a-luck, seven-up, and the telling of inferior twice-told yarns. Lacy told Charity that the minor offenses also included manslaughter committed before or during the war and wife desertion, but she didn't believe him, especially since Morgan was trying very hard not to laugh.

The offense punished the most often was that of poor storytelling. Good storytellers were camp favorites, but woe to the man who told a yarn that wasn't up to their exacting standards or was something that most of the crowd had already heard. The end of his tale would be greeted by dead silence, and he'd know he was doomed. Anyone accused of a crime was convicted. The high-muck-a-muck usually sentenced the offender to being "throwed in the creek with a two-hundred-pound rock tied around his neck." After protests and pleadings from the man's friends, the rock part would be omitted from the sentence, and the man would be tossed in the creek. If he resisted, he would probably hit the water more than once.

Contrary to the rule of fun, the court didn't handle all the arguments. Some, mostly over poker games, almost became shootouts. Morgan didn't try to stop them because he was more concerned about getting Charity to safety, and the conflict usually ended anyway when the men realized she was present.

One argument was more heated than the others, due to long-standing animosity between the participants. Morgan was aware of their hatred and knew it would probably end one day in bloodshed. He was desperate to get Charity away from the situation. He tugged on her arm. She didn't budge, only kept sketching furiously. "Come on, Charity, let's get out of here. These two have been workin' on trouble ever since they got here."

"Not yet. You make me leave every time. I want to see what happens." She pulled her arm away, ignoring his angry scowl. "I need to get this for the story."

"What you're gonna get is a bullet. Come on."

"Don't worry so much. With all the arguments we've seen, nobody's done any actual shooting."

"These two might. They've hated each other for years. I want you to leave now."

Charity didn't hear him. She was concentrating intently on what was being said by the other two men. She wanted to remember every word for her article—well, almost every word. A few were a bit coarse for the *Century*. Suddenly Morgan stepped in front of her, bent down, hoisted her over his shoulder, and quickly started to move out of the camp. "Morgan! Put me down!"

Her shriek caused every head to turn in their direction, including the men involved in the potential gunfight. She kicked her legs and slapped his back with her drawing pad, dropping her pencil. He didn't slow down.

"Morgan Kaine, you brute. Put me down!"

He grabbed her legs and feet, pinning them to his chest and stomach so she couldn't kick him. "Be still, you stubborn woman."

The cowboys around them guffawed as she kept wiggling and pounding on his back with one hand. Her hat fell off, and when the pins jiggled from her hair, it cascaded in a riot of dark waves across the back of Morgan's thighs. The laughter faded. A young cowboy picked up her hat and, trailing along behind them, handed it to her with a timid smile. She shoved her hair out of her eyes, smiled at the boy, took the hat, and looked to see if the altercation had ended. The two men were staring at her and Morgan as if they weren't quite sure whether to continue their fight or not. She smiled at them and shook her head. "G-good n-night," she called, being jostled with Morgan's every step. "S-see you in t-the morn-ing."

Morgan stepped away from the camp fire's light into the darkness. His pace slowed, but he didn't put her down. He kept walking toward the buggy. Her stomach was getting sore, and it was too hard to talk, so she tried a tactic she had read about once in a novel. She tugged the back of his shirt from his pants and trailed a thick, silky strand of hair back and forth across his low back. He stopped abruptly. Bending forward, he lowered her feet to the ground with a thump.

When he straightened, he glared at her. "You can't put

yourself in danger like that, Charity. It's got to stop. If you don't have enough sense to get out of harm's way, at least let me do my job and protect you."

She dropped her drawing pad and hat on the ground, resting her hands on her hips. "You've been doing your job too well. Anytime there's the tiniest squabble, you hustle me away as if I'm a child. I can take care of myself. I can judge when things are getting out of hand, when I need to run or hide."

"When bullets start flying, it's too late."

"Morgan, there hasn't been any gunplay the whole time we've been here." She didn't count the shots fired in the air at the races. "It was just a little disagreement over a poker game. It ended like all the rest—peaceably."

"Usually half of those little disagreements end with a man dead or close to it. This one had nothing to do with a poker game. Those two have been at each other's throats for over a year, ever since Jack ran off with Henry's bride-to-be. They hate each other's guts. The only reason they didn't shoot it out last night was that the cook hit Henry over the head and knocked him cold."

"Well, why didn't you tell me?"

"I tried to tell you, but you were too caught up in your confounded story to listen. You ignored me."

"Oh." She frowned, trying to remember what he had said. She had to admit she hadn't paid very close attention. "I didn't ignore you intentionally. I just didn't want to miss anything that was going on. I guess you have to be more insistent."

"I think I was." He tried not to notice the way the moonlight danced in her hair.

"You could call it that." She smiled and walked her fingers up his chest, teasing his chin with her fingertip. "I'm sorry, Morgan. I'll try to listen better and take your advice."

Every night on the trail he had watched her brush her long hair and braid it into one thick braid. Every night he had ached to run his fingers through it, to bury his face in its fragrant softness. She looked up at him with smiling eyes, her hair loose and gently blowing in the wind, and his anger seeped away. He combed his fingers through her hair, curling it around his hands. When he spoke, his voice was ragged. "I was scared half to death that you'd be hurt."

His kiss was deep and desperate, born of fear, need, and confusion. A part of him wanted to push her away, to shield himself from caring, so he wouldn't be afraid for her, couldn't be hurt. Yet another part wanted her, needed her, loved her, would die without her.

She was shaken by the intensity of his kiss but not frightened by it. When he buried his face in her hair, she clung to him. "What is it? What's wrong?"

He shook his head and pressed his lips gently against her neck, sliding his hands down her back and holding her tight. A storm raged within him, a torrent of conflicting emotions. There was only one thing of which he was certain—if he had any sense, he'd send her home by stagecoach.

# Chapter
## Twenty-two

On the third night at the VP Ranch, everyone bedded down early because they would be leaving the next morning. Lacy came up to the ranch house to see Charity in case he missed her in the confusion the next day. They walked out into the yard arm in arm, while Morgan sat on the porch steps.

"We'll probably be gone a month to six weeks. Will you be at the ranch when I get back?"

"I don't know. I'd like to stay that long, but I don't want to wear out my welcome."

Lacy draped his arm across her shoulders. "I don't think that's goin' to happen. You're like one of the family." He felt her tense, and he knew the time had come for some questions to be answered. "Maybe I'm a little off on that. Do you seem like part of the family because you are?"

"Yes."

He drew in an unsteady breath. He had wondered about it from the third or fourth day after her arrival at the ranch—the way she looked at Jacob when his attention was elsewhere, the way his father studied her, and the way Addie watched them both. It hadn't been hard to see her resemblance to Jacob or some of the little mannerisms that were so much the same as his father's, but he hadn't been sure if those things were real or imagined. When Morgan had been so shocked by his comment about a brotherly hug, he figured he hadn't imagined them. "I'm your brother?"

"Yes," she whispered, thankful that he hadn't made the

distinction of only being her half brother. It was more reassuring somehow.

He couldn't believe his father had kept her existence a secret all these years. Had he lost track of her? Had he been married before? He dismissed that idea immediately. "Why didn't he tell us about you?"

"Because he didn't know. My mother was Will Davenport's older sister. From what I can gather, she swore him to secrecy, too. I wasn't even sure whether Joshua or Jacob was my father until Joshua and I talked." She told him about finding the chest and the things it held, as much of the story as she knew and what she had done so far.

"I set Mama's chest out on the dresser before I left. I didn't have the courage to put his picture and the letters in it. They're in my drawer. I don't think Addie would peek inside, but she might simply open it to admire the box, and I didn't want her to stumble across those things. I'm hoping he might see the chest and recognize it."

"I think he knows, Charity, or at least he has a strong suspicion. That's why he got so mad at Morgan when he suggested bringing you down here."

"I didn't know he got angry with Morgan."

Lacy smiled and ruffled her hair. "That's because you and Mother were so busy planning the trip. Dad was fit to be tied. He's worried sick what might happen between you and Morgan on the way home. He was acting just like a father, telling Morgan you couldn't come. I wasn't tryin' to eavesdrop, but I heard part of the conversation in passing. I can only think of a few times that I've seen him so mad. Poor Dad, no wonder he's been a little edgy lately."

"Do you think I was wrong to look for him?"

"No. It's right that you should find each other." He squeezed her shoulder. "And I like having a sister. My folks had a little girl, but she died before I was born."

Charity had seen her photograph, taken when the girl was about a year old. "I can't take her place. I wouldn't want to try."

"No, but once the shock wears off, I think they'll feel blessed at having another daughter. My mother may not have given birth to you, but you know how she is. She'll love you like her own. I think she already does."

Charity turned and hugged him. "I hope so, Lacy. I didn't come here to cause problems. I didn't come here for money either. I want you to know that. Mother left me well situated."

"Good. Maybe you can give me a loan." He laughed and hugged her again. "Well, sis, I've got to get back down to camp. I'm glad you told me. It will all work out, you'll see."

"I hope you're right." They said their good-byes, and Charity promised to write him if she had to leave. They vowed to keep in touch no matter what happened with Addie and Jacob.

Morgan walked out into the yard and stood beside her as she watched Lacy ride off into the black night. Light from the kerosene lamps inside the parlor shone through the window, but they were in the shadows. "He knows?"

"Yes."

"Looks like he didn't mind."

"I think he's glad." She suddenly felt drained, sad, and surprisingly close to tears.

"You don't sound very happy."

"I wish he didn't have to leave tomorrow."

He put his arm around her. "He'll be back."

"But will I be there? I wish everything were settled. I'm so tired of secrets and worrying about it all."

"Then talk to Jacob when we get home. I'm sure he knows, honey. He's just having a hard time accepting it."

"You didn't really want to bring me here, did you?"

*Uh-oh.* "I thought if I suggested it, Jacob would start acting like a father and everything would come out in the open. Actually he did protest like a father would, only it wasn't in the open. I was a little fuzzy from bouncin' off the ground that day. I didn't think you'd want to come. Didn't figure you'd want to leave him. Then when you jumped at the chance and got so excited about it, I couldn't back down. I'm glad we came. It's been a pleasure to see you enjoy it so much."

"I have enjoyed it, most of it, at least. Can't say that I

liked being hauled around on your shoulder. For such a muscular man, you've got pointy bones."

"Knobby knees, too."

"I believe it." She giggled when he tried to tickle her, and wiggled away from him. "And I bet you've got corns and bunions."

"Maybe a corn or two." Laughing, he caught her. "How about you?"

"Nope. Just cold feet."

He put an arm around her, mindful of others inside the house who might come out at any time. Even an embrace would be unwise. "I know a way to get them warm."

"Oh?" Her experience was limited but her imagination wasn't. "How?"

"Wear thick wool socks."

Morgan and Charity went down to the outfit before dawn so she could be part of the excitement as the men broke camp and set out. When they arrived, it first appeared that everything was in a turmoil, but as Charity watched, she realized the men knew exactly what they were doing. It was basically the same in every outfit. They first rolled and tied up their bedrolls, then rushed over to the chuck wagon and grabbed a tin plate, cup, knife, and fork and helped themselves to fried steak, a thick chunk of bread, and hot, black coffee. Morgan and Charity waited until the Double J crew all had their breakfast before they filled their plates.

While the men gobbled down their food, the horse wrangler for each outfit brought their remuda up fairly close to the chuck wagon. Some of the men formed a loose circle around the horses. Standing about thirty-five feet apart, men stretched their lariats between them, forming a temporary corral.

"Usually only one or two men in the outfit will do the roping," explained Morgan. "Someone with a gentle throw. They don't want to spook the horses with too many ropes flying at once. One spooked horse could cause the rest to break and run. Every day each man tells the roper which horse he wants, and he'll get it for him. Once ridden, a horse won't be used again for four or five days, so it can rest up from the hard work."

They watched as one by one the men picked up their horses and began saddling them. "Let's go watch from the buggy so you can see more of the camp." When Morgan drove back a little way to give them a wider view, she understood why he had suggested it. Seeing three hundred men mounting their horses within minutes of each other was impressive, but watching about forty or fifty of those horses try to dismount their riders was hilarious. They pitched and bucked and caused general mayhem until the cowboys brought them under control. "Some of those horses do fine once they're out working, but they have to be reeducated every morning."

Around the chuck wagons, as the cooks put away the dishes, and the bedrolls were thrown on the wagons, half the chuck-wagon mules were objecting to the whole situation. Jingling trace chains and cuss words filled the air as each contrary mule took two or three able-bodied men to get it harnessed to a wagon.

Suddenly the cowboys took off, most of them riding past the buggy, doffing their hats or touching the brim in a salute to Charity, before galloping off across the prairie with a wild Texas whoop. Lacy stopped for a minute, hopped off his horse, and gave her a hug. "Be there when I get back." He looked at Morgan and smiled, but his words were spoken with all seriousness. "I'm depending on you to make sure she stays. Take good care of her, and mind your manners on the way home."

A hint of a smile touched Morgan's eyes. "You're sounding like a brother."

"Yep. Kinda like the role." With a smile and wink at Charity, he ran along beside the horse Indian-style before leaping on its back with a yell. Charity laughed and wiped the tears from her cheeks with the heel of her hand. Morgan handed her a clean handkerchief and patted her shoulder.

The chuck wagons fell in line behind the man assigned to pilot them to the first night's camp. They, too, drove past Morgan and Charity, the men calling their good wishes and bidding her a fond farewell. Deeply touched by their cowboy gallantry, tears stung Charity's eyes once more, but she held them at bay. After the last wagon rolled away from camp, the remudas fell in behind them, a majestic herd of over a thousand horses. The young horse wranglers stayed near the chuck wagons or drifted behind the herd, encouraging the horses along if they lagged behind. The creak of the wagons, tinkling of bells, and rattling of hooves mingled with a farewell refrain sung by the cooks and wranglers to the old campground and the pretty woman they were leaving behind.

As the entourage disappeared amid churning dust, and the sounds of their departure floated away on the wind, Charity wiped her eyes and blew her nose again. "You didn't tell me I was going to cry like a baby."

"There's nothing wrong with honest tears and the feelings that go with them." Morgan felt unusually sentimental himself. It had been a long time since he'd been on a roundup. In some ways he wished he could have gone along. "They do depart in style. They're excited and anxious now, but before long they'll be wishin' they were home and the work was done. A lot of them don't know what they're heading into, but I've been there. It's some of the roughest country in all of Texas, and I doubt if there's much more than a cup of water between here and the Devil's River. They've got a mighty hard drive ahead of them."

He glanced at the trail of dust moving farther off in the distance. "There were some boys who rode out of here—too young to shave more'n once every month or two—but they'll come back men. Some of them will stay with it the rest of their lives, and some will hightail it back to the farm or the city, wherever they came from. Either way, they can say they've been a cowboy, and they'll say it with pride. They'll have those memories for a lifetime."

"I believe you miss it."

"Yeah, sometimes I do." He tapped Biscuit on the back with the reins and turned the buggy toward Mitchell County. They had thanked their host and said their good-byes the night before.

"Morgan, what happened to your father's ranch?"

"Mother sold everything—even his clothes—a week after he died."

"Didn't some of it belong to you?"

"The ranch should have been mine, but Dad was so deep in debt that selling it was the only way to pay the creditors. Mother took the rest of the money and left Austin."

"She didn't leave you anything?"

"Twenty dollars and her thanks for setting her free."

"Oh, Morgan, how horrible."

"I was too full of guilt and grief and anger to care. I didn't want anything of theirs." He touched the watch in his vest pocket. "Addie bought some of my father's things and saved them for me. I was finally ready to take them a few years ago."

"Do you ever see your mother?"

"No. I think she's living in California. I haven't heard from her in years, and to be honest, I don't care if I ever do."

She laid her hand on his arm. "It's understandable."

He glanced at her hand, comforted by her touch. With each passing day—sometimes with each passing moment— he grew more aware of how much she meant to him.

"Jacob, are you sure you don't want to come to town with us?" Addie tied her bonnet strings beneath her chin.

"No, you go on with Josh and Serena and have a good time. I've got some things to do around here." He stretched his arms above his head. "I thought I'd take a ride and see how widespread the rain was last night. We've got some puddles down by the barn, but I want to see if we got any over at the bluff."

"Well, you take care crossin' that river. I don't want you to get over there and not be able to get back home." She smiled, knowing he needed some time alone. Every so often he needed to ride off by himself for a while. He'd always been that way.

He'd been fidgety since Lacy and the men left. It was Lacy's first time at running the roundup crew entirely on his own, but she knew Jacob had confidence in him. Of course, he worried about something happening to him; that was only natural. She did, too. But they both knew he had grown up and was ready for the responsibility.

She suspected most of his worry was over Charity. Jacob had taken a powerful liking to that girl, which suited Addie fine. She adored her and prayed every night that Charity and Morgan would find happiness with each other. Charity was strong and independent, but she had a heart of gold. She was the right woman for Morgan. She'd give him enough of a challenge to keep him interested, but she would also shower him with the love and affection he so desperately needed. As for Morgan, well, Addie had always thought the sun rose and set in that boy.

"I won't cross the river if it looks like it's rising fast." Jacob grinned and dropped a peck on his wife's cheek. "I'm not as dumb as I look."

"Never thought you were." Addie grinned back. "Want anything from town?"

"What do you think?"

"Yes, I'll bring you some taffy. And a box of chocolate bars, but only if you share them. I don't want to have to turn the house upside down every time I want one."

"Now, honey, I only put them in the springhouse so they wouldn't melt."

"That was last summer, and it was a good idea. I'm talkin' about the box I brought home in January."

"I just put them in the desk so they'd be handy when I was workin'."

"And conveniently forgot to tell anyone else." She smiled and tweaked his nose. "You old scalawag. You were saving them for yourself."

"Then get a dozen boxes. We can afford it."

"Braggin' again." She laughed and hurried down the porch steps.

Jacob waited on the porch until the surrey was out of sight. There were only a couple of men still at the ranch, and they were busy. He had the house to himself and wouldn't be disturbed. Turning, he walked purposefully down the dog trot and opened Charity's bedroom door. He had been waiting for this moment since Morgan and Charity drove off to the roundup.

Her desk was near the door, but only drawings and writing supplies were on the top of it. There might be something in the drawer, but he would check it later. He looked across the room at the dresser. Sitting in the center of it was the small walnut chest he had given Marion. It had been unique, made by a craftsman who never made two the same.

In his heart he had known Charity was his child, had suspected it from their first ride around the ranch. He'd seen Marion's smile in her smile, heard her laugh in Charity's laugh. The memories had been powerful, bringing back intense feelings that he had long thought buried. Marion had been his first love. On the day he gave her the chest, he had thought she would be his last.

Heart pounding, he crossed the room. There were two pictures of Charity's mother on the dresser—one of the woman he had known, one of the woman she had become. He picked up the one taken six months before he met her. He could still remember where it had sat on the mantel, next to the one of Marion and her late husband.

She had been so beautiful, so lonely. A bittersweet smile touched his lips. He had brought her joy when she had only sorrow. She danced with him, laughed with him, sang with him, made love with him. He couldn't believe she wanted him. He was so young. She couldn't believe he desired her, wanted to love her. She felt so old. During their night together, he gave her pleasure, heard her cry out in delight, and held her as he dreamed of their life together. But in the morning, she wept in shame and asked him to leave, never to return.

Swallowing a lump in his throat, he set the picture down on the dresser and picked up the other one. The years were kind to her. According to the date in one corner, the picture had been taken shortly before she died. She was still beautiful. He tipped the picture slightly toward the light, reading an inscription on a small white piece of paper tucked in with the photograph. *To my darling Charity, the joy of my life and my most precious gift. I bless your father for giving you to me.*

Joy and sorrow mingled in his heart, rising in a swell of emotion. A tear slid down his cheek. She had written those words for him. She knew her daughter would try to find him, and she reached out to him the only way she could. "Thank you, sweet Marion, for your forgiveness."

He opened the box and found only jewelry. When he searched the top dresser drawer, he found what he had been seeking, barely hidden beneath a stack of petticoats. He gazed at his picture, the one he had had taken especially for Marion. He read the note he had sent with the box. Oh, how grand he had felt buying it and having it delivered. He read Will's letter and immediately understood the efforts Charity must have gone through to find him.

Every time he looked into Charity's eyes, he had known. Now, at last, he accepted it. He put the picture and other things back in the drawer, laying them on top of the petticoats. He sensed that she had left them there for him to find; she might as well know that he had.

Jacob quietly left the house, saddled his favorite horse, and rode hard across the prairie. He crossed the river, which had risen about a foot, and galloped across the grassland to the ridge. Judging from the puddles, he knew it had rained even more there. That pleased him. There should be some green grass when Lacy and his men got the cattle home. It wouldn't be enough to last long, but it would be a good start.

He rode back to the river, noting that the water wasn't any deeper than when he had crossed earlier. That meant there hadn't been much rain to the northwest where the headwaters of the Colorado were. They might not have gotten any rain on their grazing land above the Caprock.

He spent most of the day riding over the ranch, thinking. Marion might have been his first love, but Addie had been his love of a lifetime. He might have sweet memories of Marion and still hold a tiny place for her in his heart, but his love for Addie filled the rest of it. He tried to think of a way to tell her about Charity, but he couldn't come up with any. No matter what he did, Addie was going to be deeply hurt.

He'd worked hard all their married life to be a good husband, sheltering her from pain every way he could. How could he intentionally hurt her? How could he tell her that after he met her, he had found another woman he thought he loved and had given her a child?

As much as he hated to do it, he decided his only choice would be to talk to Charity alone and ask her not to say anything to Addie or Lacy. In private, he would legally acknowledge her as his child and would promise to do all he could for her. She couldn't stay—maybe visit on occasion, but not live at the ranch and become part of the family. His heart ached at the thought, but he could see no other way. Addie was his soulmate, the woman God had given him to love and cherish all his days. *What if Charity marries Morgan?*

Focusing on Morgan and Charity's relationship, Jacob's thoughts whirled around in his head like a wasp caught inside the crown of his Stetson. The more he thought about the way they looked at each other, the worse he felt. Morgan was a good man, but confound it, he was spending night and day alone with Jacob's daughter. Jacob knew how it felt to be out under the stars alone with the woman you loved. He and Addie had come close to going too far more than once before they were married.

He rode back to the ranch house, rubbed down his horse, and fed and watered him. All the while he thought of Morgan and Charity alone on the trail. He should never have allowed her to go off with him. She might be a woman, but she was his daughter. He should have stepped in and shouldered his responsibilities. By the time Addie got home, he was in a sorry state.

They ate a light supper and retired to the parlor. She looked through the mail while he stared out the window. "Jacob, you might as well quit lookin' out that window. It's already dark. They're not going to get here this late."

"They could if Morgan pushed it."

"You don't even know that they've left."

"Well, they should have. The outfit likely rode out three or four days ago."

Addie shook her head. "You know as well as I do that yesterday was probably the earliest day for them to break camp. I doubt Charity would leave until it was over. They won't be home until tomorrow, if then."

"They'd darn well better be home tomorrow. He doesn't need to keep her out on the trail alone more than two nights."

Addie laughed. "Why are you gettin' so worked up?"

"Don't you remember how it was when we were courtin'? Tarnation, Addie, we had a heck of a time stopping once we got started. He'll have her bedded before she knows what's happening."

Addie shook her head. "I swear, Jacob, the way you're acting, a body would think you're her father."

Stunned, he stared at her and felt the color drain from his face. Her gaze locked with his, and he could no more hide the truth than he could out-and-out lie to her.

Her eyes grew wide, and the magazine she held slid from her hands to the floor. "Dear Lord, it's true," she whispered.

"You suspected?"

She nodded and looked away as quick tears formed. "Not at first." She swallowed the lump in her throat and drew in a harsh breath. "But you're alike in so many ways. I thought I was imagining it. I had hoped I was. Who was her mother?"

"Will Davenport's sister, Marion. It happened before you and I started courtin', honey." Jacob moved across the room and sat down beside her on the sofa, not touching, but close enough to do so if she let him.

"You got her pregnant and didn't marry her?" Incredulous, she looked at him. "How could you do such a thing?"

"I didn't know. Addie, I spent time with her for two weeks. One night we went to a dance, and when I took her home . . . I wound up stayin'." He raked his fingers through his hair. "She was a widow and terribly lonely. She was older than me, and I was real flattered that she found me attractive. Tarnation, Addie, when a man's that age, sometimes his body overrules his good sense. It was the only time we ever had sex."

"Where?"

"Galveston."

She sat perfectly still. A tear slid down her cheek. "Did you love her?" she asked softly.

He hesitated. "Yes, but not the way I love you, sweetheart. The feelings I had for her were like a little rosebud. What I feel for you is like that whole trellis on the porch filled with roses."

"Did you want to marry her?"

"For a while I did. Especially after spending the night with her."

"It must have been some night," she muttered.

Jacob cringed. "I can't deny that I cared for her, but there was a lot of guilt mixed up in my feelings, too. She was ashamed of what we had shared. She was a good woman, Addie. Not the kind to go to bed with a man without benefit of marriage, but her husband had been gone for two years, and she was mighty lonely."

She looked at him in surprise. "How old was she?"

"Thirty, I think. Maybe thirty-one. Old enough not to want to marry me when she was thinkin' clearly. After she sent me away that morning, I never saw or heard from her again."

"And you never knew about Charity?"

He shook his head. "Not until she came out here, and I started noticin' things about her that reminded me of myself and of Marion."

"Seems like you remember her well."

"Besides you, she was the only woman I ever cared about. The only one I ever spent more than a few hours with. I was surprised by the memories, honey. When we got married, I pretty much put her out of my mind. Oh, I thought about her every once in a while, but I just wondered how she was doin' and hoped she'd found a man she could love. I thought about her as an old friend, nothing more."

"Have you talked to Charity about it?"

"No." He explained about what he had found in Charity's room. "From what I can tell, she only knew my initials and had the picture to go by when she first got here. I think she may have talked to Josh. He's said a few things that indicate he knows. I guess she was waiting until we got to know her better." He took Addie's hand, relief rushing through him when she didn't pull away. "I'm sorry, Addie. I didn't want to hurt you. If havin' her here will hurt you more or bring you shame because I had an illegitimate daughter, I'll send her away."

"You could do that?"

When it came down to it, he wasn't sure he could. He took a deep breath, releasing it in a heavy sigh. "I don't want to, but if you ask it of me, Addie, I will."

She put her other hand on top of his. Poor Jacob. He sounded as if his heart were being ripped in half. He had always been such an honorable man. He tried so hard to do what was right. "A man should stand by his children, whether they were born on the right side of the blanket or not. It'll take a little while to get used to the idea, but I'll not have you send your daughter away. I need to get a breath of air."

He found her half an hour later in Charity's room, looking at Marion's picture. He walked up behind her and slid his arms around her waist, resting his jaw against her temple. Will's letter and Jacob's note to Marion were lying on top of the dresser alongside his picture.

"She was very beautiful," Addie said.

"Yes, she was. But you're the one I've loved all these years, the one who has my heart."

"I love you, too, Jacob. Always have and always will."

# Chapter
# Twenty-three

In unspoken agreement, Morgan and Charity refrained from any touch more personal than rubbing shoulders in the buggy. When they bedded down the first night, Charity took the west side of the fire, and Morgan took the south. They lay awake a long time, chatting about nothing important, and finally drifted off to sleep from sheer exhaustion.

The second day, Morgan drove the buggy in the morning and rode Cactus most of the afternoon. Rubbing shoulders wasn't enough, and it only made things worse. They set up camp in silence and didn't say more than two words to each other during supper. By the time they unrolled their bed-rolls—two blankets each on top of waterproof tarpaulins— they were both wound tighter than an eight-day clock.

It was their last night alone.

Charity sat on her blanket, her shoes neatly lined up above her pillow. Morgan was stretched out on his bed, leaning against his saddle, watching her slowly brush her hair.

She always massaged her scalp with her fingertips the instant she took out the pins. "Does it hurt to pin it up all day?"

"Not unless I pin it too tight. Then I get a headache. It feels good to take it down anytime."

She pulled her dark hair forward over her shoulder and ran the brush through the length of it. Morgan watched the movement of the brush as it skimmed over her bosom and down almost to her waist. His mouth went dry. She ran the brush through her hair again and, with a regal toss of her head, flung it back over her shoulder. She met his burning gaze and went still.

He broke eye contact first, desperately trying to think of something to talk about, something to divert his thoughts from how badly he wanted her. "Uh, do you know how cowboys tell time by the stars?"

"No." She looked up, suddenly fascinated by the heavens. Conversation. Yes, that's what they needed. An interesting, stimulating—no, not stimulating—enlightening discussion. She was an excellent conversationalist. "How?"

Morgan smiled. She wasn't doing any better than he was. "By the position of the Big Dipper as it rotates around the North Star."

She looked up. "There it is. What time is it?"

"About eight o'clock. On a trail drive or when they have some cattle rounded up and have to hold them overnight, the men ride guard in two-hour shifts. I go by the star in the Big Dipper where the handle connects to the dipper. It's the fourth star down from the top of the handle. At ten o'clock, that star is just about where ten o'clock would be on a regular clock."

"And when it's twelve, would it be straight up?"

"No, ten and six are the only ones that are the same. It goes backwards and doesn't move as much. Midnight is where nine would be on a clock. Two A.M. is at the eight, and four A.M. is at the seven."

"So, six A.M. would be at the six, except the sun is probably already up, so you couldn't see it."

"True. It makes one complete rotation in twenty-four hours."

"That's nice to know. Now when I wake up and it's dark, I'll be able to tell the time." She put her brush in her small satchel and set it beside her shoes.

"Only if it's not cloudy. Then you hope your horse can tell time."

"What?"

"We had a horse that knew exactly when he had been on guard for two hours. Sometimes we had to do longer shifts, and the only way we could get that horse to cooperate was to take him back to the chuck wagon and dismount. The same man, or a different one, could get right back on him and he'd go out for another two hours. When his time was up, he'd head back to the chuck wagon. We sometimes used him for more than the normal stretch because he could see good at night. Some horses are better at night work than others."

They chatted about horses for a while and a few other safe topics before deciding to try to go to sleep. Morgan watched her toss and turn. She had done the same thing on the trip down. He knew that this time it wasn't only because she wasn't used to sleeping on the ground. Finally around midnight she fell asleep.

Morgan gazed at her face, reflected in the flickering light of the fire. Looking at her was nice, but he ached to hold her. A thunderstorm came up to the north of them. He watched the lightning flash in the distance and heard the faint rumble of thunder. It wasn't long until a chilly breeze swept through the camp. He got up and put more wood on the fire, but when he checked on Charity, she looked cold.

He couldn't have that.

The storm was moving toward the east. He didn't think it would reach them, but just in case, he fetched a spare tarp from the boot of the buggy. He moved his bedroll over beside Charity, placing her between him and the fire, and laid the extra tarpaulin down at their feet. If it started to rain, he could pull it up over them quickly. Instead of moving his saddle, he rolled up his jacket and used it for a pillow. He placed his gunbelt beside it, so the gun would be within easy and quick reach.

He pulled off his boots and set his hat on one corner of the tarp, with the boots on the brim so it wouldn't blow away. Stretching carefully out behind Charity, he loosened her top blanket from where it was tucked around her back and scooted up against her, her back to his chest, drawing both of the blankets up to cover them. She mumbled something in her sleep and snuggled up against his warmth.

Morgan closed his eyes and smiled. He'd be tired and cranky from lack of sleep—and more frustrated than ever—but lying beside her and holding her filled him with sweet pleasure and contentment. He rested his cheek against her silky hair and inhaled deeply, enjoying the lingering fragrance of lily of the valley. For the first time, he understood how a man could lose himself in a woman, how easy it would be to let her become the most important thing in his life.

He tried to resist. He honestly did. It was the firelight dancing on her cheek that tempted him. That smooth, soft cheek. So inviting. He kissed it gently. That's all. Just once. He couldn't help it that she smiled at his touch. Was it his fault her lips were so full and soft, so inviting? If she hadn't smiled, he might not have noticed. He might not have been tempted. He might not have brushed a kiss at the corner of those sweet lips.

She sighed softly and turned toward him. He kissed her again, gently, but fully, on the lips. When he raised his head, her eyelids fluttered open. She gazed sleepily up at him, her eyes darkening with desire.

"You were cold."

"Not now." She slid her hand around behind his neck, spreading her fingers across the back of his head. "Now I'm on fire."

With a groan he pressed his lips firmly against hers, seeking, taking, giving. He smoothed his hand up her ribs and higher. She gasped with pleasure as he touched her breast and moaned softly as he deepened the kiss. He kissed her again and again, caressed her with gentleness and with fervor, and when he unbuttoned the bodice of her wrapper and skimmed his hand from throat to waist with only the thin chemise separating her skin from his, she trembled with need.

She unbuttoned his shirt, aching to touch him, and when she slipped her hands beneath it and pressed her lips to his chest, he cried out her name in a ragged whisper. With trembling fingers, he guided her face upward, capturing her lips in a kiss that branded her soul.

"I need you. Be mine, Charity. Only mine."

The roughly spoken words wrapped around her heart,

filling her with unbearable longing, not only for physical satisfaction, but for a lifetime of love, a lifetime of belonging to him alone. He kissed her again, and she lost herself in his touch, his caress. Yes, this was what she wanted, what she needed—to be his love and give him all the love in her heart. More than anything in the world, she wanted to be his wife, to have his child.

*Have his child.* Charity froze. He hadn't mentioned love. And she wasn't his wife.

"Charity?" She hadn't moved, but he felt her withdrawal. In desperation, he held her close, cradling her head against his chest. He could calm his passion. He would get himself under control if it killed him, but he couldn't bear for her to pull away from him, leaving him cold and abandoned. Alone.

"I can't do this. It's not right," she whispered, fighting back tears. She tried to pull away, but he wouldn't let her. His hold tightened.

"It's all right, sugar. I'll stop. Just don't move right now. Hold me. Please."

His plea almost broke her heart. She slid her arm around him, holding him as if she would never let go. She wasn't sure she ever could. "I'm sorry, Morgan. I won't make the same mistake as my mother. I couldn't bring up a child alone."

"You think I would expect you to?"

"No, but I don't want a forced marriage. I don't want Jacob coming after you with a shotgun."

"He'd do it, too. At least we'd get him to admit he was your father."

"I think we could think of a better way to accomplish that."

"But it wouldn't be near as much fun."

His tone was wistful, but she felt him slowly relax. Stopping their lovemaking was hard enough for her. She knew it must be torture for him. From all she'd read and heard, it was more difficult for a man. Of course, according to a lot of what she had read, she wasn't supposed to feel the wonderful things he made her feel, either. That part she didn't believe, not for one minute.

"No, it probably wouldn't be as much fun. You make me feel things that novels barely mention and marriage guidance books avoid completely. It's amazing how they skirt around such an important part of life."

"Been reading up, have you?" He eased his hold, but he wasn't ready for her to move away. He was curious to see where this conversation was going, and he wanted to hold her until morning. He also figured that talking was her way of getting herself under control.

"Not lately. Several years ago I was curious so I tried to find some books on the subject. What's on the market is disgraceful."

"I thought they didn't say much."

"Exactly. How's a woman supposed to know what to do? Or a man for that matter? No, don't answer that. I can guess."

"Most men just do what comes natural."

"Well, most of these books hint or sometimes blatantly tell a woman that what comes natural isn't right, that she's not supposed to enjoy it."

"Maybe you should write a book about it."

"Maybe I will someday. When I know what I'm talking about."

He considered volunteering to give her lessons, but that probably would lead to talk of marriage, and he wasn't ready for that. He loved her and wanted her to be his wife, but there were some things to work out first. The situation with Jacob and Addie had to be resolved, and he had to decide if he could be a lawman and have a family at the same time.

He changed the subject since that one might lead into dangerous territory. They lay in each other's arms and talked until the sun came up, not an activity as satisfying as the one they would have preferred but far more prudent.

When they arrived at the Double J, Addie and Jacob welcomed them warmly but with underlying nervousness.

Charity noticed it right away. She glanced at Morgan. When she saw his narrowed gaze, she knew he'd picked up on it, too.

"Did you have a good trip?" Addie bustled them inside the family parlor. "Did the roundup crew have any problems?"

"It was a good trip. Good weather. No problems. The roundup got started right on schedule." Morgan watched his aunt nervously clasp and unclasp her hands. Jacob was rubbing his throat as if his collar were too tight. The top button wasn't fastened. "How about around here? Everything all right?"

"Oh yes. We're fine. We got some rain last night and the night before." Addie's gaze darted between Jacob and Charity and back again.

"I saw lightning to the north last night. Thought you might be getting a shower."

"Morgan, why don't you take your things on into your room? Charity, dear, I'll take yours for you. Sit down and rest a bit. I'll go make a pot of coffee." She took Charity's bag from her hand and plucked her hat from her head before she could say a word. "Come along, nephew. You can tell me about the trip."

Morgan caught Charity's eye, silently asking if she wanted him to stay. She shook her head. With a single nod and a tender, encouraging smile, he followed Addie from the room. Charity turned to where Jacob fussed with a figurine on the mantel and walked over next to him. "How are you?"

"Fair to middlin'. I've been working through some things."

"That's good. At least it is if they're working out the way you want them to."

"I think they're going to." He took a deep breath and met her gaze. "I went into your room yesterday. I found the things I gave your mama and the letter from Will. She never told me we had a child. Will never mentioned it, either. I guess she had made him promise that he wouldn't." He held out his arm, and she went to him, hugging him, blinking back tears. "I'm sorry, Charity. If I'd known, things would have been different."

"Did you love her?" she whispered.

"Yes, honey, I did. But not the way I love Addie. I didn't know your mama long enough for it to become that kind of love. I only knew her for two weeks."

"Two weeks?" Charity drew back, searching his face. He dropped his arms, and she stepped away. All her life her mother had preached against making love outside of marriage. She had harped on it, over and over again. *She had had a good reason.*

"Don't judge us too harshly, Charity."

"Help me understand."

"Let's sit down."

They moved to the sofa. "What we did was wrong, Charity. I reckon that's why those kinds of rules were set up in the first place, to keep people from being hurt—the two involved and the innocent one that comes along because of it. I was young, but old enough to know better. All I can say in my defense is that your mama knocked me right off my feet the first time I saw her.

"At first she was just being nice, showing me around town and doing things with me because Will had left. She was a very lonely woman, Charity. She hadn't stepped out with a man since Henry died. One night we went to a dance, and when I took her home, I wound up stayin'. The next morning I asked her to marry me. She refused. I cared for her, and I was worried about the possibility of a baby. She told me not to worry, that she'd been married to Henry for ten years and never gotten pregnant.

"She felt bad about what we'd done, guilty like me, but she wouldn't use that to corner me into marriage. Not that she would have had to. She said there was too much difference in our ages to make a marriage work. She didn't want to grow old while I was still young. She told me to leave and never come back, that there could never be anything more between us. She was upset, but she meant every word. I did what she asked.

"After the time I spent with her, I knew I wanted a wife.

I waited awhile to get over my wounded pride and to see if she would write. She never did. I started courtin' Addie and married her a few months later. I reckon I was already married by the time Marion knew for certain she was carrying a baby."

"By saying I was Henry's child, she protected me, and herself, from those who would have scorned me because I was illegitimate. Still, I wish she had told me about you."

"I think she wanted you to know. How did you find Will's letter?"

She explained about going through the trunk and what she had found.

"I wish it had been a little easier for you. It would have helped if you'd known my name."

Charity laughed. "Yes, it would have. Do you have any idea how many men around here have the same initials?"

"I can think of three or four," he said with a smile.

"What about Addie? How is she?"

"She was hurt and upset at first, but you know Addie. She's got a heart as big as Texas. She wouldn't turn you away for anything. So now that everything is out in the open, think you can call me Daddy?"

She grinned and clasped his hand. "I'd love to, Daddy."

He leaned over, kissed her forehead, and tipped her face up so she met his gaze. "Did anything happen between you and Morgan? Do I need to send for a preacher?"

Charity smiled, warmed by the love and concern in her father's eyes. "No, he was a perfect gentleman."

"Hog-slop. If you think I believe that, gal, then you haven't gotten to know me very well."

"Well, maybe he wasn't a perfect gentleman, but nothing happened to warrant a quick wedding." When she saw the skepticism in his eyes, she gave him her most winsome smile. "It's true, Daddy. There's no reason to worry."

Jacob shook his head and smiled, thankful he didn't have a whole houseful of girls.

# Chapter
## Twenty-four

Morgan strolled up the walkway of the house Jacob had built for the family to use when they were in town. He had been back at work for a week and intended on spending his first day off taking Charity and Sam to the amusement park. They were sitting on the porch steps, heads together, petting a tiny white kitten. Charity looked up when he approached, her face lighting up with happiness. "See our new friend. He belongs next door, but Mrs. Jennings said we could play with him."

Morgan bent down and tickled the kitten's stomach with his finger. He was instantly attacked by four clawed feet and a mouthful of tiny teeth. "Ferocious critter, ain't he?"

"A veritable mountain lion. We'll have to guard the calves before long."

Morgan smiled and drew back his hand. "I think they'll be safe for a while. Sam, why don't you return the kitten to Mrs. Jennings? We'll be ready to go in a few minutes."

"Sure. She should be takin' that pan of cookies out of the oven about now. Come on, Pepper." Within seconds, the boy and the kitten had disappeared around the corner.

Morgan and Charity went inside the house. He gave the door a shove, not closing it all the way, but blocking them from view of the street. Drawing her into his arms, he kissed her thoroughly and leaned his forehead against hers. "I've missed that."

"Me, too. How are you?"

He shrugged. "It's been boring with most of the cowboys

gone. I'd rather have been out at the ranch. At least then I could have seen you. What have you been doing?"

"Writing the article about the roundup. I finished it last night and mailed it this morning. I'm so glad you took me to see it. Jacob says there probably won't be many more like it." She stretched up on tiptoe and brushed a quick kiss across his lips. "I've been looking forward to today. Sam must have told me about the zoo a hundred times."

"I hope he didn't make it sound better than it is. It's not much as far as zoos go. I'm sure you've seen ones a lot better."

"I'm certain I'll enjoy it."

Morgan wasn't so sure she would. It wasn't anything spectacular. It didn't even resemble a real zoo. He released her and reached in his pocket. "I was at the depot when this telegram came in for you. Since I was coming right up here, I brought it."

Charity unfolded the telegram and read it quickly. "Oh my."

"What's wrong?" Morgan couldn't tell from her expression whether she was upset, excited, or both.

"Nothing. Richard wants me to go to England to do a story."

"England?" He felt the floor drop right out from under him. "When?"

"As soon as I can get away, but at least within a month."

"Sounds like quite the opportunity." What would she do if he begged her to stay? How could he ask her to give up a chance like that?

"Well, yes, it is." She wanted to go—who wouldn't? Yet she didn't want to leave her family, and she certainly didn't want to leave Morgan right now, not when she was hoping he would propose sometime soon.

"Is that hesitation I hear?" He tried not to sound hopeful.

She shrugged. The least he could do was act as if he didn't want her to go. "I just hate to leave my family so soon."

"Do you have to give him a reply today?"

"No. I can think about it for a few days. Let's go ahead to

the amusement park. I'll worry about this later." She hooked her arm through his. "Right now, I want to enjoy the company of two of my favorite men."

It was dumb to be jealous of a kid. Morgan gave himself that sage advice and asked if she was wearing comfortable shoes.

"Yes. Why? Sam asked me the same thing."

"We'll be walking around a lot, and I intend to do plenty of dancing later." He also reminded her to wear something to keep the sun out of her eyes.

She disappeared briefly into her bedroom and returned wearing a wide-brimmed straw hat trimmed in bright yellow ribbon and silk daisies. It matched her yellow calico fitted shirtwaist and skirt. Her choice of clothing brought a smile to his eyes. He hadn't seen her in anything that required a corset since she moved out to the ranch. She could wear one with this outfit, he supposed, but she sure didn't need it, and since he intended to spend the evening dancing with her, he didn't want it.

"How's this?"

"Nice. You look mighty fine today, darlin'. Mighty fine."

She grinned and dropped him a shallow curtsy. "Thank you, kind sir." He looked good, too. His rust-colored shirt brought out the red highlights in his hair. "So do you."

"We're liable to be a little too purty for the likes of this town." They laughed and walked out the door, ready to have a good time.

With Sam talking a blue streak, they walked down to the corner of Second and Oak, where they caught the trolley in front of Snyder's store. "Did you bring a drawing pad, Miss Charity?"

"Not this time. I intend to simply enjoy myself and my friends. I can come back another time and sketch anything interesting I see."

Morgan put his arm across the back of her seat, making certain the men on the trolley knew she wasn't just on an outing with Sam. Morgan was mildly surprised at the number of cowboys on board. It appeared that every man who hadn't gone on the roundup had chosen to come into town. Several of them had their sweethearts along, and two were taking a couple of girls from the district out for the evening. They were easily blowing their whole month's pay on one night's companionship and probably didn't figure a cent of it was wasted.

The little mules plodded along Second, dutifully pulling the car along the tracks at a steady pace. They crossed the bridge over Lone Wolf Creek and started up East Hill, but slightly more than halfway up the hill the trolley came to a halt.

"Sorry, folks, but you'll have to get out and walk to the top. The mules can't make it up the grade with anybody on board."

Charity looked at the twinkle in Morgan and Sam's eyes and burst into laughter. "Now I know why you told me to wear comfortable shoes. I should have worn toe-pinchers and made you carry me."

They all piled out of the trolley and walked. The little mules and the trolley car beat them to the top. They climbed back on board, and traveled another mile or so, going past the Odd Fellows Cemetery and on to the gate of the amusement park.

To Morgan's amazement, Charity was delighted with the animals in the zoo. She spent time at each cage, watching the animals with interest and asking questions. They saw coyotes, badgers, antelope, white-tailed deer, and bobcats. Charity was fascinated by the small prairie-dog town. Those quick, quizzical little animals seemed to be equally fascinated by the people. She gazed in awe at a mighty buffalo, sad that the breed was almost extinct, and laughed at an animal that was half-cow and half-buffalo.

"Shows you what happens when a lady wanders too far from home. No one to protect her from amorous advances," murmured Morgan in her ear.

She thought he might be talking about her going to England. Then again, he could be talking about her trip to Texas—with him making the amorous advances.

They watched a baseball game for part of the afternoon. She and Sam shared a bag of fresh roasted peanuts and cheered and jumped up and down every time the home team scored a run. She even gave the umpire a piece of her mind now and again when she disagreed with a call.

Sam looked at her with new respect. "You've been to baseball games before. You're the first girl I've met who knows what's goin' on."

Charity laughed and ruffled his hair. "I love baseball. I go to the games every chance I get, which unfortunately isn't often enough."

Her enthusiasm rubbed off, and Morgan found himself standing and yelling his encouragement to the team on more than one occasion. He shook his head, thinking Dick would laugh himself silly if he saw him. The local team was victorious over the team from a neighboring town, leaving the townfolk in high spirits.

The horse races rounded out the afternoon, and since Charity didn't know any of the people or horses involved, she gave her support to the underdogs. A couple of her favorites won.

"Holy Moses, Miss Charity," Sam said, "if you had bet on those horses, you would've won a pile of money."

"Yes, but I could as easily have lost. The best way to win money gambling is not to gamble."

"Yeah, that's what my pa says, too." Sam glanced at the sinking sun. "I'd better head on toward home. You gonna stay?"

"Is it all right for you to go home by yourself?"

"Yes, ma'am. I come out here to the baseball games by myself sometimes. I've got my ticket for the trolley, and I'll go straight home when it gets to town. Ma will have supper ready 'bout the time I get there."

"I'll see you soon. Thank you for the drawings you brought me." Charity watched the youngster leave through the park gate and board the trolley. He turned and waved to them, grinning from ear to ear. "Will he be safe going by himself?"

"Should be. I've seen him out here alone during the day before. He usually comes with some of his friends, but not

always. Now, pretty lady, shall we go try out our dancin'
shoes?''

"My feet are already tapping.''

Moments before they reached the dance pavilion, the
fiddler struck up a lively tune, luring everyone inside.
"There won't be any fancy dances here, but they'll be
lively.'' Morgan twirled her out onto the floor, where a
square dance set was forming. Charity had never done Texas
square dancing, but it didn't take long to catch on, especially
when the caller gave directions.

She was very glad, however, that not all the dances were
lively. Slow dancing with Morgan Kaine was about the
closest thing to heaven she could think of—except for
kissing the way they had that last night on the trail. She
didn't dance with anyone else. Neither did he. Finally the
fiddler declared he was "plumb wore out, and everybody
can go home.''

As they walked to the trolley, Morgan put his arm around
Charity and kept her pressed against his side. The boys over
in the beer garden were growing rowdy, and he was glad to
get her away from there. The little trolley was crowded,
which gave Morgan a good excuse to keep his arm around
her. He also knew they had a bumpy ride coming, and he
wanted her secure.

The little mules complacently began the trip back to
town, plodding along at their same steady pace. Shortly
before they reached the long, steep grade of East Hill, the
driver stopped the trolley and moved the mules to the rear of
the vehicle.

"Why is he doing that?''

"They act as brakes to slow us down on the hill. Be
warned, they usually can't hold it. We'll probably go off the
tracks.'' He tightened his arm, pressing her against his side.
"I'll hold on tight so you won't go flying.''

She glanced up at him and breathed a sigh of relief when
she saw his smile. "Anybody ever get hurt on this thing?''

"Nope. Just relax and enjoy the ride.''

She relaxed and enjoyed the feeling of his body against
hers, the faint woodsy smell of his cologne, the whisper of

his breath against her cheek. She forgot about the ride until she glanced back and saw the little mules digging in their heels, trying to slow the trolley car. They helped for a few minutes, but it was soon more than they could handle. She glanced back again and laughed nervously. They were running as fast as they could, trying to keep up with the speeding car.

"Here we go," yelled Morgan with a grin. His grip on her tightened even more. There were screams and shouts and giggles as the car flew off the tracks and lurched to a sudden halt in the sand. "You okay?"

"Yes." She looked back to see how the mules were doing. They stood behind the car, sides heaving. "But I believe those two think this whole idea is ridiculous."

Morgan looked at the mules and laughed. If mules could look disgusted, those two did. "I think you're right. We have to get off now."

"Don't tell me we have to walk down the hill, too." She groaned as she stood and joined the procession departing the car. "My feet are sore already."

"I didn't stomp on your toes this time."

"No, but I'm not used to jumping around so much."

"We don't have to walk. We just have to put the car back on the tracks." He left her for a moment with the other women beside the tracks and helped the men lift the trolley back into the proper position. Within minutes they were on their way, moving much slower because the grade was not nearly so steep here.

Morgan walked Charity home, trying not to think about how nice it would be to stay awhile. When they walked up onto the dark porch, he asked if she'd like to sit in the porch swing. "It's late and all your neighbors are in bed. We wouldn't disturb them. And they won't disturb us."

"I'd like to sit with you a spell."

He chuckled softly. "Now you're startin' to sound like a Texan." They sat down, and he turned toward her, putting his arms around her.

"Ever done any kissin' in a porch swing?"

"Can't say that I have."

"I hear it's nice."

"You can't believe everything you're told. I think we should investigate it thoroughly and judge for ourselves."

"Thoroughly, huh?"

"Mm-hmm."

"Like this?" He kissed her tenderly.

"That's nice. But we really can't conclude anything with one example."

"Definitely not." He kissed her again. And again. They lost count and didn't care. The kisses grew more fervent, and the swing swayed wildly, but they didn't notice—until they almost fell out of it. Morgan steadied the swing and buried his face in Charity's hair to keep from laughing out loud. She pressed her mouth against his shoulder to stifle her giggles. After a few minutes, he raised his head. "I forgot about the part where you couldn't get too carried away."

"At least we didn't land on the porch with a thud," she whispered.

Someone lit a lamp next door.

"No, but I think we made some noise. I'd better go. Let me check the house and make sure it's safe." He followed her inside, lit a lamp, and turned it down low. Together they walked through the house, making certain it was empty. He left the light in her bedroom, and they walked back to the front door. "I'll come by around one and drive you out to the ranch. Thanks for going today."

"Thanks for taking us. I had a wonderful time." She wondered what it was going to take to get this man to say what was in his heart. "Good night."

"Good night." He dropped a kiss on her forehead and ran a fingertip slowly down her cheek. *I love you.* He wanted to tell her, but he thought about her trip to England and couldn't bring himself to say the words. She wanted to go. He could never give her something like that, not on a lawman's salary. He was scared to try ranching full-time. All the cattlemen were worried.

Disappointed, Charity watched him walk out the door and across the yard to the street. She thought she saw love in his eyes. Why didn't he say something? Was he still afraid she would be like his mother? Was he too bitter, too afraid to love?

She shut the door and changed into her nightgown. Lying on the soft feather mattress, clutching the spare pillow to her chest, she stared out the window at the Big Dipper and the North Star. It was almost two A.M.

"Confound it, Morgan Kaine. I hope you don't sleep a wink."

She knew she wouldn't.

# Chapter
# Twenty-five

When Morgan came to pick up Charity the next afternoon, they were both out of sorts. Neither one had gotten much sleep. The more Morgan thought about her going off to England, the madder he became. It had occurred to him sometime in the wee hours of the morning that she might not go if he told her he loved her. Addie had explained to him recently that most women put great stock in hearing those words.

When they had returned from the roundup, Addie assured him she accepted the fact that Jacob was Charity's father. "I can't deny he had strong feelings for Charity's mother. He wouldn't have been with her if he hadn't. I also know that my husband has told me he loved me every morning and every night for twenty-eight years. I reckon a man doesn't say those words unless he means them, especially not that many times."

As he led Princess from the small enclosure behind the house and over to the waiting buggy, he decided that they would take a side trip on the way to the ranch. He knew some pretty places along the river where a man could say important things to a woman in private. He might even ask her to marry him—if he could work up the courage. Thoughts of his parents had nagged him during the night. What went wrong? Could their troubles have been prevented? Could he make Charity happy, or would they end up as his parents had?

He had tried to focus on Jacob and Addie's marriage and their happiness, telling himself that he and Charity would be

302

like them, but the old fears ran deep. He couldn't support her very well as a deputy, but he might be able to land a sheriff's job in another county not far away. And if he could move up to United States marshal in a few years, he could provide her with a good home. He still worried about being a lawman and having a family, but he knew plenty of men who had made it work. Between that and raising cattle or horses, he should be able to give her a decent life. He would have to keep running his herd with Case's, but perhaps someday he could set up a ranch of his own.

The trip to England still worried him. He wouldn't feel right asking her not to go. He had enough money saved up to pay his way to go with her, but it would be foolish to spend it on a trip. They could get engaged and wait to get married until she got back. The thought of letting her go off by herself as a single woman—engaged or not—to be wooed by rich English noblemen was just plain stupid. Marrying first and sending her off alone wasn't any better.

The trip to England was on Charity's mind, too. She wanted to go, but she didn't want to go alone. She had the urge to tell Morgan to quit dragging his feet and propose. When she came out of the house, he had already hitched Princess to the buggy. Cactus was tied to the back of it. "I have to stop by Laskey's Grocery and pick up some cheese for Addie," Charity said.

Making plans for later, Morgan only nodded and helped her into the buggy. He drove to the store on Second and parked the buggy, tying the horse weight to the bridle to keep Princess from leaving. The hitching rail in front of the store was filled, plus there was an ordinance against simply tying up a horse attached to a vehicle. Too many of them got away and wrecked things.

They were no sooner inside the store than a commotion down the street brought them rushing out again. It appeared that a brawl had broken out in one of the saloons and spilled out into the street. Morgan ran half a block down the boardwalk, scattering the townspeople in his path, jumped into the street, and waded into the melee. Throwing men left and right, he made his way to the two main troublemakers. He jerked them apart, and both men stumbled to the ground.

"What's the problem here?"

"He was cheatin'. I don't let nobody cheat me." One man got to his feet, swearing at the man still lying on the ground. He turned his scathing gaze on Morgan. "I don't like nobody stopping my vengeance, neither."

Morgan watched his eyes. This one was trouble. Full of hate, full of his own importance. Another man stepped up beside him, wiping blood from a cut on his lip. They were two of a kind. Morgan sensed the bystanders running for cover, including the other men who had been fighting. The one accused of cheating crawled away, leaving Morgan to face these two alone. That was just as well.

"This ends here. Now. You take the money you've lost and get out of town." He knew from experience to keep his eye on the first man. Heart pounding, he waited for his next move. There was always some fear—it made him alert, gave him an edge—but it was always overshadowed by the exhilaration of being in control, of being in power. *Where's Charity?* The exhilaration didn't come. He wasn't sure he was in control. The man saw his uncertainty.

Morgan forced himself not to think of her. He hardened his heart and his expression. He searched inside for the hate that had made him coldly defy death over and over. It wasn't there. But now he saw the flicker of uncertainty in the other man's eyes. He had fooled him. Maybe.

Out of the corner of his eye, he saw the bright blue of Charity's skirt as she stood on the boardwalk. His heart thudded against his chest. He couldn't breathe. Fear wrenched his gut—pure, unadulterated terror. She was too close. He couldn't let shooting start. One stray bullet— Suddenly, as if sensing his distraction, she moved, taking cover behind a buckboard. Safe. Unless he was shot. If he went down, she wouldn't stay put. He had to end this now.

He focused his will, blocked out everything but the two men in front of him. "I'm Morgan Kaine." His voice was soft yet like steel. He saw recognition in the man's eyes. His friend shifted uneasily. "Is a card game worth dying over?"

Still the man hesitated, calculating his chances. "If you think you can take me, go ahead."

"And get tried for murder? No, thanks." The man held his hands out away from his gun.

Morgan pulled his Colt from the holster so fast the man blinked and went pale. Morgan called to the bartender peeking around the saloon doorway. "Eldon, come relieve these gentlemen of their guns."

Eldon came out of the doorway shaking his head. "I told them, Deputy Kaine. I told 'em it was against the law to wear those hoglegs." He took the pistols from the two men. "Want me to take these guns over to the sheriff's office?"

Morgan nodded. "How much did you lose in the card game?"

"Twenty-five dollars. Jim here lost thirty." The man had lost his bluster after seeing Morgan in action.

"Eldon, get their money for them. I'm not saying anyone was cheating, but I don't want this row to start up again. They can use it to pay the fine." He ignored the men's groans.

As the bartender went inside for the money, Sheriff Ware came hurrying down the street and stepped up beside Morgan. "Anybody hurt?"

"No, but these two were carrying pistols in town and had the itch to use them. They were also involved in a fistfight, but I think half the men in the saloon got in on that."

"I'll take these two over to the calaboose. You go see to your lady," Dick added quietly.

Morgan slipped the gun back into his holster with an unsteady hand and turned toward Charity. She stood beside the buckboard, her face ashen, her eyes wide and filled with horror. Her anguish cut him to the quick. He slowly walked over and put his arms around her, a lump clogging his throat when he felt how she trembled. He cleared his throat and held her close. "It's all right, sugar. It's over."

She looked up at him, searching his eyes, touching his soul. "Until the next time. Please take me home." She pulled away and walked back to the buggy. Morgan followed, his heart heavy.

Neither of them thought about the cheese Addie wanted from the store. They rode out to the ranch in silence, each lost in private thoughts. Morgan knew that he could not remain in law enforcement if they married. He couldn't put her through that kind of anguish day in and day out. Nor could he face it himself. The worry that she might be hurt or killed because of him would torment him day and night. Anxiety over being killed and leaving her alone would be like an infected wound, sapping his strength and distracting him when he most needed a clear head.

Even if she wouldn't marry him, he didn't think he could remain a peace officer. He wasn't sure he had what it took anymore to do the job. He surreptitiously lifted his hand. It still trembled slightly. Had fear taken root so deep inside of him that he would never be rid of it? Or was it only because he had been so frightened for her? It was too soon to tell.

He realized with some surprise that he wouldn't mind changing careers. The problem was how to provide for her. He wouldn't marry her and give her a lifetime of hardship.

Charity was terrified. She could not live her life knowing that one day he wouldn't come home or that he might be gunned down right before her eyes. She couldn't bear it. It would eat away at her heart and soul, day by day, minute by minute. It would destroy their love, destroy their marriage. Love? Marriage? He had never mentioned either one. Perhaps his mother had wounded him so deeply that their chance for happiness had already been destroyed.

She couldn't ask him to give up his career for her. She understood about dreams and goals. He had a reputation throughout Texas. His very name commanded respect and obedience. He was fearless, daunting. How could she ask him to give up something at which he excelled, especially when there was such a need for good peace officers? If he gave up his life's work, he would come to regret it. He would hate her for taking it away.

By the time they reached the ranch, she had convinced herself that she didn't need him. Her mother had done fine without a man. She could, too. Besides, she would make a lousy wife. Her career was her life. It couldn't hurt her. It couldn't break her heart or chisel it away slowly with fear and worry. She hadn't been brought up to cook or wash clothes or pick up dirty socks. She was a writer, an illustrator. That was her world, and it was safe.

Morgan dropped her off at the house and took the buggy down to the shed. He brushed Princess, gave her some oats and water, and turned her into the corral. Cactus nudged him in the back, so he fed him a bucket of oats, too. He thought about rubbing him down but didn't. It would only have been an excuse not to go to the house.

Addie met him on the back porch, her brow etched with worry. "What's this about Charity going off to England? She's in there packing her trunk right now."

"It's an assignment for the magazine." He wondered how many bottles of whiskey it would take to drown the pain.

"Did something happen in town?"

"I had to stop a fight." He held out his hand. Almost steady, but not quite. "I'm goin' back to town. I'll see you in a few days."

"You're leavin' now? Use the sense God gave you, boy. Go in there and talk to her."

"I can't. I've got to work some things out, Aunt Addie."

When she stretched up on tiptoe, he bent down so she could kiss his cheek. "Get rid of your ghosts, Morgan. Spend a little time on your knees—and I don't mean scrubbin' the floor, although it could probably use it. Ask for help. You just might get it."

"Did she say when she's leaving?"

"Tomorrow morning."

His heart dropped to his ankles. He took a deep breath. "I'll be there to see her off."

"Morgan Kaine, what's got into you?"

"Good evenin', Addie. See you tomorrow." He left without another word.

After he rode out through the gate, Addie marched to Charity's bedroom. "What happened in town?" she asked.

Charity turned away, picking up a skirt and folding it. "There was a brawl. Morgan almost got into a gunfight. He could have gotten killed because of me."

"What did you do?"

"I distracted him. Not intentionally, but I could see it in his face. I've never been so terrified in my life. I couldn't live with the fear, Addie. I couldn't bear waking up every morning and wondering if that was the day he would die. I can't ask him to quit his career. He wants to be a United States marshal." She looked at Addie, tears brimming in her eyes. "I'm sorry to leave you and Daddy, but I have to go. I'll come back as soon as I can, but right now I have to leave."

"You're running away."

"I know, but I'm going, just the same."

Nothing any of them said that night could change her mind.

When Morgan got to the depot the next day, he was afraid he wouldn't get to speak to her. The whole family was there except for Lacy. Sam and Sheriff Ware had come to wish her well, too. Charity had dark smudges beneath her eyes. Her face was pale, her smile forced. Everyone else was trying too hard to be cheerful, until they saw him. Then they all frowned.

The conductor shouted the first call to board the train.

Morgan was late. "Charity, could I speak with you a minute?" She stepped away from the others, and he drew her to one side.

"I thought you weren't going to come."

"I almost didn't. I never thought I was a coward until today. I hate to see you go."

"I don't want to miss the England trip. If I don't go, he might give it to someone else." She called on every ounce of willpower she possessed not to throw herself into his arms.

"Will you be comin' back?"

"I'll come for a visit. It may be six months. I don't know how long I'll be in England."

Six months of misery. The beginning of a lifetime of misery. How could he stand it? "I'd like to see you when you come back."

"Of course. I'm sure I'll stay awhile." The pain in his eyes mirrored her own. Oh, Lord, how could she live without him? "Until Richard sends me someplace else."

"Maybe things will be different then." He was thinking of his job. He would always feel the same about her. He would always love her.

"I don't think so. Morgan, I have to go. Thank you for all you've done for me, for helping me find my family."

"I don't think I helped much."

"Yes, you did. And you didn't stop me even when you knew what I was doing. I'll always be grateful for that."

He didn't want her gratitude; he wanted her love. When she came back, things would be different. He'd have another job, something safe and secure, even if it meant working as a store clerk.

He stood apart from the others as she hugged her family and Sam and shook Sheriff Ware's hand. She looked at him, unable to hide her longing. Before she could turn away, he closed the distance between them and wrapped his arms around her. He didn't dare kiss her; he'd never stop. He'd never let go. They clung to each other until the engineer blew a long blast on the whistle. Stepping apart was almost impossible. His heart breaking, Morgan watched her board the train, wiping tears from her cheeks.

Seconds later, the train began slowly to move away from the depot. As soon as she could be heard above the noise, Addie lit into him. "How can you stand there and let her leave? I can't believe you didn't even try to get her to stay. I thought you had more gumption than that."

"I can't tell her not to go on that trip. It's important to her."

"She's not leavin' because she wants to go on a trip, you churnhead. She's scared. Scared for you to be a lawman, but she won't ask you to quit. She'll give up what she wants most so you can be happy."

"Happy? Do I look happy? I'd quit my job in a minute if I had something else to offer her, but I don't. Ranching is the only other thing I know. Last fall I had five hundred head of cattle. There's no tellin' how many I've got now. Not enough to stock a ranch, that's for sure. I won't make her live a life of just scrapin' by because I can't live without her."

Jacob stepped up beside him and rested a hand on his shoulder. "Can you live without her, son?"

"No, but I won't ask her to marry me until I've got a decent job—one we both can live with. I'd rather let her go now than have her leave later because I failed her."

"Morgan, you know I've loved you like a son. I always intended to leave you part of the ranch or take you in as a partner if you showed any interest in ranching again. With Charity's portion, you two would be well set."

Morgan was dumbfounded. "Jacob, I can't accept something I haven't earned. I don't want to take anything away from Lacy." He glanced at Serena and Joshua. "Or from any other children that might come along."

"Jacob can do whatever he wants with his half of the ranch, Morgan. He's had you in his will ever since we established the Double J. You might as well have it now instead of waitin' until he kicks the bucket. Our family has a bad habit of living a long time." Joshua smiled. "You'd better make up your mind before you can't catch that train."

"Even if you don't marry my daughter, you're family. As of this minute, I'm giving you stock in the Double J whether you want it or not. 'Course it would make me happier if you came out and lent a hand in runnin' the place."

Excitement raced through him. He had never dreamed he'd be a part of the Double J. It wouldn't be liking having a ranch all his own, but he could be happy there. On a ranch that size, there was plenty of work to go around, plenty of decisions to be made, room for him to be his own man. Equally important, Charity would be happy there. Except she wouldn't get to go to England. He could go with her, but if he paid his way, he couldn't build her a house.

"I can't make her miss her trip."

"Heck, boy, I'll pay your way, and you can go, too. Make it your honeymoon." Joshua grinned as Serena nodded in agreement. "That's our wedding present to you. Can't have her mopin' around the house, dreamin' of castles and nobility. Get a move on."

Morgan felt a tug on his arm and looked down.

"Please, Mr. Kaine, go after her. Don't let Miss Charity go away. She might get to England and not ever come back." Tears swam in Sam's eyes, though he tried valiantly not to cry.

"She's not goin' anywhere, Sam. At least, not without me." He squeezed his shoulder and grinned at the sheriff. "I'm resigning in about half an hour."

"Why not now?" Dick grinned back.

Morgan began backing up. "Because I'm going to borrow a horse, and I don't want to be arrested for stealing."

"Whose horse?"

"The first one I come to." He turned and ran out of the depot. Several horses were tied to the hitching rail in front of the Lone Wolf Saloon across the street. He grabbed the reins of a beautiful palomino. The animal looked fast and would be easy to spot. As he swung up into the saddle, a rancher he knew ran from the saloon, a drink in his hand.

"Where you goin' with my horse?"

"To stop a train. I'll bring him back."

"Fine." The man waved and turned back toward the door. Suddenly he spun around. "To stop a train! Kaine, you come back here with my horse."

Morgan was already a block down the street, turning the corner at Oak and Second. He trotted down Second until he was past Elm, touched his heels to the horse's flanks, and the animal shot to a gallop. Morgan let him have his head, and the stallion responded by going all out, racing up East Hill as if it were level ground. He cut across to the railroad and stopped. If Morgan judged correctly, the engineer would spot him before he built up any speed and could halt the train without too much problem.

As the engine came in sight over the top of the hill, Morgan urged the horse onto the tracks, between the crossties. He stood up in the stirrups and waved his hat in a wide arch over his head. The engineer gave a long pull on the whistle, making the horse shy, but when Morgan kept him under control and on the tracks and waved again, the engineer put on the brakes. He stopped the big steam engine a good fifty feet from them.

Morgan guided the horse off the tracks and rode up beside the engine.

"What's the problem, Deputy Kaine?"

"One of your passengers is wanted back in Colorado City."

The engineer grinned. "And I bet I know which one. Go ahead. I'll wait."

Morgan rode alongside the tracks. By now people were leaning out of every window, speculating on the problem. He stopped at the last passenger car and dismounted. The horse wandered over to a patch of grass and started eating, acting as if waiting beside a stopped train was an everyday occurrence. Morgan hoisted himself up to the first step at the back of the car as the conductor opened the door.

The conductor was grinning from ear to ear. "She's up at the front of the car, Deputy Kaine—the only one that ain't hangin' out the window."

Suddenly Morgan was scared spitless. She might turn him down. He might make a fool of himself for nothing. Those thoughts made his expression somber when he stopped in front of her. "Miss Charity Marie Brown?"

"Yes?" She watched him warily, hoping, praying he had come to tell her he loved her, but from the stern expression on his face, she was afraid someone in the family was hurt.

"Would you please stand up?"

She stood, her heart pounding, her breathing shallow.

"Ma'am, you're wanted back in Colorado City. I'm placing you under arrest."

"You're what! What on earth could you be arresting me for?"

"For stealing my heart." His expression grew tender, and his eyes filled with love.

"Oh, Morgan." She reached up, resting her hands on his chest as a collective sigh went up from all the ladies in the car. She shook her head. "I can't—"

He stopped her with a gentle finger on her lips. "I

resigned, darlin'. As soon as I return a stolen horse, my lawman days are over." He glanced out the window. She did, too. "Cactus wasn't handy, so I borrowed that one."

"I can't ask you to give up your career." Even her troubled expression couldn't hide the love in her eyes.

"You didn't ask me to. I made the decision all on my own. It wasn't hard, once I knew I had another job waiting for me. Your daddy made me a partner in the Double J. As he said, with your share we should do all right."

Quiet murmurs filled the car. Hushed speculation ran rampant, but everyone concluded that she must be Joshua's daughter.

"He's such a good man. He told me that he and Addie have always loved you like a son."

Several passengers gasped, but Charity and Morgan barely heard them.

"I love you, Charity. With all my heart and soul. I can't spend my life without you. Will you marry me?"

She smiled up at him, her face glowing, her eyes sparkling with happiness. "I think I need a little convincing."

"Yes, ma'am." He bent his head, touching her lips in a kiss filled with all the love in his heart. She returned it in full measure. The kiss lasted until they finally became aware of the passengers' loud whistles and laughter. He raised his head. "I love you. Will you marry me?"

"I love you, too, with all my heart. And I'd be honored to marry you."

A cheer went up.

Charity glanced around, her face turning pink. Everyone in the car wore a beaming smile. Several of the ladies fanned themselves and looked envious. All the doors between the cars were open, and people craned their necks trying to hear what was going on. "I guess we've held the train up long enough."

"Reckon so." Morgan took her small bags from the rack over the seat and arranged with the conductor to have her trunk set out beside the tracks. Morgan would get a buckboard from town and retrieve it. As they reached the doorway, he turned and touched his hat politely. "Have a good trip, folks. Sorry about the delay."

"Land's sake, boy, I ain't seen a kiss like that in years. You can stop my train anytime," called an elderly lady from the middle of the car.

"I ain't never seen a kiss like that," muttered another woman, glancing at her husband in irritation.

He leaned over to her with a twinkle in his eye. "We'll rectify that when we get to Fort Worth, buttercup." She turned pink but smiled anyway.

Morgan and Charity left the train amid more laughter and good wishes. The conductor and baggage man put her trunk about fifteen feet from the tracks and reboarded the train. Morgan set her other bags beside it and fetched the horse. The engineer blew the whistle as the train started up again, and everyone on the train waved. Arm in arm, Morgan and Charity waved, too.

The elderly lady who had teased Morgan earlier hung her head out the window. "Kiss her again, sonny. I need to get my blood pumping."

Morgan grinned. "Mustn't disobey my elders." He pulled Charity into his arms and kissed her until only the red caboose was in sight.

When they finally broke apart, Charity laughed and shook her head. "Well, Morgan Kaine, that was some proposal."

He grinned. "Not bad, huh?"

"I'd given up. For this time around, at least. How about England for a honeymoon? I've got more than enough to pay your way."

"No need to use yours or mine, for that matter. Joshua and Serena are giving us the money for the trip as a wedding present." The creak of wagon wheels caught their attention. They turned to see Jacob and Joshua riding up in a buckboard.

"We figured you'd need a way to get Charity's trunk back to town."

"Confident I'd say yes?" Charity smiled at them.

"Well, we figured you would, and if you didn't, we knew

we'd have to carry Morgan back in the wagon. He'd have been too low to sit up."

They loaded her things in the buckboard, and Morgan and Charity climbed in back as well. Jacob and Joshua teased them all the way back to town.

# Chapter
## Twenty-six

Jacob posted the announcement in the newspaper himself, inviting everyone in the county to his daughter's wedding. Other personal invitations went out to ranchers and other friends across West Texas. Many people tried to guess how he had come to have a daughter, but all he would say was that he had known Charity's mother before he married. He and Addie's obvious love for Charity quickly put an end to any malicious talk.

Neither Charity nor Morgan could bear a long engagement, but they wanted Lacy and the Double J cowboys to share their joy, so they waited, setting a date for a week after the men were expected home.

When the herd was within a day's ride, Jacob, Joshua, and Morgan rode out to meet them. They were greeted with grim news. Thirty percent of the cattle had perished. Of the nearly fifteen thousand Double J cattle that had drifted, only ten thousand returned. It was the same for most of the other ranchers. Although Lacy had driven them slowly home from the Concho, the cattle were still gaunt and weary. He and his men were exhausted and deeply troubled by what they had seen.

"We can't let them drift like that again." Lacy's eyes bore the haunted look of a man who had seen things too dreadful to describe. "Fencing will have its own problems, I know, but we have to avoid this." When pressed, he told them how it had been.

Afterward, at dusk, Jacob asked Lacy to go for a walk. When they went around a little hill and everyone else was out of sight, Jacob turned and embraced his son, telling him without words of his love, silently sharing the burden of what he had been through. Lacy wished every man in the outfit could be given a portion of his father's understanding and strength.

Since Lacy knew about Charity being his sister, Jacob told him how things stood between them. Lacy was thrilled and proud of his father and mother. When Jacob told him Charity and Morgan were getting married, he barely stifled his excitement quick enough to avoid a stampede.

The women drove out to meet them when they returned to the Double J. Even to Charity's untrained eye, it was easy to see that the cattle and the men had not fared well. Still, that many Longhorns made a spectacular sight even if they were far too lean.

The cowboys had not been told of the upcoming wedding. Morgan and his family had decided they would let Charity do the honors. The workers who had remained at the ranch during the roundup were asked to keep the secret. That evening when the men finally returned to the bunkhouse, she and Morgan paid them a visit. The cowboys trudged outside—no way were they going to let her set foot in that smelly place this time—and gathered around them. Before she said a word, they began to smile.

"Gentlemen, I know you're ready to collapse, so we won't keep you long. Morgan and I want to personally invite you to our wedding, which will be held here on Saturday." In spite of their bone-aching weariness, the men gave a respectable cheer. "It's going to be quite a celebration. Jacob and Addie have invited everyone in the county and then some. Of course, I don't know if they'll all attend, but there should be plenty of food and dancing to keep everybody happy.

"Jacob asked me to tell you something else. I'm his daughter." Dumbfounded, the men stared. Every one of them knew how much Jacob loved Addie. "He knew my mother before he married. For her own reasons, she never told him about me, but he and Addie have graciously accepted me as part of the family."

Morgan spoke up. "I've quit my deputy sheriff job. We'll be living and working here at the ranch. I'm sure Jacob and Joshua will be talking to you, too, but Charity and I know you've been through a rough time these last weeks, and we wanted to thank you for your hard work and diligence in seeing it to the end. You're a fine group of men, and we're proud to be associated with you."

With their hearts a little brighter and their steps a little lighter, the men bade them congratulations and good night.

Charity and Morgan were married on the front porch of the ranch house on a beautiful sunny morning. The earlier rains brought green grass, and a profusion of buttercups, red and yellow Indian blankets, daisies, sunflowers, and fragrant lavender and purple wild verbena turned the prairie into one giant bouquet. The Baptist preacher from Colorado City performed the ceremony. He was assisted by the circuit-riding preacher who visited twice a month at the little community church on the ranch.

Charity made a beautiful bride, dressed in an original white satin gown covered in Brussels lace designed and personally sewn by Madame DeFontaine. Her father gave her away with a gentle kiss on the cheek and a loving countenance. When she looked into Morgan's eyes and recited her vows in a strong, clear voice, her radiance brought mist to many an eye and wistfulness to lonely cowboy hearts.

Dressed in his best suit and a shiny new pair of boots—a gift from Fred Myers, who actually had them ready on Monday—Morgan stood straight and proud. Gazing down at his woman with unabashed love, he pledged his troth in a clear, loud voice, a voice no longer cold and hard but rich with warmth and caring. There were many soft little sighs heard among the ladies.

Jacob and Joshua's brother Augustus and their mother were in attendance. Charity was a bit in awe of the feisty woman, but Grandma Hunter wouldn't have any such nonsense. Upon her arrival, she had leaned on her cane, looked Charity over from head to toe, and proclaimed,

"Your last name may be Brown—soon to be Kaine—but you're a Hunter. Just look at those eyes. Any dang fool should have seen that right off. Now, come here, child, and give your old grandma a hug."

Richard and Helena came out from New York City. They arrived a week before the wedding bearing two trunks filled with gifts from Charity's friends — including one from Mark Twain, along with a note reminding her that he had warned her about Texas cowboys — and a thousand free copies of the newest *Century* magazine, the issue containing Charity's first article about Colorado City.

Some three thousand people witnessed the ceremony and stayed clear into the next day for the festivities. Rowdy Kate and Jake Maurer hung a "Closed till the party's over" sign on the restaurant door and brought their employees out to help with the cooking. Most everyone brought food of some sort, but Jacob and Joshua spared no expense when it came to feeding their company. Most of the folks who attended were ranchers or cowboys or prominent citizens of the town. There were also some who were not so prominent, people like Mrs. Gilbert, the dressmaker, and Ester, the telephone operator, the desk clerks and bellboys from the St. James, store clerks and trolley drivers, and the old cowboy Charity had first met on the train.

Sam and his family were there, as were Case and his mother. Smokey, who still worked for Case, brought his own new bride, Lucy. If anybody knew where they had met or what she had been, they chose to ignore it, especially after Charity hugged them both. Sheriff Ware roamed the crowd, keeping the party-goers from spiking the punch too much, happy for his friend and pleased with the role he had played in bringing them together.

The folks in the district stayed away, although they had been included in the open invitation, which they appreciated. Mr. Kaine, the Hunters, and Miss Charity might not have had a problem with them being there, but a lot of other folks would, and they didn't want to dampen the festivities. Archie Johnson threw a party in his saloon in honor of the wedding. With free drinks for all, they toasted love and the newlyweds, independent women, and gallant Texan men who stopped trains to catch them, fathers who publicly accepted their illegitimate daughters, and anything and everything else they could think of.

Charity and Morgan left in the middle of the afternoon. They had hoped to sneak away, but it proved impossible with so large a crowd. They were spotted moments after they drove through the main gate. Everyone thought they were going to town, either to stay at the St. James or in Jacob or Morgan's house. To insure their privacy, they went to Zeke Davis's old place instead. The family had been in on their plans and had helped them clean it up earlier in the week and prepare for a few days alone.

When the crowd spotted them leaving, a number of them rushed to saddle their horses or hitch their buggies to follow. With Case and Lacy's "help," their departure was delayed long enough for Morgan to take Charity on a bouncing ride across the prairie and hide behind some mesquites until the jovial group thundered past. Case and Lacy led the group halfway to town before declaring they would never catch the couple. When they suggested going back to the party and getting busy dancing and eating, the crowd promptly turned around.

By that time Morgan had tucked Princess and the buggy away in the barn and carried Charity across the threshold. He didn't put her down until he reached the bedroom.

She smiled ruefully as he carefully set her on the floor. "Not hard to guess what's on your mind," she said.

With a wicked smile, he drew her very, very close. "Same thing that's been on your mind for a month or so. Nervous?"

"A little. You?"

"Yeah, a little, but I reckon we'll get over that soon enough."

"I expect we will." She reached up and pulled the pins from her hair, one by one, and shook it loose.

He ran his fingers through the long, soft strands, massaged her scalp with his fingertips, and kissed her tenderly. When he raised his head, he cupped her face with one hand and gazed at her, his eyes shining with love. "I never thought I'd have a wedding day or feel this way about anyone."

"I guess I'd kind of given up on it, too. I love you." She turned and kissed his palm. Curling her hand around his, she brought it to her heart. "And I always will."

"I love you, too. And I will forever."

He leaned down and touched his lips to hers in a sweet kiss that soon turned to fire. He was not patient. Neither was she. They had waited too long for this moment. They undressed each other quickly, sharing kisses and caresses, whispering promises and words of love. He took her hand and led her to the bed, teaching with gentleness and love the things she had read about and so much more.

Later, they lay curled up together and looked at the moon through the bedroom window. Charity raised up and rested her hands on his chest, then kissed him.

"Howdy, pardner." He smiled lazily, a contented, happy man.

"Howdy. I think I'm going to like being your wife."

"I know I'm going to like it. You being my wife, I mean."

She toyed with the hair on his chest. "Are you going to like being a husband?"

"Yes, ma'am."

"I'll be a good wife to you, Morgan. I'm not very good around the house—"

"You do fine where it counts most."

A soft blush filled her cheeks. "Well, that's nice to know. I won't be unfaithful, not ever. I'll be true to you in every way."

"I know you will. I trust you, sweetheart." He smiled and ran a fingertip down her cheek. "And comin' from this old cowboy, that just about says it all. You're the only woman I'll ever love, Charity. The only one I'll ever want or need." He rolled her over onto her back, and the lovin' started all over again.

A coyote howled out on the prairie, and another answered the call. In the distance the cattle stirred, lowing softly. And as mockingbirds sometimes do, one landed in a mesquite tree outside the window and serenaded them with every song he knew.

Morgan didn't notice. He was oblivious to everything going on around him. The loving woman in his arms made him forget about everything but her.

Dear Reader,

I hope you've enjoyed *Yours Truly,* which you've probably guessed by now was set in my hometown of Colorado City, Texas. (Pronounced Col-o-ray-do, rhymes with tornado.)

The name of the town has varied over the years from Colorado to Colorado City. It was called both in its earliest years and still is today by local residents. It was officially known simply as Colorado, Texas, but many citizens and ranchers unofficially added "City" to give it equal status with Dodge City, Kansas, another cattle town. It was originally incorporated as a town, but a few years later met the requirements for a city. I don't know if that designation was officially added then. Since that's what it is called today, I chose to add city to the title.

I picked 1885 because it was the heyday of the cattle boom. It was also when the Stockman's Ball was held. Everything I wrote about the ball is true. Wouldn't it have been grand to attend? I've portrayed the town as accurately as I could according to available records. It was all there—except for Mayfield's Blacksmith Shop and the Waterin' Hole Saloon.

Except for those mentioned above, the businesspeople were real, as was Sheriff Dick Ware, a former Texas Ranger. The telephone operator's name is unknown, but there were telephones in the town at the time. The major and secondary characters are fictional, and a few of the minor ones as well.

Richard Gilder was the editor of the *Century* magazine. He and his wife Helena seem to have been the type of people who would befriend Charity. The *Century* included articles by women, as did other magazines of the period.

Sadly, the grim roundup of '85 only heralded the problems that were to come for West Texas ranchers. Droughts, harsh winters, and dropping cattle prices took their toll, and the cattle boom collapsed a few years later. Many of the ranchers and businessmen went bankrupt or moved on to other areas. Other railroads cut through Colorado City's territory, ending its days as one of the biggest shipping points in West Texas. Some ranchers and businessmen survived and eventually prospered. Many of the county's first families still have descendants living there today.

Like all small towns, Colorado City has had its ups and downs. Right now they are coming out of a low time, and the economy is picking up. The old buildings of downtown, many of them built during the time frame of this story, are taking on new life as enterprising citizens turn them into antiques stores and other businesses.

So if you're traveling in West Texas along I-20, stop off in Colorado City. Drop in and visit the Heart of West Texas Museum and the Heritage House, then wander on downtown and see what you can find. Take a minute to imagine what it was like in the 1880s when Rowdy Kate rounded up the girls to dance in front of Jake's and a piano-poundin' professor played a lively tune. If you listen carefully, you might hear the jingle of gold and silver spurs and the swish of satin gowns as the cowboys escorted their ladies down the red carpet to the Stockman's Ball.

I would love to hear from you. You can write to me at 4910 S. 287th Street, Auburn, Washington 98001.

My best wishes to you all,
Sharon Harlow
May 1993

*Come take a walk down Harmony's Main Street in 1874, and meet a different resident of this colorful Kansas town each month.*

# A TOWN CALLED
# ❧HARMONY❧

__**KEEPING FAITH** by Kathleen Kane
  0-7865-0016-6/$4.99  *(coming in July)*
From the boardinghouse to the schoolhouse, love grows in the heart of Harmony. And for pretty, young schoolteacher Faith Lind, a lesson in love is about to begin.

__**TAKING CHANCES** by Rebecca Hagan Lee
  0-7865-0022-2/$4.99  *(coming in August)*
All of Harmony is buzzing when they hear the blacksmith, Jake Sutherland, is smitten. And no one is more surprised than Jake himself, who doesn't know the first thing about courting a woman.

__**CHASING RAINBOWS** by Linda Shertzer
  0-7865-0041-7/$4.99  *(coming in September)*
Fashionable, Boston-educated Samantha Evans is the outspoken columnist for her father's newspaper. But her biggest story yet may be her own exclusive–with a most unlikely man.